A SANCTIFY NOVEL

Queen of
WANDS

A SANCTIFY NOVEL

Queen of WANDS

KATEE ROBERT

Entangled Publishing, LLC
2614 South Timberline Road
Suite 109
Fort Collins, CO 80525

Visit our website at www.entangledpublishing.com.

Edited by Heather Howland and Kari Olson
Cover design by Heather Howland
Interior Art by Tom Morris, All American Tattoo, Spokane, WA

Print ISBN 978-1-62266-359-0
Ebook ISBN 978-1-62266-360-6

Manufactured in the United States of America

First Edition June 2014

10 9 8 7 6 5 4 3 2 1

To PJ Schnyder - You never fail to help me pinpoint the good in any bad situation, and your conversations brighten up my day. Thank you!

CHAPTER ONE

Screams sliced through the air, each higher than the one before. They cut off abruptly, followed by the voice of a very angry Diviner. "Give me the Ladydamned drugs!"

Jenny O'Keirna's brother paced outside the door to the bedroom, back and forth, over and over again, until she wanted to slap him silly. "Just go in there, you big oaf."

Boone spun around, gray eyes bloodshot and on the far side of crazy. "I can't. They won't let me."

"They" being the three midwives closeted in the room with the Diviner. Why Ophelia needed three was anyone's guess. Jenny refused to dwell on it. Hells, she wished she could forbid Boone from her presence, too—he was climbing the walls like a caged animal—but he was the last of her family left alive and, for once, he actually needed her. She might be an ass, but she wasn't going to leave her big brother alone the one time he was totally and completely out of his element.

Still, enough was enough. "She's your woman. Go get her."

"I am respecting her wishes." Each word came out sharp

enough to cut. "You should do the same."

She ignored the threat with the ease of long practice. "Just because she can read the future in her creepy cards doesn't mean she knows everything."

Boone had only recently come to terms with the fact that the Diviner wasn't bullshitting when she used her cards to commune with her goddess, the Lady. If the tic in his cheek muscle was any indication, he didn't appreciate the reminder.

She grinned. "Want me to kick down the door?"

They turned as one and eyed the thick wood. The castle was their family home, had been for ages. When Boone killed their sadistic half brother, Kristian, and took the throne, the first thing he wanted to do was burn it to the ground, but the Council forbade it. Truth be told, Jenny was glad it had. There were plenty of crap memories haunting these hallways—especially in the year leading up to their exile—but it was her last link to her father.

In her head, she realized he was a monster, but in her heart he was something else altogether. She couldn't wipe out those memories any more than she could the ones of him hurting Boone. Or of him encouraging Kristian to do the same.

But that was Hansarda for you—bittersweet on the best of days. Or maybe she was just bitter because she'd spent the last ten years as an outcast and now the asshats on the Council were welcoming her and Boone back with open arms. As if they hadn't sat idly by while Kristian aligned with the monsters of Sanctify, and did his damnedest to kill everyone on the planet.

If Boone hadn't attacked when he did…

She pushed the ugly thoughts away. Both Dad and Kristian were dead and gone—end of story—leaving only this castle behind. As the only permanent building on Hansarda, it had been created to last. Dad made sure of that, and he didn't do anything half-assed. It was a trait he and Boone had in common, though if she ever compared him to their father out loud, her brother might have a stroke. He was a drama queen like that.

Jenny sighed, deciding the door was a lost cause. "I don't like our chances."

"It may be best if we wait it out."

Gods help her, but he actually sounded scared. Trust Boone to face down suicide mission after suicide mission in his quest to take the throne, only to quail before his pregnant woman giving birth.

"Chickenshit." She smacked him on the shoulder and danced out of reach when he turned on her. "Come on, big brother, scared of a few itty-bitty women and a baby?"

"Jenny."

"Bo-oo-one." She loved watching the vein in his forehead pulse when she stretched his name into three syllables.

"I am not afraid." His gaze shot to the door again, belying his words.

"Boone!"

They both jumped at the shrieking quality of Ophelia's voice. The woman was freaking scary before she went into labor, with her eerie knack for knowing things she shouldn't and her sweet skills with a knife. Now she was just plain terrifying. Thank the gods keeping her happy wasn't Jenny's burden to bear.

She patted him on the shoulder. "Have at it." Then she turned and ran away.

"Jenny! Jenny, get your ass back here." Boone sounded so damn panicked that she laughed. Seeing her brother's machine-like composure finally break was too satisfying.

"Sorry," she called as she rounded the corner. "I didn't knock her up."

Ophelia screamed again and then Jenny was on the stairs, sprinting toward safety. If she had any doubts before, she didn't now—there was no way in hells she would pop out a kid. Or lock herself in with a man. As happy as her brother and his Diviner seemed, there was no force in the universe that could convince Jenny to climb into that particular trap. She'd rather gnaw off her own leg than spend her life chained to a single person.

She flew through the thick wooden door at the bottom of the stairwell, skidding to a stop in front of a giant furball. "Here kitty, kitty."

"One of these days, I'm going to show you my claws."

Yeah, like that would happen. Cole was just too damn adorable, with his feline features and brindled coloring. The Beshmaiite hated it when she compared him to a cat, despite some pretty obvious similarities. Well, obvious similarities if she ignored the fact that he was a foot taller than her and had fangs designed to gut his enemies.

His lethalness wasn't enough to cow her into submission. And he should know better by now than to show just how much it bugged him. "Come on, pretty kitty. Stop lurking in dark corners and live a little."

His fur stuck straight out for half a second before he got control of his temper. "How are things with the lady?"

If she listened closely, she could still hear the screams. Or maybe that was just her imagination. "Remind me never to have kids."

"The thought of you reproducing…" Cole shuddered, his hair rising in waves. "Just don't."

"Pop off, Cole."

She started to shoulder past him, but his next words stopped her. "There's a problem. Boone can't deal with it because…" Because he was dealing with a breeding Diviner who had the tendency to attack first and ask questions later.

"Spit it out."

Cole looked away. "I think he'd like to hear it first."

Jenny rolled her eyes. "Stop toying with my emotions and tell me. Boone doesn't need this right now and you know it, or you wouldn't have brought it up in the first place."

Cole's hair flattened to his body, revealing his powerful limbs. She had him and he knew it. "A distress call came through the secret channels."

"Which secret channels?"

"Azure Enterprises."

She wasn't sure if it was a relief that it wasn't her people or a worry because it was the Diviner's. "Is it her father?" This was the last thing they needed after what happened when Boone took the throne. Ophelia had barely recovered from the loss of her mother. If something happened to her dad, too...

"No."

Jenny checked her sigh of relief because Cole was still so damn tense.

"It is their inventor, Mac Flannery."

The one responsible for turning Azure Enterprises into the major player it was today. His weapons and armor were cutting edge, the stuff of action vids and imagination. Except they worked in real life. She'd seen the antimatter gun fired only once, but once was more than enough.

If any of their enemies got their hands on him...

"What's going on? Where is he?" She didn't know much about the guy, other than the fact that he was a genius and his location was kept secret. She'd once suggested it might be a good idea if she were kept up to date on all this top-secret crap, but Boone shot her down pretty damn quick. It didn't matter that she'd sacrificed everything right alongside him—he'd always see her as his kid sister.

Cole shook himself, reminding her more of a dog than a cat. "He's probably just being paranoid. The guy spends his time locked up in a room, working on gadgets. People like that aren't exactly well-balanced."

"You don't think I can cut it." His obvious doubt hurt

more than she would ever admit. No one took her seriously—they never had. Hells, she could outshoot both her brother and Ophelia, but no one seemed to remember things like that when it came down to the line.

"I didn't say that." His voice took on a purr.

Great, now he pitied her. If there was one thing she hated more than being written off, it was being pitied. Jenny's hand went to the bracelet on her left wrist, twisting it. The metal shifted, ready to spring around her hands and form gauntlets. "Tell me, Cole."

For a moment, she thought he would argue. Then he eyed her bracelet, hackles rising as he recognized the move for the threat it was. "He's on Terra II."

Jenny's eyes widened. Terra II, called T-II by anyone who'd actually been there, was a shit hole. The only reason people stopped there at all was because of the lack of law enforcement. If you wanted shady dealings with merchants carting everything from drugs to forged ship docs to weapons, T-II was the place to be. Everything was gray, coated with the pollution from the factories—gray air, gray streets, gray people.

Jenny had never had the pleasure of visiting, which wasn't surprising. She'd been only twelve when Kristian drove Boone off-planet. He spaced, and took her with him. Jenny didn't blame her brother for taking her away—she had no illusions about what a sadistic shit like Kristian would have done to her—but now she wanted freedom more than anything in the universe. It was a damn shame, because *freedom* was the one thing she could never have as a member of the ruling family.

Which meant there was no way she could pass up the opportunity to take off for a while. Who knew when she'd get a chance like this again? It might be months or, worse, *years*. "I'm going."

"Jenny…" She stared at Cole until he took a step back and

bowed, the move far more fluid than any human could have managed. "I don't know why I bother. Fine."

"Send the coordinates to *Psyche*." Jenny headed down the hall, unable to quell the bounce in her step. She was spacing. Thank the gods. She needed *Psyche's* controls beneath her hands again, the universe and all its possibilities laid out before her.

"Jenny."

She froze at the sound of her brother's voice. Crap. She forced a cheery smile as she turned around, ready to argue him to a standstill if he tried to stop her from leaving.

But her stoic, brooding brother was grinning like an idiot. "It's a girl."

It took a moment for her mind to switch tracks. "A girl?" A niece. Her smile widened and turned into something real as she pictured a miniature Ophelia running around, getting into trouble and scaring the castle staff. Being auntie to that little hellion was going to be great fun.

"A girl." He practically skipped over and grabbed her to spin in a circle. "I have a daughter."

As quickly as he started, Boone set her down and took a step back. "Come see."

"Sure thing." As much as her skin itched with the need to get off-planet, Mac could wait a few hours. It wasn't every day Jenny got a niece. She bounded up the stone stairs, barely able to keep up with Boone. When was the last time she'd seen such unadulterated joy on her brother's face? Gods, she couldn't remember.

He flung open the bedroom door, revealing a sweat-stained bed and a half-naked Diviner. Ophelia yelled, "Close the Lady-damned door."

Boone kicked it shut without hesitation, and they all winced when the baby let forth a startled shriek. The kid had a serious set of lungs. "How are you feeling?" he asked.

Ophelia never took her gaze from the tiny bundle resting in the cradle of her arms. "I just popped out a baby. How the hells do you think I'm feeling?"

Jenny sidled closer, peering over her brother's shoulder. The baby was wrinkled and red and looked a bit squashed, and she hoped to the gods the little mite would get cuter as she got older. If not, well, she was still family. "She's...adorable."

"Shut up, Jenny," Ophelia said without looking up. "She's perfect."

The baby blinked, revealing the brilliant violet eyes that characterized the Diviner species. Boone was going to have a handful with two card readers in his family. His life would have been so much simpler if he'd found a nice Hansardian girl to settle down with instead of saddling himself with another of Sanctify's so-called "ultimate enemies." Those bastards would just *love* to get their hands on another Diviner.

Jenny smiled. "Yeah, she is."

He reached out, running a single finger down the baby's face. She turned her head to the side, mouth searching. The expression of sheer hunger gave Jenny the willies, and she almost missed her brother speaking.

"What did Cole want?"

"Cole?" She sighed, watching her chances at spacing without Boone finding out swirl down the drain. But if she lied to him and took off, he'd hunt her down, baby or no. Jenny wanted to be taken seriously, and that meant manning up. "We got a distress call from Mac."

Ophelia finally tore her attention away from the kid. "Mac's in trouble?"

"Something like that." She shrugged, going for nonchalance. "I figured since you two were busy, I'd head that way and see what's up."

"No." Boone stood, towering over her. The intimidation

move stopped working when Jenny turned six and realized he'd never willingly raise a hand against her. "Absolutely not. You are not going to T-II."

"Afraid I might get corrupted?" Jenny laughed, the sound high and light, free of the bitterness clawing its way up her throat. In a way, it was sweet that he still wanted to protect her. Annoying as hells, but sweet. "Don't you know me better than that, big brother?"

"I know *exactly* what you're capable of."

"Bo-oo-one." There went the vein, right on cue. "I stayed out of the way and *safe*"—she spat the word—"on Valneci while you came here and almost *died* to save our people. This is just a pickup. Nothing fancy. I'll go get Sir Genius and be back here within two weeks. Cake."

"Jenny—"

"Enough." Ophelia snarled, the sound identical to what came out of Cole's mouth when Jenny went too far in her teasing. "You'll upset Clarice."

"Clarice?" Jenny's eyes nearly bugged out of her head, her anger temporarily derailed. "Please tell me you didn't actually name your daughter that. Boone, what in the seven hells were you thinking?"

Ophelia handed the baby to Boone, and he took her like she was the most breakable thing in the universe. The picture they made—her big brother whom she'd seen damn near cut an Abura-Sumashi in half and this tiny bundle of podness—was the strangest thing she'd ever seen. And she'd seen some weird shit.

"Get my cards."

"Ophelia," Boone and Jenny said at the same time. They shot each other nasty looks.

"Shut up, both of you." Ophelia pointed at the desk across the room from the bed. "Jenny, my cards. Now."

It was on the tip of her tongue to tell the Diviner where to shove her damn cards, but curiosity got the best of her. What was the harm in indulging Ophelia's beliefs? Just because she didn't worship the same gods didn't mean she had to be as close-minded as *some* people.

And if she got something out of it, well, that was okay too.

Jenny handed the cards over, watching as Ophelia shuffled them a few times and then passed them back. "Cut the deck."

"If you say so." She did as commanded, cutting it high.

Ophelia looked at her for a long time, her violet eyes distant, until Jenny had to fight the urge to squirm. "Three cards are enough, I think."

"Three? That seems like a rip-off."

Boone smacked Jenny lightly on the back of the head. "Show some respect."

"You first."

"Children, focus." Ophelia flipped over three cards in quick succession.

Jenny leaned over, gaze skating over the badass winged woman holding a wand, the dude with a stick about to walk off a cliff, and the couple...growing out of a tree? The cards were pretty enough, but she couldn't make heads or tails of them. "What in the hells does that mean?"

A triumphant smile blazed across the Diviner's face. Jenny didn't like *that* smile one bit. "You need to be the one to go." Ophelia held up a hand as Boone opened his mouth. "She's an adult and more than capable of kicking my ass, let alone doing a run to pick up Mac. I know it and you know it, so stop being so damn stubborn."

"Ophelia—"

"No, Boone." She met Jenny's gaze. "I'll see that you have the pertinent information. Get your ass in gear."

The hairs on the back of her neck stood up in warning, but she decided to get out while the getting was good. "Yes, ma'am."

CHAPTER TWO

"Mac? Damn it, Mac, where are you?"

Mac Flannery startled, nearly dropping the handful of wires he'd so carefully separated from the tangle on the floor. So typical that his first call in a week would happen right now, while he was in the middle of something. He reached over and grabbed a second set of pliers to hold the wires in place.

Pausing to glance at the messages flitting along the screens around him, Mac stepped out of the virtual room and grabbed his handheld from the cluttered table in the center of the equally cluttered room. Boone's face greeted him, the man looking more pissed off than ever. Which was saying something since he always looked as if he'd swallowed a prickly bearnut.

"I'm sending someone for you."

"Sending someone?"

Boone's jaw clenched so tightly it was a wonder his teeth didn't shatter. "Did you or did you not send out a call for help?"

"Yes." Mac thought over the facts he painstakingly gathered over the last two months to the vital piece of the puzzle that fell into place three days ago. Dangerous didn't begin to cover it. "I need to be relocated."

"Listen, you—"

The link screen tipped, Boone disappearing, and righted itself to show Ophelia. She looked amused, a half smile pulling at the edges of her lips. Everything about the woman screamed delicate and cultured, but Mac knew better. He'd seen her fight only once, but once was more than enough to scare the living shit out of him. "Ophelia."

"Tell me."

As much as he wanted to make this someone else's problem, he was nearly 100 percent sure he was being monitored. "The signal waves—"

"I'm not an idiot." Ophelia's carefree manner melted away, her expression as cold and unfeeling as the blade she kept on her wrist. "I don't need details, just a general idea."

Mac recognized a command when he heard one. With anyone else, he would have cut the transmission and sent a bug to every piece of electronics they owned. But she was Gerard's daughter, and her father was good to Mac.

"There's large movement within the organization your father has me watching." Sanctify. Those bastards had become one of the heaviest hitters in the universe over the last thirty-five years, and they were showing no signs of slowing down. Which didn't bode well for any nonhumans under their control. "The death of one of their vital members has left a vacuum of power, and the individual rallying to step in has personal interests. Personal *vendettas*."

She frowned, shoving back her mass of black hair. "How personal?"

"Very." Sanctify's new High Priest was out for revenge, by the looks of it. And for whatever reason, Mac was square in their crosshairs. As was Azure Enterprises, Hansarda, and everyone connected with them.

Ophelia cursed, turning to glare at someone—probably Boone—off to the side. She glanced back at Mac. "Do I need to call in our people?"

The analytical side of him whispered that he was being paranoid, that he needed to check the data one more time before confirming what he'd found. A few more days. A few more days and he could be sure...

No. He wasn't wrong. They were all in danger and the longer he hesitated, the more time those monsters had to find, torture, and burn innocents in the name of their god, Ba'al. It meant taking a leap of faith, which was something he hated to do, but he couldn't risk it with lives on the line. "Yes. As fast as possible. I think they have the coordinates of every major facility you use."

Her pale skin went chalky. "Lady save us."

There was no telling how fast Sanctify would move, but Mac figured it was a good time for those who believed in such things to start praying.

Ophelia made a visible effort to regain control. "Your pickup will be there in roughly twenty-four hours. If they know where our people are, we can't congregate in one place—too easy to target. Pick one of your foxholes and hide away for a while."

Mac didn't ask how she knew about his escape routes. He and Gerard had worked together for years—it made sense that the old man told her everything about his habits. "I have a few in mind."

"Good. If things get too hot, I need you to take Jenny with you."

Boone voiced a protest in the background, but Ophelia didn't acknowledge him.

"Jenny O'Keirna?" Mac's heart skipped a beat, and he prayed his expression gave nothing away.

"She's your pilot. You do exactly as she says and she'll get you out alive." Ophelia's brows rose. "Is there a problem with that?"

She was a Diviner; of course she would see below the surface of his reaction. He mentally cursed and forced a smile. "No. I'll bounce you a message when I have more information."

"Sooner rather than later, Mac."

"Will do."

He cut off the transmission, slumped into his chair, and ran his hands through his hair. Nine months ago, when Ophelia paired up with Boone, the then-heir to Hansarda, Mac went through his usual protocol. He dug up everything there was to know about the royal family—their past, their habits, the skeletons in their respective closets that could potentially hurt Azure Enterprises. Everything.

At first he hadn't paid much attention to the daughter, the youngest of the three siblings, since she wasn't as large of a threat as her brothers. But after Boone killed Kristian, he'd done a deeper search on her, looking for anything that popped. Ophelia's report on how dangerous Jenny was in combat was enough to have Gerard worried that she was dangerous as a greater whole. At first all Mac found was the expected—she flew under her brother's direction on a ship named *Psyche* with a crew of identical triplets and an Evarven. Nothing special.

Then he'd run across surveillance videos of an assortment of bars. Jenny always seemed to be dancing on tables or getting into fights. It made her a potential problem to be watched, but what caught his attention were her mannerisms—the woman put on personalities similar to the way normal people put on clothes. One moment she was all smiles and snarky remarks, the next she was downright deadly, the next something else altogether. In short, she was a brilliantly put-together puzzle.

And he was intrigued, despite himself. *Very* intrigued.

It didn't help that she was beautiful. Perhaps not by the

current universal standards, not quite curvy enough, hair too dark and plain, face all unforgiving angles. But those cool gray eyes caught and held him better than any snare. And her lips, a bit too full for her face, a little too kissable, were always lifted in a lilting smile.

And she was coming here.

Mac looked around at the half-repaired machines littering the place, their insides spilling over onto every available surface and a good portion of the floor. There was a basic cot shoved into the corner, its single blanket wadded up near the foot of the mattress. Impressive. Very impressive. Even the virtual room was a mess of connections no one but he would be able to figure out.

He needed to get moving, to figure out what he could leave, what he needed to take, and which of his hideaways to aim for. Instead, he crossed to the nearest screen and pulled up the video of Jenny that had originally caught his curiosity. She was with Ophelia in a hole-in-the-wall club on one of the Far Reach planets. The night had begun much the same as so many others— drinking with her mad grin firmly in place. It wasn't until the fight broke out that the switch flipped, all joking demeanor gone in an instant, replaced by a stone-cold killer.

She hadn't even hesitated before going up against one of the Abura-Sumashi with only metal gauntlets as a weapon. It didn't matter that the male of the legendary warrior species was well over two meters tall, with tusks long enough to gore. She'd waded into that fight with no hesitation, and she'd held her own until Boone showed up and put an end to it.

He couldn't imagine her here, surrounded by all his paraphernalia, under the harsh lights scattered across the ceiling. This was a place for shut-ins who had more brains than sense.

People like Mac.

He spent half a second imagining what it would be like if Jenny hid with him. What they could possibly do to while away the long hours, unable to leave for fear they might be seen…

He shook off his thoughts and stood. It didn't matter if he had a schoolboy crush on Jenny. What mattered was the danger they were all in. When Ophelia's mother killed the High Priest, it brought out the worst in an already terrible organization. Word was the new, younger priest who'd taken charge was out for blood, and he planned on killing every last person under Ophelia's protection.

On the surface, it made sense that they would avenge the death of the High Priest, especially since it was at the hands of the hated Diviners. But the more he dug, the more he suspected that there was a personal element involved. It was never more than a hint, but he couldn't shake the feeling that he was missing something.

He just hoped to gods he figured it out before Sanctify showed up to collect their vengeance.

CHAPTER THREE

As *Psyche* sliced through Hansarda's atmosphere, Jenny took her first full breath in weeks. She still couldn't believe Boone had let her go. Ophelia's superstitions really did come in handy from time to time.

She brought up the star map and plugged in the coordinates to T-II. The nearest warp point was roughly twelve hours away, and from there they'd need to jump a single time. Not too shabby.

"So what's the plan?"

Jenny glanced at the man sitting next to her. Hadriel was the oldest of the triplets—the only way to tell them apart was their hair coloring, each a different shade of brown. Even after flying with them for five years, Jenny still didn't know if they dyed their hair on purpose to help people out, or if it was natural. All three were attractive in a nondescript sort of way that sneaked up on a person. Open features and quick smiles—and all too smart for their own good. "You know, I think I like you better when you're pretending to be mute." Both of his brothers were, so usually Hadriel didn't speak in a show of solidarity—and because he liked screwing with people.

"Don't be like that. I'm just up here to help out."

"I don't need your help." She waited, but he just sat there grinning. "Scat."

He snorted and stood. "What are the orders?"

"We're doing a standard pickup, getting one of Ophelia's people to safety." And having a bit of fun while they were at it. If you liked your fun with a sharp edge, T-II was the perfect place to go. She couldn't wait. "Get Shad working on the intercom as soon as possible—the static is getting freaking ridiculous." She was never letting Boone fly her ship again—*Psyche* came back all dinged up after being in his not-so-tender care.

"Yes, ma'am." He ignored her growl and walked out the door.

Jenny turned back to the controls, running her hands over them. The last time she'd spaced for what was supposed to be an easy run, she'd ended up sneaking onto Sanctus itself in a rescue mission. "I'm back, baby. I know it's been a long time, but it will be just like the old days—you, me, and the stars."

The controls vibrated gently under her hands, and she could almost believe the ship was answering. Almost. After double-checking their course and making a few tweaks, Jenny sat back with a sigh. *Psyche* had been her one and only ever since she became a pilot. It was the only thing in the entire universe that was hers, and hers alone. Here, there were no controlling men, smothering her with their protection. Here, she was as close to free as she ever got.

There was nothing left to do before they warped. Normally she'd go play cards with the boys or lounge around in her cabin, flipping through the newest fashion vids, but the thought of doing either made her twitchy. She stood and paced along the narrow corridor leading to the cockpit, her skin feeling too tight. It was Boone's fault. Thanks to her darling big brother's overprotectiveness and determination to keep her close, she hadn't gotten laid in *forever*.

"Eight months, twenty-five days, and some-odd hours." Jenny rolled her shoulders, but it didn't help the tension riding her.

One day. She could handle one more day.

Hells, it wasn't like she had a choice. The only other people on this ship were the triplets, and she'd be damned before she crossed *that* line. They were friends, not random men she could use for a night and then space, never to see again. Sex with friends was complicated. Too complicated. It caused more stress than it took away, which defeated the whole purpose.

The comm unit beeped an incoming message, and Jenny flicked it on. Ophelia's face appeared on the screen. Her hair was pulled back into a messy tail, but she was dressed in actual clothes—not the sweats she'd grown so fond of during her last trimester of pregnancy. "Look at you, all dolled up."

The Diviner glared, but the expression didn't dim the happiness radiating from her violet eyes. "If you weren't Boone's sister, I'd kick the crap out of you."

"Tried and failed, big sister." She smiled as she thought back over her single sparring match with Ophelia. They used real blades and nearly gave Boone a heart attack. The way he'd freaked out was priceless—and worth the price of Jenny's losing.

"For the record, I won the match. And don't call me that. I am not marrying Boone anytime soon."

No one out-stubborned a member of the O'Keirna clan. "Whatever you say, *big sister*."

The Diviner's eyes flared. "I am not your sister, Ladydamnit."

Jenny waved away the comment, idly wondering if steam could really shoot from someone's ears. "So what do you have for me?"

"You know, if I didn't think he'd do the same thing to me, I'd have Boone put you under full lockdown." Ophelia pushed back the hair already escaping her ponytail. "But it's irrelevant. I need you to behave yourself on this run."

As if Ophelia didn't attract nearly as much trouble as Jenny did. For all of Jenny's shenanigans, *she'd* never managed to get kidnapped by a ship full of Abura-Sumashi mercenaries. Neither Ophelia nor Boone seemed to appreciate it when she pointed out that little tidbit. "Sure thing."

"You know, if you want people to believe you're actually going to do something, you shouldn't give in so easily." She smiled a little. "I'm bouncing over the coordinates of Mac's current location. Even though he's got twenty-four hours to prepare, don't expect him to be ready. The man is worse than a woman going on vacation when it comes to packing."

"Want me to throw him over my shoulder and carry him to safety?"

"Jenny, be good." Ophelia gave her a stern look, her violet eyes dancing. "I'm worried you're going to give the poor man a stroke."

She clasped her hands over her heart. "I would never!"

"Bullshit."

"So what exactly do you want me to do?" At the Diviner's raised brows, she laughed. "I'm not saying I'll follow the plan, but I like to know what it is so I can trample all over it."

"We need you to get Mac, take him to one of his foxholes, and then come back to us."

Back to Hansarda and her gilded cage. Jenny made a face. "Sounds boring."

"Just stick to the plan. You haven't seen what Sanctify can do when they're pissed. What happened to Boone was child's play compared to what they do when they're truly angry. It's—" Ophelia shuddered, gaze going distant, seeing horrors Jenny had only heard about. "It's not something I'd wish on my worst enemy, let alone someone I consider family."

She nodded, but she couldn't help one last dig. "I knew you

wanted to be my big sister! We can have sleepovers and watch sex vids. It'll be great."

Ophelia shook her head. "You're crazy, Jenny."

"You love me for it."

"Yeah, I know. Be safe and report in when you have Mac." The transmission cut off, leaving her alone once more. It was becoming more than a passing trend these days. She tried to convince herself that it didn't matter, but feigning indifference was becoming harder by the day.

Twisting her hair into a knot that didn't need a tie, she said, "Computer, bring up all information on Mac Flannery."

The computer obeyed, displaying several screens worth of information. Most of it was blah—the inventions he was responsible for, his contributions to Azure Enterprises, stuff that didn't tell her much of anything. Biting her lip, she moved past those pages, pausing briefly over the account of how Ophelia's dad had found him.

He'd stumbled upon Mac during one of his runs—the details of which were pretty damn vague—and decided to save the boy from the men who'd killed his mother. After having met the old man, Jenny figured he must have seen some potential in the thirteen-year-old. Gerard saved him, set Mac up with his own place, and then gave him free rein, the only condition being that all his inventions went to Azure Enterprises. Not a bad gig, as such things went.

Jenny did a quick calculation in her head. That meant Mac was barely thirty, if that. Somehow she'd pictured him as an old fart with a cloud of crazy white hair, bent over his mad experiments. What man in his prime chose to spend all his time holed up inventing stuff? Not a sane one, in her opinion.

She brought up the last file, containing only a picture. Jenny liked her men big, pretty, and dumb—so much easier to leave them behind that way—but even though he veered more toward interesting than burly, she had to admit Mac was attractive. He had the kind of chiseled jaw that just begged to be nibbled on. She wondered at his ancestry since his skin was the palest she'd seen outside of an albino. There were even freckles smattered over his nose and cheeks, and she had to fight against the urge to try to count them. The skin combined with a mop of careless red curls on his head meant he would stick out like a sore thumb anywhere they went. And then there were his eyes. She leaned forward, trying to figure out what color they were. Green, then brown, then some mix of the two. Strange.

They seemed to stare straight through the screen at her.

Boone would die if he knew she was ogling Mac. Her sudden desire to find out exactly what kind of heat the inventor was packing aside, it would almost be worth it to hook up with Sir Genius just to see her big brother's face when he found out. But this wasn't the time for rebelling. Boone actually consented to a solo run without Cole looking over her shoulder, so she needed to be on her best behavior, or run the risk of him locking her up for months to come.

She could do it. Really.

"Jenny?"

She shrieked and jumped out of her chair, spinning around to find three pairs of identical brown eyes staring at her. As one, the triplets burst into laughter, the picture made downright eerie because sound emerged from only one of their throats. She reached behind her to minimize the screen with Mac's information, hoping they wouldn't notice. "What the hells were you thinking, scaring me half to death?"

Shad, the middle-haired one, moved his hands in a blur, spelling out, *Stop mooning and come play cards with us.*

Apparently she hadn't moved fast enough. "I'm not mooning over anyone." She was sitting in the cockpit, ogling a man she couldn't have. Big difference. Jenny stood, brushing imaginary dust from her black pants. "Fine, fine. But only if you go easy on little ole me."

Caeden snorted. *As if we've ever believed that innocent act. You clean us out every time.* Then he blushed, which kind of detracted from his attempt to be a hard-ass.

"Not every time." She had to let them win occasionally or they wouldn't play.

"Whatever you say." Hadriel laughed and threw his arm over her shoulders. "Come on. We have a good ten hours before we warp, might as well make good use of it."

"Truer words were never spoken."

Unbidden, Mac's image appeared in her mind, those damned strange eyes seeing far too much. What kind of trouble could the two of them get into in ten hours? There were plenty of surfaces in the *Psyche* that she'd yet to christen. Maybe they'd start right here in the cockpit...

Hells. She hadn't even met him and he was already trouble.

CHAPTER FOUR

*M*ac hurried around his apartment, trying to tidy up. He'd been packing for hours, yet there were still things everywhere. It hadn't taken long for his clothing—he didn't own much—but he'd gotten distracted with the solution to the new laser he'd spent the last few weeks working on. It took twelve hours, but he managed to add in a heat sink to allow more shots to be fired before it needed time to charge. Another victory, but the alarm he'd set up to track *Psyche's* arrival went off before he had time to revel in the joy of it.

Jenny's ship had passed Control and was entering the atmosphere.

Which meant he had maybe half an hour before she showed up at his door. Mac paused long enough to look around. The place was more cluttered than when he started, but the irreplaceable tools were packed away. Now he just needed the network.

He walked into the virtual room, checking to make sure nothing of importance happened while he was working. Sanctify had its virtual storm walls up again, but they wouldn't matter once he had the opportunity to sit down and concentrate. Mac took a step toward the wall of information before he caught himself. There wasn't time. He was supposed to be getting ready for transfer, not sinking into a new project.

Steeling himself, he moved to the opposite screens and brought up a file on each of his foxholes. He needed to make a decision, but without running a risk comparison, there was no way to tell which was the safest option.

With a sigh, he dismissed the three located on Far Reach planets. Sanctify had too much of a presence beyond the four Quadrants. Hells, they were a presence everywhere. But most of the Far Reach colonies didn't have ironclad governments set up, which left them open to outside influence.

Nitriph was out. Sanctify had taken it just under a year ago, and things were still stirred up. He briefly entertained the idea of hiding in plain sight on a controlled planet, but it was too risky.

That left Terra III and Terra IV.

Mac ran his hands through his hair. Neither were great choices. The Star Council just convened on Terra III, so security would be off the charts. And Terra IV was a prison planet. He looked between the two files, wishing there was time to do more research before deciding. As if to reinforce his lack of time, Mac's link beeped. He jumped, knocking over things in his hurry to find the damn comm unit. When he finally came up with it, he clicked it on with a huff.

The male pictured in the screen was covered in spikes, his brow heavy with built-in armored plates. Combined with the long snout, the Bolkerian gave off the impression of an angry armadillo. "There are three fleshies heading up. Look like trouble. Thought you might want to know." He spoke in their native tongue, a series of clicks and whistles. The Bolkerians were notorious for their refusal to bend to anything the Star Council recommended, including implanting vocalizers.

"Thank you, Beq." Mac butchered the language, but Beq nodded, giving a grunt of approval. When they'd met years ago, the Bolkerian had agreed to teach him the language for entertainment value alone. Mac had stuck with it despite some initial setbacks—being human, he lacked certain necessary physical attributes—and an unlikely friendship had formed.

The warning made him frown. *He* might know she was trouble, but a stranger would look at Jenny and see a striking woman who drew the eye in any room she walked into. Most people wouldn't automatically assume she was a threat.

Mac walked straight to the door and eyed the camera he had looking out into the hall. Three men approached, hands hovering over their lasers. Between the white robes and forbidding expressions, there was no mistaking their identity.

Sanctify.

"Oh, shit." Trouble was a serious understatement of having these men show up on his doorstep. He glanced at the clock ticking down the seconds. The timing couldn't be worse, with Jenny's ship no doubt already docked. She would come to pick him up and walk straight into a trap.

With the defenses he had in place, he could hold them off indefinitely—as long as they didn't call in reinforcements. But that wouldn't do a damn thing to help his allies on *that* side of the door.

Mac knew all too well what Sanctify did to people they considered their enemies. Since Jenny wasn't a Diviner, she'd probably be saved from the public dismemberment and burning, but that wouldn't stop them from shooting her. If he stayed holed up in his safe place, he'd most likely be forced to watch her and her team die.

Not again. He wouldn't stand by, helpless, while another woman he cared about died.

He took a deep breath and keyed open the door. He didn't

bother with a smile of welcome. They'd know exactly how fake it was. "Gentlemen."

"It is time for you to repent, Mac Flannery," the man in the middle said. He was older than his teammates, his bronzed skin giving off a weathered look of countless years spent in the sun. The other two were pups—this man posed the most danger.

"I don't owe allegiance to Ba'al." Not that it would stop them from trying whatever they had planned. Members of Sanctify weren't exactly known for their religious tolerance.

The man barely blinked. "It is time you saw the truth and joined the brotherhood."

It all clicked together—their showing up on his doorstep and using words instead of charging in with lasers raised. They wanted to take him alive. Mac laughed, the sound coming out bitter and harsh. Of course Sanctify wouldn't want to waste his talents. It wasn't something he'd factored into the threat, and he was a fool for missing that potential outcome. "And if I don't?"

All three of them shifted, their hands dropping to their lasers and their gazes hardening. That answered that. They would attempt to take him by force if he fought. So be it.

He took a few steps back and motioned them forward. "Come into my parlor."

• • •

Jenny eyed the Bolkerian lounging just inside the door to the apartment building. Well, as much as their species ever lounged. She gave him a nod, meeting his eyes a few seconds longer than most people did, acknowledging that he could very literally eat her for breakfast if he were so inclined.

Caeden followed as she bypassed the lift, taking the stairs

two at a time. They reached the fourth floor in time to hear the distinctive whine of a laser being fired. "Crap." Thank the gods she hadn't pushed back picking up the inventor until after she scratched her itch.

Jenny jerked her chin at the opposite wall, and Caeden slid soundlessly to the other side of the door. She pulled out her laser, powering it up, and then smacked the door lock. It flashed green, which would have been a warning even without sounds of a struggle coming from the other room. This guy was way too smart to leave his front door unlocked.

She dived, going low while Caeden went high. There were two men on the ground and a third pointing a laser at Mac, whom she recognized from the pictures. All the intruders wore distinctive white robes of those Sanctify bastards.

She didn't hesitate, shooting the final man in the back. It wasn't honorable and wasn't nice, but these pieces of shit had taken her brother captive and tortured him. She wasn't in the mood to take chances—or be forgiving. As he collapsed, Jenny scanned the room, ready to deal with anyone else who decided to be a pain in her ass. The scent of charred flesh hit her full in the face, and she wrinkled her nose but powered through it. They didn't have time for her stomach to rebel, not when Sanctify was on the ground. Satisfied there was no other threat in the room, Jenny strode over to check the other two men.

Both dead—and not a mark on their bodies.

Jenny glanced to where Mac stared at the one she'd shot, his face a little on the shocked side. He'd better get used to it. They were on the brink of war, and battle never came wrapped in a pretty package. She looked back at the two he'd taken out and reconsidered—apparently sometimes it did.

"How did you kill them?" Professional curiosity, of course.

"Nerve gas. Didn't extend as far as I thought it would—I'll have to perform some experiments to correct the flaw."

Jenny blinked. He really was a geek. And yet the fact that he took out two members of Sanctify with one of his inventions was kind of hot. She shook her head and stood, motioning Caeden into the room. "These three wouldn't be alone. We need to get the hells out of here."

Mac cleared his throat. "But—"

"Not buts. I'm supposed to keep you alive, and Sanctify already tried for you once." And they weren't the types to run from a loss with their tails between their legs.

He seemed like he wanted to argue, and Jenny wondered if she really *was* going to have to throw him over her shoulder and haul his ass to the ship. A quick glance at his body changed her plans—he had muscles under that threadbare T-shirt. Nice muscles.

Now was so not the time to be thinking about all the delicious things her charge could do to her with muscles like those. The room was so chaotic, she wondered if Sanctify had trashed it before Mac got off the smoke bomb or whatever it was. Piles of random crap covered the floor, until it was a trial just to get from one wall to the other. Not that she wanted to go any deeper than the meter she stood from the door. "Please tell me you're packed."

"More or less." He waded into the room and came up with three bags nearly the size of Jenny. She tried not to notice how easily he carted them around. "There are a few other things—"

"No time." She motioned for Caeden to take one of the bags, leaving Mac with the other two. "We need to move."

His mouth tightened, but he nodded. "I have one last thing to accomplish." Before she could argue, he moved to the wall of screens and flipped up a keypad.

"What are you doing?"

"I'm implanting a virus. I can't leave information like this lying around for anyone to find."

Right. Geek. She shook her head and checked her laser—plenty of charge left to do some damage. They bypassed the lift and hurried down the stairs, earning a grunt from the Bolkerian. The streets were crowded with people selling and buying everything from weapons to the latest sex vids. Dust coated the back of Jenny's throat as she led their little group down a maze of alleys, her laser held at her side and ready for trouble. Mac had no problem keeping up, even hauling the damn bags.

Jenny stopped at the mouth of the alley nearest the shipyard, scanning it for problems.

Empty.

Warning bells pealed through her mind. A shipyard should never be empty, especially not at this hour. Which meant either a trap…or a trap. "Goody."

Caeden went tense next to her. *What's the plan?* At least he trusted her, even if her idiot brother didn't.

The breeze sent a lone scrap of cloth drifting across the ground until it disappeared behind the nearest ship. Four more ships separated her group from *Psyche*. If they could get there and off-planet, no one could catch them.

Getting there might be a problem.

So really, there was only one option. "We use the ships for cover and run like crazy over the open ground. Shoot anything in a white robe." She waited until Mac met her gaze, the shock of his eyes like a punch straight to her chest. Stupid, idiot hormones. She really needed to get laid, because this strange attraction between them wasn't going to be anything but trouble. "Let's go."

They moved as one, sprinting over the open ground to the first ship. Jenny's senses were on hyperdrive, aware of everything around her without focusing on any singular aspect. They skirted the edge of the ship, lasers up and ready.

Hair along the back of her neck stood at attention as they rounded the last ship. There was *Psyche*, looking perfect and untouched. And wrong. Hadriel should have tracked them here and had the hatch down. She held a hand out, stopping Mac from moving forward as three men slipped around the edge of her ship, lasers pointed directly at her group. Those bastards had the drop on them.

"Godsdammit." Jenny considered going for the shot anyway, but there were too many—one of her people would get hit.

The man in the middle stepped forward, too-white teeth turning his smile into a skull's grin. "Put down your weapons."

She could feel the men looking at her, waiting to follow her lead. How the hells did Boone deal with this shit? No wonder he walked around like he had a stick up his ass. He'd always been too aware of the responsibilities that came with ruling—whether he wanted to or not. It was why he was a great king.

But Jenny wasn't Boone. She'd deal with this in her own way. She gave a mad grin of her own. "You're in my way."

"And you have something of ours." His pale eyes flitted over Mac before centering on her once again.

"Don't think so. He's mine." The words sent a funny thrill through her, but with this asshole waving his laser around, there wasn't time to worry about it.

The huge man on the right moved forward a step. "Drop your lasers. Now."

Jenny's smile got wider. "Do as he says." She glanced over her shoulder at Mac. "Be a good boy and get on the ground."

He frowned for a long moment before going to one knee and setting his bags down. Obviously the man needed to learn how to take orders, but she couldn't worry about it now—she had to trust that Caeden knew what she intended.

The center man was still smiling. "Very good. Now come here."

Either Sanctify had next to no information on her, or this guy was stupider than he looked. Jenny beamed as she strode toward him. "Yes, sir."

"Get the other two in the ship." His eyes raked over her, pausing briefly on her nonexistent chest. "I'll be along shortly."

This guy really was a special snowflake if he thought he was going to take any kind of advantage of her. Oh well. He wasn't going to be a problem for long.

CHAPTER FIVE

*W*hat in the gods' names was she thinking? Mac's chest constricted as Jenny waltzed across the open space to stand before the oldest of the Sanctify soldiers. The red stripe on his sleeves marked him as an executioner—he must be the leader of the group on T-II. She laced her hands behind her back, leaving herself completely vulnerable as the monster looked her over like he wanted to eat her alive.

Mac started to rise, but the triplet next to him—Caeden, he suspected, judging from the man's near-black hair—kept him in place with a hand on his shoulder.

How could the man expect him to stand by and watch her be hurt?

The two enforcers on either side of the executioner started toward their group, passing Jenny without hesitation. Mac caught a glint of metal on her wrists, but the men blocked his view before he could see more. Caeden's hand tightened on his shoulder, forcing him to stay in place.

"What—"

The triplet pulled out a laser in a move too fast to follow, taking aim at the priests. First one man and then the other jerked, red spreading over their white robes as their bodies slumped to the ground. The burned-flesh smell hit Mac, and he pressed the back of his hand against his mouth in an effort to keep from vomiting.

A feminine laugh made him look up from the mutilated bodies.

Jenny punched the executioner, her fists encased in gauntlets that seemed to have appeared out of nowhere. Blood flew as the man stumbled back. He raised a hand to his jaw, gingerly touching his split lip. "You'll die for that, bitch. You and the Diviner whore."

Fear surged, icy and thick in Mac's throat. He looked to Caeden, but the man seemed content to let Jenny take the lead. What the hells was wrong with him? She was 53 kilos, tops—the executioner probably weighed double what she did. "Do something."

Caeden barely spared him a glance. His hands motioned out a form of sign language, but Mac had no idea what he was saying. When the man seemed to realize that, he shrugged and jerked his chin toward Jenny, raising an eyebrow.

She'd rocked forward on her toes, fists raised. "Hey asshole, guess what?" She feinted left, dodging back when he swung at her head. She ducked, popping up inside his reach and delivering a devastating uppercut to the executioner's chin. Blood and teeth flew as the man landed on his ass. "Nobody calls my sister a whore."

After one last kick to his face, she turned and gave Mac a huge smile, as if she hadn't just delivered a devastating attack to a member of Sanctify. "Let's get off this hellshole of a planet, yes?"

He could only stare, unable to decide if he was turned on or scared shitless. He'd known Jenny was dangerous, but seeing it in person was something else altogether.

They had to keep moving. Getting off T-II was the immediate priority. Once they were aboard *Psyche*, he would have plenty of time to navigate his unexpected reaction to her actions. He grabbed his bags and stepped over the smoking bodies of the two priests. He could feel her gaze on him, but he wasn't about to stop and talk within view of the bodies.

"Get your ass on the ship before something else goes wrong."

He knew *exactly* what else could go wrong from personal experience—everything. One moment life would be tottering along, happy as can be, and the next everyone around him was dead and his world was falling apart. Holos never caught the true brutality of death, the smell of it, the way it narrowed the world down to a fine point, one second stretching into an eternity. Mac remembered all too well the way the smell of blood clogged the back of his throat, settling in until he could barely breathe past it.

He blinked, trying to focus. This was bullshit. They weren't out of danger and he needed to be functioning on all cylinders— not taking a nightmare walk down memory lane. Jenny needed him *here*.

She grabbed his hand, the touch of her skin doing more to bring back his senses than anything else so far. She was so warm, the calluses on her palms rough against his own. She was real, more so than the memories threatening to suck him under. Tugging him forward, she adjusted the bags on his shoulders and set his hands on the ladder hanging from the hatch. "Hey. I need you to move. Now."

"I can do that." The world came back into focus a centimeter at a time as he climbed. The sharp breeze cutting through his too-thin clothing. The bite of the ladder against his hands. The straps of the bags cutting into his skin. Hauling himself into the ship, he found another triplet standing in the corridor.

The man looked at him for a brief moment before he offered a hand and pulled him to his feet. He cleared his throat, hands moving incomprehensibly. Another mute—fantastic. Mac sighed. "Show me where to go and I'll get out of your hair." The triplet jerked a thumb over his shoulder, motioning down the hall.

Jenny popped through the hatch, Caeden hot on her heels. She shot Mac an unreadable look. "I want him up front with me."

"There will be more." He started down the hall, his equilibrium returning with each step. They weren't safe, no, but the metal walls helped ground him. "They put five on a squad and, by my guess, we just encountered two partial squads. There will be four more men around—possibly more."

Jenny started down the hall. "Caeden, get your ass on the cannons. Hadriel, you know what to do."

"Cannons?" Mac dogged her heels, trying to take in everything as they rushed down the hall and through the hub to the cockpit. Though the ship looked barely workable from the outside, every part of the interior was shiny and new. Obviously someone knew how to fly under the radar. "Since when does *Psyche* have cannons?"

Jenny threw herself into the pilot's seat. "Since Sanctify became a gigantic pain in my ass. Sit down and strap in."

He dropped his bags on the floor and buckled himself into the copilot's chair, watching her out of the corner of his eye. Even with the danger hanging over their heads, she moved with a careless grace, hands flying over the controls as the ship jerked into the air. He grabbed the chair's arms when they swooped up, heading for space. Gods, it had been years since he flew anywhere. That pilot had been focused more on a smooth ride than a quick one. Jenny's approach made him feel as if he'd left his stomach dirtside.

She brought up a view of their tail and cursed under her breath. "Of course it would be a warship they sent. Talk about overkill."

"I don't know if it's overkill, considering who they're coming up against."

"Who?" She gave a wicked grin. "An inventor and little old me?"

Having seen Jenny in action, Mac would have recommended Sanctify send three warships—at minimum. Even that many might not be enough to stop her. She sent them hurtling straight through the atmosphere and into space. He was so focused on keeping his stomach in check that he nearly missed her sigh. It was such a soft, sweet sound, more reminiscent of lovemaking than flying a ship. Then again, what did he know? He was nearly as happy tweaking his inventions as he was with a woman.

A tiny voice whispered it was because he hadn't found the *right* woman, but Mac quashed it. There was no right woman for him. Between the countless hours his workshop demanded and the planet-full of emotional baggage he came with, he considered himself fortunate to make time for the occasional one-night stand.

"Hang on, kids." Jenny jerked them into a barrel roll, sending Mac's stomach somewhere north of his heart. Vibrations from the cannon shook the deck. "Godsdammit, Caeden—stop flirting with them and *kill* something. And don't even try to tell me you're lulling them into a false sense of security—you'd have a better chance of dazzling them with those wide shots. I need them off my ass. Now."

Her smile was firmly in place as she put the ship through a series of maneuvers that left Mac's head spinning. He'd never get used to space. The lack of concrete rules offended him on a personal level—down was never down...except sometimes it was. Ludicrous.

"What's the plan?"

"Does your mother know you have a nasty habit of asking questions at inappropriate times?"

Mac clenched his fists. Just because he knew Jenny's history didn't mean she was aware of his own. "My mother's dead."

Her smile dimmed. "I'm sorry."

"Why?" His breath hissed between his teeth when the entire ship shuddered.

She glanced at the flashing panel lights and flicked on the comm unit. "That better not be my fucking bulwark smoking. Do something about it, Hadriel. *Now*."

Time passed as they continued their crazy path, punctuated only by Jenny's cursing and the occasional maneuver that left him feeling sick. Finally, gods alone knew how much later, she said, "We warp in ten."

As if on her command, the warp point opened up in front of them. Rationally, he knew it was just a doorway to several roads—for lack of a better word—with set destinations. Science, plain and simple. But his heart pounded at the vicious colors he had no name for, all boiling into one another and out again. Here, this deep in space, it didn't matter how intelligent he was. It didn't matter if he'd created some of the most fantastic weapons in the known universe. There was no control. No pretty equations to solve. He was completely at the mercy of nature. He wiped his palms on his pants, unable to tear his gaze from the warp point looming ever closer.

"Mac." Even if her voice wasn't enough to yank his attention away, Jenny's knuckles rapping on his head was. She frowned at him, the tiny line between her brows doing nothing to diminish her beauty. "What the fuck is wrong with you?"

This lanky woman possessed more balls than most men he knew—and less common sense. Some things were better left unsaid. "I have no idea what you're talking about."

"Bullshit." Jenny glanced at the warp point, hit a few controls, and turned back to him. "I, of all people, know crazy when I see it. And I'm supposed to protect said crazy ass, so I need to know how far in over my head I am right now." She reached for him again, but he caught her wrist. The touch sent a zing straight to his toes. He was half surprised every hair on his body wasn't standing on end.

"Stop smacking me." She'd only done it twice, but even the casual sting was more than enough reminder of everything he'd gone through. He didn't want to associate that with Jenny. Not now. Not ever.

"Oh, please. It was just a love pat."

"Don't do it again."

"Or what? I hate to be the one to tell you this, but I can take you with one hand tied behind my back." She gave him a saucy grin and pulled against his grip.

Mac held on, even though every instinct yelled for him to do the opposite. "I'm serious." He might be a closeted shut-in, but he was more than capable of taking care of himself.

"I get it. You're a freak and I'm your caretaker." She struck, fingers hitting his pressure points and breaking his grip. "So store that little tidbit of information somewhere in that freakishly large brain of yours and be a good little genius until I save our asses."

CHAPTER SIX

*J*enny tried to focus on the jump. Those bastards were still on their heels, and *Psyche* might be fast, but she wasn't as bulky as Ophelia's ship, *The Dutchman*. If they took on too much damage, they'd be floating helplessly, waiting to be picked off. She triple-checked the coordinates. They'd pop out near Terra I, exactly the opposite direction Sanctify would expect them to run if they were trying to get out of the Inner Second Quadrant. Hopefully it would be enough to lose their tail, but she'd do what was needed to get them out of this alive.

As they hit the warp point, the entire ship shuddered in protest. Her skin broke out in gooseflesh and she shivered. There were thousands of theories about what kind of space or plane of existence or whatever connected warp points—hells, she suspected Mac was the type of person who could quote every single one—but she'd always believed it was dead space. A place where the souls of those who'd passed away could touch the living. It would explain the way her body temperature dropped and her breath ghosted from her lips. Here, she could almost believe she'd see Dad again, see the way his lips quirked up when he was proud of her.

But that was just a temporary flight of fancy. In reality, the only thing that mattered was living to fight another day.

She could sense Mac's eyes on her as they popped back into straight space, but Jenny had no time for him. Wheeling the ship around, she scooted forward in her seat, ready to jump again if Sanctify made an appearance.

A heartbeat passed, then another.

Could they really have lost them after only one jump? Last time Sanctify was this close, it took her nearly seven jumps to lose them—and she'd almost killed Ophelia in the process. Thinking about how pale the Diviner had been, all vitality drained from her face, still made her skin crawl.

"What's wrong?"

Everything. Nothing. She couldn't decide if suspecting a trap meant she was being smart or paranoid, and the indecision didn't help her temper any. It was almost enough to make her wish for home.

Almost.

The only warning she got was a ripple in colors, and then the giant hull of a white warship shot out of the warp point. "Shit." She veered to the left, cutting so close, she was sure she could feel the wake of its passing. "Now, Caeden!" The warship shuddered as he unloaded shot after shot into it, and then they were back in the warp point.

It hurt to breathe, but the discomfort barely registered. Those wily bastards were onto her, and even with Caeden poking holes in their ship, she couldn't risk waiting outside the warp point again.

They shot into straight space. "We're not done yet." She wheeled around and hit the warp point again, this time heading for the Outer Third Quadrant. It put her too damn close to

Sanctify for her liking, but it was the only way to escape the Terra planets.

They had to take a chance.

Another heartbeat of straight space, and then they dived back in. Her lungs felt like ice, but it wasn't enough to slow her down. "One more!"

This time, she waited, poised to jump again if they had somehow tracked her progress. It should be impossible, but Sanctify had the nasty tendency of surprising her. A full thirty seconds passed without anyone showing up, and then a full minute, and only then did she sit back. "Everyone okay?"

No one answered, but she had monitors on the triplets, and the ship seemed none the worse for wear. Thank the gods.

Now she just had to deal with the inventor beside her. "Where are we going?"

"Terra IV or Terra III."

A prison planet or one with the Star Council sitting in session—both in the quadrant they'd just ran away from. "Have you lost your godsforsaken mind? You know what? Don't answer that. It doesn't matter—we're not going to either."

Mac's eyebrows dropped. "Excuse me?"

Great. Another male who had issues with women opposing him—just like her big brother. If she let him, she had no doubt he'd be railroading her just like every other man in her life. Well, this was her godsdamned ship and she ruled here. "I said, Sir Genius, that you need to pick another planet."

"No." He shook his head. "They are the only valid options where we have a reasonable chance of remaining undetected."

"Find a different option." She thought she sounded quite reasonable, but he just frowned harder, as if he thought she might be joking.

"There *are* no other options."

Obviously the man had never dealt with the O'Keirna family

or he wouldn't have bothered arguing. He wasn't going to win, but his blind denial grated on her nerves. She turned to the screen in front of her, fingers caressing the keys while she considered. "Hmmm."

"What are you doing?"

"If you won't pick a place with some decent entertainment, preferably *not* in the quadrant we just left Sanctify trolling, then I'm going to do it for you."

"Entertainment shouldn't even be a factor."

"So says you. I say different." Keiluna was out—ever since Sanctify found out Ophelia's family used the planet as a base of operations, it'd doubled the number of patrols in all the cities and settlements. She wasn't nuts enough to try to get through *that* net. She liked her skin where it was.

"Jenny." Gods, he sounded like Boone when he said her name like that—as if she was acting crazy, and he was going to make the decision for her...for her own good, of course. Well, she wasn't completely crazy and he wasn't her brother. Crazy was staying where they were any longer than necessary.

Hansarda was an obvious choice, but she kind of doubted Boone would greet them with open arms. He wanted to protect Ophelia and their new kid, so giving Sanctify more reason to attack their home planet wouldn't be smart.

An idea stopped her in her tracks. A terrible, wonderful, treacherous idea. It was quite possibly the worst notion she'd ever had, but she couldn't shake how bloody perfect it would be.

Sisilean. The planet where dirty little boys and girls went to get their kicks—where every sexual fantasy could become reality. The kind of place not even Sanctify could touch.

Who in their right minds who expect her to take Mac there? Most people looked at Sisilean as an impossible dream because of the hefty price tag that came with it.

She, on the other hand, had an in—friends who wouldn't

hesitate to open their home to her and her crew. Under normal circumstances, she wouldn't be willing to bring trouble to their doorstep by even asking, but desperate times called for desperate measures.

No way could she spend gods knew how long on a planet like Terra IV.

She looked up and found Mac staring at her as if she'd grown a second head. "What?"

He opened his mouth, shut it, and sighed. "It doesn't matter what I say. You're going to do what you want either way."

Obviously. She started to program the coordinates to Sisilean and then thought better of it. The twins wouldn't thank her for showing up unannounced, entourage in tow. "I have a call to make, so I need you to either get out or shut the hells up."

He raised an eyebrow, curiosity sparking in his eyes. "I'll be good."

His words sent a shiver of something dangerous through her before she smothered it. There would be plenty of playmates on Sisilean. *This* man was off-limits. "Better be."

The call went through, saving her from having to come up with a decent threat. Gwendolyn and Lucien were known as the Golden Twins, and they played to it with every ounce of their inexhaustible energy. Those two could out-party Jenny most days of the week, which was saying something because she left most people in the dust.

The static cleared, revealing a petite woman squinting into the screen. On anyone else the expression would be pinched and ugly, but Gwendolyn made it endearing—like a godsdamned puppy. A sexy puppy. "My eyesight must be going because I could swear I see my long-lost friend Jenny. But that's impossible. She's supposed to be on lockdown. At least that's the excuse I keep getting every time I try to see her. Could it be the delicious Boone actually let you out to play?"

She ignored the thread of disappointment that it'd been Gwen instead of Luc to answer the call. "Oh shut it, Gwennie. You know damn well my brother will never get that stick out of his ass." She drew herself up, letting the last of her worry about Mac go. "I'm on a mission."

"Boring." Gwen faked a yawn. "Tell me something juicy."

Jenny slanted a look at Mac. To his credit, though he was watching the conversation with interest, he didn't seem love-struck like most males when they got an eyeful of Gwendolyn. And she was offering up an eyeful now—her robe barely covered the essentials and, as it was see-through, she might as well have not even bothered. Her friend's serious lack of modesty wasn't new, but she found herself gritting her teeth at the dark nipples that kept flashing around. "Cover yourself up, hussy. We have company."

Gwen laughed, the low, throaty sound worth millions on its own. "Where did you pick this one up? Want to share?"

Fuck no. She smiled to cover up her insane gut reaction. "Perhaps another time."

"Now you're just teasing me."

It was so easy to fall back into their banter as if the last year of separation had never happened. "Would I do you false?"

"Oh Jenny, you do me false every time. You'd think I'd stop playing cards with you after the hundredth time you took me for all I had."

No one wanted to play cards with her anymore. "It's because you're a dumb blonde, and not even a natural one."

"At least I have tits." Gwen leaned forward, peering down. "Have you hit puberty yet or still living in hope?"

Jenny laughed. "Sad to say, I think that ship has flown."

"Oh, sweetie, I missed you terribly."

"I missed you, too. That's why I'm coming to visit."

Instantly, all joking was gone from Gwen's demeanor. She

perked up, her dark eyes wide. "Truly?"

"Truly. You're going to be my supersecret hiding place."

"As if I haven't heard *that* line before."

She let the smile drop as if it'd never existed. "In all seriousness, you need to know the situation. We have Sanctify on our ass. It might not be safe for you, but I couldn't think of anyplace else." Mac cleared his throat and she glared at him. "Anyplace I could survive. This smart-ass wants us to bunker down on Terra III."

Gwen shuddered. "Gods, we can't have that. When can we expect you?"

She'd hoped for the invitation, but relief hit her harder than she'd expected. This was a bearable solution. Ophelia's precious genius would be safe, and she'd be free to sow some wild oats. "Twenty-four hours. Maybe a little more if we run into trouble."

"Then don't run into trouble. Oh, this is so fabulous. Luci is going to be tickled pink."

Picturing the cultured other half to Gwen's over-the-top personality, she laughed. "Oh, I'll just bet." Truth be told, she'd missed him even more than Gwen. It had been way too long.

"Why are we still talking? I have too much to do. Get your ass over here. Now."

"Yes, ma'am." Jenny cut off the call when she squealed in protest. "Gets her every time." The blonde associated "ma'am" with being old and no one could tell her otherwise. So of course Jenny had to stick her with it occasionally, just to watch her squirm.

"Explain what the hells just happened." The borderline panic in Mac's voice made her laugh harder. He waved his hands, as if he could cut off the sound like a maestro. "Tell me that wasn't Gwendolyn Devine."

"Why wouldn't it be?"

He shook his head. "You're friends with a sex vid star."

"Of course." Jenny smiled all the brighter for the small thread of hurt worming through her at his words. She lifted her chin, meeting his eyes. There was nothing wrong with her friends, and there sure as hells was nothing wrong with her. "You'd better hang on, princess. We're in for a few jumps."

"You're not seriously planning to go to Sisilean, are you?"

"I am. And why can't I?" She set in the coordinates for the first jump—there were three jumps from their current position to Sisilean. The chance of anyone following them successfully there was slim to none.

"Sisilean is a Far Reach planet. The natives are reptilian creatures of highly unusual intelligence who like the taste of human flesh." Mac ticked the points off on his fingers as if she gave a damn. "Even inside the gated communities, it's still dangerous. Not to mention the colonists themselves. They're…"

"*Freaks* would be the word you're looking for. Which makes it the perfect place to hide from those holier-than-thou bastards." She winked. "And you'll fit right in once we get you in some leather."

"For your information, 'freaks' wasn't the word I was looking for."

"Sure it was." She gave a mock shiver. "Bondage and role-play and whipping, oh my. Stop being such a stick-in-the-mud."

Mac shrugged as if they were talking about the freaking weather. "I couldn't care less what consenting adults do to entertain themselves."

"Then what's the problem? The planet is invite-only and the exceptions get shot out of space."

"That's…true." He gave a blatantly reluctant nod. Silly man, thinking he could outmaneuver her. Even Boone would beat a hasty retreat when Jenny got going, and her brother was one of the smartest people she knew. Not that she'd ever tell him so, but still.

"Then it's all settled." She cut off his protest by cranking on the intercom. "Better get strapped in, boys, and hang on to your dangly bits. Here we go."

CHAPTER SEVEN

An invitation to Sisilean. It was something most boys dreamed of as soon as they hit puberty—to be surrounded by sex vid stars, each more beautiful than the next. Mac never shared that particular fantasy, but even he could see the attraction. It was a place where every desire was indulged, no matter the flavor.

And he was going there with Jenny.

"Hang on, princess."

Mac closed his eyes as they coasted through the third jump, his stomach cramping. He wondered at the purpose of all the nicknames she used. Probably another wall she erected between herself and the rest of the world. Just like the damned grin. He wanted to see her smile with genuine feeling, rather than just a mad gleam in her eye. Taking a deep breath, he tried to gain some mental distance. His ridiculous infatuation with the woman had to stop. Where they were going, there would be plenty of eerily perfect men to dote on her. It made him more than a little sick to think about. Or perhaps that was all the jumping.

They slid into straight space and it was as if a weight lifted from his chest. He inhaled deeply. "Are we there yet?"

"Do I look like your freaking mom?"

It was too much on the heels of recent events. The memories hit him full force, dragging him under. The ropes biting into his wrists and neck, holding him immobile against the chair, unable to look away. The long spill of his mother's crimson hair, its beauty in stark contrast to the horror the rest of the room contained. The men's jeers and laughs as they did things to her…

Mac nearly startled out of his chair when Jenny knelt in front of him. It wasn't until she wrapped her arms around him that he realized he was shaking. He tried to push her away, but she was having none of it. "Why are you hugging me?" Not that he was complaining, exactly, but it didn't seem like a rational response.

"Because you're shaking and it's my fault. Now stop being such a macho jerk and let me cuddle you for a minute. I fucked up. I'm sorry."

"It's nothing." The words tumbled from numb lips, but he stopped trying to make her move. It was too right to have her holding him like this, her cheek pressed against his chest. Warmth soaked into his skin through the shirt he wore. Mac suddenly wished it were thinner or, hells, gone completely.

"It's not nothing, you idiot. Gods, can't you even let me apologize?"

He leaned down and rested his chin on her head, the last traces of the memories fading away. It was always like this. They struck with the fierceness of an attacking Bolkerian, and were gone between one breath and the next. He'd never come out of them with a beautiful woman in his arms, though. "Sorry I'm not letting you have your moment."

"That's better." She gave him one last squeeze and leaned back, taking her warmth with her. "I'm generally an asshole, and I get a bit chatty without really thinking it through. Feel free to smack me." She shrugged, her gaze searching his face as if assuring herself he was okay.

She was, hands down, the strangest creature he'd ever encountered. With so many facets of personality to explore, she represented a challenge like Mac had never experienced before. And when she knelt so close, her scent wrapping around him, seeming to soak into his brain and muddle his thoughts, it was everything he could do not to kiss her.

As soon as the thought crossed his mind, he wondered at it. Why resist? Why not kiss her when she smelled so wonderful and felt so amazing against him? He moved before doubt could set in, hooking the back of her neck, and towed her closer. Jenny's sound of protest died when her lips met his.

Her entire body went taut, hands coming up to grab his upper arms. He maintained his grip, using his free hand to stroke down her back, marveling at the play of muscles under his fingertips. So much strength, so much dedication, so much *life*, all wrapped in a package he couldn't resist.

It had been so terribly long since he kissed anyone. But worry had no place here. He caught her bottom lip, raking his teeth gently over it. She gave a little groan and opened to him, tasting of mint and woman. Her tongue danced with his, until he was sure his head would explode. Shifting his grip, he gathered a fistful of her hair and used it to tilt her head back. She gave way willingly, a sigh slipping free as he kissed along her neck.

He needed her closer, needed the feeling of skin on skin, simply *needed*.

The franticness of his thoughts slammed Mac back into reality. He froze, distantly aware they were both breathing hard and clutching each other. This was wrong. He shouldn't be making advances on Jenny—and certainly not in the godsdamned cockpit of her ship. He was supposed to be an intelligent man and yet here he was, pawing her like an adolescent boy with more hormones than sense.

He jerked back, releasing her so quickly she fell against him. "I'm sorry."

"Don't be." She pushed to her feet and shoved her hair off her face, grin firmly in place. "It wasn't that bad of a kiss."

"Jenny—"

She held up a hand. "We're good. Just leave it." Dropping into her chair, she turned to the controls, flipping to a screen showing the lightest-brown-haired triplet, who greeted them when they boarded—Hadriel. "All right, boys, we have twenty-three hours until we get dirtside. Feel like a game of cards?"

His hands went through a series of motions and Jenny gasped. "I'm offended! I don't have to cheat—I'm just that good."

They shared a smile that Mac had no part of, and he immediately resented the other man for it. She had a history with her crew, a history he couldn't hope to compete with.

Taking a large mental step back, he made an effort to analyze his reaction. The kiss had affected him more than he anticipated, but it was merely a hormonal reaction. He'd have to be dead not to be attracted to Jenny. The borderline jealousy, however, was equally unexpected. Irrational. There was too much to think about, too many options to consider. And emotions only made things more complicated.

What he needed was a clear head.

It took all of five minutes to find the crew quarters and the room with all his personal belongings. He palm-locked the door and settled onto his cot, staring at the bags he'd brought along. His hands twitched, itching to take apart or build something. With twenty-three hours he might be able to put the finishing touches on the laser.

Confident that was exactly the distraction he needed, Mac settled down to work.

• • •

So tell us about this one. Shadrach paused to toss a blue chip onto the table. *He's pretty, but I don't think he's dumb enough for you.*

"That's not very nice." Even if he was right. What did someone like Mac have in common with someone like her? She shouldn't have let things get so carried away in the cockpit, wouldn't have even gotten that close in the first place if she hadn't acted like a bitch. Jenny matched Shad's bet and gave him innocent eyes. "Maybe I'll just keep his mouth too busy to talk."

They laughed just like she hoped they would. Hadriel cocked his head at her as he folded his cards. "You like him."

"That's crazy talk." Damn it, she'd answered too quickly. All three perked up like freaking hound dogs.

Caeden leaned forward, dark eyes lighting up. *You* do *like him.*

"And you need a mint—your breath is nasty." She looked around the table. "Are we gossiping like schoolgirls or are we playing cards?"

"It's your option." Hadriel's lips quirked. "You nervous? I think we're dancing a little too close to the truth, boys."

Her foot started tapping, but she stilled it. If the triplets got the best of her now, they'd never let her live it down. Besides, they were wrong. Mac was a job. Nothing more, nothing less. No matter how good of a kisser he was. Dredging up every bit of sass possible, she laid down her cards. "I win."

You can't know— Shadrach's hands froze. *How in the hells do you do that?* He motioned at the full house in front of her.

She shrugged as she gathered up the stack of chips. "Just lucky, I guess."

Then you're the luckiest person I know. He pushed back from the table and stood. *I'm done. You've cleaned me out.*

"Aw, Shadrach. Don't be a poor loser. It's all fun and games until someone gets hurt."

You know what, Jenny? I love you, but fuck off. He disappeared through the open door, leaving her staring in shock after him.

"What the hells was that all about?"

Hadriel and Caeden looked at each other and shrugged. "His ex has been sending messages again. Makes him cranky." Hadriel started shuffling the cards.

"That bitch? Can we just kill her already? I know plenty of places to hide an inconvenient body."

"The scary part is I don't think you're joking."

She gave them a blank look. "Why would I be joking? She might as well have torn out his heart and spaced it. That bitch deserves to die." When they didn't say anything, she sighed. "Come on. Seriously. Do you really think I'm going to hunt her down and string her up?"

"Actually, I could see that happening," Hadriel said.

Caeden nodded. *You're kind of scary like that.*

There was nothing to do but laugh. "Fine, fine. I promise to do her no bodily harm as a result of this new shit with Shadrach. That's as good as you're going to get."

"Fair enough." Hadriel dealt the cards. "Don't think we've forgotten about you."

Of course they hadn't. That would be too easy. "There's nothing to remember. I'm keeping him safe. Enough said."

Want to know the sad thing, Hadriel? Caeden discarded two cards and drew replacements. *I think she almost believes that.*

She didn't. Not really. Even if Mac hadn't held some freakish attraction before, the kiss had done her in. Hells, her head was *still* spinning. If he hadn't pulled away, she would have been in his lap and getting naked inside of three seconds. It was *still* a fight not to abandon this card game and go hunt him down for a redo.

But then his look of horror flashed in her mind, effectively dousing her desire. Why had he looked like she'd just sucker punched him and then killed his dog? She was a good kisser, damn it, and gods knew she wasn't ugly. Most guys would have jumped for a chance to get their hands on her.

Mac wasn't most guys, though, which was the problem.

"You're thinking about him again, aren't you?" Hadriel leaned over and tapped her forehead. "Focus. We're playing a game."

She slapped his hand away. "I'm all in."

"Jenny—"

If she wants to throw away credits, let her. Caeden shoved his stack in to meet hers. *I call.*

It was a stupid move, but she wasn't in the mood to play anymore. She flipped over her cards and stared. Two pair.

Caeden tossed his cards on the table. *If you weren't so damn distracted, I'd accuse you of cheating.*

"I'm not going to apologize for rocking at cards." She offered a saucy smile that she didn't feel. "But if it helps, we're on our way to Sisilean."

A slow blush started up his neck, spreading over his face. Just like she'd known it would. *You're joking.*

"Nope." She slapped Caeden on the back hard enough to send him staggering and danced out of the room.

The boys would definitely want some freedom to pursue whatever tail would have them—the exception might be Shadrach, but hopefully some pretty thing could sex some sense into him. They deserved it after the last few years of running and fighting, and then being stuck on Hansarda for so long. The triplets were human, but they weren't native to her planet and some of the customs still made them queasy.

She could only hope Gwen and Luc's antics would be enough to distract her from thinking about that stupid kiss.

CHAPTER EIGHT

*J*enny barely made it off the hatch ladder before she was lifted off her feet in a hug. "Oh my gods!" The pitch of Gwen's voice was high enough to shatter glass. "You're really here!"

"Weird how that works. I say I'm coming and I show up." She laughed and wiggled from her friend's grip. "Holy hells, you really pulled out all the stops, didn't you?"

Across from *Psyche* was a stretch-hover, penned in by two military-looking vehicles with more weapons than she could count in the three seconds she had before Gwen started talking again. "Of course. As if I do anything halfway."

"Where's Luc?" She angled around her friend as if he'd appear from thin air. She'd fully expected him to be here, since he didn't have a lot of faith in his twin when it came to keeping out of trouble—rightfully so—and it wasn't like him to miss an opportunity to try to boss Jenny around.

"Oh, he's just finishing up a shoot. He's thrilled you've come to visit." She laced an arm through Jenny's and towed her toward the stretch-hover. The damn thing was a brilliant white, sure to stand out in the thick green jungles they had to travel through to reach their destination. While she could appreciate how bright and shiny it was—not to mention the fact there was sure to be alcohol inside—she still didn't like calling so much attention. They were supposed to be hiding out, after all.

Speaking of that…she turned, gaze flitting over the triplets and coming up empty. "Where's our little techno geek?"

Hadriel shrugged. *Thought he was with you.*

Damn it. The last thing she wanted was to go fetch the man, but it wasn't as if she could leave him here. She sighed. "I bet that's what you told your mother every time Caeden fell down the stairs and landed on his head."

Hey!

Jenny patted Gwen's arm. "Hold that thought—I have to go get my man." It was only when her friend raised dark eyebrows that she realized what she'd said. "Godsdammit, not like *that*. I'm babysitting, remember."

"I remember what you said. I also remember what *your man* looks like." She licked her lips. "I wouldn't mind babysitting him if you get bored."

Over her dead body. She ducked out of the blonde's grip. "Be back before you can miss me."

She was up the ladder in record time, annoyance twisting deeper with every breath. Damn him for making her feel like her skin was overheating. It had been her every intention to make sure they weren't alone together, and that lasted all of a minute. And it wasn't even her shoddy self-control to blame. It was Mac. The lock to his room was blinking a dull red, but no door was barred to the captain of the ship.

Or so she thought until the computer ignored her command to grant access. "This is what I get for having a freaking genius on my ship. He screws with everything."

Smacking the door, she yelled, "Hey, Sir Fuck-With-My-Ship-Again-And-I'll-Stake-You, let me in." Sexy or not, she wouldn't hesitate to shove a stake up his ass and leave him on the edge of the desert if he messed with *Psyche*. Boone would be so proud. Annoyed all over again, she kicked the door. "Open up."

Nothing.

Jenny stared at the blinking light, wondering what her brother would do if she killed Azure Enterprises' little pet. Hells, what was she thinking? It wasn't Boone she would have to worry about—it was Ophelia.

With another sigh, she marched to the nearest intercom and slapped it on. For once, no static sounded. "Connect to Gamma Cabin." She crossed her arms over her chest, foot tapping while it thought about her request. This ship might be one of the fastest in the universe, but the damn thing needed a complete overhaul of its comm system.

"Yes?" Mac sounded harried and pissed off.

She blinked. "Excuse me for interrupting whatever the hells you have going on right now, but you need to get off my ship. We're here."

"I need another hour. Maybe two."

Oh, hells no. Jenny's foot started tapping faster. What happened to the mild-mannered guy she'd picked up on T-II? Sure, he'd taken out two members of Sanctify all by himself, but there wasn't any other indication that the dude was a force to be reckoned with. Except the little glints of stubbornness and strength she got when they argued. Shit. "How about this? You get out of that cabin now or I cut down the door and you leave my ship in pieces."

The pause stretched out so long she started to wonder if he planned on ignoring her. Obviously the man had no idea who he was dealing with.

Finally Mac sighed. "You aren't going to leave me alone, are you?"

Right. Because she was the crazy one in this situation. Jenny let her voice fall into singsong pattern. "Of course not, silly. Now get your cute ass out of that cabin and let's go meet some sex vid stars."

Another, longer, sigh. "Five minutes?"

Her jaw started to hurt from clenching her teeth so hard. "Try it and see what happens."

"Fine."

The door to the cabin slid open, and she didn't give him a chance to change his mind before she charged in there.

"What in the seven hells?" It looked as if some giant gadget had vomited its innards all over the room. "You know how to make yourself at home, don't you?" Maybe it would be better to stuff him somewhere for the time being instead of bringing him around the twins. Gods knew, Luc would have a tizzy fit if his perfect home was messed up.

Though it might be worth the headache to watch those two go head-to-head.

He actually had the grace to look sorry. "I got a little carried away."

A little? There was no way she wanted to take the time to clean this with everyone waiting for them. "If you say so."

"Jenny—" He hesitated and, for once, she was in no hurry to fill the silence. "I'm sorry I was short with you."

It seemed they were destined to be forever apologizing to each other. She snapped her mouth shut before she made a careless response. Best to get this conversation out of the way as soon as possible and then never look back. "Listen up, because I'm only going to say this once. Are you listening?"

He nodded, watching her like she was a rabid animal. "Yes."

"Stop apologizing about stupid shit. I'm not breakable and I won't go cry myself to sleep because mean old Mac thought kissing me was a mistake." There were plenty of other reasons to cry herself to sleep, but none of that bore thinking about now. "Got it?

He nodded again. "Yes."

Well, that was easy. They could stand here all day arguing about it, but there was no point. Jenny shrugged. "Whatever. Get what you need and let's boogie."

Talking done, he moved around the room, tossing random items into his bag. She crossed her arms and leaned against the doorframe, watching him. It was her job, wasn't it? If she spent some time wondering if his hands were as clever on a woman's body as they were on machines…well, what did she expect? He was smoking hot, and she was only human. Shit happened. It was a pity their kiss ended before she had the chance to find out how those fingers really felt.

He went still when he met her gaze. "If you could see the way you're looking at me right now…"

"Don't need to." She tried to shrug away the buzzy feeling in her stomach. "You ready? I think we've taken long enough."

"Yes," Mac said slowly. He grabbed a laser as he stood and offered it to her. "I'd like you to be the first to have one."

Jenny took the weapon, examining it carefully. It looked like any other laser, except the cartridge glowed blue instead of green. Aiming it at the far wall, she widened her stance, getting a feel for its weight. It fit in her palm as if it were made for her. "Nice."

"It doesn't overheat as quickly as normal ones." He stepped closer, showing her a switch on the side. "It also has a setting for stun, which ups the number of shots as well."

"Mm-hmm." Her mind got sidetracked by those hands again, his calluses different from her own but no less present. Standing next to each other, the differences in their sizes only became more apparent. He was half a head taller than her, which put him easily over two meters, and his shoulders dwarfed hers. Gods, who knew they grew geniuses so damn sexy? She finally dragged her gaze away from his body to find him watching her, as if she were a puzzle he didn't have the answer to.

"I would give a lot to know what you're thinking right now."

She licked her lips. Now was the time to brush him off, or make a smart-ass comment that would kill the tension welling up between them. Or, hells, even take a step back so she wasn't in his personal space. It would be the right thing to do. The *responsible* thing to do.

But faced with those shifting eyes that saw too much, she couldn't stop herself from telling the truth. "I was thinking that you're one sexy son of a gun."

The shock on his face would have made her laugh under any other circumstances. Instead, Jenny kissed him. Stupid, unforgivably stupid, but it seemed like the thing to do.

This time there was no slow exploration, no cautious opening to each other. Instead, Mac's tongue met hers stroke for stroke, so closely miming a different kind of penetration that she moaned, her free arm going around his neck while she held the laser away from them with the other. For his part, he had no such restrictions. His hands were under her shirt in seconds, rough palms sliding over her back and pulling her closer. She went eagerly, hooking one leg around his waist and writhing when his arousal pressed against her, right where she wanted it. Or it would be if there were a few less layers of clothes between them.

"Oh my." Gwen's laugh held even more delight than her words.

Shit. Jenny shoved Mac so hard, he tripped and landed on the cot in a heap. Spinning to face her friend, she pointed accusingly. "Your timing hasn't gotten any better."

Or maybe it had. What was she thinking, kissing him again? Telling him she thought he was sexy? The idea was to put some distance between them, not try to jump his bones every time they were alone. It hadn't even been thirty-six hours since she picked him up—it didn't exactly shine a golden light on her chances of making it through this mission without getting naked with her charge. Which meant Boone would never trust her to do another solo run without a babysitter.

Gwen peered around her to where Mac struggled to his feet. "*Au contraire*, my timing is impeccable. Two minutes later and you would have been boning like bunnies, and then where would we be? We're wasting daylight and the natives tend to get… restless…once darkness falls."

The idea of killer lizards getting restless was enough to make the small hairs on the back of her neck stand on end. "Then let's get this show on the road. Is everyone else ready?"

"Of course, sweetie. We're just waiting on you and your man." Gwen's dark eyes danced with mischief. "I do think my darling twin is going to be jealous."

Mac shouldered his bag, somehow managing to hide the massive tent in the front of his pants. "Twin?"

Jenny cracked her neck, grateful for the chance to get back in control of the situation. "You didn't know our friend Gwendolyn Devine has a twin?" She tapped her bottom lip, pretending to think. "I'm surprised you've never seen his films before. Then again, he does cater to a different clientele than Gwennie here."

"Stop teasing the poor man." Gwen grinned. "Dearest Lucien is rather famous in the male-on-male circuit, with a specialty in BDSM."

"I see."

"You don't have a problem with that, I hope?" Jenny gave him innocent eyes. She didn't run across many heterosexual males who didn't get a little squirmy at the thought—hells, even Boone avoided Lucien. Then again, that might be because Luc made it a point of groping her brother whenever he was within touching distance. Tomato, tomahto.

"Why would it be a problem?" Mac carefully stepped around her and strode from the room. It was everything she could do not to check out his ass as he walked away.

"I like this one. He doesn't ruffle easily."

Which was a problem in and of itself. What was Jenny supposed to do with a man who didn't get all huffy when she was outrageous? She straightened, switching out her old laser for the one Mac had given her. It didn't matter if it was a prototype—he had made it, so it was bound to be freaking perfect. "Sure he does, Gwennie. I just haven't found the right buttons yet."

CHAPTER NINE

*T*hick heat plastered Mac's clothing to his body, making him profoundly grateful his physical reaction to Jenny had passed. The triplets gave him appraising looks as he climbed down the hatch, and there was a distinctly hostile gleam in Hadriel's eyes. He was one to watch out for. If Mac could win him over, it was highly probable the other two would follow. Something to consider once he figured out a plan of action.

They piled into the stretch-hover, easily fitting with room to spare. Every aspect of the vehicle screamed luxury, from the minibar stocked with high-end liquor to the plush red velvet seats. Personally, he would have felt more comfortable in one of the armed hovers, but he doubted anyone else would agree from the way the triplets lit up at the sight of liquor.

Jenny and Gwendolyn sat on the opposite seat, watching him with eerily similar expressions. Whatever they had up their sleeves, he wanted no part of it. Even the oh-so-casual way they brought up Gwendolyn's twin was calculated. As if Mac was one to sit on a pedestal and look down on anyone else. How the man chose to make his living was no one's business but his own. And if he preferred men to women? More power to him.

"So, Mac, tell me a bit about yourself." Gwendolyn leaned forward, offering up a healthy view of her breasts, her dark skin making them stand out against the white shirt she wore.

"I work for Azure Enterprises." He kept his eyes firmly on her face. He would not play these games with them, not when there was so much at stake and his reactions to Jenny were so damn unpredictable. Back on the ship, he'd only meant to show her the laser, but then she'd looked at him as if it was everything she could do not to touch him. He'd never had a woman watch him with that expression on her face.

Granted, her shoving him halfway across the room as soon as her friend showed up wasn't the best sign, but the spark between them only seemed to grow stronger every time they got close. Even now, he wanted time alone with her to see what it would take to coax that sweet sigh from her mouth.

Mac rubbed a hand over his face, forcing himself back on track. "There's nothing particularly exciting about what I do." Not to anyone else, though seeing Jenny's eyes light up when she held the laser had felt pretty damn exciting. Gods, he didn't need this fascination with her.

No, what he really needed was a place to set up a temporary comm room to get his feelers up and running again. No doubt Sanctify hadn't stopped moving forward with whatever it was planning, so Ophelia and Boone needed all the information they could get.

"Oh, that's no fun." Gwendolyn pouted. On anyone else, the expression would look sulky and childish, but somehow she managed to make it extremely sexy. Part of the overall effect was the way she was dressed, a white shirt tucked into gray slacks—not overtly attention-grabbing, but the fit was tighter than necessary, the vee of the shirt a bit too deep to be strictly professional. A more ruthless man might play one woman against the other, flirting with the sex vid star to make Jenny jealous, but Mac had no time or patience for such games, even as an experiment.

There was only one woman who captivated him.

She crossed those impossibly long legs. "He's being ridiculous."

Gwendolyn gave a coy smile. "That's okay, sweetie. We have plenty of time to work on him."

"I don't know. He'll be a tough nut to crack."

Mac sighed. "You do realize I can hear you?" He glanced at the triplets, but they were no help, obviously preferring to watch the drama play out, rather than participate.

When he looked back at the women, he found them staring. "What's your point?" Jenny recrossed her legs. Was she doing that solely to drive him out of his mind? Because he couldn't look at her without wondering what it would feel like to have those legs wrapped around his head.

Focus. He needed to focus.

He closed his eyes, dredging up the necessary information to reestablish his comm room. It wouldn't be easy since he'd left most of his supplies behind, but it could be done. And it would keep him distracted and occupied for at least several days. Gods only knew the trouble Jenny could get into during the intervening time, but at least he wouldn't make a fool of himself again by pinning her against the nearest available surface. He hoped. "I'll need some space to set up shop."

Gwendolyn stared at him in horror. "Surely he isn't talking about *working* while he's here?"

"You see what I'm dealing with?" Jenny waved a careless hand in his direction. "It's no biggie—I'll have enough fun for two people."

"Only two?" The blonde laughed. "You're slowing down in your old age."

"Them's fighting words, Gwennie." Jenny cocked her head. "Have you been keeping up with the knife? Or has being a sex vid star made you lazy, too?"

Gwendolyn gasped and laid a hand against her chest. "Just because I left Valneci as soon as I could find a ship willing to carry me doesn't mean I stopped practicing. Do you think I keep this body by lazing around?"

Mac refocused, gaze jumping between the two. Obviously his knowledge of Jenny had larger holes than he'd originally anticipated. He hadn't been aware she knew Gwendolyn until yesterday, let alone that they apparently had a history. And gods knew the sex vid star didn't advertise she was Hansardian—it was a fact some people would pay good money to know. With her distinct features and dark coloring—fake hair color aside—he categorized her as one of the Drieya clan. They were particularly bloodthirsty, even for Hansardians, and had a reputation that made the other clans wary.

He filed the knowledge away, making a mental note to dig deeper and then ensure that any digital evidence of the truth was well hidden from searching eyes. Any connection to Boone and Ophelia would be exploited, and this was one he hadn't known existed. Hopefully their enemies remained equally in the dark.

"Good. I'm still going to kick your ass, but I'm glad to hear you aren't bringing shame on our people."

Gwendolyn flipped her hair over her shoulder in an expert move. "Luci's better than I am, but he's always had a way with blades."

"That's because you two haven't fought against anyone with sweet skills like me in a long time." Jenny cracked her knuckles.

"Your idea of fun leaves something to be desired." She gave a delicate shudder.

Jenny laughed. "Don't worry, Gwennie. We'll still drink ourselves stupid and make questionable decisions."

"Oh, thank the gods. I was worried you'd grown up on me."

"Never."

And yet for all Jenny's bubbly speech, she still had her fake smile firmly in place. The exchange only heightened his curiosity. There was obvious affection between the two, but he couldn't tell if her show was for him or for Gwendolyn or just because she was so used to pretending that she didn't know how to drop the mask. If it was even a mask. At this point there wasn't enough evidence to confirm which Jenny was the real woman, and which was the mask. And he *wanted* to know for more reasons than to simply satisfy his curiosity. She was a puzzle, to be sure, but there was a thread of something deeper than he couldn't help but want to pluck. That wasn't even taking into account the sheer desire he felt for her.

It would take time, but he fully intended on unraveling the riddle that was Jenny O'Keirna.

The rest of the ride passed quickly, the women chatting about inconsequential things until the stretch-hover bumped to a stop. Then the blonde took charge. "Welcome to the place where all your dreams come true." She winked. "Or at least your wet dreams."

Whatever Mac expected, it wasn't for them to step out into a perfectly normal-looking home. Well, normal if you were a member of the upper financial tiers of society. The huge house curled around the circular drive, naturally dividing itself into three wings that he could see from here. Gods only knew how far it stretched back into the surrounding jungle. A seven-meter-tall fence ran around the border of the property and, judging from the occasional spark lighting its surface, it was electrified. Hardly the most welcoming sight, but knowing what he did about the native wildlife, he was glad for it.

"This is our patron's residence on-planet," Gwendolyn said as she threw open the front doors. "He doesn't come through often, but I'm required to stay on-site to entertain as he sees fit."

Her grin widened. "Though I'm more than welcome to entertain myself as I see fit in the meantime. There are a few others who serve a similar purpose, but keep your hands to yourselves, boys," she said to him and the triplets. "Unless they give you permission to do otherwise, of course."

Curious. While he wasn't particularly plugged into the sex vid industry, he hadn't been aware that Gwendolyn Devine had a patron. From the secretive look on her face, there was more to the story…though it was entirely possible that she simply wanted them to *think* there was more to the story.

The triplets looked around the white marble room in awe. He couldn't blame them. It was huge and expensive, from the sweeping grand staircase to the mural painted onto the domed ceiling. It depicted an orgy of such massive proportions, it was a wonder someone hadn't been smothered. But that most likely wasn't what the viewer was supposed to think when looking at it.

Mac shook his head. "This place is nothing but trouble."

Gwendolyn arched a perfectly shaped brow. "We wouldn't have it any other way. We'll keep you more than entertained during your visit. Won't we, Luci?"

He did a double take at the sight of the man who stepped through an archway on the right. He was much taller than his twin, his skin the same dusky tone, his shoulders nearly as wide as Boone's, and he walked with an ease of being at home in his surroundings. Beyond that, he was beautiful in a way even Mac had to acknowledge. The close-cropped black hair only accented how flawless his bone structure was—premium genetics at their best. Mac couldn't have created a more perfect specimen if he'd tried.

Lucien turned to face him as if sensing his thoughts. "Welcome—"

That was a far as he got before Jenny squealed and threw herself into his arms, wrapping her legs around his waist. Mac clenched his hands, using every ounce of self-control to stay rooted in place. His vision bled to red when she planted a solid kiss on the man's lips.

"I missed you so much, Luc. My life's so empty with only one overbearing brother figure in it."

"I missed you, too." He carefully set her down, maintaining a grip on her waist. "I've been hearing all sorts of rumors about your comings and goings. You need to fill me in."

"Then let's not waste any more time." They turned and strode from the room, leaving everyone else staring after them.

Gwendolyn smiled wickedly. "I do believe Luci is getting tired of men. His tendencies change on a whim, you know. Maybe he'll go back to preferring women again for a while. What do you think, Mac?"

He nearly jumped out of his skin. "What?"

"Just wondering what your thoughts were about my brother. I'd quite forgotten how familiar he and Jenny were."

No, she hadn't—he could tell from how closely she watched for his reaction. This woman was playing with him much the same way a cat toyed with a mouse before ripping its head off. So he gave her nothing. She might not act like a danger, but Gwendolyn was still a predator. Which might be a problem, since they were currently at the mercy of her and her brother, isolated from *Psyche* and their only way off-planet. The thought wasn't a comfortable one—there was too much he didn't know, couldn't plan for.

Shifting his bag higher up on his shoulder, Mac said, "Is there a room where I can set up my electronics? I've been offline too long." Once he had a better view of their situation, he would feel better. Safer.

She pouted, obviously put out by his lack of reaction, but there wasn't a whole lot she could do to stop him and still maintain her role as gracious host. Mac was supposed to be a guest, after all. "This way. Boys, stay here and I'll make sure all your needs are taken care of."

Caeden signed something and all three fell into a silent conversation. Or—from the angry looks on Hadriel's and Shadrach's faces—an argument. Mac was going to have to learn sign language as soon as possible. He hated being ignorant.

Gwendolyn led him up the curving staircase and down a long hallway decorated in shades of lilac. Everything about the house was perfect and untouchable, the color scheme all pastels that left him feeling as if the life had been leached from every room. She pushed open a door to a pink room, smiling triumphantly. "Here you go, sweetie. Do whatever you want with it."

Mac ignored the sexual invitation in her voice and shouldered past her into the room. It was equipped with a basic comm unit, which was all he needed to get started. "Thank you."

"Jenny was right—you're no fun." Her lower lip stuck out, just a bit.

Reminding himself not to burn any unnecessary bridges, Mac reined in a sharp reply. "No, I'm not."

He shut the door in Gwendolyn's face before she could test his control any further. After setting down his bags, he began inspecting the room in earnest. These people were Jenny's friends, but he didn't trust them or their motivations. They might not be enemies, but that didn't meant they had anyone's best interests at heart but their own.

Ten minutes later, he'd found not one, but three hidden cameras. It made sense. This was the home of a man who employed sex vid stars, so of course he would want to see his investment at multiple angles. All the same, Mac had no intention of being monitored every moment of his stay here. He couldn't do anything about the rest of the house, but this room was now camera-free.

After unpacking his bags, he settled down to get to work. He needed to set up and get another report to Ophelia. Gods only knew what Sanctify had been up to while he was offline.

CHAPTER TEN

"I hardly believed Gwen when she said you were coming, and yet here you are." Luc maneuvered Jenny back a few paces, keeping his hands on her shoulders. "You've lost weight."

"Wow, five minutes in and you're already mothering me. That's a new record." She crossed her arms over her chest, as if that would hide her body from his view. When he just gave her an impassive look, she sighed. "It's only a few kilograms." So what if she forgot to eat some days because she was running around, putting out fires? He wasn't her mother. Her throat closed at the thought. It hadn't been her mother who protected her and made sure she was eating healthy while growing up. It had been Boone.

Well, Boone and the man gazing at her, concern lighting his dark eyes. "You can't afford even that much. Come along—you can update me while you eat." He grabbed her wrist and started for the kitchen.

Being towed along brought back all sorts of memories from their childhood. When Boone had fled Hansarda and taken her with him, a small contingent of his people had followed. Luckily for Jenny, the twins' parents were part of that group. Valneci's stark landscape wasn't like the sand dunes of home, but she, Luc, and Gwen spent years exploring it and getting into trouble before the twins jumped a ship and headed for Keiluna. Since then, she'd only been able to snatch a few days every six months or so to slip Boone's leash and see them—at least she had until he took the throne.

Had it really been a year and a half since she'd seen her friends last? "I thought talking with your mouth full was *reprehensible*."

"Jenny, everything you do is reprehensible." He pushed her onto a stool. "Now sit still and try not to break anything while I scrounge something up."

She caught herself being tempted to sit on her hands and scowled. "I'm not hungry."

"On the contrary. If I remember correctly, you're always hungry." He bypassed the InstaChef and pulled out an honest-to-gods saucepan.

Who had time for actual cooking anymore? Or, to be more realistic, who had the desire for it when a full meal was only the push of a button away? Since she knew he wouldn't appreciate her thoughts, she changed the subject. "Nice digs you have going here."

Luc opened the fridge and started loading food onto the counter. He looked up long enough to raise an eyebrow. "If you hadn't noticed, what I do pays quite handsomely when you have the right backer."

"And here I thought it was because you were so damn pretty." She laughed as she dodged a thrown mushroom. "Who's a pretty boy? Our little Luci is, isn't he? He's such a pretty boy."

"I'm beginning to forget why I missed you." After dumping the diced vegetables into the pan, he pulled out some kind of meat and got to chopping.

"Because of my charming personality and dazzling good

looks." For the first tine since she left Hansarda, she allowed herself to relax, just a little. Here, in this moment, she was truly safe.

Then Gwen strutted into the room, all smiles and glitter. "Dazzling good looks? There's only space for one princess in the room and gods know it's me."

And there went her fragile peace. It was so easy to forget how catty Gwen got when the three of them were alone. A smarter woman might have merely laughed and let it go. Jenny had never been accused of being a smart woman. "Oh yes, Gwennie. You've far more experience playing the princess than I do." She'd certainly dressed down for it in enough vids.

The blonde's expression tightened ever so briefly before she turned to her brother. "We simply must have a party."

"Must we? I hardly think that was the sort of thing our Jenny had in mind when she came here to avoid detection."

"You're no fun either." Gwen turned tear-bright eyes on her. "Can't we have a party, Jenny? It would be a blast. There will be more beautiful men than even you would know what to do with."

Unbidden, Mac's face shimmered through her mind. He wasn't hers. Not here, not now, not ever…but if she didn't find something to distract herself, and soon, he'd end up in her bed. With the chemistry that snapped between them whenever they got within touching distance it was almost a given at this point. Under normal circumstances, she would satisfy her curiosity and move on, but he was different. He wasn't her usual empty-headed pretty boy.

He was the keeping kind.

And gods knew, she had no intention of keeping anyone. She had enough to worry about with Boone and Ophelia and, hells, her new niece.

Besides. As great a distraction as a party would be, it would defeat the purpose of their coming here to avoid drawing attention to themselves. "Maybe next time."

Gwen propped her hands on her hips. "And when will that be? In another two years?"

Luc was willing to forgive her for not being around, but apparently Gwen wasn't. "As soon as things calm down, I'll come back."

"Gods, you really *have* grown up." The way she said it made it sound like Jenny had come down with an incurable disease.

Luc rolled his eyes and went back to cooking. Jenny propped her chin on her fist and let the soft sounds of food sizzling wash over her and tried to ignore the woman glaring at her. She sighed when he set the plate in front of her. "Luc, honey, can I take my plate upstairs? I promise to be a good little pet and not spill on the carpet."

"Go. But make no mistake, we will speak about the circumstances that brought you here. And soon."

Not if she could help it. Gwennie was one thing—she was all glitz and glamour and as shallow as one of Nitriph's wading pools. Luc knew Jenny, and he would ferret out the whole truth in record time. The very last thing she needed was him deciding she'd be safer back under her brother's thumb on Hansarda. Which meant she had to play her hand very carefully.

"Yes, yes, I promise." She pressed a quick kiss to his cheek and turned to his twin. "Where to?"

Gwen took a deep breath and her unhappy expression melted away as if it'd never been. "This way. I have you set up in the Garden Suite."

Sure enough, the set of rooms was decorated in varying shades of pink. And there were flowers everywhere. Jenny made an effort to smile. Apparently not agreeing to a party really had pissed off her friend. "Gwennie, you tease, you. As if you really forgot I'm deathly allergic to these nasty plants."

The blonde gasped and pressed her hands to her chest.

"Gods, you must think I'm an idiot. Here, here, let's try the Sea Suite instead."

The room they ended up in was much closer to Jenny's taste. A soothing blue colored the walls, fading darker and lighter as if waves were actually rolling through the ceiling. The white furniture gave the whole place a bracingly clean feeling. She inhaled deeply, detecting a faint salt tang to the air. It might not be the searing dunes from home, but it was beautiful in its own way. "This is perfect."

"So glad you approve. Now, get settled. If you won't let me have a party, then I'll just have to put together a dinner you'll never forget." She hurried off before Jenny could decide if that was a threat or a promise or some odd combination of the two.

She strode to the small table overlooking the terrace and sat. The food was good, but then with Luc cooking she hadn't expected anything different. He'd always had a way with his hands.

Pity that he was such an overbearing asshole sometimes.

The comm unit was tucked in the corner opposite the bed, an effective reminder of her duty. She took a deep breath to fortify herself before she sent the call through. Walking the fine line meant keeping her big brother in the loop...and talking fast enough to keep the top of his head from exploding when he found out where they were.

Instead a pair of bloodshot violet eyes greeted her. "What do you want?" Ophelia snarled.

Jenny took in the messy hair and huge circles underneath her eyes. "Hey, big sis! I missed you."

"Do you know how long I've been sleeping?" The screen tilted as Ophelia sat up, charging on before she could say anything. "Two hours. *Two*. Babies don't sleep, Jenny, not even a little bit. And I need my Ladydamned sleep, so tell me what the fuck you want and tell me now, so I can go back to sleep."

She blinked. "Um."

In the distance, a baby wailed, and Ophelia's shoulders slumped. "Lady help me, but I'm going to wring your neck."

Yep, she was definitely never going to pop a kid out. "I'm just reporting in like a good little solider."

"Bullshit." Ophelia disappeared from the screen for a moment, coming back with the baby in tow.

"Language, language." She lowered her voice and leaned in. "There are innocent ears around."

"Look at my face. Does it look like the face of someone you want to screw with?"

Damn it all to the seven hells, but Jenny was starting to wish her brother had been the one to answer the call. Taking a deep breath, she dropped all pretense of teasing. Obviously Ophelia's tolerance was at an all-time low. "Here's the deal...and try not to freak out."

Ophelia gave her a flat look. "If you don't spit out whatever it is you're dancing around, I'm going to crawl through this comm unit and slit your throat."

Okay then. "We ran into some trouble of the white-robed nature on T-II while picking up Mac. He's fine. Everyone's fine. But I didn't feel any of his choices prudent so I made the executive decision to hole up with him as a secondary barrier of protection until things calm down."

That violet gaze missed nothing. "Where?"

"See, that's the thing..." She was supposed to be being good, which meant if Ophelia or Boone ordered her home, she'd have to listen. And the last thing Jenny wanted was to run back to Hansarda with her tail between her legs. Lifting her chin, she decided it best to just get it over with. "Sisilean."

For a long moment, Jenny was sure Ophelia would try to follow through on her threat. Instead she started laughing. It was just a dry chuckle at first, quickly devolving into fits of hysterical giggles.

She watched the process in dawning horror. Gods, she'd broken the Diviner. Boone would never forgive her for driving the love of his life insane. She was still searching for something to say when Ophelia finally stopped laughing and looked up. "That's the funniest thing I've heard in a long time."

"Uh…thanks?" She was usually the person setting everyone else on edge—she wasn't sure she liked being on the other end of things.

"Boone will have a fit, but it's too late to do anything now." She smiled and the expression raised the small hairs on the back of Jenny's neck. "Don't screw this up or there will be consequences."

She swallowed hard, forcing a shaky smile. "That's the spirit, big sister. You're learning to fit right in on Hansarda. Next thing you know, you'll be staking people."

"You know better."

She did. If anything, Ophelia was more vicious than the average Hansardian—and that was *before* she popped out a kid. Jenny'd always heard motherhood made women soft and gentle and whatever. Obviously the general universe was sadly misinformed because she was freaking scary. "Look, it's not like I plan on getting your precious genius killed."

"I know, but trouble follows you around like a stray puppy. Stay out of it and keep him safe."

"I will. You can count on me, big sis."

"Lady help me, but if you call me that again—"

"Love you, too. Tell my brother I said hi!" She disconnected the call before Ophelia could threaten her again.

But her respite didn't last long. The door slid open, Luc stepping quickly inside and shutting it behind him. From the guilty look on his face, he'd just sidestepped his twin. She could relate—Gwen was a force of nature once she set her mind on something.

She sat down and patted the bed next to her. "Want to braid each other's hair and decide once and for all what constitutes a giant cock?"

He laughed. "Nice try."

Silly her to think she could get out of talking so easily. "I'm babysitting the big, brawny redheaded guy and Sanctify is on our heels. We lost them, but that doesn't mean a whole lot to those butchers. He's smarter than smart, and I can't let them have him." *Wouldn't* let them have him.

Luc sighed, seeming to hear her unspoken thoughts. "I figured as much when I saw the way he watched you." When she gave him a blank look, he sighed again. "Jenny, I love you but sometimes you're as dumb as a box of rocks. The man is clearly smitten."

Her stomach gave an uncomfortable little flip. "Whatever. The point is that we need a place to stay and I missed you, so why not kill two birds with one stone?"

"You're in serious denial." He maneuvered her around and started rubbing her shoulders, nimble fingers working out the knots that plagued her. "Tell me about Hansarda."

Hansarda was the last thing she wanted to talk about, but he was a friend, practically family. Hells, he was more brother to her than Kristian had ever been when that monster was alive. Brushing her hair aside to give him better access to her neck, she said, "It's over. Ten years of running and fighting and suffering under Kristian's heel and it's over in a single day. And I wasn't even *there*."

His grip tightened ever so briefly. "He should have suffered years for what he put you through."

"Me?" Her laugh came out harsher than she intended. "I hadn't seen the bastard since we were exiled. It wasn't *me* he got his jollies off by cutting up. All this time I had to sit back and watch Boone take hit after hit in his effort to protect me. I should have killed Kristian years ago."

"No."

"No?" She tried to turn, but he was too strong, easily keeping her in place. "Let me go."

"Stop throwing a tantrum and listen. Boone had to be the one to end things between them and you know it." Luc resumed his massage and, despite her best intentions, she gave a muffled moan. "What of this woman he's dead-set on marrying?"

Of course he knew about Ophelia. Everyone did at this point. "She's already turning our lives upside down. She's…good for him. Really good for him. Hells, they have a kid now—it's all domestic bliss and shit."

"Sounds delightful. Now take off your shirt and let me get at this damned knot between your shoulder blades."

Jenny started to comply when the palm lock flashed green and the door opened as Mac strode into the room.

CHAPTER ELEVEN

They were in this house a handful of hours and the man already had Jenny halfway out of her clothes. Mac's hands dropped to his side, the reason for his visit forgotten. "What's he doing here?"

Damn. He hadn't meant to sound so accusatory.

She looked over her shoulder at Luc as if seeing him for the first time. "Luc? He lives here."

When Gwendolyn told him the location of Jenny's room, he'd misread the smirk on her face. Obviously the woman meant for him to find her like this. "I'll just be going then."

Luc slid off the bed, as graceful as one of the huge jungle cats populating this planet. "Oh no, don't leave on my account." He sent Jenny a meaningful look that Mac couldn't decipher. It made him want to hit something—preferably the smug face of a sex vid star who was too pretty by half.

"Luc, you don't have to go." She wiggled back into her shirt and hopped off the bed. "We still have a ton to catch up on."

Gods, every word out of her mouth was a knife in Mac's gut.

It didn't make any logical sense. He'd met her less than two days ago. Knowing she was with another man shouldn't fill him with such a horrific feeling. "I'll just talk to you later."

"I think not." Luc sidestepped him, pausing long enough to wink at her. Then he was gone, leaving only awkwardness in his wake. Mac wanted to ask her what her relationship was with the twin, but he couldn't force the words past his dry throat. It was none of his business who she touched or who touched her. While it was plain she was attracted to Mac—evidence had proven she was a pleasure seeker, so she wouldn't kiss him if she didn't enjoy it—it didn't mean she felt anything for him.

"So…" She clasped her hands together and bounced on her toes. "What's up?"

It took more effort than it should have to drag his gaze from the door the sex vid star had just exited. "Excuse me?"

"Well, I'm a smart kid most days. And you managed to drag yourself away from your beloved work to come find me. So what gives?"

It took a second to backtrack to his original reason for seeking her out. "I want to know what your intentions are."

Her eyebrows rose. "Your virtue is safe from me."

"That's not what I meant and you know it." He sank into the cushioned seat across from the bed. "You wanted to come to Sisilean, and now we're here. What's next?"

"Alcohol and good times, of course." When he just stared, she relented. "Did you notice how many checkpoints we had to go through to land here?"

"Four." Their thoroughness was actually incredibly impressive. But that was part of Sisilean's charm—it was exclusive and incredibly discreet.

"Silly question. Of course you did. Do you think Sanctify can get past all four without triggering Control to shoot them out of the sky?"

"Theoretically, it could be done." Given enough time and the right equipment, *he* could do it. But Sanctify obviously didn't have anyone like him or they wouldn't be pursuing him so hard. "But it's unlikely."

"Exactly." She took a seat on the edge of the bed. "Even if they did, don't you think we'd notice a bunch of white-robed freaks running around?"

"Most likely." Sanctify wasn't exactly known for being subtle.

"Gwen and Luc's invitation isn't going to wear out any time soon, so all we have to do is wait for the search to die down and then figure out the next step. If the way is clear, it will be no problem to deliver you to one of your original foxholes."

And once he was safely set up, she'd space and be gone from his life forever. It made sense, even if he didn't like thinking about them coming to that point. "Seems logical."

She frowned at him, the line appearing between her brows. And just like that, all seriousness was gone. She gave a perfectly carefree laugh. "Yes, I am aware of that. It might surprise you, but I can be pretty damn logical when I want to be."

He hated watching that mask go back into place. This was the first real conversation they'd had, even if it was about their enemies. "Why do you do that?"

"Do what?" Her grin faltered, but she reclaimed it almost instantly.

"That." He waved at her face, then at her clenched fists. "Why do you pretend you don't care?"

"Who says I'm pretending?" She shrugged, the tension riding her shoulders giving lie to the act. "Maybe I just don't give a shit."

If he backed off now, she'd build up her barriers and keep him out indefinitely. "Don't do that. Not with me."

She narrowed her gray eyes. "What makes you so special?"

That was the question, wasn't it? One he didn't have an answer to. He could point out that they could barely keep their eyes off each other. Even now, she'd somehow moved closer to him, until they were a few short steps apart. Closing that distance and reaching for her would have been the most natural thing in the world—if he were sure of his welcome.

Since he wasn't, he returned to the original point. "You care more than anyone I've met. You have a natural propensity to take people under your wing and defend them with everything you have."

"Bullshit. I'm all sunshine and rainbows and glitter." She paused, cocking her head to the side. He had half a second to recognize that things were about to go downhill fast, and then Jenny slid several steps closer to him. "And sex. I'm all about hot, sweaty sex, too."

He retreated, silently cursing at the lack of furniture to maneuver around. There was too much open space in this room. She shadowed his steps, her expression taking on a decidedly predatory edge. "Don't you like what you see, Mac?"

The shock of her actually using his name went straight through his body. On her lips, it sounded like the most decadent dish, something she savored. His traitorous mind couldn't help wondering if she'd savor another kiss the same way. He tried to adjust his clothing, but she saw the effect she had on him.

"So you *do* like what you see? Do you want to touch me?" She hooked the bottom of her shirt and pulled it off in one smooth move. Gods, she was even more magnificent than he could have guessed.

Her skin looked exactly as soft as it felt, a direct contrast with her strength as she stalked closer. Her pants hung low on her waist, offering a glimpse of a tat just inside her hip bone. Before he could identify what it was, she stood before him, close enough to touch. "Do it, Mac. Touch me."

He wanted to. Gods, how he wanted to. Every time she said his name, she delivered a devastating blow to his already-fractured self-control.

"Fine. You won't touch me, then I'll touch you." She reached out and cupped the front of his pants, the contact going through him like a bolt of electricity. He staggered, doing his damnedest not to come in his pants when she stroked him. "Like that, don't you?"

It would be so simple to take her up on her offer. To fall into Jenny and forget the world for a time.

Except...

Looking at her past actions, all evidence pointed to her habits of sleeping with a man and then walking away, never to be seen again. Judging from that, he had the strong suspicion if he gave in and had sex with her now, he'd never get the chance to do so again. It was the only logical conclusion given the data he possessed. Which was completely unacceptable.

He wanted more than a single night with her. A whole hells of a lot more.

She gave him a squeeze, jarring him out of his analysis. "I like my men present and accounted for when I have their cock in my hand, thank you very much."

Which only served to reinforce the fact that she didn't see him as different from the men she'd had in the past. But if he could change the game, throw in a new variable, it may be enough to attract her mind the same way he apparently attracted her body.

Which meant he couldn't give in to her seduction—not now.

That alone gave him the strength to draw her hand away and press a kiss to her knuckles. Hurt flickered over her face before she covered it with a smile. He couldn't let her think he was actually rejecting her. This was too important. *She* was becoming too important. "I want you. So much that I'll be walking around with blue balls for the foreseeable future."

She raised an eyebrow even as she tried to pull away from him.

Mac tightened his grip, needing her full attention. She tried for the same move she'd pulled back on the *Psyche*, but he caught her free hand before it made contact. She went still, eyes widening as if she were actually seeing him for the first time. "Let go."

"One more thing." He stepped forward and crossed her arms behind her back, bringing them chest to chest. The move wasn't meant to harm, so when she gasped, he went still. Until he realized it was desire quickening her breath. "Are you listening, Jenny?"

She blinked slowly, obviously fighting against the pull between them. "Yes…"

"Then let me make something perfectly clear. When we finally are together—and we will be—there won't be any lies or barriers between us."

She flinched. This time, when she yanked on his hold, he released her. "You're nuts. I'm not a liar."

"You lie to every single person in your life." The more he interacted with her, the clearer it became that she was a woman who only respected strength. Mac would never be a feared warrior like either of her brothers, but he wasn't weak. He had to make her realize that strength came in all different forms. Setting clear boundaries for them was the first step. Not allowing her to stampede over those boundaries to get what she wanted was the next. "But I won't have it between us."

"There is no *us*. I'm your babysitter, you're the freaky genius I'm protecting. End of story."

Another lie, but he let this one go. She'd been pushed enough for one day. It was Jenny's MO to charge into any situation without thinking twice, so the fact that she was currently retreating spoke volumes about how deeply he'd affected her. She wouldn't underestimate him again. Mac smiled. "If you say so."

"I do." She crossed her arms over her chest, which only served to frame her lace-covered breasts to perfection. He caught the barest hint of her dusky nipples and bit back a groan. The woman was temptation personified.

He laced his hands behind his back in an effort to remind himself that he couldn't touch her again just yet. "I have things to take care of. But we'll talk again soon."

"Don't count on it." But there was the slightest waver in her voice.

He turned and walked from the room, careful to keep a measured pace even as he felt her glare pinned to the back of his neck. The fact that she hadn't gone for her knives once during the conversation was a good sign. But he couldn't let himself become too confident. Jenny was cagey and had no intention of being tied down, which meant he'd have to go about this carefully.

He was so busy thinking, it took him a full ten seconds to realize his room wasn't empty—Gwendolyn and an unfamiliar man were waiting for him.

The little blonde turned to him with a smile. "There you are, darling. I was worried you'd gotten lost along the way." She hurried over and grabbed his elbow, tugging him over to the stranger. "This is Javier. He's our resident wardrobe master."

The man in question was taller than Mac and thin nearly to the point of emaciation, the bones of his shoulders and ribs easily discernable through the pale straps crisscrossing his chest, a direct contrast to his blue-black skin. Silver buckles connected them to pants so tight he wasn't sure how the man moved.

For his part, Javier had been giving him an equally thorough examination. "You've brought me quite the gift this time."

"Gift?" He rotated as the man circled him, not comfortable enough to let Javier at his back.

"Of course, silly." She ran a hand down his arm, pulling at the shirt fabric. "You see what I'm talking about? These clothes will simply not do."

"I absolutely agree." He stepped so close it was everything

Mac could do to hold his ground. "Something this magnificent should be clothed in..." He cocked his shaved head to the side. "Leather. Leather and silk."

That startled a laugh out of Mac. "Exactly what am I dressing for?"

Gwendolyn's smile made the hair on the back of his neck stand on end. "Why, dinner, of course."

"And dinner in this household requires leather?"

"And silk." Javier gripped his chin, turning his face this way and that as Gwendolyn stood by and watched. "You are on Sisilean, darling. Dinner is never simply dinner—it is *entertainment*."

He couldn't determine what worried him more—her words or the satisfied smile on her face.

CHAPTER TWELVE

*J*enny smoothed a hand over her red dress, wondering how something as simple as pretty clothes could lift her mood. But it was a beautiful thing, the cut somehow giving the illusion of curves where she had none. The deep vee nearly hit her belly button and she had to keep the straps in place with some sticky tape. From the waist, it flowed around her legs, the long slits in the side showing a ton of skin with every step.

Mac was going to shit his pants.

"Stop thinking about him." She sat down to pull on strappy heels nearly the same tan color as her skin. "He might be freaking brilliant, but he's still just a pretty man, and there are plenty of pretty, stupid men in the universe."

But he was the only one to ever call her out so thoroughly. With a few pointed sentences, he'd stripped bare every mask she had. Even her family, whom she loved even though sometimes she hated them, had never once questioned her the way *he* had. They took her at face value, the same as everyone else. She was Mad Jenny, Crazy Jenny, Jenny Who Has Sweet Knife Skills and

Is Good in a Fight.

Mac alone had called her out and had the audacity to demand she show him what lay beneath. "You don't want to play with my demons, Sir Genius. They'll eat you alive."

"It's generally considered bad form to mutter under your breath."

It didn't matter that the man made her feel off-center and vulnerable. Right now she was going to have fun and let her worries slide away for a few hours. She finished hooking the back of the right shoe and stood up. "Everything I do is considered bad form, Luc. Don't know how you forgot that."

He made a spinning motion with his finger and she obliged, a small smile pulling at the edges of her lips when the dress flared out with the movement. "Beautiful. He won't know what hit him."

Jenny ignored the comment and gave him a once-over. "You've pulled out all the stops tonight."

He wore a perfectly fitted pin-striped suit over an ivory silk shirt that contrasted sharply against his dark skin. He smiled, a quick flash of white teeth. "And you're changing the subject. Why so skittish?"

"I'm not skittish." She checked to make sure her hair was still in its purposefully messy updo, and then there was nothing left to stall with. "I just want you to mind your own godsdamned business."

He raised an eyebrow. "I'll let it lie for now. But I have it on good account that Gwendolyn sicced Javier on your inventor. The results should be quite startling."

"He's not *mine*." Gods, even those three little words felt like a lie. What the hells was she going to do? "Besides, I can't imagine the man in anything other than his utilitarian pants and shirts. They fit his equally dull personality so well."

Another dirty lie. She'd spent considerable time imagining him naked. And he'd stopped being dull about two seconds after she met him and realized he'd taken out two members of Sanctify without even drawing blood.

"As you say." He offered his elbow and she gingerly placed her fingers in the crook, sighing when Luc rearranged her hand to the correct position. "You'll need to brush up on your social skills now that Boone has taken over as king. It's expected."

It might be, but Jenny had still dodged every tutor her brother sent her way over the last eight months after he declared that if he had to relearn the ropes, then she should, too. She had planned on taking off as soon as he was distracted with running the planet, but it hadn't worked out so well. At least she was free of those damned lessons for the time being.

"A lot of things are expected." She sighed again. "It's no fun."

"Indeed. Being an adult has its disadvantages." A twinkle sparked in his dark eyes. "But there are perks as well."

"Perks? Perks are good."

"For example, tonight's dinner is very specifically for an adult audience."

That sounded promising. Between Mac and Sanctify and all the responsibility waiting back home, she was in desperate need of distraction. "Would it scandalize my big brother?"

"Oh, most definitely."

"Coming here really was a fantastic idea."

They descended the staircase as if they were royalty greeting their subjects—even if no one was around to witness it. Luc led her into a grand dining room. The table was huge, able to fit at least fifty people comfortably, though only the far end of it was set.

Jenny's gaze jumped over the triplets—all dressed to dazzle in varying shades of gray—and settled on the broad back of the inventor. Then he turned around and she tripped over her own feet. It was only Luc's smooth handling that kept her from tumbling into a heap on the floor.

Mac was *gorgeous*.

A loose V-neck shirt draped to reveal a pale chest that had to taste nearly as good as it looked. And gods, those pants. They were so tight it was as if Javier had painted them on, not even rippling where they tucked into knee-high boots. She had the sudden insane urge to lick the stiches that crossed over a not-so-subtle bulge.

He gave her a crooked smile and her thoughts tripped over themselves much the same way her feet had. The man knew the effect he had and damned if he wasn't amused. Though amusement didn't quite cover the heat of those green eyes as they raked over her skin in an almost-physical touch.

Luc cleared his throat and she had the presence of mind to wonder how long she'd been eye-fucking Mac. Too long, because everyone in the room was now staring.

Awkward.

"What's that you were saying about stupid men?"

Mac's gaze hardened when it switched to Luc, his eyes going icy. As they walked toward him, for the first time in as long as she could remember, she couldn't find words to speak. Luc patted her hand and abandoned her, sauntering off to chat up the triplets.

She started to cross her arms over her chest and abandoned the gesture halfway through. "Hi." Oh, that was weak. But she couldn't look at him without remembering how he'd pinned her arms behind her and stared into her godsdamned soul just a few hours ago.

The crooked smile reappeared. "You look ravishing."

What was she supposed to say to that? Something witty and snarky and fun. But all Jenny could come up with was a faint, "Thanks."

Gods, what was she thinking? This was bad. So very, very bad.

Gwen, of all people, came to the rescue. "You look outstanding. I was totally right in picking the ruby shade for your coloring. Though you're a little pale, dear—you might want to hit up a tanner while you're on Sisilean."

She turned partially away from Mac, though even seeing him out of the corner of her eye was still distracting. "Haven't you heard? Pale is the new tan." She laughed, wincing at how forced it sounded.

"If it was, I'd be the first to know. Come, come, it's almost time for dinner." She grabbed Jenny's hand and dragged her to the table. "You're just going to die when you see the entertainment."

Only if she managed to keep her eyes off a certain inventor whose chest shouldn't be so freaking cut. *Nothing* about him was as it should be. She pasted a smile on her face and Gwen paused in her babbling, obviously waiting for an answer. "Fabulous."

"You're not listening to a word I'm saying."

"Can you blame me? Everyone is dressed to impress." Including Gwen, who was outfitted in a slinky black gown that hit her just above the knees but was so tight, it was obvious she wasn't wearing any form of underwear. "You look fantastic."

"I know." Gwen giggled.

Jenny couldn't help a little choked sound when Mac slid into the chair next to hers. Bad enough if he sat across from her where she would have no choice but to ogle his goodies. This close it was as if her entire body was tuned to his like a divining rod.

She turned to find Luc on her other side. "You abandoned me."

"A little abandonment is good for the soul."

"Bullshit," she hissed. "What game are you playing at, Luc?"

"No game." The little shit actually winked at her. "Or rather, no game you can win. Might as well give in now."

"As if that would ever happen." She scooted away from him, which only brought her closer to Mac. The fresh, clean scent of him teased her. What the hells? Did the guy just jump out of a Clotheshorse or something? He smelled as if he'd soaked in laundry detergent…except more. Better.

And Jenny had officially lost her damn mind.

Gwen perched at the head of the table and daintily clinked her wineglass with a fork. They went silent as she beamed. "I have a special surprise in honor of our guests."

Luc gave an almost-silent sigh next to Jenny, but there was no opportunity to ask him what was going on. Not that she would—she wasn't exactly a happy camper where he was concerned, either.

"On that note, dinner is served."

The doors behind the blonde opened and two men and two women filed into the room. Naked men and women. She eyed the bulging muscles on the men as they set trays on the table, uncovering them to reveal a variety of food she'd never seen before. When her attention finally circled back to the women, her stomach lurched. They were beautiful, the very essence of perfection. She'd never been bothered by other woman's beauty before. Jenny was normally a firm believer in the more the merrier.

Their tits were so damn…perky. And huge. Abso-freaking-lutely huge. She glanced at Mac out of the corner of her eye, wondering if he liked what he saw. It shouldn't matter. If he was staring at these painfully perfect bodies, it was only because he was human. It wasn't something that should upset her. Maybe if she thought it enough, she'd actually start to believe it.

But he was staring directly at *her*.

She stopped breathing long enough to get light-headed. Any second now, he'd turn and ogle the sparkly nipples on the woman dishing up his plate. Any second…

Jenny finally exhaled—and got annoyed that she cared so much to begin with. She glared. "What are you looking at?"

"You."

Damn. The man really knew how to steal her thunder.

She faced forward and started filling her plate, determined to keep from making a bigger ass of herself. Gwen should have sat next to her so they could girl-talk or some shit. Instead she was stuck between one man she wanted to throttle and another she wanted to get naked with. And gods alone knew what was going on with this food. She probably wouldn't even enjoy it.

Her first bite shot that theory all to hells and back. Sweet and tart and a little bit of spice… It was strikingly familiar. She took two more bites, rolling the flavor over her tongue in an effort to figure out what it reminded her of. "Gwen—"

"Isn't it fabulous, sweetie? It's your favorite, if I remember correctly."

She froze, nearly throwing her fork across the table at the grinning blonde. "You bitch."

Gwen jerked back as if she'd physically reached across the table. "Why would you say something so mean to me?" Her lower lip trembled, but Jenny refused to feel bad.

She looked at everyone stuffing their faces and wanted to throw up. But puking wouldn't stop the drug's effects, a fact she knew all too well. "Stop. *Stop eating.*"

The triplets dropped their forks at her command, but Mac and Luc only carefully set theirs on the table, twin expressions of curiosity on their faces. Luc swayed a little bit, reaching out to grab the edge of the table. "I seem to be feeling a bit off."

It was only going to get worse. Even as she fought it, a delicious looseness worked its way through her muscles. She slumped in her chair, a giggle slipping free. "I hate you so much right now, Gwen. I'm going to kill you."

"Jenny…"

It seemed to take forever for her to turn her head. "Mac?"

He looked so lost, now-brown eyes wide. Eventually a smile spread over his face. "What's happening?"

"It would seem my darling sister has drugged us." Luc swirled his wine, somehow managing not to spill a single drop. Jenny watched the red liquid in fascination. "Just couldn't help yourself, could you, Gwendolyn?"

"Relax, Luci, and take that stick out of your finely tanned

ass." Gwen laughed, stretching. "Where are my beautiful boys and girls?"

The men and women crowded around her. In the low light, their skin looked oiled. She wondered how it would taste. "No, no, no. Bad Jenny."

She listed sideways, using Mac's shoulder to push herself to her feet. Or that was the plan. Instead she ended up sitting in his lap. "Hey there, handsome."

"I feel so odd. Fantastically odd. I'm angry, and yet all I want to do is strip you naked and kiss every inch of your body." A frown marred his face, gone almost as quickly as it'd come. "Why am I verbalizing everything that comes to mind?"

Reaching up to cup his face, she ran her thumbs along his full bottom lip. He really was far too hot to be so smart. It wasn't fair. "My dear, dear friend dosed our food with Butterfly's Kiss. It's a damn sexy drug."

"Sex sounds fantastic."

She laughed when he put his arms around her, and tipped her face up so he could nibble along her jawline. "It does, doesn't it?" Big hands cupped her hips, dipping down to play along the edge of the slits in her dress. The heat of his skin made her shiver. "That feels nice."

"I agree."

Jenny hummed under her breath, wiggling against Mac as pleasure sparked over her skin. She wanted to move, to dance, to run. Gwen must have felt the same way because she jumped to her feet. "Let's go play. Something…" Her eyes seemed to glow in the low light. "Something *scandalous*."

"Stop toying with our emotions, Gwendolyn." Luc's voice slid through the room, strumming something deep within Jenny. He'd have the answer. She was sure of it. He shifted slightly, drawing the attention of everyone in the room. "Shall we dance with the lightning bugs?"

"Oh, Luci, what a wonderful idea." Gwen clapped, bobbing in place. "They're attracted to skin. Last one covered is a prude." Laughing, she raced from the room, faster than Jenny had seen her move in years.

Mac's hands tightened on her hips. "Don't go. Stay with me."

"Don't be such a sourpuss." She pushed to her feet, and gave him an absent pat on the head. Gwen disappeared through the door and it was too much—Jenny had never been able to sit back when a competition was on the line.

Wildness pressed against her skin, wanting an escape. She slid from Mac's grip easily and flipped her hair off her face. "You heard her, boys—wouldn't want to lose to a pair of girls, would you?" With that she sprinted out of the room, ignoring Mac when he called her name.

CHAPTER THIRTEEN

$\mathcal{M}$ac watched the crimson fabric disappear through the door, every cell in his being demanding he give chase. He rose even as a small part of his rational mind said that this was a terrible idea. It wasn't safe—there were far too many unknown factors to go frolicking around outside during a Sisilean night. Not to mention being under the influence of an unknown hallucinogen.

"What are you waiting for?" Luc pulled off his shirt, revealing a chest to make a bodybuilder jealous. "They're bound to get into trouble. Then again…so are we."

Jenny being in trouble was unthinkable. Mac stopped trying to fight the urge to run, and knocked over the chair in his haste to get out of the room. The sound of his feet pounding the tiled floor echoed strangely in his head as he followed the chorus of feminine giggles.

Colors pulsed and merged, giving him the eerie feeling of being inside a warp point. The only steady part of the shadowed hallway was the door leading into the night. He picked up speed, suddenly sure he could feel something terrible exhaling on the back of his neck. Something he most certainly didn't want to catch him.

Bursting into the humid air was like entering a new world. It jarred his senses so violently that Mac stumbled to a stop, staring about in wonder. The high walls hid the jungle, but he could sense it just beyond sight—a dangerous and beautiful enemy who shouldn't be trusted. Above him, the sky opened into eternity, an infinite number of possibilities stretching forth. He was struck by the urge to board a ship and jump through warp point after warp point just to see where he ended up.

A giggle brought his attention back dirtside. Jenny danced out from behind a twisted tree, her dress floating out with each exaggerated movement. She looked like a fire nymph who had wandered into the wrong realm.

"Perhaps that's exactly what she is."

He jumped, nearly falling in his effort to get away from Lucien. "How are you reading my mind?"

"Mind reading is hardly necessary when you speak every thought aloud." He inhaled deeply, tilting his head back. "Don't fight it—it's better for everyone if you just relax and let the trip take you where it wants to go. It's only a finite amount of time."

Let the trip take him where he wanted to go. It made perfect sense.

"Yes, I know. That is why I suggested it."

A lightning bug drifted between them, alighting on the man's chest. He moved closer, drawn by the warmth its light gave Lucien's skin. Reaching out, he held perfectly still as a second lightning bug landed on his wrist. "Fascinating."

"Hey." Then Jenny was there, sliding between them, frightening off the lightning bugs and taking Mac's hands. "Hands off, Luc. You have plenty of beautiful toys—this one is mine."

Over her shoulder, Luc raised an eyebrow. "Careful there.

This man is no one's toy."

He opened his mouth to agree, but she was off again, dragging him behind her as if he were exactly what she called him — a well-loved toy. "I want you to see this." They moved around the tree and into the makeshift garden, the thick foliage cutting off the starlight and leaving them in nearly complete darkness.

"I can't see."

"Sure you can. Just *look*."

And then, just like that, he truly could. All around them lightning bugs flared to life, making the small clearing look as if it were bathed in candlelight. It was like existing in one of the stories his mother had read to him as a small child — where fairies roamed, ready to grant a wish or lay a curse, depending on their whim. He turned back to Jenny and smiled. He was in the presence of one right now. "You're beautiful."

"You'll turn a girl's head with those kind of compliments." She took a step away and he followed the movement. Her eyes lit up as he stalked her across the clearing. There was something so perfect and primal about this, something that couldn't be denied.

He grabbed for her, but she laughed and dodged his hand. "Ah, ah, ah. Not so fast. You have to catch me first." Still giggling, she squeezed through the trees, a trail of crimson cloth flowing behind her.

Blood pounded furiously through his veins, and he gave chase, ignoring the branches that clung to him, trying to slow his progress. All that mattered was her laugh and the glimpse of bare skin and red fabric he followed.

She turned long enough to meet his gaze and then she was off again. "Is the big bad inventor getting tired?"

"Never." He could run after her for hours. Days. Forever.

Between one step and the next, the trees fell back and the ground gave way beneath his feet. Mac tried to backpedal, but he was already going over the ledge. He hit the water two meters down, colliding with enough force to drive the air from his lungs. Liquid closed over his head, strangely peaceful despite the violence of his entry. He sank into the darkness, spreading his fingers in wonder as glowing fish emerged from the cubbies in the rock wall and circled him.

Then he remembered he needed to breathe.

He pushed off the bottom, clawing his way to the surface. Nothing tasted so good as that first breath. He treaded water, fighting against the pull of his heavy boots, and looked around. This body of water could only be called a lagoon. It had obviously been crafted to instill a feeling of isolation and romance, the trees leaning over the water in places and giving the whole area an intimate feel. As he swam closer to the edge, he saw there were dips and seats dug into the smooth rock. A perfect place to engage in a watery tryst.

Shaking his head, he pulled off his shirt and tossed it onto dry land. There was nothing to be done about the pants and boots, but at least he wasn't being strangled by clothing anymore.

"You godsdamned idiot." Jenny leaped into the water, coming up sputtering as she waded over and took him by the shoulders. "What in the hells were you thinking? I think you just scared me sober!"

Her dress became completely transparent, her chest rising and falling in her agitation. Agitation on his behalf. "You were worried about me."

"Don't let it go to your head." She moved closer, her dress flaring along the surface of the lagoon in waves.

It drew his attention up past her hips, over her ribs, to her breasts. She had truly magnificent breasts. "I can see your nipples."

She looked down and then smacked him in the shoulder. "Of course you can see my nipples, dumbass—I'm wearing a sheer dress and I'm in a freaking lake."

"Lagoon."

"What?"

"A lake would be much larger. We're in a lagoon."

"Gods above and below. You're such a pain in my ass. I could just—just—hells, I could just kiss you." And then she did, plastering herself against him, arms twining around his neck.

It had only been hours since she was last in his arms, but it felt like eternity. He was supposed to be holding back, but it would take a stronger man than Mac to push this woman away. Instead, he touched her like he'd wanted to ever since she'd shown up to save him from Sanctify. Taking a fistful of hair, he pulled just hard enough to make her gasp, opening her mouth to him. She tasted of the dinner they'd just eaten, sweet and tart, and that indefinable thing that was pure Jenny. Her tongue darted into his mouth before retreating, teasing him.

That wouldn't do.

He maneuvered them around, pressing her against the ledge. She wrapped her legs around his waist, grinding against him. It was so good, so right. Except there were far too many clothes between them. Mac broke off the kiss long enough to look down to where the water lapped at their hips. "It just had to be fucking leather, didn't it?"

She laughed so hard she vibrated against him. "Gods, I've never heard you swear before."

"Well, damn it, your friend couldn't have chosen better if she outfitted me in a fucking chastity belt."

"There you go again." She tried to lean forward, but his hold kept her in place. A little whimper escaped her mouth when he tightened his grip on her hair. "Gods, you're making me so hot right now."

Hot didn't come close to covering it. "Hells, if you keep moving like that, I'm going to come in these cursed leather pants."

"Tell me more."

He was about to do just that, but the long line of her neck

distracted him. Leaning down, he kissed his way over the sensitive skin, bending her farther backward as he did. The position arched her back until it would have been a crime not to pay attention to those breasts.

She moaned when his lips finally closed over a nipple through her dress. Gods bless whoever chose this fabric and left out the bra. It was almost enough to make him forgive the damned leather pants. Jenny clutched his head, holding him in place—as if he would have willingly gone anywhere. Cupping her ass with his free hand, he pulled her more tightly against him. He would have given damn near anything to be out of these pants and inside her. But this was enough for now.

He bit down gently, gauging her reaction. She went wild, hips moving against his, fingers digging into the back of his head. "More. Now. Give me more." There was no ignoring the demand, even if he were so inclined. So he set his teeth against her, tongue stroking her nipple as she whimpered for him.

Gods. He'd do damn near anything to get her to make that sound again.

Relinquishing his hold on her hair, he lifted her from the water and set her on the ledge in front of him. Yanking off her shoes was more difficult than it looked, but it was worth it to have all that skin available to him. But it wasn't enough. One good rip and the fabric parted to reveal the tops of her thighs. Another rip and she was bared completely for him. He went still, unable to tear his gaze away. "Why the hells aren't you wearing underwear?"

"I have a better question." She laughed, the sound borderline hysterical. "Why the hells are you talking about it instead of putting your mouth to good use?"

"A valid point." Her laugh was cut off when he pushed her legs farther apart and licked up her center. Gods, she tasted just as good here as she did everywhere else. Better. So much better.

He focused on her clit, urged on by her cries.

Mac lifted his head, looking up her body. The picture she presented was almost enough to finish him then and there. She met his gaze squarely. "If you don't make me come *right now*, I swear by all that's holy, I will cut you."

She whimpered when he gave her a love bite on her inner thigh. "Make all the threats you want. I see you." He rubbed his face on her other thigh, enjoying the chance to tease her when she was so close to the edge.

"See me, my ass." She tried to wriggle free, but he kept her hips pinned easily. Not that she seemed to be trying that hard. She licked her lips. "You aren't going to leave me like this…are you, Mac?"

She knew how much it affected him to hear his name on her lips, knew she could get free if she really wanted to, but she was here, with him, and practically begging. Holding her gaze, he dragged his tongue over her. The intimacy of the moment was nearly unbearable, her wide gray eyes hazy with a potent mix of passion and vulnerability.

He gave himself over to the glory that was Jenny, feeding on her cries as he pushed her closer and closer to the edge. Unable to help himself, he plunged two fingers inside her. She screamed as her body clamped around him. He drew it out, changing his rhythm, her breathless shrieks the most beautiful sound he'd ever heard. Finally she went limp, gasping, her body seemingly unable to take more. Because of how *he'd* made her feel.

Pressing kisses to each of her hip bones, he rested his forehead against her stomach. He was so hard, it was a wonder he didn't burst the damn pants at the seam. But no, that would be too easy. Instead he was stuck in misery.

She gave a little sigh, so similar to the one he'd heard on *Psyche*, and he suddenly decided it was all worth it.

CHAPTER FOURTEEN

Footsteps crunched somewhere above Jenny's head, but she didn't have the energy to move. Which was bad and so very, very good, all at the same time. A throat cleared. "I see you two haven't wasted any time." Luc laughed when Mac cursed.

"Shove it, Luc." Jenny started to sit up, the move making Mac's hands dig harder into her hips. The feeling sent a shiver through her entire body. Mac had kept her pinned with a minimum effort, and she hadn't been able to fight it. Hadn't *wanted* to fight it. That should have filled her with fear—if he was this controlling when it came to sex, it was only a hop, skip, and a jump to be that controlling in the rest of his life—but the majority of the feeling pushing against her skin was sheer, unadulterated lust.

And gods help her, a little sliver of trust.

Mac pulled her into the water, maneuvering her until even her chest was covered. Which was silly—Luc couldn't care less if she was naked, because he didn't see her as anything other than a sister. But her heart gave a funny jump at the thought of him trying to protect her.

Mac's thumbs teased the tension from her shoulders even as his voice went hard. "Go away."

"Hey!" She tried to rise, but he easily held her in place. Again. "That's my friend you're talking to."

"Your friend needs to leave." There was no compromise in his tone.

Luc laughed. "Don't worry, I understand how it is. Young love and all those unmentionable things. Enjoy your man."

Her thoughts turned into a terrifying static. "Love" was not a word she wanted thrown around. Not now, not ever. "It's not like that—" Mac went tense behind her, but she rushed on, shouting after Luc as he disappeared through the trees. "Damn it, he's not my anything!"

As soon as Luc was out of sight, Mac released her, moving away. She felt his absence like a kick to the stomach. "Look—"

He held out a hand, stopping whatever she'd been about to say. Probably a good thing, because she didn't know how to go about making it better. Hells, she wasn't sure why she was so worried about hurting his feelings in the first place, only that the look on his face made her stomach drop.

He shook his head when she took another step toward him. "It doesn't matter."

Ouch. She rubbed a hand over her sternum, a strange ache starting in her chest. This was all so wrong. The mission had started so great, and yet things had gone sideways as soon as she laid eyes on him. It only seemed to get getting worse as time went on. "What does that mean?"

"It means exactly what it sounds like, Jenny."

She flinched when he said her name, the ache getting stronger until it was like a gaping hole in her chest, ready to suck in the unwary. "But it does matter."

"Does it?" He pulled himself out of the lagoon and stood. She got temporarily distracted by the streams of water running down his pale chest. He even had freckles there, too. And it was a very nice chest. Even now, when he was obviously pissed as hells, there was still a huge bulge in the front of his pants. Mac was packing some serious heat.

She licked her lips. It would be really easy to make a joke right now, but he demanded honesty before, and after what he just did to her, she could hardly deny it. "Yes, it matters."

He stared for a long time before finally turning. "No, I don't think it does." Then he walked away. Hurt flared, pinpricks of heat dotting the back of her eyes. For one eternal second, she thought she might actually cry.

Then reality kicked in and anger took over. She shoved her hair back and climbed out of the pool, marching after the idiot. He thought he could just walk away from her? Not freaking likely. No one walked away from Jenny, not successfully. She was the one who decided when she was done, not the other way around. And she sure as hells wasn't done with this asshole inventor who made her come so hard she saw stars.

Shoving branches out of her way, she stormed back into the lawn area where the rest of their party was. Mac stood as far away from her as he could without leaving the grass, his head tilted back and eyes closed. He looked almost peaceful.

It was a shame she was going to rain on his parade.

Gwen grabbed her arm as Jenny tried to sidestep her, speaking low enough that the others couldn't hear. "Looks like you had a good time."

Glancing down, she sighed. Between the soaked fabric and the tear up the center of the dress, there could be no doubt in anyone's mind that she'd been dipping. "Back off."

"But I want details. Is he as good as he looks like he'd be?"

A crack sounded in the direction she'd just come from. The knot between Jenny's shoulder blades spasmed so hard she almost went to her knees. Gritting her teeth, she ignored

Gwen and turned to watch the trees. It was hard to tell, but she'd thought she heard...

"Because he looks like he'd be fucking fantastic. That ass—"

"Shut up, Gwen. *Now*." Her tone must have been enough to clue in the blonde, because she stopped talking.

With no distraction, total and complete silence reigned. No birdcalls, no rustle of small animals, even the lightning bugs were gone. The hairs on the back of her neck stood up as the heebie-jeebies shot down her spine. Taking a measured step back, she dragged Gwen along with her. "Please tell me you have weapons in the house."

"Weapons?"

Gods above and below. Jenny mentally cursed herself for bypassing her laser when she got dressed this evening. Stupid, so terribly stupid. "Yes, weapons. We're going to need them."

A branch cracked almost directly in front of them. Whatever it was, the thing was moving. "*Go*." The blonde gave a shriek and sprinted for the house.

Now she could see the slinking shape moving through the trees. It was hard to tell size with the shadows, but the damn thing had to be at least as big as Jenny. "Shit."

Mac and Luc appeared on either side of her and she felt the triplets at her back. "What's coming?"

"I can't be sure, but...I think it might be one of the natives. Please tell me you guys have weapons." She'd heard stories about these lizards. They were wicked fast and between the claws and the nasty double-rowed teeth, they made quick meals of their prey. Well, she had no intention of being anyone's meal tonight. All the same, she didn't particularly want to fight this thing with only her gauntlets.

Hadriel pressed a laser into her hand and she spared him a glance. *I have a few more.*

Thank the gods for her paranoid men.

Luc spoke quietly as the thing circled just behind the edge of the trees. "It will come for us quickly and try to separate one from the herd. The claws are poisonous. And watch out for the tail."

She turned, tracking the lizard's movement. "I'm tired of waiting." She took aim and fired a shot into the trees.

The thing yowled and rushed them. The group scattered, and she found herself next to Luc and Caeden. The triplet had a laser in each hand and Luc had scrounged one up from somewhere. For a minute it was so much like the old days, before the twins took off, that Jenny couldn't breathe.

Then she saw the lizard go for Mac.

"Oh, fuck no." She shot it in the leg, causing it to stumble before it reached him. He jumped out of the way of those snapping jaws, and then Shadrach was there, calmly aiming down his laser at the lizard's head. The shot charred the thing's scales, but judging from the way it went after him, it didn't do any lasting damage. "How the hells are we supposed to kill it if we can't use lasers?" The shots might slow it down, but they'd overheat their guns before too long and then they'd be screwed.

"We aren't supposed to kill it." Luc shoved her out of the way as the tail came whipping past them. "The guards will take care of it once Gwendolyn gets them."

"Then she better hurry up." Jenny dived over the grass just as the lizard flipped around, apparently deciding she was the easiest target. Typical.

It came after her, covering the ground at a terrifying pace. She got off one shot and then it was on her, claws flying. She dodged and ducked, using every single trick she owned to stay ahead of its strikes. Instinct demanded she turn and run, but the moment she did she'd be dead. So instead she circled it, desperate to keep the lizard turning so it couldn't catch her.

Things were going fine until her foot caught on an uneven

section of the ground. She went down hard, trying to roll out of the way. But a suffocating weight landed on her back, pinning her as sharp teeth ripped into her shoulder. She screamed and flailed, trying to flip the lizard off. It was no use—the thing was too damn heavy. Distantly, she could hear men's voices yelling and smell the charred scent of lasers. The lizard gave her a shake, teeth digging in deeper as wetness covered her back.

Blessed numbness soaked into her skin, wrapping itself around her. A small part of her mind screamed that it was bad, so very, very bad, but she couldn't dredge up enough energy to care.

The weight suddenly disappeared from her back, a terrible scream filling the air. Jenny wanted to look, to make sure Mac was okay, but she couldn't seem to move her head.

Hands turned her over and arms she could only half feel lifted her from the ground. Someone was arguing, but she couldn't focus long enough to figure out what the big deal was. She just wanted them to shut the hells up so she could sleep.

The arms tightened around her, and a sharp tingling started in her shoulder. A sane part of her whispered that it would get so much worse, but she couldn't hang on to the thought.

She blinked at the chest pressed against her cheek. Such a nice color, so pale and smooth. Trying to lift her hand to run a finger along those muscles was a terrible mistake, though. Pain lanced through her entire body, fire coursing along her veins, spreading agony in its wake. "Oh gods. That hurts."

"Hang on. You're going to be okay."

Mac shifted her in his arms and it was too much. The abyss pulled Jenny under, smothering her even as it dulled the agony.

• • •

There was so much blood. Too much. Mac looked to the twins, trying to ignore the way Jenny's head lolled against his arm. Their skin was unnaturally gray, but only Gwendolyn was showing signs of cracking. "Tell me you have a medic."

"Why would we have a medic? This is a protected place." Her voice spiked with each word. She'd be in hysterics before too long.

Lucien seemed to realize it as well. He jerked his chin at one of the half-naked women huddled in the doorway. "Get her a tranq."

"I don't need a freaking tranq. My friend is hurt and it's—" She shuddered when the woman jabbed her with the needle. "Damn you, Luci. This isn't fair."

"Go to bed, love. We'll talk in the morning." He gave her a little push and she tottered out of the room. When Lucien turned to the remaining men and women, his dark eyes were deadly serious.

"Get that table cleared, you bloody idiots." Hadriel shouldered around the black haired man. Mac had half a second of shock at the fact the triplet could speak—could all three of them talk?—before he moved to follow the order.

"My equipment. Go." Shadrach and Caeden hurried out of the room and he turned back to Mac and Lucien. "I need her facedown. And I need you to tell me about these damn lizards."

He didn't want to let go of Jenny, but his chest was already wet from her blood. She needed help. Now. Help he couldn't give, even with his skill set. Gritting his teeth when she made a small sound of pain, he set her on the dining room table. Hadriel immediately shoved him aside and took his place near her shoulder.

Lucien moved to the other side of the table, helping the oldest triplet cut off the remaining pieces of her dress. "Their claws have poison that can kill a man in less than an hour."

"It wasn't the claws that got her." Hadriel leaned over and examined the wound. "I need this cleaned and then I can see what the damage is. Get some water and towels."

Mac started to argue but Lucien stopped him with a hand on his arm. "Stay with her. I'll take care of it." Then the man was gone, replaced by Shadrach, who rushed into the room and dropped a box on the table. He flipped it open, pulling out a stack of med patches.

"There's something wrong—her shoulder is bleeding more than it should." Shadrach signed something, brows drawn down over his eyes. Hadriel shook his head. "We can't risk it."

Mac's stomach lurched at how casually they spoke while she lay there, unconscious and bleeding. Too much blood. Memories pounded against him, threatening to pull him under completely. He clenched his jaw and forced words out. "Stop talking."

They glared at him, but before anyone could do something they'd regret, Lucien was back with the water. He handed it to Hadriel, who carefully washed her wound, cursing when the blood only ran faster. "This needs to be patched up." He lifted his hand without looking at his brother. "Not med patches, dumbass. I don't know how they'll react with the chemical in the saliva— they might make it worse."

Shadrach made a face and switched out the med patches for actual cloth bandages. He handed over an IV, along with a packet of blood. After checking the label, Hadriel handed it to Mac. "Hold this. Keep it above her body." Then he inserted the needle into Jenny's forearm.

So much blood. Too much.

Memories blindsided him, sucking him under before he had a chance to throw up defenses. His mother, one hand held out in a plea while the other cradled her stomach. The man advanced on his mother with the knife, started cutting her up…

A slap to his face jarred him back to the present. He blinked at Lucien. The dark man's eyes were too wide, but the rest of his face was perfectly under control. "Do you need me to help you hold the blood?"

It would be such a simple thing to hand it over and flee the room. But then he caught sight of Jenny's face, her eyes closed and skin too pale. He met Lucien's brown eyes and shook his head. "I'm fine."

"As you say."

Hadriel finally stepped back from stitching up the wound and wiped his hands. "That's all I can do for now. We'll have to check the bandages and keep them clean."

Mac took the blanket that Lucien offered him. "I'll take care of her." With the help of the man, he got her wrapped up and in his arms once again.

"That's bullshit." Hadriel started to say something else but Caeden slipped through the door, signing madly. "You're sure?" When the other man nodded, he sighed. "Looks like we have bigger problems than a pissing contest between you lads."

Lucien's eyes flashed. "Explain."

Mac's skin crawled at the look on Hadriel's face. "Caeden found one of the guards dead, and the exterior doors left open. That thing didn't crawl over the walls—it was let in on purpose."

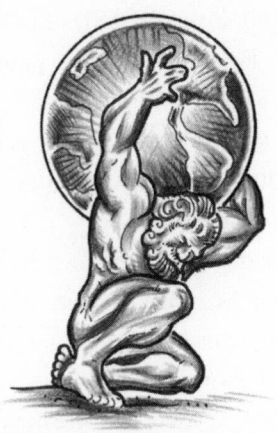

CHAPTER FIFTEEN

*J*enny opened her eyes slowly, hating life with the hate of a thousand fiery suns. Her shoulder was one big lump of pain, and she was pretty sure she had beard burn on the inside of her thighs. So instead of jumping up and demanding that someone tell her what the hells was going on, she lay there and stared at the gently shifting colors on her ceiling.

"How are you feeling?"

Of course he couldn't just sit there and be quiet. Whoever said geniuses were the strong, silent type was an idiot. Or maybe no one said that and she was just making things up. "Like I had the best sex of my life and then got trampled by a Bolkerian."

Mac gave a half smile. "So you're better than you were."

"Yeah, sure. Great deduction." Considering she'd been passed out cold, it wasn't saying much. He moved into her line of sight, freckled skin streaked with mud and blades of grass. Jenny turned her head enough to see that he still wore the leather pants from the night before. "Dude, you really need a sans shower or something. I can smell you from here." She was such a liar, but she couldn't draw a full breath looking at all those stupid muscles, perfectly defined by his stupid leather pants. She was going to smack Gwen silly the first chance she got.

"I'm going to let that pass since you've been seriously injured." He gave that crooked smile that made her toes curl. "But I've changed my mind."

She briefly considered pretending to pass out again, but discarded the thought. Mac had proven to be nearly as stubborn as she was—he'd just wait her out. Heaving a sigh, she gave in. "Changed your mind about what?"

He pinned her to the bed with a single heated look. "Last night wasn't nothing, and it does matter."

Yikes. "I—"

"No point in arguing." He walked across the room as if he didn't have a care in the world. "I'm sure the twins and the triplets will be in shortly. How we got stuck with so many multiples is beyond me." Then he was gone, door swishing shut behind him.

We. Such an innocent little word when left all on its own, and yet it was like he'd taken all the air in the room with him when he left. Not cool, not cool at all. Because sometime in the last few days she'd started to feel like he was part of the team. More than that, like it could be him and her against the universe. Stupid, silly thoughts. The kind of thoughts she should have grown out of when she put away her dolls and started learning knife fighting. But there was something about Mac that called to that part of her, the part she never let anyone near.

And the fact that he refused to have sex intrigued her even as it infuriated her. She was such a mess.

She huffed and stared at the ceiling again, willing the waves to calm her. Instead, Jenny's agitation only grew. Where the hells did he get off putting irrational thoughts like these in her head and then bouncing out? The least he could do was stick around so she could yell at him. Or ask him to hold her. "I need a drink."

"You know, we just talked about this."

Jenny startled and then cursed when the move made her shoulder scream. She'd been so busy jumping through mental hoops, she hadn't heard him come in. "You keep saying that, and I keep not listening."

"Obviously."

Luc stepped aside, and then Gwen was there, rushing across the room. "Gods, Jenny, I was so worried about you. Then they gave me a tranq and I just passed out. Are you okay? You're not dying or anything, are you? Because I really couldn't handle that."

"Gwendolyn, take a breath. As I said before, she'll be fine."

"Fine isn't good enough." She turned back to Jenny, all big brown eyes and pouty red lips. "The party is in three days and if you miss it, everything will be *ruined*."

"*Gwendolyn*."

They both flinched at the barely restrained violence in Luc's voice. He didn't get pissed often, but when he did, he was scarier than Boone. But Jenny had bigger things to worry about. "What party?"

The blonde dredged up a shaky smile. "Your surprise party."

The room seemed to turn a full circle even though she didn't move. "Gwen, I told you we couldn't have a party. It'll bring too much attention, and the whole reason we're here is to hide."

"I know." She shot a nervous glance at her twin. "But I mentioned it to my patron—"

"Gods, Gwendolyn. What were you thinking?" Luc looked like he wanted to shred something. "You're putting Jenny in danger."

"It's just a party. And it's too late now. Our patron loved the idea." She shifted from foot to foot. "I can't stop it, even if I wanted to."

It was like the universe was out to get Jenny. She closed her eyes, and sighed. There had to be a way around this, if she could just have a second to herself to think it through. Neither of the twins was apparently interested in giving her that, though. She heard Luc's heavy footsteps. "Get out."

"But—"

"You've done enough. Just get out."

Gwen made a sound dangerously close to a sob and the door slammed behind her. Only then did Jenny open her eyes. "You didn't have to make her cry."

"It's a superficial emotion. I doubt she shed a tear before she started making calls to get all the details in place for her party."

Gods damn Gwen for going ahead with it the one time Jenny actually made a responsible decision. "There's an easy fix—I'll just keep my team in a room up here. No one has to know we're here."

Luc shook his head. "I wish it was that easy. If our patron knows you're here, he'll insist you attend."

The room was a little too warm, like the walls were closing in. She didn't like being trapped and forced into situations she didn't choose—even if they were parties thrown by one of her dearest friends in the world.

"We have other problems as well." Luc dropped into the overstuffed chair opposite the bed. "The guard at the outer gate was killed and the door left open."

Her mind tumbled over itself at the change in topic. "No shit?"

"I have no idea if it was an inside job or an outside attack, or some combination of the two." Luc rubbed a hand over his face, and for the first time, she noticed how tired he looked. His normally dusky skin was damn near gray, and there were lines around his mouth and eyes that had never been there before. "And now my fool sister has sneaked a party into the mix."

She wished she could be surprised, but Jenny really should have seen this coming. Gwen didn't like hearing the word "no."

"She's pretty one-track-minded when it comes to stuff like that."

"Stop making excuses for her." Just like that, the signs of tiredness disappeared and he was all fire and brimstone again. "She knows bringing so many near-strangers into this house is a mistake, especially after you explicitly told her not to. But do you think she cares?"

"Stop it. Just stop it." She flinched. "Gods, that hurts."

"Can you please resist ripping your stitches? I'm rather attached to this comforter, and bloodstains are a bitch to get out." He sighed and stood. "I'll call your first mate and have him check the bandages."

"Hadriel did this?" He was never going to let her live it down.

"Is he not a medic?"

The man in question came through the door, and Jenny threw up her hands, wincing at the move. "Fine. Great. Let's just have a freaking party in my room. Too bad I'm so messed up or I'd take advantage of you two."

"As if that's ever stopped you." Luc sat again, crossing his arms over his chest. "Now be a good girl and sit still for Hadriel."

"Don't you know by now? I'm never a good girl."

Hadriel snorted. "Stop trying to distract us, or I'll tranq you."

"Since when are you so chatty?" He just stared at her and she sighed. "Damn. You really do sound like a medic." She let him turn her around, trying to keep the sheet pressed to her chest. It was one thing for everyone and their dog to see her naked when she was passed out cold—it was totally another for Hadriel to ogle her boobs here and now.

She held her breath while he peeled away the bandages covering her shoulder and made a pleased sound. "At least the bleeding's stopped. That's something."

"Wait—what the hells are you talking about? I wouldn't stop bleeding?" She started to turn around, and got smacked upside the back of her head for her trouble.

"You're fine," Hadriel said. "The poison should be out of your system by now so we can risk using med patches."

"Poison?"

"What are you—a parrot? Yes, poison."

She looked at Luc, but he just stared. "A little help here would be nice."

"You need more help than I'm able to give." He settled back in the chair and popped his neck. "But you'll make a full recovery."

Thank the gods for that. "So are you going to explain what happened with the guard or do I have to beg?"

He lifted an eyebrow. "No begging required, though that's an entertaining concept. But, yes, the guard. He was found outside the north gate, savaged by one of the natives. It's not clear if the native killed him or just took advantage of the body. I suspect the latter. We believe his killer used his access keys to leave the gate open, and the body as bait. From there it was only a matter of time before one of the natives followed the scent of blood and found their way in. Frankly, we're damn lucky it was an adolescent or you wouldn't be running your pretty mouth right now."

That thing was an adolescent? Jenny fought back a shiver at the thought of a full-grown one and tried to think. "I don't know, Luc. Are you sure this is about us? Don't you have enemies?"

"Of course. More than I care to count. But none of them are the type to do something like this."

"So who else is there?" When he only stared at her, she shook her head. "Look, I get it—Sanctify is on my ass. But they don't know where we are. Even if they did and somehow managed to get through the gauntlet that's required to even make it through the atmosphere on Sisilean, this is hardly their style. Those bastards would have shown up, guns blazing, and tried to skin us alive. This has to be an inside job." It wouldn't take much for a familiar face to lure a guard into relaxing long enough to kill him. Then again, there were plenty of people out there with the skills to be damn near invisible so the guard wouldn't see them coming. There were too many variables in place to know for sure.

She flinched when Hadriel bopped her on the head again. "I swear to the gods, if you hit me again, I will not hesitate to beat the shit out of you."

"Temper, temper." But he finished wrapping her shoulder and wadded up the bloody bandages. "We'll be close to keep you out of trouble."

"Did everyone forget that I'm in charge here? Go back to pretending to be mute." She slid off the bed, only wobbling a little until she locked her knees, and gave them both death stares. "I am the fucking captain. Stop undermining me or I swear by all that's holy, I will shoot you both."

The men exchanged a glance. That shit seemed to happen a lot around her. Hadriel shrugged. "Have fun with that." Then he left.

"Godsdamned coward." Jenny gave in and leaned her hip against the bed so she didn't fall on her ass.

"You know, you'd be a lot more convincing if you didn't have to prop yourself up." Luc crossed the room and gave her a gentle push. She tried to fight the pull of gravity, but she ended up in a heap on the bed. *Oh gods, oh gods, oh gods.* She bit her lip to keep in a moan of pure agony.

He gave a mirthless laugh. "My point exactly."

"I don't need you talking to me like I'm a freaking child." She even felt like one when he stood over her like that. "I'm not stupid. I know that trouble is trouble, no matter if it was here before we were or not."

"Gods, Jenny, I know you're not stupid. If you'd get over your pride for half a moment, you'd realize as much. I love you, and I don't want to see you hurt."

It was Boone all over again. He wanted to protect her, didn't believe she was capable of doing it on her own. Well, she had agreed to be left out of the action for her big brother's sake when he swooped in to save Ophelia and steal the throne—she'd be damned before she let Luc take the fire for her.

Inhaling deeply to give herself time to think, she dredged up a smile. "I know. Honestly, I'm fine. I have this covered." And if she stayed in this room another minute, she was going to burst into tears or start screaming—neither was an option right now if she wanted him to take her seriously. She pushed out of bed and staggered toward the door, clutching the sheet to her chest.

Luc's sigh was like a kidney punch. "Where do you think you're going?"

"If the guard was killed and the lizard let in, I need as much information as I can get. And we need to double the guards if possible."

"Jenny—"

"Don't worry. I won't skip out before the party and make you look bad in front of your patron." No matter how terrible an idea this party was. But she'd put Luc and Gwen in this position when she asked them for a place to hide. She couldn't take off and leave their careers in shambles. She slapped the palm lock, pausing to summon the strength to leave the room.

"Damn it, that's not what I meant and you know it."

She did, but there was no room for softness now. If she learned anything from growing up with him and Boone, it was that showing the slightest weakness would result in being railroaded by these well-meaning assholes. "Leave it alone. I'm done."

As she walked down the hall, she could feel him watching, just waiting for her to stumble. Well, he could wait for days, because she wasn't going to give him the satisfaction.

Trying to remember where Gwen said Mac's room was, Jenny turned left down the hallway, mentally cursing when she tripped over a set of stairs. "This is so not my day."

"What are you doing?"

Horror-vid-slow, she looked up to find the man in question

at the top of the stairs. He'd showered and changed into a fitted pair of black pants and a knit navy sweater that did wonders for his well-muscled shoulders and arms. He looked good enough to eat. She wobbled, throwing a hand against the wall to keep from falling. Except she used the injured arm, and it sent white-hot agony searing through her body. "Shit."

He flew down the stairs three at a time, catching her just as she fell. He lifted Jenny, cradling her against his chest. "What are you doing out of bed?"

"Don't take me back there." If Luc saw her like this, it would just reinforce his belief she couldn't take care of herself.

"Okay."

She loved him just a little bit for not questioning her in that moment. Anyone else would have. Instead, Mac climbed the stairs and headed to his room.

CHAPTER SIXTEEN

*H*olding Jenny in his arms again settled something deep inside Mac. He'd been stalking the halls, ready to snap, when he saw her at the bottom of the stairs, wearing nothing more than a sheet. Right now, in this moment, she actually needed him. It soothed a primitive part he hadn't been aware even existed.

Careful of her injured shoulder, he tucked her more firmly against his chest. "Why are you out of bed?"

She tensed, but finally sighed and relaxed against him. "Luc and Hadriel are trying to take over. They think I can't handle this mess."

A thread of underlying pain ran through the words, but he couldn't begin to guess how to fix it. He wasn't particularly good at comforting—hells, he didn't interact with people enough to have to. But for her he would try. It would help if he knew what she was talking about, though. "What mess?"

"Oh, just that the guard might or might not have been killed to let that thing onto the grounds." She turned her face into his chest. "And apparently Gwen went behind my back to plan a party that we can't get out of because her patron is backing it."

He held her closer, careful of her shoulder. "We'll make the best of it." He wasn't sure how, yet, but if he had some time, he could hop a signal into Control and put his own alarms into the checkpoints. It wouldn't stop Sanctify from coming dirtside if they somehow found a way in, but it would at least give them a chance to do something about it before those bastards came knocking on their door.

She finally looked at him, her face drawn with exhaustion and stress. The fact that she wasn't bothering to smile shouldn't have warmed him, but it did. For once, she'd left the masks behind. "I should have listened to you when you said this place was the wrong choice."

If she had, who knew if he would have been able to get through to her as well as it seemed he had? Mac didn't like the feeling of being coerced into situations not of his making any more than she did, but he was here with her. He pressed a kiss to her forehead. "It will work out."

"Did you figure that out with your supersweet probabilities?"

"No. But I know *you*. You won't stop until the mission is successful." He turned down the hallway to his room.

"I hate to say this, but you might have too much faith in me."

"You're wrong. No one else could have saved Boone from Sanctus when they took him captive. No one else would have thought to even try." And she'd done more than attempt to save him—she had actually succeeded. It was the first time in living memory that someone had pulled off an escape from Sanctify's home world.

"Ophelia would have gone without me." But she was looking at him as if he'd just told her a valued secret. "But maybe you're right. We were a pretty badass team."

"Without equal." That mission had cemented his fascination with the woman, even though he hadn't known about it until months later. Shifting his hold on Jenny, he pressed a hand against the lock.

Jenny gave a muffled snort when they walked in. "Gwen really outdid herself with this room."

He turned, taking it in for what felt like the first time. The pink walls were ghastly, even without the floral bedspread. Add in the lace curtains hanging on either side of the window, and it couldn't be more feminine if it tried. "I think it suits me."

She laughed and then winced. "Oh, stop. Don't make me laugh—it hurts."

"I'm sorry."

"I'm fine, I'm just bitching." Her breath hitched as he set her on the bed. "I need to know everything you can tell me about the new High Priest. Gwen's more than proved that we can't stay here, so I need to know how he thinks so we can find a way around his patrols when we move to get you to safety."

He sat, unable to quell the protective urge that demanded he pull the sheet higher around her and then smooth a hand over her arm and down her hip. Mac moved to her stomach, amazed at how much strength could be stored in such a lean package. It wasn't that she felt breakable, exactly, but having her in his bed and injured drove home just how vulnerable Jenny was right now. When she strutted around, running her mouth, she was larger than life. Here, now, she was so much more real. "You need rest."

She smacked his wandering hand. "Stop mothering me. The new High Priest. What do you know about him?"

Not nearly enough. "From what I can gather, Oberon's the youngest person to ever take the position. There are whispers he's related somehow to the former High Priest, but I can't pin down how."

"Great. So he's looking for revenge?"

"I suppose so." Mac shrugged. "It might also just be the usual desire to eliminate all Diviners. Hansarda is now home to two of them, which would be considered quite the coup."

She frowned. "And he's looking to use you to do it."

All evidence seemed to point in that direction. "It seems like overkill."

"Right. Overkill. It couldn't possibly be because you're a genius who has a knack for coming up with really nifty ways to kill people."

Okay, it might be as simple as that.

She frowned. "I don't like it that we're not sure of this Oberon guy's motives, or what he's capable of. At least with the last High Priest, we were dealing with a known entity. If there's even the slightest chance that they could make it dirtside, we have to get out of here. Soon. I won't have my friends hurt because of this."

He mentally cursed himself in three different languages for bringing up this possibility, but it had to be said. "The twins may be in danger because of their connection with you, even if you leave."

"So they might fuck with my friends to draw me out. Gods, I hate those monsters." She settled more firmly against him, moving her head to his chest. He shifted, putting his arm around her, careful to avoid her shoulder. Jenny sighed. "I want to kill them all."

"I do, too." And he would in a heartbeat, if it meant keeping her safe.

She yawned. "I'll talk to the twins about it before the party. I really, really wish Gwen hadn't put me in this shitty position."

"If you have to make an appearance, make a quick one." The chances of them coming into danger from an hour of socializing shouldn't be that high. But he didn't like it, not when this forced attendance came so closely on the heels of the native's attack. There was danger here, even if it wasn't the same danger they'd fled on T-II. Mac pressed a kiss to the top of her head, earning another sigh from her.

"You know what, Mac? I think I might actually like you."

That surprised a laugh out of him. "I'm glad to hear it."

She lifted her head, gray eyes sizing him up. "No, I'm serious. I don't really like all that many people. And I sure as hells don't trust them."

It occurred him that she wasn't wearing her mask—hadn't been for the entire time they'd been alone. He reached up and ran a single finger along the edge of her jaw. "I know."

"I just...I don't know what to do with *this*."

For all that he wanted Jenny with a fire he never could have anticipated, he was no more experienced in this than she was. But that wasn't going to stop him from pursuing this. "We will figure it out together."

She kissed him. Just the briefest brushing of lips, and yet it somehow seemed more intense than any kiss they'd had up to this point. She shivered. "You make me so damn crazy."

The feeling was most definitely mutual. Every one of Mac's nerve endings crackled, demanding he flip her over and finish what they started in the lagoon. But memories of last night hit him square in the chest, the thought of all that blood dousing his desire. Right now Jenny needed to rest and recover.

He smoothed back her hair, guiding her head back to his chest. "Rest. We can talk more tonight."

She yawned again. "Most men wouldn't turn down sex for sleep."

Of course they wouldn't. Mac had the feeling she didn't spend too much time in bed talking. The woman had more walls than T-IV and twice as much security around her heart. But she had let him in—not all the way, but it was a start. "I'm not most men."

"No shit. I kind of figured that out ages ago. I think I'm going to sleep now. I'm freaking exhausted."

"I'll watch over you while you do."

She gave him a soft smile as her eyes slid closed. "Thanks."

They lay there for a long time before Jenny's breathing finally evened out and the last of the tension eased from her body. He waited a good half an hour more, luxuriating in the ability to hold her. It went a long way toward assuring him that she'd be okay.

But there were still things to do, no matter how much he wanted to stay like this forever. Something nagged at him, a missing puzzle piece. He needed more information to figure out exactly what it was, and the only way to do that was to get his systems up and running again. He'd hack Sanctify's network, and use that to figure out how close they were.

First, though, he had to report in.

Slipping out of bed, he pulled the comforter around her shoulders and turned to the comm unit. It was impossible to tell who would be worse to deliver the news to, but he didn't have a choice—Ophelia and Boone would find out sooner or later, and they wouldn't look kindly on his withholding information.

Routing the signal to bounce from three separate locations was child's play and probably unnecessary since Sanctify wasn't supposed to know where they were, but Mac didn't want to take any risks. There was also the added bonus of so many bounces disfiguring the signal and making it difficult to translate for anyone attempting to listen in.

Too short of a time later, he was staring at *both* Ophelia and Boone. As if they were waiting for his call. "I have a report."

"We know." Ice was warmer than Boone's tone.

Ophelia's wasn't much better. "What happened to Jenny?"

He didn't ask how they already knew. Spending as much time interacting with Diviners as he had, nothing really surprised him anymore. "She's fine."

"I know she's fine, Mac, which is the only reason I'm not on a Ladydamned ship to come save your asses. What I don't know is how she was hurt in the first place." In the background a baby squalled. "It's your turn, Boone."

The man didn't argue, just leveled a baleful stare at Mac. "If anything happens to my sister because of you, I will stake you myself."

The mention of Hansarda's practice of staking criminals in the desert to bleed out and be eaten by the sand worms made his stomach lurch. "I don't want to see her hurt."

"Then do something about it." Boone left the screen and a few moments later the crying turned to a contented gurgle.

Ophelia rubbed a hand over her face. "I don't know how he does it—the man has a magic touch."

Since Mac didn't know the first thing about babies, he switched back to business. "I don't have anything definite, but I can tell you what I do know."

"Do it."

"We were attacked last night. From what I can gather, someone killed a perimeter guard on the estate and used his access keys to open one of the outer gates with the intention of letting Sisilean natives onto the property. One of them came hunting us and Jenny was bitten in the ensuing fight. A small amount of anticoagulant poison was left in her system, but she's fine and recovering now."

"I see. And who exactly do we think killed the guard?"

"I don't have enough information to make a guess." Under her hard look, he relented. "As far as I can tell, our location is still secure, which would lead me to believe that this attack has nothing directly to do with us—if it weren't for the fact that we're currently being hunted by Sanctify. I don't know. There are too many variables."

She drummed her fingers against the arm of her chair. "I don't like you staying on Sisilean. I doubt that pleasure palace you're staying in has nearly enough security to deal with any kind of threat beyond the natives."

"It doesn't."

She nodded. "What's the plan? And where's Jenny?"

Before he could stop himself, he turned to look to where she still slept in his bed. When he faced Ophelia again, she wore a strange smile. "What?"

"Just the Lady's business. Would you like a reading, Mac?"

He wanted to say no, but traditionally it was bad luck to refuse an offered reading. Diviners didn't extend invitations like that very often, even if they couldn't turn down a request. And while his faith lay in anything he could create for himself, he wasn't naive enough to doubt the existence of something *more*. He'd seen too many odd things while working with Azure to discount Diviners as anything other than uncanny. Still, he couldn't help but ask, "Will I like what it says?"

The strange smile appeared again. "Who can tell?"

His skin broke out in gooseflesh. "Then with all due respect, I'd rather not."

"You may change your mind later on."

His throat closed at the terrible knowledge in her eyes. Sorrow and pain and hope and fear. "I don't understand."

"I know. But you will. Contact us again when you space from Sisilean and we'll discuss your next move."

CHAPTER SEVENTEEN

"I don't know what we're supposed to do with this." Gwen turned Jenny around, eyeing her shoulder. "It'll look tacky as hells with what I planned on dressing you in."

Javier frowned and it was all she could do not to throw up her hands and offer to go to the party naked. Knowing these two, they'd think it was a brilliant idea and then she'd be screwed. It had never bothered her that her friend had blinders on when it came to some of the harsher realities of life, but she couldn't help wondering how the blonde rationalized her current priorities. One of *her* guards had died and *her* home had been infiltrated. But all she was worried about was dressing Jenny in something that wouldn't embarrass her patron.

The clothing expert circled her. "I think I have an idea. It's not what we imagined, but it would hide the scar."

She pinched the bridge of her nose, just wanting this to be over. "Sounds fantastic. Let's do it." Then she could get back to the things that really mattered.

If she had to cut herself out of the outfit later, so be it. They just needed to get through tonight and figure out the next step—which would already be done if she hadn't slept the majority of the last three days. She'd woken up and her first thought was to wonder how Mac had transported all the techno junk from his apartment on T-II to this room. As it was, she'd had to clear a path to the door when Gwen and Javier descended on her this morning, banishing Mac from his own room. He'd gone off without even a good-bye, leaving her feeling much the same as she had in the lagoon. *Bereft*.

It didn't make any sense, and she was kind of afraid to look too deeply for fear of what she might find.

"Stop thinking so much." Gwen tapped a perfectly manicured fingernail against her forehead. "You're going to give yourself wrinkles."

"Gods forbid that happens—who would want me then?"

Mac. She shut down the thought before it could take root.

The little blonde cocked her head to the side. "Sweetie, you need to stop. I get that Luci has you all riled up and you're worried about your yummy man and whatshisface with the ugly white robe, but tonight is for fun." She winked. "And for forgetting."

"It's not as easy as that." Once upon a time, it had been. Hells, even six months ago she wouldn't be stressing about things she couldn't control. Instead of worrying about how they were going to survive, she'd be drinking with Gwen and gossiping over the eye candy who'd be at the party tonight. She probably wouldn't have said no to the party in the first place.

Gods, she was turning into Boone.

"I need a drink."

"That's the spirit." Gwen trotted over to the InstaChef and returned with a glass of clear liquid. "It'll be just like old times."

The last time her friend had promised a good time, Jenny ended up being mauled by a giant lizard. "What's being done about the security? And who the hells did you invite?" There shouldn't be anyone too dangerous, since certain infractions—like murder—could get one banned from Sisilean for the rest of your life. Most of the people who could afford to make use of its entertainment wouldn't bother with something so mundane.

That hadn't stopped someone from killing the guard and letting a native onto the grounds, though.

And there were plenty of ways to kill someone without getting blood on your hands. Not to mention, it would just take one careless word to the wrong person, and Sanctify would zero in on their location faster than she could say, "We're fucked."

An hour. She could do an hour and keep her head down. It would have to be enough.

"Oh, that. Yes, yes, Luci has taken care of everything. And the guest list is extremely exclusive." Gwen waved away their safety as if it were no concern.

Even the attack three nights ago wasn't enough to penetrate the perfect little bubble she called life. She wondered what she'd say when Gwen found out she was going to be leaving with them. Or what Luc would say for that matter. Maybe she'd just tranq them both and lock them in *Psyche's* unused cabin. Stuff like that seemed to work well enough for Boone.

She should probably call him to report. Damn it, why hadn't she done that the morning after the attack? They'd gone four days since her last contact—he was probably ripping his hair out and making plans to come save her by now. Shit. Being responsible sucked. "Hey, can I have a minute? I need to get a hold of my brother."

Gwen's eyes lit up. "He still as delicious as always?" She tugged at her top, baring another few centimeters of skin and sending her in public indecency territory.

"Gross, Gwennie, just gross."

"I'm just saying…I'd so hit that."

"He just had a baby with the love of his life."

"So what? Love fades and a bitch's body never bounces back from that kind of trauma."

She shook her head, hating that she no longer agreed with that mentality. She'd *seen* Boone and his Diviner. Their love only seemed to go stronger with time and every barrier that showed up in their path. She was *it* for him, and vice versa. It was almost enough to wish she'd end up with someone who looked at her like that, who thought she was beautiful and strong even when she was at her worst.

Gods, could she be any more maudlin?

"I wouldn't mess with her if I were you." Though watching the blonde go head-to-head with Ophelia would be entertaining. It'd be a great show for all of three seconds—until the Diviner ripped out Gwen's throat.

"You're no fun anymore."

"That's what I keep hearing. Seriously, though, I just need a few minutes."

"Fine, fine." Gwen pouted, but seemed to realize the quivering lip didn't work on her. "I'll go get that sexy Mac ready. By then Javier should be done with your getup."

"Thanks." She waited until the door shut and then palm-locked it. She caught herself holding her breath and sighed. The longer she waited, the worse it would be—better to rip the med patch off quickly. She dialed home, half hoping to find Ophelia instead of Boone.

But no, the gods never smiled on her like that.

Her brother appeared in the screen, his arms crossed over his chest and a muscle in his cheek jumping. "You're making a mess of things."

That was how he wanted to play things. No hello. No "hey Jenny, heard you were injured. How are you feeling?" Nothing but stern disapproval. Fine. She grinned. "Just want to keep life interesting—you know how bored I get."

"Now is not the time for your bullshit. There's a lot riding on your ability to keep the inventor safe."

It was bad enough having Luc and Hadriel on her ass—she didn't need Boone, too. The only person who seemed to have any faith in her abilities was the inventor himself. "I can handle it."

"Oh, I have no doubt you can handle it. I wouldn't have agreed to your leading the run if I thought any different."

She took a measured breath. At least Boone believed she was capable, even if he was an ass about it. "I have things under control."

"So getting attacked by a giant godsdamned lizard was all part of the plan?"

"About that—"

Boone ran his hands through his hair, making it stand on end. "It was a bad call to go to Sisilean, and you know it. But it's too late to worry about it now. What are you going to do to fix this?"

It was on the tip of her tongue to make a snarky comment, but she smothered the urge. He was actually treating her like an adult for once in their lives—the least she could do was attempt the same. Dropping the grin, she said, "We space in twenty-four hours. As far as we can tell, Sanctify still has no idea that we're here, but I'm not as confident in my ability to keep Mac safe here as I was before." To keep *anyone* safe if there was someone using the natives to attack.

His face betrayed none of his thoughts. Dad used to be able to do that, shut down all his emotions and look at a situation from a completely dispassionate stance. Seeing it on her brother brought back too many things she didn't want to deal with.

"And then?"

She gave him a saucy smile. "I figured I'd just wing it."

"Jenny—"

"I'm just kidding. I don't know yet because I need to have a sit-down with Mac. He's got plenty of hidey-holes to choose from, and he's even more paranoid than you are. I'm sure you'd approve." Though she seriously doubted he'd approve of where Mac's mouth had been the other night. But what Boone didn't know wouldn't hurt her.

He started to say something and seemed to think better of it. "You won't come home now, even if I tell you to, will you?"

And add to the threat around Ophelia and her new niece? "I made a bad call coming here. Bringing the inventor to Hansarda would be a worse call."

Boone sighed. "How's the shoulder? Any permanent damage?"

A flash of fear nearly paralyzed her. She hadn't even considered the possibility of permanent damage. How could she fight and shoot with her dominant arm screwed up? She wasn't anywhere near as good with her left as she was with her right. Taking a deep breath, she made an effort to slow her panicked thoughts. Hadriel would have told her if that was something to worry about—he knew how much these things mattered. "It itches like crazy, but I'm practically at one hundred percent." It wasn't strictly the truth, but it would make him feel better to think that.

"Well...I'm glad you're okay."

She wrapped her arms around herself. "Yeah, me, too. Er, I mean thanks." Gods, they were so terrible at this crap. Then again, considering their older brother had been a complete sociopath and Dad hadn't been much better, she figured they were doing okay.

"Take care. And keep me updated, godsdammit."

"Oh, fine, since you asked so nicely. Go take care of your family, Boone, and tell my big sister I said hi."

That finally teased a smile from him. "You know how much she hates it when you call her that."

"Yep. But you'd think, being a Diviner and all, that she'd realize the whole marrying-you thing is going to happen."

He laughed. "One would think."

"No one out-stubborns an O'Keirna. That's what I always say."

"You never say that."

She shrugged. "Well, maybe I should start. It's pretty catchy."

"Get some rest, Jenny, and I'll talk to you soon." He made it both a threat and a promise and cut off the call.

She unlocked the door and staggered over to the bed, more tired than she wanted to admit. A glance at the clock told her there wasn't time for another nap. This party planning crap was seriously overrated when her shoulder throbbed in time with her heartbeat, and she could practically *feel* Sanctify breathing down her neck. Maybe she should say to hell with it and lock the damn door before…

As if summoned by her thoughts, Javier breezed into the room, trailing a length of shiny black material behind him. He helped her wrestle into it, and made quick work of her hair and makeup, muttering all the while. She put up with it, because this was a battle she wasn't going to win. If she didn't submit, Gwen would be back in here and wailing about her ruining the party again. Better to just let them have their way. This time.

Javier stepped back. "It is the best I can do."

Well, that was encouraging. "Thanks."

He gave her one last look-over and then turned and left the room without another word. She checked herself out in the mirror and sighed. Perfection. Any other time, she'd be strutting around and planning on leaving a trail of broken hearts in her wake.

Now? Now, she just wanted to get through the night and out of this place.

Even so, a part of her couldn't help wondering what Mac would think of the catsuit that hugged every curve of her body. Would he like it? Hells, would he even care?

She wished she could keep on pretending that his demands

for honesty and refusal to sleep with her were all that intrigued her about him, but it wasn't the truth. She *liked* the big stupid genius inventor. Hells, she even trusted him enough to let him have glimpses of the part of her she never showed anyone. He hadn't flinched, hadn't backed off, hadn't done anything she expected. Instead, he'd stood rock-steady against the storm that was Jenny, and then turned around and demanded *more*.

They were spacing tomorrow, taking her crew and hopefully the twins, and heading for a safer location. Tonight, though? She ran her finger around the heart-shaped cutout that made the most of her breasts. Maybe after she made a quick appearance at the party, she'd make a trip up to his room and see exactly how determined he was to keep his hands off her.

CHAPTER EIGHTEEN

$\mathcal{M}$ac finished lacing up his ridiculous pants—leather again—and pulled on the shirt Javier had left for him. Going down to the party and mingling with a crowd of people like Gwendolyn and Lucien was the last thing he wanted to do, but he couldn't leave Jenny alone. An hour, she'd promised, and he'd hold her to it.

He started to turn for the door and checked himself at the last second. So far the searches he'd run had brought him nothing suspicious, but it didn't hurt to check one more time. None of the alerts he'd placed on the checkpoints had shown anything, either.

It *should* have comforted him, but he couldn't shake the feeling that he'd missed something important. There was no reason to link the native attack to Sanctify, and he was all too aware of running the risk of blaming all the attacks on the known threat. And yet…

He went back to his comm unit and pulled up the most recent reports that had come through Sanctify's main server. A secondary colony founded on Psrida. A high-profile target taken out. A trio of warships deployed to T-II. Another trio sent to T-IV.

Mac frowned, his fingers flying over the holo-keyboard. That couldn't be right. Those warships had been sent to T-II days ago to pick *him* up. Why would they send another group? And, for that matter, why the hells would they be sending troops to T-IV? It was a prison planet. Sanctify had never held an interest there.

He dug deeper, pulling the code from the message regarding T-II, comparing it to the original message. On the surface, it seemed identical, but...

The small hairs on the back of his neck stood up.

The code wasn't the same.

He sat back, steepling his fingers and tapping them to his lips. Sanctify had a handful of decoding algorithms they used when they were trying to fly under the radar—which wasn't often, admittedly. He leaned closer to the screen and ran each of them against the code of the most recent message.

It fell into place a line at a time.

Three warships

It made sense. They'd copied the first message because it was the same number of troops being deployed.

With the High Priest

He stared. That didn't make sense. He'd been tracking and decoding Sanctify's movements for years now, and he'd only ever seen the old High Priest leave the safety of Sanctus three times—all to secure Sanctify's supremacy over a new planet.

But that was the problem—they weren't anywhere near taking full control. Nitriph was still fighting with everything it had, and the rebellions didn't show signs of dying down any time soon.

So why the hells was that bastard traveling so soon after taking over?

To Sisilean.

His entire body went cold. Gods above and below, the High

Priest of Sanctify was coming *here*? Mac scrubbed his hands over his face and ran the algorithm again—and a third time. Nothing changed.

Shit.

He had to tell Jenny. There was still time to get them off-planet if they moved now. Even at top speed, the soonest those warships could be here was three days from now. Unless…

The tingling on his skin got worse. Holding his breath, he pulled the coded message apart, aiming for the time-date stamp. What he found made him curse.

The message was dated three days ago.

Though every instinct demanded he go find Jenny and get her to safety, he forced himself to go through the same process with the second trio of warships. He cursed as the lines came clear. *Three warships to Sisilean*. Those sneaky bastards. They had to know he would be watching for them, so they'd split the six into two groups and faked their destinations.

Adrenaline coursing through him, he took a deep breath and minimized that screen and pull up the ship logs that had been registered with Control over the last twenty-four hours. If Sanctify was dirtside, his alarms should have gone off. He had every single one of their ships' log-ins, and that's what they should have used to try to gain access to Sisilean.

Nothing.

"Now, why don't I find that reassuring?" He scrolled through the ships that had landed, the number higher than he'd expected. Ten had come in today alone.

He found what he was looking for—and hoping *not* to find—immediately. Seven of the ships had come in individually, but there was a cluster of three that had approached at the exact same time. They weren't any log-ins that he recognized, but he'd have to be a fool to think that they weren't the same warships. "Fuck."

Sanctify was here.

• • •

Jenny prowled from one room to the next, trying to pretend she wasn't looking for Mac in the crowd. It had been over an hour, and he still wasn't downstairs. She downed the rest of her drink and set it on the tray of a passing—very naked, very oiled— waiter. Damn it, she was so annoyed she couldn't even bother to check out his ass as he walked away. This was so messed up.

"Are you looking for someone?"

Jenny jumped, tripped over her own feet, and was forced to catch herself on the shoulder of the man who'd spoken. "What the hells is wrong with you? You can't just go sneaking up on people like that."

He smiled and she blinked. The dude was gorgeous. Oh, not in the pretty-boy way she usually went for—more like the type to see a woman he wanted, club her over the head, and drag her back to his ship—but those lips, framed so nicely by a close- cropped beard, were positively sinful. And that hair, gods—she'd kill for hair that luxurious and thick.

And she was staring at him, mouth hanging open. Awesome.

For his part, the man's smile just widened, but she noticed it didn't reach his black eyes. "I didn't mean to startle you."

"Um…right." Her gaze skated down, taking in a massive chest and tight leather pants similar to what Mac had worn the other night.

"Something I could help you with?" The words were filled to the brim with innuendo.

She was already shaking her head before he finished. Whoever this guy was, he was trouble in a way she wanted nothing to do with. Her life was more than complicated enough at the moment. "Thanks, but I'm good. I'm just looking for a friend."

"I could be your friend." His dark eyes were intense on hers.

Even if she were looking to get some action, she wouldn't touch this guy with a ten-foot pole. She'd have to be blind not to recognize a predator like the one who stood before her. He was as out of place in this room full of beautiful, vapid people as one of the Sisilean natives would be. "Thanks, but no thanks."

His smile died, leaving his face terrifyingly expressionless. "We haven't been formerly introduced. I'm Oberon."

It was like all the air had suddenly been sucked out of the room. She *knew* that name—the same name of the new High Priest of Sanctify. Jenny swallowed hard, fighting to keep the polite smile on her face while she searched for another explanation—*any* other explanation. There had to be more than a single man running around the universe with that name. This guy could be one of them.

But was she willing to risk Mac's life on the possibility?

Not by a long shot. "Your mother actually named you that?"

He didn't so much as blink. "No, it was my father who named me. He had an odd sense of humor, I'm told."

Keep talking until you can make a smooth exit. Easy enough. Or it would be if she could manage to draw a full breath. "Your father, huh? I bet there's a story there."

"There is." He tilted his head to the side.

Her gaze landed the people around her, all with cups in their hands, and her escape plan fell into place. "Why don't you grab me another drink and then tell me all about it?"

"I'll do that." He brought her hand to his mouth and pressed a kiss to her knuckles. The feel of his lips against her knuckles made her entire body break out in gooseflesh. The High Priest of Sanctify had just kissed her hand. She needed to find a bathroom and wash that shit off immediately. He turned, somehow managing to disappear into the crowd even though he stood half a head taller than anyone else in the room.

As soon as he was out of sight, she headed in the opposite direction, against the tide of colorful people. Some were dressed in leather, some in silk, some in outlandish gear that most people would balk at. *Keep breathing. Get to Mac. Get the triplets. Get out.* She turned a corner and almost ran over Shad. He was so busy trying to fend off the hands of a drunk man, he didn't see her until she yanked the guy off him. Shad signed, *I had it covered.*

We have bigger problems. For the first time, she thanked the gods they were able to communicate in sign language. It meant she didn't have to mince her words. *Sanctify is here, as in, in this house.*

His eyes went wide. *Shit.*

My thoughts exactly. Get your brothers and meet me in Mac's room.

Done.

At least that was taken care of. She hoped like hells that Mac had just gotten distracted with some project or other, and wasn't wandering around the party looking for her. She headed for the door leading into the hallway, but froze when a familiar woman caught her eye. Impossible. The chances of the Abura-Sumashi being here were astronomical.

Still…

Changing direction, she slid through the crowd, following the cascade of shining white-blond hair. It didn't mean anything. There were plenty of other women in the universe who had the same color. But then the space in front of her cleared and she saw the way the woman was dressed—fitted, serviceable clothes that still managed to cost more than Jenny's entire wardrobe. It really *was* her. She picked up her pace until she was a bare step behind the other woman. "Sadie?"

The Abura-Sumashi froze before turning slowly to face her.

Holy shit, it *was* Sadie. The pale female didn't look like much— she barely came to her shoulder and appeared damn near fragile.

Jenny knew better. She might not share the tusks or towering height of the males of her species, but Sadie was one tough bitch. Hells, she could probably come close to taking Boone down.

She narrowed her creepy black eyes. "What are you doing here?"

"Me? What are *you* doing here?" What were the odds of both the Harpy Queen and the High Priest of Sanctify being on the same planet—in the same godsdamned house—at the same time?

"I'm here on business."

"What kind of business?"

Sadie sighed and flipped her hair over her shoulder. Jenny had practiced that move more times than she cared to admit and she still couldn't make it look half as effortless. "I'm playing babysitter. You?"

It could be possible. Some of Gwen's guests were terrifyingly rich. It would be like the Abura-Sumashi to contract out on one to make a quick credit. Still… She didn't like that Sadie was here. "To who?"

"None of your damn business. On that note, I'll be going." Sadie took a step sideways and went still. She reminded Jenny so much of Cole in that moment that she shivered. He got the same look on his face when he saw something he wanted to eat and thought it might put up a fight.

The tingling of gooseflesh on her skin got worse she turned around, finding Oberon cutting through the crowd toward them, a drink in each hand. Judging by the way he moved, he'd had some kind of formal combat training. Was it too much to ask for that Sanctify pass on their leadership to another doddering, drooling old man like the last High Priest had been? Not only did this guy have an army of zealots at his back, but he seemed to be pretty deadly in his own right.

"What the fuck? Did he see you?" Sadie cursed, sliding

closer. "You have to go. Now."

She'd never seen Sadie nervous about *anything*, and the woman looked like she was half a second from bolting. Oberon was seriously dangerous if he was able to make *her* nervous. She whispered, "You know who that is?"

The Abura-Sumashi looked at her like she'd been dropped on her head as a baby. Hells, maybe she had. She'd take that up with Boone the first chance she got. "That's Oberon, you godsdamned idiot."

Jenny pressed, needing to know if she knew exactly what position he held. "And?"

Sadie grabbed her arm and dragged her out of the room and into the hall. "And he's the fucking High Priest of Sanctify. So if I were you, I'd run for safety like a good little rabbit."

The insult stung, but she had more important things to worry about than her pride. Like a chance to off the new High Priest of Hansarda's enemy—and make the world a safer place for her niece.

"Don't even think about it," Sadie said. "Even on personal business, he wouldn't be allowed to attend without guards."

"What's he doing here?"

"He has...kinks."

Well, then. Maybe he was here for pleasure and had no idea that the inventor he'd sent two of his death squads after was hiding here...but she didn't like her odds. They had to get out and they had to get out now.

Sadie peered around her at the door they just came through. "You need to get out of here. If he doesn't already know who you are, he will soon. And Sanctify will do damn near anything to hurt the Diviner and pay Boone back for breaking their hold on Hansarda before they could get their claws in deep."

So it *was* personal. "I can't leave Mac."

The Abura-Sumashi looked ready to strangle her. "Who in

the hells is Mac?"

Part of Jenny screamed to keep her damn mouth shut, but personal antagonism aside, Sadie loved Boone. Not in an ooey-gooey way, but she'd gone out on a limb more than a few times for him. If she had a loyal bone in her body, it was attached to her feelings for him. "Ophelia's inventor."

Those dark eyes might as well have been deep space for all the emotion they showed. "The one responsible for the antimatter gun."

In for a little, in for a lot. "Yes."

"It would just figure that my first cake job in years, you have to come along and fuck it up."

Was the universe really that twisted to throw all of them into the same place at the same time by sheer chance? Jenny wasn't willing to bet on it. "How is this my fault?"

"It doesn't matter. Get your ass upstairs and retrieve your shit. What's this inventor of yours look like?"

She ignored the niggling voice in her head demanding she rely only on herself to get out of this. Even Boone got help from other people on occasion and, if there was ever a time to call in a favor, it was now. "Tall, pale, handsome, mess of bright-red hair. Probably wearing leather."

Sadie rolled her eyes. "So are half the men here and most of the women. Whatever, don't worry about it. With that kind of coloring, I'll find him no problem. You have transport through the jungle?" She ran her hands through her hair. "What am I saying? Of course you don't."

"I can steal—"

"Don't bother. I have my own. My hover is around the west side of the house." She hesitated, as if considering something. "If for some reason you can't get to your ship, the coordinates for *The Harpy Queen* are programmed into the navigation system. I'll get you off-planet—but only if you're there before eighteen hundred."

Jenny glanced at the clock on the wall next to them. A little under two hours. "If I'm not there, it's because we got out."

"Or you're dead. Either way, I'm not waiting. This job sure as fuck doesn't pay enough for me to be worrying about your sorry ass." Then she was gone, disappearing back through the door they'd just come through.

She frowned at the door for half a second before she spun and ran for the stairs. Whatever was up with Sadie would work itself out. Right now, Jenny's only priority was to get Mac and her crew to safety. She stopped at the top of the stairs. Shit, what about the twins?

"Jenny!"

She breathed a sigh of relief when Mac grabbed her arm. He was okay. He didn't give her a chance to say anything before he hustled her into his room. "We are in serious trouble. Sanctify is on Sisilean."

She laughed, because it was the only thing she could do. "Yeah, no shit. They're *here*."

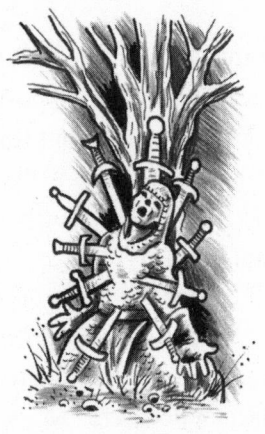

CHAPTER NINETEEN

Jenny kept checking the hallway while Mac threw his stuff into bags. Her third time out, she had to bite her lip to keep from yelling at the triplets for taking so long and worrying her. The reason for the delay danced nervously in front of all three men as they strode down the hall, reminding her of a yapping little dog—but with better hair. "The party's going. I need to be downstairs. Why do I have to come with you?"

Luc's voice came from behind Caeden. "Because Jenny is your friend, and if something happens to her, you'll never forgive yourself."

At least the gods were smiling on her now. She hissed loudly enough to catch their attention. Gwen threw up her hands. "There she is. See—nothing to worry about."

"Hush." Luc grabbed her wrist and towed her over. "Hadriel said you sent Shad to round us up?"

"There's been a change of plans. We have to go—and you're coming with us."

"But the party!"

Luc slapped a hand over his twin's mouth and frowned. "What are you talking about?"

A clock ticked in her head, winding down the time they had to escape—which was ridiculous since the only time she'd seen a non-digital clock was in the vids. She wanted to hustle everyone along, but the set of Luc's shoulders told her he wasn't going anywhere without an explanation. She took a deep breath. "See, it's like this. The Big Bad of Sanctify is in your living room— which is bad—and he knows who I am—also bad—and since he's got a hard-on for Boone and Ophelia, it's pretty freaking likely that even if I bolt now and take Mac with me, he's going to torture and kill both of you—and that's badder than bad. So you need to come with me. Like now."

His frown deepened and Gwen squawked. But then he came through for her, just like he always had in the past. "What's the plan?"

"Run like hells. There's a transport on the west side of the estate. If we can get there, we have a chance of reaching *Psyche*." And if for some reason they couldn't reach her ship, they had a contingency plan—even if she wasn't going to say shit about it unless she had to.

"Fair enough." He gave Gwen a little shake. "Do not even think of arguing, Gwendolyn. I promise to make this up to you."

She gave another sound of protest but took one look at his face and nodded reluctantly. When Luc released her, she turned tear-filled eyes on Jenny. "I'm not happy with you."

"I know. I really am sorry." She shook her head. What was she saying? Survival mattered a whole hells of a lot more than a party, especially a party she hadn't wanted in the first place, and managed to lure *the High Priest of Sanctify* into their living room. She leaned into the room and nodded at Mac. "Time to go."

"I have everything I need." He handed off one of the bags to Caeden and hoisted the other two over his shoulders. The man knew how to pack in a hurry.

"And here I thought we were going to chat all night." Hadriel motioned with his laser. "After you."

Gods, when was he going to go back to the silent gig? "Right." She turned, but Luc was there first. She followed, making sure to keep close to Mac. He'd proved that he could take care of himself, but if they got out of here before anyone knew they were gone, it wouldn't come to that. In the meantime, it was up to her to make sure they didn't get him.

Luc set a quick pace, leading them down the stairs and into the servants' quarters. Everything was less snazzy, but no less expensive, the carpet thick and the walls painted a soothing yellow. Jenny actually preferred it to the glitz and glam of the rest of the house, but she'd never admit that to Gwen.

"How did you know Sanctify was here before I did?" Mac kept up easily, even though he was carting around a bag nearly as big as she was.

"The head dude from Sanctify showed up at the party." And he'd kissed her damn hand. Gross.

"*What?*"

She glanced at him. "I thought you knew."

"I knew three warships landed today, but they sent two sets here. I assumed that, as High Priest, he'd stay back in relative safety." He frowned. "But then, I wouldn't have thought he'd leave Sanctus in the first place."

Six warships? Apparently they weren't taking any chances this time. "Yeah, this guy doesn't seem like he's following any of the old rules." Which made him doubly dangerous.

They wove through the kitchen, earning nasty looks from the people rushing in and out. Jenny didn't like how close they were to the main party, but Luc knew where he was going better than she did. A door tucked into the corner spit them out into the shadows of the back of the building. Jenny fought a shiver at the sight of so much open ground between them and the wall. They'd be sitting ducks.

Luc must have thought the same thing because he skirted the side of the mansion, keeping close to the wall. As they followed, she noted how well Gwen kept up—apparently she *had* been training after all. Good.

Before she had a chance to say anything—and, really, what was there to say?—they reached the corner of the building and saw the hovers. Jenny's gaze coasted over the ritzy ones, vehicles aimed more at looking pretty than at function. Ideally, she'd pick one of the escort hovers, but that option wasn't likely since the guards never strayed far from them. As they crept closer she caught sight of what could only be Sadie's hover. It was beefier than the others around it, and painted a dark red that she suspected matched *The Harpy Queen*'s. Nudging Luc, she pointed.

He nodded. "Guards?"

She shrugged. It wasn't like she and Sadie had had time for a heart-to-heart. "No idea."

"Hadriel, stay with them. Jenny, come along."

She bristled at his taking charge as if he had a right to it, but getting out of here was more important than her bruised ego. Look at her, acting like a responsible grown-up. It was becoming a habit.

She followed closely on Luc's heels, flicking her wrists to engage the gauntlets. They circled the hover—a monstrous thing with nearly as many weapons as the escorts had—finding no sign of movement. She scrambled up the side, trusting him to watch her back while she was exposed. Dropping through the mini-hatch into darkness did nothing good for her blood pressure, but there was no one waiting to slit her throat at the bottom. A quick check told her what she already suspected—the entire thing was empty.

But who knew how long it would stay that way?

She climbed back to the top and leaned over. "Clear. Get everyone over here."

While they got situated, Hadriel took the controls and she chose one of the two gunner seats. From this high up, she sat inside a protected bubble. The plastic wasn't perfectly clear, which made it hard to see. Who the hells invented this shit? Jenny slapped the button to retract it, inhaling the warm jungle scent. This was more like it. While the idea of the plastic staying between her and the jungle was a nice thought, it wouldn't hold up against the claws of the natives. And then she'd be trapped inside the tank with an angry reptilian. Being up close and personal with one of those monsters once was more than enough, thank you very much. It was better to be up here where she had a chance to ward off an attack before they got too close.

On the other side of the hover, Caeden situated himself in the remaining gunner seat. She nodded to show her approval— he was a fantastic shot even if he couldn't see a pair of tits without turning into a blushing virgin.

She motioned to Hadriel. "Let's go." The clock was ticking and, though she hoped she wouldn't need to hitch a ride with Sadie, she wasn't going to lose their last resort because they dawdled.

She found herself holding her breath as they started forward, picking up speed after they crossed through the gate, giving a little wave to the guards. No one tried to stop them—they seemed more concerned with someone getting in than people leaving.

Jungle whizzed by, an indistinguishable blend of shadows that could be hiding everything or nothing—and that was what she could see through her hair flying around her face. There was no way to tell if they were being attacked unless something jumped out, going for her throat.

"Gods, I'm just a bundle of sunshine."

A hand on her knee startled her. Mac handed her a tie, and she used it to pull back her hair, her heart warming that he'd thought of something as small as this. He squeezed, offering a grim smile. "It'll be okay."

She spared him a smile—a real one. "Just hang in there. We'll be out of this before you know it."

"Of that I have no doubt."

"Hey, how do you want me to come up on the shipyard?"

At least Hadriel was asking for her opinion, rather than Luc's. It was on the tip of her tongue to tell him to come in fast with guns blazing, but something held her back. Caution might be the better part of valor right now. "Slow. I want to make sure we're not running into a trap." These days those bastards in Sanctify were even shadier than she was and, while she could hope and pray that they didn't know Mac was here, she wasn't going to bet their lives on it. "Does this thing have a scanner on it?"

"Damn, I should have thought of that." Hadriel's head disappeared as he fiddled with the controls. "There we go. Heat scanner. Not a huge range, but enough so we aren't flying blind."

The hover slowed until she could pick out the individual trees around them. Jenny rotated her seat in a circle, senses on full alert. They weren't safe—not by a long shot—and she didn't want to get jumped right now by some nasty-ass lizard with a taste of her blood. She had no doubt Sadie's hover was equipped to deal with them, but it wasn't a fight she looked forward to having.

"Shit."

That one word told her all she needed to know. Someone was waiting for them at the shipyard. "How many?" If they had a chance to fight their way through, they were going to have to take it—she'd rather have her own ship than beg a ride from *The Harpy Queen*. Looking down at the tight expressions on everyone's face, and she wondered if that was the smart course.

Her job was to keep Mac—and everyone else—safe, and that was pretty damn hard to do when jumping into a full-scale battle.

Hadriel cursed. "At least twenty, and from what I can tell, two warships."

In other words—suicide. A wild part of her wanted to tell him to go for it, but the rational side of her held the command back. It wasn't a legitimate option, and it would get her and everyone under her command slaughtered. Which meant they had only one option. "There is a set of coordinates programmed into the navigation system. How far is it?"

Hadriel squinted at the screen. "Twenty kilometers, give or take. Where do they lead?"

Twenty kilometers through the jungle with no escort hovers to keep the natives away. It would be better if they could kill the running lights since the pale-green glow drew those bastards like a fly to honey, but that really would be suicide. Jenny rolled her shoulders. "A ride, but only if you can get us there fast."

He hesitated for a full ten seconds. "You got it."

"Everybody else, keep low and strap yourselves in to something. This is going to be a wild ride. Caeden, you good?"

He gave her a thumbs-up before rotating his seat to cover their rear, which left her with the front. Good enough. "Let's do this."

The hover picked up speed again and she had a few minutes to be thankful for the hair tie before a strange sound filled the night. It raised the small hairs on the back of her neck and she fought back a shiver. "What the hells is that?"

"Lyiaks' hunting calls." It was Gwen who answered. When Jenny spared her a glance, she found the blonde curled up in a ball in the corner seat. "They're coming for us."

Great. What was a pack of hungry lizards against her natural charm and good looks? Oh wait, a freaking pack of hungry lizards. She gritted her teeth. It didn't matter. They weren't going to be feeding anyone tonight.

She checked to make sure the guns were powered up, sparing a moment to wish for something more familiar. There was no telling how long these suckers would last. But at least Abura-Sumashi were paranoid types, so the guns probably had every upgrade imaginable.

The thought had barely crossed her mind when she caught sight of movement on the edges of the running lights. Every instinct screamed for her to fire and keep on firing until every one of those things were dead. But that was a rookie mistake and Jenny was no damned rookie. She held her breath, waiting.

They came from both directions at once, clawing up the side of the hover. Jenny shot the first one, the kickback making her shoulder ache, and turned in time to get a good look at a mouthful of teeth before she blasted that bitch back to wherever it came from. There was barely a chance to draw a full breath before the next wave came, each one trying to take a bite out of her face.

One after another, she shot them down, distantly aware of Caeden doing the same. All the while, a small part of her was screaming in panic. The monsters in the night were real and they were coming for her. Dad taught her a long time ago that emotion in battle could get you killed, and she was a big fan of living, so she locked away the fear threatening to overtake her, just like he'd shown her. There would be plenty of time to freak out if they lived through this.

No. Not if. *When*. Important to keep the right vibes going.

"What the fuck am I thinking?" Jenny's shot knocked three from the side of the hover, and she whipped around in time to hit another. Something wet hit her face. But that was wrong. Everything was supposed to be flying *away* from her.

She looked over and screamed. Caeden was out of his seat, his arm halfway down a lizard's throat. It chomped down, a bump from the hover knocking it from its position...and taking

Caeden's arm with it. He slumped sideways, blood pumping from his body at an alarming rate. "*Caeden!*"

Then Mac was there, pulling him from the seat and getting him to the bench seats. That was all Jenny saw before she was forced back into shooting. These bastards just kept on coming, and if she missed a beat, she'd be worse off than Caeden. They all would.

She was vaguely aware of someone shouting "Tourniquet," and the other gun firing, which meant someone had taken Caeden's place, but there was no room for thought beyond keeping those monsters off her side of the hover.

She pulled the trigger again and again and again, until her hands starting cramping and then went almost completely numb, until the world narrowed down to tooth and claw and scale.

And then they were gone.

Muscles shaking, she tried to get control as they flew into a clearing that was double the size of the one where they'd left *Psyche*. All she wanted was to give in to the sudden exhaustion coating her body and rest for a second, but a whine cut through the night.

Laser fire.

"Everybody *down*." She took the laser Mac handed up to her, and went to her knees so the hover would protect the most of her body. "Hadriel, bring her around the side of the ship. Slowly."

"Is that—"

"*The Harpy Queen*. Yes. Now, go."

He obeyed, winging the hover out close to the tree line and around the edge of the massive ship. There were two other hovers there, one on its side and the other sporting a really pissed-off-looking male Abura-Sumashi. He roared at the only standing robed man—who looked about ready to pee his pants. Jenny didn't blame him. At well over two meters tall and built like a tank, the male's size alone would give a smart man pause. Add in the tusks and nasty temperament, and that was one son of a bitch you did not want to mess with.

The member of Sanctify didn't get a chance to regret his mission, though, because Sadie strode up behind him and shot him in the back. "That's the last of them."

Apparently they didn't need Jenny's help after all. She stuffed the laser into the waistband of her pants and stood. "You sure know how to throw a girl a welcome party."

"You're late."

"Yeah, yeah. We had some trouble along the way." She stumbled to where Mac and Shad held an unconscious Caeden. Or at least she thought he was passed out. The alternative was… No, she so wasn't going there. "How is he?"

It was Mac who answered. "We stopped the bleeding, but he needs medical attention as soon as possible."

"Thank you." He'd helped save one of few people she actually cared about in this world. She started to stand and her legs went out. He caught her easily, moving to the far seat.

"You need a doctor, too."

"I'm fine." Or at least she would be as long as he didn't let her go. The warmth of his arms around her felt good, especially since she couldn't stop shivering.

She looked around the hover, noting Gwen helping Shad wrap up Caeden. A quiet chatter above their heads was all she could hear of Luc and Hadriel. Against the odds, they'd made it to *The Harpy Queen*.

So why did she have the feeling that *this* had been the easy part?

CHAPTER TWENTY

As much as Jenny would have liked to sit right there and sleep for a few days, they weren't out of danger yet—not by a long shot—so she squeezed Mac's hand and stood. "We need to move, people. We've got to space before they send someone else to shoot us out of the sky."

Sadie watched as they approached, as unruffled as ever, her cool black eyes taking in their ragtag crew. A small smile twitched at the corners of her lips, and Jenny wondered if the Abura-Sumashi's face would shatter from the unfamiliar expression. Before she could find out, Sadie pressed the button to open the ship's hatch. The air that rushed out smelled faintly of mint, cooling her skin even as it sent a zing through her system. What the hells?

She sent a questioning look at Sadie, who shrugged. "It mimics the atmosphere on Abura-Sumash."

She filed that information away. There wasn't much known about the Abura-Sumashi species as a whole, and she was pretty sure this fell into that unknown category. "One of my people needs medical assistance."

"Then you're lucky you're on *my* ship instead of that little rust bucket you're so attached to." Sadie led the way into the loading area of the main ship. "Efim, take him to the med bay and see what you can do about that arm."

The male Abura-Sumashi shouldered past Hadriel and glared down at Shad, who was carrying Caeden. For half a second, Jenny thought she might have to step in and be the voice of reason, but then Shad handed his brother over. The giant male took him with more care than she would have expected, but she still met and held his gaze as he walked past, Hadriel and Shad trailing behind him. She turned to Sadie. "That man's like a brother to me."

She rolled her eyes. "If I wanted him—or any of you—dead, all I had to do was leave without offering my help."

It was a valid point, but she still hated the feeling of relying on a dubious ally for help. "Let's go."

Luc and Gwen came next, their arms wrapped around each other. That, more than anything else, told her how rattled they were. Luc nodded at the doorway. "We need to speak, as quickly as is prudent."

"We will."

Mac came last. He ran his hand over her arm as he passed, and that little touch gave her the strength to straighten and start thinking about their exit strategy. He, at least, believed in her. He trusted her to get them out of this alive without stepping in and demanding to know how the hells she was going to do it.

Aside from the oddly flavored air still giving her an energy high, *The Harpy Queen* was the same as every other warship out there. Oh, of course it was freakishly clean and outfitted with cutting edge-gadgetry—even the palm locks on the lifts. There were a couple lights on them she didn't recognize, which made her curious—for the amount of time Jenny'd spent locking up her brother and Ophelia, she was more than a little familiar with them.

Speaking of Boone and his darling woman...

She needed to get a hold of them when she had a second. It was amazing the sheer amount of information that could show up and change everything. Like, say, the fact that apparently the High Priest liked to get his kinks met on the same damn planet where they were hiding. She took half a second to wonder what Ophelia's dad would think of all this. As a former lieutenant of Sanctify, Gerard would know if sneaking off to a sex planet was breaking some sort of rule. She'd have to ask him...eventually.

Focus, Jenny.

She shook her head, trying to focus. Sleep would help, but she didn't have the luxury right now. Being a fearless leader was shit. "How are you planning on getting past the three warships just outside Control's perimeter?" Even *Psyche* would be hard-pressed to escape the net Sanctify had closed around them. Sadie could talk all the shit she wanted, but her ship blew *The Harpy Queen* out of the water when it came to speed.

Sadie headed toward a set of stairs. "I'm going to shoot those fuckers out of the sky."

"Why didn't I think of that?" She smacked her forehead. "Oh, yeah, because there are *three* of them—and that's if they keep the *other* three already dirtside grounded. You've got some sweet weapons on this rig, but they aren't that sweet."

There was that tiny smirk again. On the Abura-Sumashi, it might as well have been a belly laugh. "Let me worry about that. You take care of your injured man."

What was she going to do that the people already with him couldn't?

As much as she hated to admit it, she'd be worse than useless in the med bay. "I'm coming with you. You're going to need my help."

"I won't." Sadie paused at the top of the stairs and hit the palm lock to open the door. "But if you want to see how a real captain pilots their ship, you're more than welcome to watch."

And there went the claws. "You'd better be careful. With that kind of talk, I might mistake you for being sweet on me."

"Hardly."

The bridge doubled as a cockpit, the chairs settled in front of more screens than Jenny would know what to do with. There were easily triple the number *Psyche* had—why in the gods' names would they need so many? She checked out the row of seats along the opposite wall. Forget the screens, she decided—there was no way she wanted so many people looking over her shoulder while she flew. It was bad enough with Hadriel from time to time.

She took the seat next to Sadie and watched her power up the ship. Part of it was curiosity, part of it was wanting to know if she could fly it if things went wrong. A few minutes later, they were in the air, Sadie rattling off commands in a language Jenny didn't recognize. The male voices responding must be the rest of the crew, and she had to wonder if they were all Abura-Sumashi. She'd bet money on it.

Sadie was mean enough that the only people who'd want to spend time with her had to be even meaner.

They hit the atmosphere and then straight space. Jenny held her breath, gripping the arms of her chair and hating that it wasn't *her* hands on the controls. She barely had time to shift in her seat and the entire ship shook.

Sadie cursed. "Two on our ass."

Which left one unaccounted for. "I hate to say 'I told you so,' but—"

"Shut up." She pulled a move that left Jenny's head swimming, spinning them up and around until they centered directly behind the warships. "There you are." Sadie barked out two short commands and the cannons boomed, peppering the sides of both warships.

Jenny immediately took in the trajectory pattern and the fact that they were aiming for the propulsion systems. "It won't work. They have reinforced…" What the hells?

A small explosion came from the side of the nearest warship, sending it spiraling toward Sisilean. As she watched, it hit the atmosphere and was immediately attacked by the bots powered by Control. Despite the size of it, they had it reduced to flaming ruins inside of fifteen seconds.

"Guess you really don't come onto Sisilean without an invitation."

"Why are you still talking?" Sadie flipped them into a roll, evading the scattered shots coming from the remaining ship, and returned fire. Seconds later, it joined the first one.

What. The. Fuck?

Sadie leaned back with a contented sigh and caught Jenny staring. "I'm the baddest bitch around. Don't forget it."

"You're something. That's for damn sure." The flying had been spectacular, but those Sanctify pilots had to have been rookies to be taken down so quickly. Every time Jenny had clashed with them, they'd made her work for her escapes. The only time she'd seen one shot out of the sky was as a result of Mac's antimatter gun.

"Don't you have a man to check up on?"

Yeah, she did. She also had some serious shit to think about. She didn't like the worries circling her head right around now, but it wasn't like she could accuse Sadie of…what? Being too badass? If she was being some kind of shady, it couldn't have to do with Sanctify. No matter how badly they wanted Mac, Jenny couldn't see them allowing the sacrifice of ships for no damn reason.

She'd talk to Mac about it. He'd know if it meant something.

In the meantime… "I need access to a comm unit."

Sadie raised her eyebrows. "If you think that's wise."

She knew what *wouldn't* be wise—skipping a check-in with Boone and Ophelia. "It's nonnegotiable."

"In that case, tell the bitch I'm still waiting for replacements for the boots she ruined."

She grinned. "I'll be sure to do that." Ophelia had a unique way of getting under the Abura-Sumashi's skin that even *she* couldn't match. But then, she knew better than to screw with a chick's genuine sand-snakeskin boots.

Jenny bypassed the lift and headed for the stairs, doing her damnedest to convince herself that they hadn't just jumped from a bad situation to a worse one.

CHAPTER TWENTY-ONE

*T*here wasn't much Mac could do to help Caeden, so he stayed out of the way as Hadriel muttered over his brother. The Abura-Sumashi who had brought him in was gone, replaced by a different one. He and Hadriel conferred in low tones, and Mac realized he was *The Harpy Queen*'s medic.

"How's he doing?"

He turned to find Jenny standing just inside the door, her arms wrapped around herself like she was going to shatter. The vulnerability hadn't been apparent when she was taking charge and getting them to safety, but now the cracks were showing. He went to her and slipped an arm around her waist. It wasn't the hug he would have liked to give her, but he wasn't sure if she'd welcome a full embrace or not. "They have the bleeding under control. The only upside to his losing so much blood was that he purged the poison from his body, so they can use med patches now that they have him stabilized."

Her breath shuddered out. "Good."

"Are you okay?"

Her smile barely curved her lips. "Me? I'm just peachy."

But she wasn't. She looked well and truly beaten down, like her light had been dimmed. "There's nothing left to do for Caeden. Why don't we find a cabin and you can rest for a bit?"

She looked at Caeden and he followed her gaze. The man was too pale, lying on a cot that was obviously meant to hold male Abura-Sumashi. It made him look smaller than normal, almost childlike. With a curse, Jenny turned away and stepped out of his hold. "There's no time to rest, but I need privacy to check in with Boone."

Mac followed her. Checking in made sense, but he'd make sure she rested if he had to lock her into a room to do it. Her energy might seem boundless, but even she had to rest at some point.

Beyond that, he didn't think she'd open up about what had put the haunted look in her eyes if she was surrounded by other people. It might be arrogant to think she'd open up to *him*, but there was a connection between them, whether she wanted to admit it or not.

Sadie stood in the hallway, her arms crossed over her chest. "Crew quarters are one floor down. I already sent the other two down there. You have the rooms on the hall to the left of the lift—split them up however you like. We'll hit a warp point in less than twenty-four hours so stay out of my hair until then. And don't screw with my shit." She strode down the corridor, bypassing the lift and disappearing around the corner.

"That chick needs to get laid."

Mac tried to picture what kind of man would be able to take the Abura-Sumashi to bed and shook his head. The man would have to be either courageous to the point of foolhardy or just a damn fool. "Do you want me to tell Hadriel where the rooms are?"

"Don't bother. He and Shad aren't leaving Caeden's side for

the time being."

Which meant there was no more reason for delay. He took her hand, warmth kindling in his chest when she squeezed it. "Then let's report and then we can talk about what's bothering you."

The walls on the third deck were all glass, allowing a decent view of a huge med bay on the right. Next to the med bay was a cafeteria with no less than four InstaChefs. Everything about this ship seemed to be cutting edge. It made him want to take some time to dig around in the engine room and see what kind of firepower it was carrying.

They took the lift down. There were four rooms to the left of the lift, and Mac waited while she poked her head into the first two until she found the twins. "Get some rest. We'll come up with a game plan in a few hours."

Mac took in the room she decided on while she headed for the comm unit. Spartan furnishings, everything bolted down so it wouldn't shift during flight. But the lack of decoration didn't mask the fact that it was outfitted in top-of-the-line materials. The bed was huge, easily taking up the far wall while still leaving room for a small InstaChef and a tiny door that must lead to a personal bathroom.

"The Abura-Sumashi obviously likes her pretties."

"Jenny—"

"Not yet." She bit her lip. "I'm not trying to be a bitch, but I have to keep moving or I'm going to dissolve into a bumbling mess."

"It's okay to be affected by what just happened."

"I know." Her smile was too damn fragile for his peace of mind. "But not yet."

Gods, she was something else. He crossed the distance between them in a single stride and pulled her into his arms. He kissed her, trying to put all the words he didn't know how to say into the movement of his tongue against hers. She was a force of nature, and that was something that he never would have expected to want with such fierceness. But he did.

Mac pulled away just enough to say, "You amaze me."

She leaned her forehead against his. "I've fucked up this mission from the beginning. You're right—that is pretty impressive."

He wasn't going to tell her that he would have made different decisions. There was no point. He'd spent the years since his mother died taking the cautious route. But that didn't mean the blame for this lay solely on her. "There were too many variables in play for anyone to know Sanctify would end up on Sisilean."

"I'm a big girl. I can take responsibility for my actions." She pressed a quick kiss to his lips and took a step back. "And now I need to do that."

"Afterward, we'll talk."

She frowned. "You're not going to let this go, are you?"

There was a time to push and a time to withdraw. This was the former. If that hellish journey through the jungle had taught him anything, it was that there was never a good time for the sort of thing that was growing between him and Jenny. It was a lesson he should have learned when he was thirteen. "No."

"I thought so. Fine. When I'm done getting my ass handed to me by my brother, we'll talk."

• • •

Jenny could feel Mac's presence at her back and she programmed the call in. She'd been so damn scattered after everything that had happened, and he'd just cut through the bullshit and given her what she needed to get her feet under her again. Sure, he'd demanded she sit down and have a conversation, but at least he'd been willing to wait until she took care of her obligations first.

The man presented such a strange balance of accepting her as she was and demanding more from her at the same time.

She liked it.

The snow on the screen cleared to reveal her brother. And—surprise, surprise—Boone didn't look happy. She cut in before he could say anything. "We had some complications."

"Define complications."

"An involved or confused condition or state."

He leaned forward as if he could reach through the screen and throttle her. "Report—and save the snark."

"You take the fun out of everything." When his entire body shook in outrage, she sighed. "We ran into some problems on Sisilean."

"Did you now?" Ophelia dropped into Boone's lap. The way she leaned against him should have made her look relaxed—instead she gave off a scarier vibe than he did. "Feel free to explain how you run into trouble on what should have been the single safest planet in the universe. For Lady's sake, Jenny, you need a password to even get dirtside."

She crossed her arms over her chest. "See, funny thing, that. Apparently the new leader of Sanctify is pretty freaking kinky. Guess where he vacations?"

Ophelia blinked. "I have to admit, I didn't see that coming."

"I know, right? I thought those dudes were all über-conservative, have-sex-under-the-covers-with-the-lights-off types. I was thinking we should ask your pop if this is normal."

"Stop. Stop right there." In the distance, a baby started wailing. Ophelia's eyes went wide. "She's crying again. Why is she crying again? Damn it, Boone, I just fed her, changed her, and rocked her to sleep. She should be out for at least an hour. I just want a Ladydamned sans shower and a motherfucking nap. Is that too much to ask?"

Holy shit, the Diviner was completely off her rocker. For

his part, Boone didn't look the least bit disturbed. "Go. Shower and sleep. I'll take care of Clarice." Apparently they still hadn't realized their error in naming her something so…square.

"Are you sure? I can—"

"Go." He kissed her and gave her a little shove off his lap. "I have it under control."

"What about—" She motioned at Jenny. As if she were this giant problem you couldn't even put into words. The sad thing was, she kind of agreed with them right now. It sure as hells seemed like the universe was conspiring against her every step of the way. Either that or she was criminally unlucky.

"I'll take care of it." Gods, he was almost smiling. Her brother was just as crazy as his woman. After Ophelia left the screen he pinned Jenny with a glare. "Do not move."

Then he was gone as well. The baby stopped shrieking and gave a happy gurgle. Before her ears could adjust to the silence, Boone was back, a bundle of white blankets in his arms. When he looked down, his entire face softened until he was like a completely different man.

It scared the shit out of her. As much of a pain in the ass as he was, her brother needed to be his normal badass self for Hansarda. Especially now, with Sanctify breathing down their neck. If he went soft…

But then he was back and down to business, as if that moment had never happened. "Tell me."

"He made me. Hells, Boone, he *sought me out*. If Sadie hadn't been there—"

"Sadie." The one word held more menace than she cared to ever have directed at her.

Damn. He hadn't been okay before, but now he was livid. Guess she should have remembered the tiff he and the Abura-Sumashi had when Sadie delivered Ophelia to their half brother. It didn't matter to Boone that the Diviner had chosen to go—he still blamed Sadie for helping.

Instead of yelling at her, he just clenched his teeth. "Continue."

She really, really didn't want to. But the whole point of reporting was to report, so she put on her big-girl panties and soldiered on. "She said she was there on a babysitting mission, but once she saw the High Priest, she decided the pay wasn't good enough."

"Correct me if I'm wrong, but aren't you on board *The Harpy Queen* at the moment?"

"About that—yes. We tried to get to *Psyche* but Sanctify was already there. They tried to head Sadie off at her ship, but apparently she doesn't take too kindly to zealot assholes who hate aliens."

He rocked slowly, but she wasn't sure if he was soothing the baby or trying not to yell at her. Hells, it was probably both. "Did you ever stop to consider it's a gigantic trap and now she's going to sell Mac to the highest bidder?"

Gods, why was everyone so sure she was stupid? "Of course it occurred to me. But it wasn't like we had a whole lot of choice. Sanctify was on our ass, and she offered us a way out. If she screws with me, I'll slit her throat."

"You can't fight your way out of everything."

"Maybe not, but I made the best of a bad situation. The only alternatives were trying to fight my way through to *Psyche* or bunkering down and hoping like hell that the High Priest didn't actually know Mac was on planet. Both those sets of odds were shit."

"If you'd gone to a location the inventor chose instead of—"

"I know. What do you want me to say? I fucked up. Now I'm doing my damnedest to un-fuck up."

He sighed. "The situation was less than ideal to begin with. Frankly, none of us could have guessed that Sanctify would have a way dirtside on Sisilean."

"Holy shit, was that actually an apology?" Common sense demanded she shut the hell up and take it, but stress had her strung too tightly. "I think I need a record of that. Mac, take care of it."

Boone's gaze narrowed on her. "The inventor is in your room?"

"Um..." Shit, shit, shit. She *knew* that look. It was the same one he'd worn the first time he caught her sneaking a guy into her room in their place on Valneci when she was sixteen.

Her room had had bars installed on the window the next day.

"Do you think I'm stupid, Jenny?"

Was there a safe answer to that?

Apparently Boone didn't need one, because he was well on his way to getting a rant going. Yep, definitely off his rocker—just like Ophelia. "You slept with him, didn't you?"

She felt Mac go still behind her. Great, this was going to devolve into a pissing contest. There had been times in the past when she wouldn't have hesitated to toss her new fling in Boone's face, but this wasn't one of them. Mac wasn't a pawn— she actually *liked* him.

More than liked.

Besides, she hadn't even slept with him yet. She wasn't going to get yelled at for something she hadn't even done. She very pointedly ignored the fact that, if she'd had her way, they already would have—likely more than once.

The silence snapped her back to the present. Boone stared beyond her and, when she turned around, she found Mac returning the deadly look. "Down, boys."

"Jenny—" They said her name at the same time and glared at each other.

Gods save her from idiot males. Spinning back to her brother—she'd deal with the inventor later—she pointed at him. "Don't even start with me, Mr. I-Boned-the-Diviner-I-Kidnapped.

I'm doing the job you sent me to do, end of story."

"Funny, but the job I sent you to do had nothing to do with jumping into bed with your charge."

It was on the tip of her tongue to protest her innocence, but doing that would just keep him thinking that he had a say one way or another in her love life. She leaned in until she was sure her face took up the entire link screen. "Get off your high horse, Boone. I called in to report — you have the report. We're on board *The Harpy Queen* and safe for now. I'll let you know when we decide our next move."

He opened his mouth, but she beat him to the punch. "Go take care of your woman and your kid. I have this under control." She cut off the call before he could see the lie on her face, and slumped against the wall. "My brother is an ass."

"It's plain he cares about you." Mac shot a glare at the blank screen. "Even if he *is* an ass."

She was so godsdamned tired, but she wasn't done yet. Bracing herself, Jenny straightened. "What did you need to talk about?"

"You."

CHAPTER TWENTY-TWO

*M*ac tried to ignore the fact that Jenny looked like she was about to walk in front of a firing squad. Her chin went up. "Okay. Let's talk."

It was hardly the response he was looking for, so he sank onto the edge of the bed and motioned to the spot next to him. "Why don't you sit down?"

"Because I feel like I'm in trouble and about to get another talking-to." She ignored the bed and paced from one wall to the other and back again. Each time she passed him, within easy touching distance, but he resisted the urge. Right now words were more important than physical comfort.

"If I say you made the best of a bad situation, are you going to snap at me again?"

Her stride hitched. "Maybe."

"Talk to me. You need to get it out, and I'm here." He waited for her to meet his eyes. "It's okay to lean on someone. It doesn't make you weak."

She gave a harsh laugh. "Right. Easy for you to say. You don't lean on anyone, but because you offered, I'm supposed to go all soft and womanly and throw myself into your arms in gratitude?"

Is that what she thought he actually wanted? "I didn't say that."

"Then what *are* you saying?" She stared down at him, naked pain in her eyes. "Why don't you lean on anyone?"

He hadn't started this talk to bare his issues to her…but if that was what she needed to prove that he was as invested in this thing between them as he wanted her to be, then he'd do it. "Because people let you down."

"That's a splendid recommendation for opening up."

Which was why he had such a hard time with it. "The only person I've ever truly depended on was my mother." Life had taught him exactly how fragile people were, and he'd taken the lesson to heart.

When she raised her eyebrows, he shrugged. "Gerard and I have a mutually beneficial arrangement. It's one step off of a business deal, and the only reason he cares about my health and well-being at all is because I'm useful to him. That's not the same thing."

She edged closer and finally took the spot next to him, close enough that their legs pressed together from knee to hip. "He's not exactly the trusting sort. Why was he okay with you on T-II?"

Her question confused him for half a second before he realized there was no way she could know the truth. "The men who killed my mother were Sanctify."

Jenny was silent for a long moment and he could almost see her putting the pieces together. "You share a common enemy."

And a quest for vengeance. Mac would never be the fighter that Gerard was—he didn't want to be. But he had another skill set that was more valuable. "I won't ever be pirating their ships or"—he took her hand and traced the calluses on her palm—"sneaking onto Sanctus for a rescue mission. But the gear I invent means the people who do are more likely to survive."

"It's pretty nifty gear."

He moved down her palm to the smooth skin on her wrist. "After my mother died, there was this hole inside me that felt like it'd swallow me whole if I didn't *do* something to make up for the loss. I'd already tried my hand at inventing small things at that point—a hack on our InstaChef that upped the quality of food was the best—so it seemed only natural to turn that skill set toward keeping the darkness at bay."

"I'm familiar with the concept."

The knowledge in her voice cut him. He used his hold on her wrist to pull her closer so he could wrap his arm around her shoulders. "You loved your father."

She took a deep breath and he thought she might confirm it, but then she went in a completely different direction. "They say he killed my mom, you know."

Mac was able to feel the slight tremor in her body only because of how close she was. He hugged her tighter. "Who said that?"

"Everyone. Though Kristian was the first who said it to my face. You know, before he went off the deep end and Boone spirited me away like the heroic savior he is. Dad made Kristian watch, he said." She shivered. "Or let him watch. It's kind of difficult to tell if he enjoyed it or not, especially considering how things turned out."

Considering her half brother had developed a taste for torture. It struck him that it was only Boone's escape into exile that saved Jenny from sharing the same fate he had. No matter what fraternal feelings Kristian started with when it came to her, he would have turned the knife in her direction eventually.

The thought made Mac doubly glad he was dead.

But he couldn't say that to her, not when her very voice vibrated with pain that had been kept inside too long. So he reached for different words. "I'm sorry."

"Me, too. Who knows if Kristian would have turned out that way if it wasn't for Dad? Sometimes it feels like he was two people—my dad and the king of Hansarda. One taught me the very things that keep me alive, and the other is the reason I was exiled from my home for ten years. It doesn't make any sense. I should have hated him—and I did—but I loved him, too." She turned her face into his chest until he had to strain to make out her words. "I miss him. I feel like a traitor for not being glad he's gone, but I can't change that."

He pressed a kiss to the top of her head. "It's okay that you loved him." The fact that she was telling him this thing that she obviously felt she couldn't say to anyone else hit him in the chest. Who could she talk to about this? Every other person in her life had been hurt by her father.

"It's so easy for Boone to move on. He hated our father. Hells, he had every right to hate the man. And I know I should, too, for what he did to Boone. But…"

"Family is complicated." The O'Keirna family was more complicated than most.

"Truer words were never spoken." She sighed, a tiny sound that made him want to build a fortification that no one could breach and take her there to keep her safe. It was a foolish idea. There was nowhere that was ever completely safe, and even if there was, it would kill a part of Jenny to be grounded permanently. Mac remembered all too well how she'd touched the controls of her ship as if caressing a lover.

For better or worse, Jenny O'Keirna was meant for the stars.

"Does it ever go away? That overwhelming feeling of loss?"

No. He bit back the word, determined not to give it voice. Somehow, though, she knew. She ran her hand over his arm, the motion soothing even if the topic of conversation wasn't. "Would you tell me about her?"

He swallowed against the instinctive response to change the subject. If he couldn't at least try, then he had no business demanding anything from her. The fact that he couldn't see her face made it easier—that, and the feel of her hand over his arm from shoulder to wrist and back again.

So he steeled himself and reached into the past. The first thing he focused on was the scent of blood choking him, of white robes soaked with a red so dark it was almost black, of a helpless scream for mercy, but he shoved that aside and went deeper. "She had the most wonderful laugh. She was so frail and small, but she laughed like someone five times her size." When Jenny stayed silent, he kept going, feeling the words out, memories rising from the deep. "She was strong. Maybe not physically, but our circumstances were less than ideal during those years, and she went without to make sure I was fed."

"She sounds like an amazing woman."

"She was. She deserved better than to die like she did."

Jenny raised her head. "You don't have to talk about it if you don't want to."

Which was the problem—he never talked about it. Gerard had found him, had killed the men who killed Mac's mother, so there was no need for words between them. The man wasn't the type to share, either.

And Mac hadn't let anyone else close since then.

But she'd opened up to him about an obviously painful subject. Strangely enough, it made him want to respond in kind. "She was the kind of women who men paid for the pleasure of her company. One of those men was a Sanctify executioner. He had no problem paying for her to be exclusive while his cell was dirtside, but when she got pregnant..."

"Oh, gods."

"Yeah." The sheer horror of that aspect of the situation was one that had only grown with time. It was one thing to murder and torture, but to do it to the woman carrying his unborn child? That truly took a monster. "He said it would be an insult to Ba'al if he let her and the child live."

"Is that really what they believe?"

It was the same question he'd asked Gerard a few years after they'd met. "No." Which made it worse, somehow. "If she'd been an alien, it would have been forbidden, but Sanctify has no laws against it if both parties are human. What they did, they did for their own reasons." Now that he'd broken the dam of silence, he had to finish it. "They killed her. Though that doesn't really do justice to what she went through. Murdered. Tortured. Butchered. Even those aren't enough. It took her a long time to die while those monsters had their fun with her. All while I was tied down and forced to watch."

"Did they die?"

The cold fury in her voice brought him back to the present. He looked down at her, taking in the icy lines of her expression, and it hit him that if they were alive, she wouldn't hesitate to hunt them down and return the favor. He loved her in that moment more than he had the words to describe. "Yes. Gerard had been tracking them for several months. After he saw what they'd done to her, he wasn't merciful." They'd taken even longer to die than his mother had.

"Good."

Yes, he loved her. Who else in this universe would care enough about what had happened seventeen years ago to go hunting now? No one. But she would have. Mac pulled her into his lap, needing to show her exactly how much he valued both her willingness to bare herself to him and to be the one to give him his vengeance. He couldn't tell her how he felt. Not yet. As far as he could tell, the only thing Jenny actually feared was being trapped, and there was no guaranteeing that she wouldn't see his love as just another cage. Which meant he had to show her that he could both love her and set her free. For him to do that, he needed time.

He just wished he could be sure the universe and their enemies would cooperate in giving it to him.

CHAPTER TWENTY-THREE

*J*enny didn't know what to do with the tangle of emotions their conversation had birthed. She felt vulnerable and furious and hurting, both from what she'd told Mac and what she'd heard come out of his mouth. It was enough to make her wish that the men who'd killed his mother were still alive so she could hunt them down and exorcise the mess inside her.

Instead, she kissed Mac.

He met her stroke for stroke, her need telegraphed back at her and multiplied by a thousand. He maneuvered her so she was straddling him, his hands stroking down her back and cupping her ass. It lined them up in all the right places and she moaned against his mouth.

Of course, that was his cue to back up. She grabbed his hair before he could go too far. "Don't you dare."

"Jenny—"

They'd already done this song and dance before, so she knew where it was going. Though part of her wanted to retreat and lick her wounds after she'd just told him something she'd never allowed herself to talk about before, she couldn't say the words that would make it happen. "I know, okay? I know this isn't just sex."

He stopped trying to slide her off his lap and finally *looked* at her. "You do?"

"This isn't my normal thing so I'm flying blind here, and frankly, that scares the shit out of me. So can you just let it go for the moment and kiss me?"

"For now."

Good enough. She reclaimed his mouth, kissing him for all she was worth. But if she expected him to jump to it, she was sadly disappointed.

Instead, he started undressing her, his mouth following the cloth, kissing along each centimeter of newly exposed skin. He pulled her shirt over her head, touch so achingly gentle that she had to fight not to beg for more. "I have the implant. I can't get pregnant." And that meant there didn't have to be anything between them. Gods, she wanted that so badly, she was shaking.

"Thank you for trusting me."

Trust? Did she trust him?

Yes, damn it. She wasn't sure when it had happened, but at some point she'd slipped over that line that kept her safe. It might have been the moment she met him, though she'd like to blame it on that first kiss. That was the moment she knew her life had taken an unexpected turn, and now she had no way to navigate back to the time before Mac.

She didn't even want to.

Tired of thinking, she reached for him, but he caught her searching hands easily, pinning them with a one-handed grip.

"Slowly." It hurt, but in a curiously good way. She pulled, a thrill going through her when she couldn't get free. Keeping his gaze on her face, he moved up her body and pushed her hands over her head. "No interruptions this time."

"I'll kill anyone who walks through the door before we're done."

His laugh rumbled through his chest. "So vicious."

"I don't like people getting in the way of what I want." She yanked off his shirt and pushed him down onto his back. He reached for her again, but she batted his hands away. "We're both wearing too many clothes." She pulled his pants off, tossed them onto the floor, and then wriggled out of her own. Before Mac could move, she settled between his legs and paused a second to take in the pretty picture he made. Muscle corded under skin that was a beautiful alabaster, his broad chest tapering down to a narrow waist and tree trunks of legs.

She took him in her hand, giving an experimental stroke and watching how even that much contact made his back arch. Jenny licked up his length, damn near gleeful when he let out a string of curses. Taking him in her mouth, she swirled her tongue around his tip. She dug her fingers into his hips, keeping him still as she teased him, using light strokes and never going nearly as deep as she wanted to.

Before she could get to really torturing him, his hand in her hair dragged her up his body. She made a sound of protest, but Mac swallowed it with a kiss. It was as far from the earlier gentle teasing as they could get. Tongues clashed, his teeth raking her bottom lip before soothing it with another kiss. She writhed against him, unable to go anywhere because of the way he held her. This overwhelming mix of pleasure and pain was almost too much to bear, and he hadn't even touched any of her hot spots.

As if sensing her thoughts, he guided her up, using his hold on her hair to arch her backward. His other hand drifted over her chest, tracing down her sternum before raising his hand to cup a breast and rubbing her nipple with her finger and thumb, carefully pinching. She cried out, her hips jerking wildly. But she was too far up his stomach to do any good. She bit her lip, fighting against the urge demanding that she beg him to touch her *there*.

To fuck her until she couldn't remember her name.

That taunting hand ran over her stomach in slow, agonizing circles, the soft touch only amplified by the pain of her position. Then—gods, *finally*—he cupped her, a single finger slipping inside, his thumb rubbing over her clit. With each stroke, he hit both her magic spots, pushing her closer and closer to the edge.

"Mac…"

He didn't so much as pause what he was doing to her. "Yeah?" At least he sounded as crazed as she felt.

She teetered on the edge, fighting not to go over. Why was she fighting it, again? She'd surrendered the second she'd admitted this wasn't just sex. "I need you inside me. Now."

He didn't ask her to say it again, withdrawing his hands and letting go of her hair. Holding her hips, he lifted her up until he pressed against her entrance.

She knew the way this would go—he'd lower her slowly, giving her plenty of time to get accustomed to his size. Screw that. She dug her fingers into his chest, using the leverage to sheath him in a single movement. Perfection.

He gasped, letting loose a string of words she didn't understand. Rolling her hips felt good. Thanks to his magic fingers, she was already so damned close. Too close. She started to withdraw, fully intending on getting some mouth action in there again, but Mac sat up, wrapping an arm around her waist. In this position, their eyes were level. And the heat there… She felt it all the way in her soul, like he was branding her as his forever. The thought should have scared the shit out of her. Instead, she came screaming his name.

Mac rolled them and withdrew, making her whimper. She lifted her head and watched him work his way down her body. He took one nipple into his mouth, rolling his tongue over the bud, and desire coursed over her in a heady surge. She had to close her eyes and let her head fall back when he moved lower, nipping her hip bone and then the inside of her thigh. Pleasure and pain. Pain and pleasure. He wove it together so flawlessly, until she wasn't sure which way was up. Her entire body shook as he licked and sucked at her, yet another orgasm looming closer with each rasp of his tongue.

"I need…"

He drew back just enough to whisper, "Give it up to me—I want it all. I want everything." Then he sucked on her clit, making stars burst behind her eyelids.

"*Mac*." She dug her fingers into his hair, the feeling doing nothing to ground her as she came harder than she ever had in her life. Waver after wave of orgasm, until words burst from her lips that had no meaning, until she was begging him to stop, to keep going, to never stop touching her.

Jenny barely had the time to register that his tongue was gone and then he was on top of her, inside her. She kissed him as he pounded into her, tasting herself on his lips, until all she could taste, could feel, could touch, was Mac.

She gave him everything.

Afterward, Mac traced abstract patterns on her back, even that innocent touch making her overstimulated body shiver. She snuggled closer, wrapping her arms more firmly around him. Gods, she felt criminally good. She slid her hand over his stomach, but stopped just south of his belly button. "Damn. I think I'm too tired to go for round two."

He laughed. "It's been thirty seconds and you're already thinking about round two? Enjoy the afterglow for a few minutes."

She ran her fingers along his chest and up to his shoulder, her thoughts slowly kicking back into action. The exhaustion and guilt that had been plaguing her since they made that run through the jungle wasn't gone, but the pleasure of sex with Mac had dimmed it enough that she could finally *think*. "That new guy—

Oberon? Think we could draw him out and take him down? We can't hide forever, and this threat isn't going to go away unless we do something drastic. If we killed their leader, that would at least give us a bit more time before some new monster takes over. And he was trained to be High Priest, right?"

"Yes, most likely for years."

"Then it's just a matter of giving him something he wants badly enough to chase us down."

"He wants me."

"Mac, no." She sat up and shook her head. "I can't let you do that." Her whole mission had been to keep him safe. No matter how shitty it'd gone, she couldn't just risk his life because it seemed like a good idea at the time.

He looked away. "We can't do anything until after we warp, so we might as well get some rest."

Oh hells no. "You can't just drop a bomb like that and expect me to take a nap."

"It's not your choice to make."

"I'm the one Boone and Ophelia sent to rescue your ass so, yeah, it *is* my choice to make. And I'm not doing it. We'll find another way." And she'd drop him at the first safe house they found.

He must have followed her train of thoughts because he was already shaking his head. "Absolutely not. This is the most logical option."

It might be, but that didn't stop her from wanting to tell him where to shove his logic. To keep those words inside, she climbed off the bed and pulled the sheet around her in a makeshift robe. She needed some space to get her shit in order. "I'll be back. I need to take a walk or something."

"No, wait." Mac moved, but she was too quick, slipping out of his grasp. He caught the sheet, though, and twined it around his fist, drawing her closer, centimeter by centimeter. "We're going to talk about this."

Like hells they were going to talk about it. If she stayed in this room, she was going to either yell at him and ruin the good thing they had going, or he was going to use his dirty sex tricks to get her to agree to use him as bait. Neither option sounded like a good one from where she was standing. She put her full weight into the sheet, but it did nothing. Damn, he was strong. Her treacherous hormones did a little dance, but she ignored them. "Let go."

His eyes darkened, changing from green to brown. "No."

If he got her back into bed, it was all over. She knew her strengths, and resisting him wasn't one of them. It wasn't even top ten. He'd put those sinful hands on her, and she'd end up agreeing to everything.

She spun out of the sheet and sprinted for the door. As it shut behind her, all she heard was his muffled curse. "Damn, damn, damn."

This hadn't gone according to plan. Considering she hadn't had a damn plan to begin with, that shouldn't surprise her. First order of business, though, was getting some damn clothes.

She turned—and nearly ran into an Abura-Sumashi. He stared down at her from a height of well over two meters, green eyes sweeping over her body. Oh yeah, she was buck-ass-naked. Fantastic. Jenny lifted her chin and gave him the same once-over. He was big in the way the males of his species were, bulky through the arms and chest, with legs that were the size of her torso. But what caught and held her attention was his hair. It hung in a glossy wave to his shoulders, and was the brightest red she'd ever seen naturally—the color of fresh blood. "I know chicks who would kill for your hair."

He blinked. The green of his eyes blazed out of the dark skin of his face—the Abura-Sumashi was closer to a true black than humans ever got. Still, even with the broken tusk and the apelike nose, he was awfully pretty.

Also…silent.

"You do speak, right? 'Cause I don't think I can deal with another mute." When he just kept staring, she just kept talking. "I mean, I have two on my ship already, and one who pretends to be mute when the mood fits—which it never fits when I'd like some freaking peace and quiet, you know? Of course you know—"

"What the fuck are you doing?"

Jenny jumped nearly out of her skin and spun around to face Sadie. The woman strode toward them, obviously not happy. "Um…having a nice conversation?"

If looks could kill, she would be a screaming mess of bones and blood on the floor. "You are standing in the hallway of my ship, naked as the day you were born, and chatting up my youngest brother?"

"It doesn't sound very good when you put it like that."

Sadie's hand dropped to the laser holster on her belt. "You have thirty seconds to get into a room and out of my sight, or I'm going to shoot your skinny ass and worry about explaining it to Boone later."

"My skinny ass? Don't you think that's a case of the pot calling the kettle black?"

"Twenty seconds."

Oh shit—she really wasn't joking. Jenny spun around and nearly ran into Sadie's little brother again. Little brother—was that a joke? She veered around him and sprinted for the twins' room, Sadie's voice ringing out behind her. "Ten seconds. Nine, eight, seven, six…"

Jenny shoved through the door and slammed the palm lock, hopping from one foot to the next until the door was safely closed. Then she set the palm lock to red and finally turned to face the twins.

Predictably, it was Luc who spoke first. "I don't suppose

there's a good reason for you to be rushing into our room, nude?"

She grinned. "I don't suppose there is."

"I thought not." Luc sighed. "I'm going to attempt to get some sleep. Try to keep the chaos to a bare minimum until it's time to warp."

"Yes, sir." She started for the bathroom—and the Clothes-horse—Gwennie hot on her heels.

"Are you okay, sweetie?"

Okay? She was so far from okay, it wasn't even funny. Or maybe it was hilarious. She was pretty sure the gods were laughing their asses off right now—the bastards. "I'm just trying to figure out what our next step is." Jenny pulled on a pair of bright-blue leggings and a long pink tunic. "If you have any brilliant ideas about where we could bunker down, I'm listening."

"I *do* have." When she frowned, Gwennie threw up her hands. "Don't be like that—I have ideas."

Yeah, she had ideas that got them into this mess in the first place. Damn it, that wasn't fair. They were in this mess because of *Jenny*. She couldn't blame Gwen for being Gwen. "What's your brilliant idea?"

"Lukrada."

"Lukrada?" She did a mental inventory of what she knew about the planet and didn't come up with a whole lot. It was one giant ocean, both the air and water too toxic to support human life. But there were a ton of resources—stuff with names she couldn't begin to pronounce—mined and harvested there, so a bunch of crazy people built floating cities. It wasn't exactly a tourist destination and, because of the minuscule population, there wasn't a market for smuggling—which was why she'd never been there.

"I have a residence on Xaigh. I rarely visit, but it's kept up. And the majority of that city is beneath the water level, so it's not like Sanctify can attack."

"Or they could just sink the entire freaking thing." Drowning wasn't high on her list of ways to die, thank you very much.

"*Think*, sweetie. There are more escape pods and underwater crafts than even you'd know what to do with. They're prepared for any eventuality—and there's no reason for Sanctify to know we're headed there in the first place."

"I'll think about it." That line of reasoning didn't hold up as well as it used to. Those bastards seemed to be two steps ahead of her from the very beginning. She had to put a stop to that shit now or Mac...

What would she do if he ended up getting himself killed? Oh, he was more than capable of taking care of himself. If she were going to be perfectly honest with herself—which wasn't a habit Jenny made—she'd admit that he didn't need her in the slightest. Sure, she'd helped when he was pinned down, but he was a resourceful dude—he'd probably have found a way out of that mess and holed up somewhere Sanctify would never find him.

But that didn't change the fact that it would feel like *her* fault for failing to protect him. She couldn't live with his death on her head. She just couldn't. Which meant she had to find a way to make sure that didn't happen.

Easier said than done.

CHAPTER TWENTY-FOUR

"Everyone to the hub. We warp in ten."

Jenny bolted awake, nearly shoving Gwen to the floor with the violence of her movement. She hadn't meant to fall asleep, but apparently Mac had been right when he said she needed rest. She wiped sleep from her eyes and shook the twins awake. "We need to go."

By the time she made it up to the cockpit, she was fully functioning and thinking hard. Gwen's suggestion actually had merit. There was absolutely no reason for Sanctify to think they'd go to somewhere like Lukrada. Not to mention the exit routes seemed way better developed than the ones on Sisilean.

The problem was convincing Sadie to take them there.

The Abura-Sumashi in question ignored the lot of them, her gaze pinned on the incoming data regarding the warp point. The only destination available would take them within the vicinity of Keiluna, which served Jenny's purposes for the time being. She'd take up their final destination with Sadie after the jump.

The rest of her crew filed into the room, each looking more

rundown than the next. Then there was only Mac. He stopped in the doorway, eyes lighting directly on her. And gods help her, but her heart sped up when he walked over and took the empty seat next to her. As he strapped in, he spoke softly enough that she had to strain to hear. "You've had your space to think. After this jump, we're talking."

What was there to say? She had enough controlling men in love with self-sacrifice in her life that the thought of adding another—even one she may or may not be falling for—gave her hives. The memory of Boone leaving her behind to protect her while he headed for Hansarda, fully prepared to die, was too fresh for her to put up with the same bullshit from Mac. She gave him innocent eyes. "The sex? Don't worry—I got mine."

He stared at her long enough that she had to fight the urge to squirm. "You can play the outrageous card all you want, but we *will* talk later."

Not until she had a better option to offer him than using Mac as bait. "Fat chance," she muttered, earning another sharp look.

But then the bastard smiled. "If you don't want to talk, then I'm prepared to compromise. I'll expect you naked and back in my bed after the jump."

"Why you—" Her hormones gave a happy little jig, lust stealing her words better than any anger could.

It was Sadie, of all people, who saved her. "Jump in three... two...one."

"That bitch sure loves to count." Cold slapped her in the face as they dove into the warp point, the ship barely shuddering. She leaned back and inhaled deeply, relishing the ice shards working their way down her throat. The only way it could be more perfect would be if she were flying this beast of ship.

It ended all too soon, the temperature in the room abruptly returning to normal. With a sigh, she unstrapped and stood, stretching out the kinks in her neck. As everyone filed from the hub, she caught Mac's gaze and winked. Instead of seeming reassured, he gave Gwen and Luc a push through the door and came back for her.

Before Jenny had a chance to say anything, he opened his perfectly shaped mouth. "What are you planning?"

"Who? Me?"

"I thought you were just avoiding talking to me, but it's more than that, isn't it?" He crossed his arms over his chest.

"Don't know what you mean." She spun on her heel and headed for Sadie. The Abura-Sumashi seemed completely focused on the controls, but she didn't so much as flinch when Jenny leaned a hip against her chair. "We have to talk."

"I'm busy. Fuck off."

She pulled on a strand of the too-white hair that had escaped Sadie's ponytail and raised her voice. "I don't think you heard me. We have to talk."

She turned slowly, as if giving Jenny time to reconsider. Yeah, like that was going to happen. Instead, her grin widened.

Those black eyes held nothing good for her. "Back off. Now."

"Don't think I will. See, you'll just go back to ignoring me and we can't have that, now can we." She gave the hair another tug, this one so hard it jerked the Abura-Sumashi woman's head sideways. A little voice whispered that this was a surefire way to start a fight.

Good. She needed one.

"Enough."

"Here's the deal, Sadie. We're going to Lukrada — and you're going to take us there." She kept her smile in place, torn between wanting the woman to agree to take them where they wanted to go and the need to get rid of some of the twisting mess inside her. Sex had been a great outlet, but she couldn't let that cloud her judgment now, so it was off the table for the time being.

A knock-down, drag-out fight, on the other hand, wasn't.

"Not fucking likely. I have a different destination in place."

"I don't think so." She gave the hair a harder yank. Sadie lunged, but Jenny was ready for her. She danced back, yanking the other woman out of her chair.

Mac stepped between them. "Have you two lost your godsforsaken minds?"

Sadie sneered. "I don't know how Boone puts up with you and the rest of this trash. He's a fucking saint as far as I'm concerned."

"Didn't your parents ever teach you not to call people names?"

"I'm not playing with you. As long as you're alive when I drop you to Boone, anything else can be healed."

Jenny bounced on her toes. "Here's the deal. I'm not going to Boone—or anywhere else you have in mind to take us. You're going to drop me and my people on Lukrada. Unharmed."

Her people. Gods, she really was turning into Boone 2.0.

They circled each other. She glanced at Mac and was relieved to see him move back to stand by the door. It struck her again that, for all his apparent need to put himself in danger, he was willing to let her fight her own battles. There was something to be said for that. A big something.

She'd never seen Sadie fight, but she'd heard stories from Boone. The woman could take a lot of damage and keep coming. That was fine—Jenny could deal a lot of damage.

She eyed the knife the other woman had pulled from a sheath in her boot. "How about this, dollface? Let's fight this out like well-adjusted individuals. Winner takes all."

"You have nothing I want." Sadie bared too-sharp teeth. "If you weren't Boone's godsdamned sister, I'd kill you and be done with it."

Jenny bounced again. A quick turn of her bracelets and gauntlets encased her hands. "Would you? I don't think so. Besides the fact that we're worth more to you alive than dead, I think you're a kind of sweet on me. It's okay, it's just part of my natural charm."

"Stop. Fucking. Talking."

The only warning she got was Sadie changing her grip on the knife. Then the Abura-Sumashi flew at her. Jenny blocked the first strike and jabbed her in the stomach. The bitch didn't have the grace to keel over—Sadie hit her right back. Gods, the woman packed a punch. She danced away, trying to move past the shrieking of her ribs.

The Abura-Sumashi was stronger, and too damn fast for this to be a fair fight. That said, Jenny didn't make a habit of fighting fair. So she kept just out of reach, in hopes that she could tire this bitch out while she figured out what to do. She ducked a wide punch and laughed. "You must be slowing down in your old age."

"Stop dancing around and fight me, damn it." Sadie lunged.

It was the opportunity she'd been waiting for. Jenny caught the hand holding the knife and struck, hitting the outside of Sadie's elbow with everything she had. A crack sounded through the room as the woman's bone broke. The Abura-Sumashi cursed when her knife fell from nerveless fingers.

She followed her retreat, hammering Sadie with blows, aiming for the broken elbow. She might not feel pain like a human, but she *did* feel it. Just when she thought she might have a chance to finish this, Sadie struck out with a high kick that took her in the shoulder. The impact spun her around and into the wall, her head smacking it hard enough that some pretty stars danced through her line of sight. It would have been really nice to lie down right about now, but she still had a fight to win.

She turned around just in time for Sadie to hit her in the side. It figured the woman was ambidextrous. Lucky her. Her ribs cracked under the powerhouse blow and she grunted—she might have screamed, but there wasn't enough air. Instead, she swayed, fighting not to pass out. "That's all you got?"

Sadie looked at her as if she'd lost her damn mind. Hells, she felt pretty nuts right about now. She spit out a gob of blood, not sure which blow caused it, and grinned. "Come on, sweet cheeks. You can do better than that."

"Don't you ever stop talking?" Sadie's breath came in short pants. At least she sounded as tired as Jenny felt.

"Never." If this didn't end soon, they'd both collapse from exhaustion before a winner could be declared. Screw that. They needed transport to Lukrada.

Jenny kicked the woman's feet out from beneath her, even though the move hurt enough that she almost passed out. Before Sadie had a chance to recover, she scrambled on top of her, using her knees to pin the Abura-Sumashi's arms to her sides.

She wiped sweat and blood from her face. "I win. Now take us to the next warp point."

"Get the fuck off me." She thrashed, wincing when her broken arm pushed against Jenny's knees.

"Not so fast. I want your word that you'll drop us—safe and unharmed—at Lukrada."

"You'll pay for this."

"But not now. And not until this crap with Sanctify and my brother is done." She leaned down, letting her weight rest on the woman's chest, choking off her air supply. "Right?"

"Fine." Sadie didn't gasp when she sat back, but it looked like she wanted to. "You have my word that you'll be delivered safe and sound to Lukrada." She leaned up, nearly toppling Jenny, her black eyes blazing. "But then you'd better run, bitch, because there's nowhere in the universe you'll be safe from me."

"Ah, ah, ah." Jenny laughed and finally looked over at Mac. He was halfway between their position and the door, as if he'd started forward to break up the fight and stopped before going through with it. For all that, his face showed nothing.

"Get the fuck off me. Now."

The hate in Sadie's voice curdled her stomach, but she'd get over it. Either that, or Jenny would have to face her again—this time with one of their deaths as the end result. As she staggered to her feet, waving Mac off, Jenny couldn't say for sure that she'd be able to beat the Abura-Sumashi again. She really was one tough bitch.

Turning her back on the woman was harder than she would have imagined, but it had to be done. If she showed any weakness now, Sadie would go for her throat—her word be damned. Jenny walked out of the room—trying not to hold her side—and stopped when she nearly ran into Mac. She straightened, waiting for him to yell at her or tell her how stupid and reckless it was to fight Sadie.

Instead he held out a hand. "Let's get you cleaned up before we jump again." He led her down the hall and into the lift, the silence settling between them in a curiously comfortable way. It wasn't until he had her in the med bay and stripped down to her underwear that he spoke. "You should have warned me."

"You would have tried to stop me."

He pressed a med patch over her ribs, sealing it with ugly pink med gel. Even though there was anger lurking in those bright green eyes, Mac's hands were gentle on her skin. "Is that what you think?"

"Why wouldn't I think that?" She held still while he wiped the blood off her face and applied a smaller med patch to the cut on her temple. When he moved to her swollen lip, she jerked away. "Leave it. I'm fine." There was too much left unsaid between them—she couldn't handle his tenderness right now.

Instead of moving away like she expected, he took her chin in an unforgiving grip and forced her to meet his gaze. "Let's get something straight. I'm not Lucien and I'm sure as fuck not your brother. I'm not going to shove you in a cage and call it protection—so maybe you should grant me the same courtesy."

She went still. "Not using you as bait isn't the same thing as putting you in a cage."

His expression didn't change. "I'm sure Boone would agree."

This time, when she jerked back, he let her go. She wasn't her brother…but he had a valid point, no matter how much she hated to admit it. And she *really* hated to admit it. "Caring if you get hurt isn't a bad thing." Even as she spoke, a thousand conversations with her brother flashed before her eyes. He'd said variations of the same thing. "Shit, you're right."

Mac stroked his thumb along her bottom lip, stopping just short of the cut. "I'm not saying we should do something halfway. I don't want to leave you any more than you want me to die."

"I—" She leaned back. Even now, with half a dozen places in her body screaming for attention, his touch was so damn distracting. "We won't make any decisions until we pull the whole crew together."

This time it was him who looked away. "In the meantime… I can't promise anything, but there's a slim chance I can give Caeden a working arm again. It might be primitive at first, but once I have some time and the appropriate equipment, I can make it fully functioning, even down to the fingers."

Holy shit. "You…you can really do that? Wait—what am I asking? Of course you can." She threw her arms around his neck and then winced when the move pulled at her injuries.

He kissed her temple and stepped away.

He acted like he hadn't just offered her a gift beyond imagining. Caeden used his hands to communicate. She didn't know a ton about prosthetics, but she'd never seen one come close to the dexterity required for him to use sign language. But Mac said it as an afterthought. Something swelled in her chest, too big for words. "Thank you. Thank you so much."

CHAPTER TWENTY-FIVE

Sadie's voice filtered through the room. "We warp in ten." She didn't sound quite right, a little too breathy.

"Guess she's going to keep her word, after all."

"It seems like it." After the beating they'd given each other, Mac didn't blame Sadie for not wanting a repeat experience.

They made their way to the hub, surrounded by confused-looking crew. Unsurprisingly, Sadie offered no explanation as they strapped in. They hit the warp point hard and fast, the cold wrapping around Mac. He shivered, but he didn't miss the smile on Jenny's face. She lived for this, for the chaos and deep space and the fights. If he truly wanted to be with her, he'd have to accept that. All of it. They were opposites in so many ways, and yet...and yet he was rapidly becoming unable to picture life without her.

"Twenty-four hours until you're on Lukrada and off my ship." Sadie turned her chair and stood, her arm held against her chest. Between that and the blood soaking her clothes from her various wounds, it was a wonder she was even on her feet.

The Abura-Sumashi turned on Jenny. "Get your fucking people out of my sight. Now."

There was no mercy in that expression. He hustled to his feet and herded everyone out the door, leaving Sadie to her family. It was only when they were on the third deck and the triplets were back in their cabin that Lucien spoke. "I'm not entirely happy with you right now."

Jenny lifted her chin, staring him down. "Don't take a high and mighty tone with me, mister. I did what I needed to do. End of story."

He shook his head. "You pushed her into a fight without even trying to talk, didn't you? And you enjoyed it."

"Don't tell me what I enjoyed."

Mac sighed. He had the feeling they could keep this up for hours, and right now, they needed to figure out what they were going to do. "Enough. Both of you. For better or worse, it's done."

Jenny raised an eyebrow. "Then shall we get down to business?"

They both dropped onto the bed, and Lucien joined them, sitting on the other side of her. What a picture. Mac took one of the chairs at the small table and tried not to stare. Next to Jenny—still covered in blood—the twins' eerie perfection was only accentuated. She should have been lost in their shadow, but there was something about her, an energy that snapped and bristled like a flame, easily overshadowing Gwendolyn. Lucien was different—he wasn't the kind of man easily ignored—but even that dimmed next to Jenny.

Or perhaps the fact that he was head over heels in love was giving him rose-tinted glasses.

He shook his head and jumped when he realized everyone in the room was staring at him. "Yes?"

Jenny gave a grin that didn't reach her eyes. "Well, Sir Genius here has a plan to end all plans. Right now we're headed for Lukrada, and operating under the assumption that if someone were to take out the High Priest, it would give us—and Hansarda—some breathing room."

Luc frowned. "That's ambitious."

"The only alternative is to hide out and hope it all blows over while Boone and our people fight Sanctify. Unless you think that's a valid option?"

His dark eyes turned flinty. "You know I don't."

"It's not for me, either. Which is the only reason I'm agreeing to use Mac as bait."

He watched her, knowing how hard it must be for her to let go enough to put this into motion. Mac wasn't too keen on being murdered, either, but he recognized that this might be the only chance they'd have at removing Oberon from the equation. "Even if we don't kill him, bringing him under Hansardian control might be enough to avert the coming confrontation, which means we need an escape route—several would be preferable—as well as a way to subdue him and whatever backup he brings. The most important element in our escape, of course, is a ship."

"I have a ship." Gwendolyn spoke up so casually, it was as if she had it stored away for a rainy day. "It's not much, but it can get us off-planet and back through the warp point."

Which would put them near Keiluna again. It wasn't a planet he would have chosen to hide on indefinitely, but for a stopping point? He could make it work. "I have a system set up that will allow us past Control, and Gerard still has several contacts dirtside who would be willing to assist us."

Jenny's gaze jumped between Gwendolyn and him. "Aren't you two just full of surprises." She tapped two fingers against her lip. "Okay, so what about escape routes? I know we talked about this, Gwennie, but I need you to draw up a map or something. I want us all taking different routes so that our chances of getting away scot-free increase."

"The problem is that only one of the groups will have

Oberon with them." Lucien crossed his arms over his chest. He didn't look happy, but at least he wasn't trying to step in and take control from Jenny.

"Sanctify doesn't have to know which group has him." Her fingers started tapping faster. "I mean, they'll probably be monitoring our links, right?"

Mac could have kissed her for her deviousness. If Sanctify was monitoring their links—and there was every reason to think they'd be doing just that—then it would be child's play to filter through false information. "That's not a terrible idea."

"Yeah, well, I have smarts, too." She made a face. "But we should probably do at least a couple dry runs once we land on Lukrada to make sure it goes smoothly."

Gwen examined her fingernails. "I'll have the maps to you by the time we land."

"Thanks, Gwennie." Jenny was practically bouncing on her toes, which made him smile. It wasn't half bad as plans went, and if they could time things right, they had a pretty damn good chance of success.

"I need the coordinates of your place, Gwennie. We have to end this, once and for all."

Gwendolyn nodded and rattled off a series of coordinates he instantly memorized. Jenny looked around the room. "Anything else?" No one said anything. "Then I'll get this ball rolling and we'll iron out any small details when we get dirtside."

He nodded at Jenny and they turned as one to head to their cabin. She staggered when the door shut behind them, slumping against the wall. When he started to help her, she shook her head. "I'm fine. Just tired. Being strong for the team is pretty freaking overrated, no?"

"You don't have to be strong for me."

She straightened. "I know. And I like that you don't immediately jump to the conclusion that I'm fucking things up beyond repair just because we've had a setback or three." She scrubbed a hand over her face. "I need a shower and a hot meal, but we have to call Oberon first."

He was already moving to the comm unit. "Give me five minutes to bounce the call through a few sets of coordinates and you'll be set."

"Oh, baby. I love it when you talk nerd at me."

. . .

As the link screen went to static, Jenny tapped her foot. She wasn't afraid, not really—there was nothing this dude could do to either her or Mac over a call. Still…this wasn't going to be pleasant. He sat at the table and she could feel his gaze on her back. Unsurprisingly, attempts to get him out of the room had failed miserably.

The screen cleared to reveal Oberon. Even knowing he was all evil incarnate and stuff, she couldn't deny the fact that he was heartbreakingly gorgeous. "Hey there, handsome. Didn't know higher-ups like you answered your own calls."

He smiled, but like last time, the expression never reached his eyes. "Perhaps I have a thing for talking with beautiful women."

"Oh, somehow I doubt that."

"Think so?" He leaned forward, propping his chin on a huge-ass fist. "You ran away while I was distracted with refilling your drink."

Jenny blinked. "Well…yeah. You're kind of like the big bad, eviler than evil, high lord of my enemy and all that. I was a little worried you were going to dismember me and purify what's left with fire."

"Unless you're hiding Diviner somewhere in your family history, that's not an honor you'll ever receive."

That's what he'd do to both Ophelia and Clarice if he got

half a chance. "Honor. Right. Because all those poor innocents should be grateful for the torture." She mentally cursed for letting him get to her. But she couldn't help it. That kind of heartless pain hadn't sat well with her even before the O'Keirna family acquired a Diviner. Pushing her hair out of her face, she lifted her chin. "I have a proposition for you."

His face gave away nothing. "This should be entertaining."

She clenched her jaw. A few minutes on the link, and he was already getting under her skin. This guy was good. "Would you like to meet up...you know, finish what we started on Sisilean?" In her head the words had sounded flirty and yet sinister, but they came out of her mouth flat and lifeless. Crap. She couldn't even do this right.

"By that do you mean sex, or fight to one or the other's probable death? Or are you offering something truly interesting as bait?"

Sex with her wasn't something he'd consider interesting? She didn't know if she should be relieved or insulted. "I do believe I resent that." She twisted her right bracelet, stopping the motion when he glanced at her wrist.

"You would like to kill or trap me. While I have no intention of killing you at the moment, I will not hesitate to do so if you get between me and what I want."

She licked suddenly dry lips. "And what is it that you want?"

"You already know the answer to that question." He leaned back and tapped his temple. "Where's that inventor of yours? I've no doubt he's in the room listening in."

Jenny started to tell him to shut up, but then Mac was at her side and there was no point. She let him take her hand, the contact grounding her. None of the anxiety she was currently feeling in his body next to her showed up in his voice. "I'm here."

"You've presented my men with quite a challenge. I'm impressed, though not surprised. Your mind is the reason I'm interested in you in the first place."

"I'd die before I gave you anything."

Oberon's smile raised the small hairs on the back of Jenny's neck. "I think you'll find I can be persuasive."

Enough. "So will you meet with us, or do you want to continue this cat-and-mouse thing we have going?"

"Of course I'll meet. I wouldn't have it any other way."

She wasn't sure she liked the sound of that, but this was the whole reason she'd called in the first place. It was too late to change her mind now. "Lukrada. I'll bounce you the coordinates."

"How kind of you." His smile widened, the sight of it twisting Jenny's stomach. "I'll be seeing both of you soon." The call cut off, leaving only static on the screen.

Jenny stumbled to the bed and sank onto the mattress, never once releasing her hold on Mac's hand. "That went well."

He laughed hoarsely. "I think we have very different definitions of that word."

Hells, she did, too. She was terrified that she was in over her head and sinking fast. The only reason she didn't march up to the cockpit and demand Sadie change course was that their options truly were that limited. It was make a stand and fight, or hide and be hunted.

She'd never been good at playing the victim, and she wasn't about to start now. If Oberon thought she was going to roll over and play dead for him, he had another think coming.

CHAPTER TWENTY-SIX

"*I* need a shower."

Mac took a deep breath and stood. He didn't like how that conversation with Oberon had gone. Everything about the man seemed to suggest that he knew something they didn't, but damned if Mac could figure out what it was. With enough time and space, he might be able to—but he had neither.

He looked at Jenny. With her ribs injured, she wasn't going to have full range of motion for at least another twelve hours. "I'll help you get undressed."

"There you go again, seducing me with your sweet words."

He laughed and let her lead him into the bathroom. Everything was decorated in rose-colored tile, the result surprisingly feminine considering the unisex colors in the rest of the room. Jenny made a beeline for the sans shower, turning it on, choosing a minty scent, and testing the water. "This bitch has everything. Think we can get away with killing her and stealing the ship?"

"Doubtful." Mac eyed the shirt and decided it was beyond

saving. He fisted the fabric and ripped it down the center.

Her eyes went wide. "I was joking before. Consider me seduced."

"You're injured."

"Like that's enough to stop me." She turned around, drawing his attention to the long lines of her back and the dimple on either side of the bottom of her spine. While he was trying to get control of his body's reaction, she kicked out of her pants.

"You coming?"

He could keep control enough to avoid hurting her. Mac undressed and joined her beneath the spray. He wrapped his arms around her and she arched against him, leaning her head back to rest against his chest, the position allowing him free rein of her body. After dispensing soap into his palm, he carefully washed her until the water ran clear. "How are you feeling?"

She whimpered as he traced circles on her skin. "Desperate."

"Good." He kept going, purposefully ignoring her breasts and the vee between her thighs. It didn't take long before they were both breathing hard and she was making little helpless noises. But she didn't try to push him or take matters into her own hands. Instead she went onto her tiptoes, rubbing her backside against him. He grabbed her hips, unsure if he wanted to hold her still or grind against her. She gave a breathless curse. "Damn it, stop teasing and *touch me*."

"I'm trying not to *hurt* you."

"You won't. Please, Mac."

Using a hand on the back of her neck, he pushed her forward until she was forced to use her uninjured arm to catch herself on the tiled wall. The water trailed down the muscles in her back, practically begging for him to follow the lines with his tongue. He ran a finger over her spine, lightly tracing over her skin until she writhed for him.

"*More,*" she moaned.

"Demanding, aren't you?" He was tempted to draw this out, but they both wanted the same thing. Using his foot to nudge her legs farther apart, he slid his hands up the inside of her thighs. He teased her, thumbs tracing her center until she was quivering. It wouldn't take much now.

He reached around and pushed two fingers into her, circling her clit with his thumb. Jenny made a keening sound, bucking against his hand. His free arm went around her waist, keeping her on her feet when her knees went out. And still he worked her, drawing it out until only the barest of shivers racked her body.

"Gods." She rotated in his arms just enough to capture his mouth, kissing him slowly, thoroughly. Like she owned him, even though he'd been on the dominating end of this encounter.

He loved this woman. *His* woman.

"Are you ready?"

"Ready?" She gave a little shriek when he spun her back around, resuming their previous positions. He didn't allow her the chance to recover, lifting her hips and shoving home.

He reached around and pressed the heel of his hand against her clit, needing to feel her go over the edge while he was inside her.

"Mac." His name was a mantra, a curse, a plea.

He bit the back of her neck, the taste of her skin on his tongue complete bliss that was only compounded when she screamed his name, milking him until he lost all control. He held her close as he pumped into her, following the call of pleasure beyond comprehension.

At least one of the heavens had to be filled with a sensation of completion just like this.

Though his legs shook, he managed to rinse them off one more time before he lifted her and carried her to the bed. She gave a contented murmur as he tucked her in and pulled the comforter up around her shoulders. "How am I supposed to walk away from you when you make me feel this good? How am I supposed to *want* to?"

You're not. But he kept the words back, because it was a conclusion she'd have to find herself. If he tried to push her, she'd instinctively dig in her heels, regardless of what she really wanted. He stroked her hair. "Try to sleep. I'm going to start working on the prosthetic." He kept up the featherlight touch until her breathing evened out and she relaxed into sleep. This, too, was an act of trust that was a gift.

As much as he wanted to crawl into bed with her, the arm needed his attention more. He dug through his bags, coming up with the bare necessities to get a prototype together. It wouldn't be pretty, but it would do until he had access to the tech he needed.

He settled at the table and got to work, starting with the bare skeleton, so to speak, and moving outward. As he painstakingly put each piece together and connected the wiring, he mentally compared it to an uninjured human arm — bones, veins, tendons, muscles. If done correctly, it would hook into the wearer's nervous system and receive messages from the brain the same way flesh would. Once he was finished, this arm would be significantly stronger than a natural one. It was a dangerous thing to give a man.

Unbidden, a memory of Caeden appeared in his mind, as the man blushed and his hands stuttered whenever he was near Gwendolyn. How much worse would it be for him in the future if he couldn't communicate? No, it was worth the risk.

Time ticked by, each hour bringing them closer to Lukrada and him closer to finishing the prosthetic. Mac saved the fingers for last. He was so close — best go slowly and ignore the impulse to rush through to the end. A dry chuckle escaped as he considered what Jenny's response would be — something snarky and sexual, no doubt. With another laugh, he rolled his shoulders one last time and got to work.

Time passed, but whether it was hours or minutes, he couldn't begin to guess. At some point Jenny woke up, but she took one look at him, gave a real smile, and left the room. He fastened the thumb to the hand, moving achingly slowly—if he botched the wiring, nothing would work correctly.

There. Done.

He sat back and wiped sweat from his eyes, his entire body groaning in protest. At some point when he was working on the ring finger, a headache had started between his eyes, and now it blossomed into full-blown agony. Not unexpected, but unwelcome. Still...

He picked up the prosthetic and ran his hands over the casing. Everything seemed to be in working order, but the only way to tell for sure was to try it on Caeden. A part of him wanted to continue to tinker, to make sure everything was perfect. He stifled that little voice demanding one more test. It was as close to perfect as it was going to get—if the thing required upgrades and tweaking, he could always do it later. Right now there was a man who needed an arm.

The triplets were in the middle cabin. They hadn't spent much time with the rest of the crew since the attack. Mac recognized it for what it was. They were closing ranks around their wounded. It seemed odd Jenny wasn't included, but then she seemed to have a knack for being in all groups and yet a part of none of them. Just another piece of the puzzle—a puzzle he was beginning to suspect he would never solve.

Just another thing he loved about her.

Caeden sat next to Hadriel on the bunk, appearing to listen as his brother's hands flew through a complicated series of sentences. Mac only caught the sign for girl and window—just enough to poke his curiosity—but he chose to ignore it. "I have something for you."

All three men perked up as if they were hounds catching scent of prey. Hadriel leaned forward. "What do you have there, inventor?"

"It's a prosthetic." He held it up for inspection. "I think I can give your brother back his speech."

Caeden went still, his face falling into a mask. It wasn't as perfect as the one Jenny wore occasionally—a little bit of fear sneaked through his dark eyes—but Mac recognized it for what it was. An attempt to shore himself up for disappointment. It was the same thing he'd do in Caeden's position, so he didn't begrudge the man his lack of faith.

"It will hurt—the sensors will automatically seek out your nerves in order to gain access to your brain's command." It was a simplified explanation, but he doubted they'd appreciate a bunch of scientific terms thrown at them.

Hadriel and Caeden exchanged a glance. The older triplet looked at Mac. "Do it." He got up and moved out of the way.

Mac sat next to Caeden and the man obediently offered his stump. It was mostly healed, just a few nasty scabs remaining. In a few days, it would be healed completely. Thank the gods he finished the arm when he did. It would hurt a hells of a lot more if attached to newly healed skin.

It was going to be agony either way.

"Caeden, when I say this will hurt, I mean it's going to feel like the Sisilean native is ripping off your arm again. Are you sure?" When he nodded, Mac motioned to his brothers. "I need you two to hold him—he has to remain perfectly still while everything is connecting."

When they took up their positions—Shad on Caeden's legs and Hadriel on his left side—Mac flipped up the control panel and keyed in the proper sequence. "I'll teach you this once you've recovered." The wires and sensors on the edge of the prosthetic lit up, waving slightly as they sensed for the body they were about to be attached to. With a deep breath, he pressed them against Caeden's stump. The man went rigid, his face draining of color. "Hold him!"

He put all his weight on the triplet's right shoulder, but even then he was lifted a full three centimeters off the cot before the man's strength went out. Caeden's eyes rolled back in his head and he fell unconscious. A thin trail of blood seeped from the edge of the prosthetic, coating Mac's hands, before the rim sealed to Caeden's skin.

They moved back, waiting for Caeden to wake up. Silence stretched as time passed, no one making an attempt to break it. So much depended on this. It didn't matter that Mac could tweak and temper the arm until it worked—if it didn't perform correctly on this first time, he was a failure. Caeden would have gone through more pain for nothing.

The man in question blinked, his gaze focusing on Mac. He sat up and stared at the arm as its fingers moved. Running his hand over the prosthetic, his eyes widened. In wonder? Concentration? Mac couldn't be sure. Slowly, oh so slowly, Caeden's hands formed words.

Hadriel translated, "There is no way I can ever thank you. I'm forever in your debt." He met Mac's gaze. "We all are. It's not enough to say thank you. Just know if you ever need us, we're there."

He started to make light of it, but the tears shining in all three men's eyes stopped the words in his throat. Instead, he stood. "It's enough to know I've helped you. We can talk later about upgrades and maintenance."

Even a blind man could see they wanted time alone. He backed out of the room. It was only when the door shut between them that he allowed himself to slump against the wall. He hadn't been prepared for the emotional turmoil, for the terrifying gratitude and vulnerability on Caeden's face — on all their faces — not by a long shot. Which was ridiculous. What had he expected would happen?

"Are you well?"

Mac looked up and almost sighed. Lucien. As usual, the

man was perfectly put together, from his fitted black pants to his formal pin-striped shirt. Even his godsdamned hair was styled. It didn't make him any less dangerous, but it still galled.

"I'm fine." He pushed to his feet and winced when his back twinged.

"I see." Lucien slid his hands into his front pockets, slouching elegantly. "You and I will never be friends."

"Doubtful."

"As I thought. But I do believe we can be allies."

"I'm listening."

"You love my dear, sweet Jenny, and she's more than passingly fond of you as well." Lucien met his gaze. The sheer ruthlessness in those sharp brown eyes surprised Mac. It shouldn't have. The man was from Hansarda—their entire culture seemed to be set up to create some of the toughest humans in the universe. "She needs to be protected."

"She can take care of herself." He'd never seen anyone as deadly—not even Ophelia. And the Diviner had scared the shit out of him on more than one occasion.

"You don't think I know that? Of course she can—she's bloody brilliant. But she's also impulsive as all hells."

Mac couldn't argue that. "Your point?"

"She won't allow me to watch her back—she thinks I don't trust her to take care of things." He sighed. "Keep her safe."

It struck him that no one—not even her childhood friend—understood just what a calculating mind she hid beneath her mask of madness. For all her talk, Jenny would never intentionally take part in a plan that would put the people she cared about in danger. If she did, she wouldn't have fought him on using himself as bait. But Luc had been right when he said they'd never be friends, so Mac wasn't about to share this particular revelation with him. "I'll do what I can."

"That's all I ask. That's all anyone can do."

CHAPTER TWENTY-SEVEN

The hairs on the back of Jenny's neck rose when she finally glimpsed Lukrada through one of the small windows in the rec room. There was something wrong with it, though gods knew she couldn't put her finger on what. It might have been the dark water that looked closer to oil than ocean. Or maybe it was the sky itself, a noxious green color. Hells, maybe it was something else altogether.

"Why in gods' names would you own a place on this planet?"

Gwen shrugged as she twined a lock of hair around her finger. "It gives me access to the wholesaler who handles most of the beauty products I own. It's not like I actually spend *time* here."

Anyone who willingly hung out here had lost their damn mind as far as she was concerned. Whatever it was about the atmosphere that made it that horrible color, it also blocked out the view of the stars. She rubbed at her arms, hating the way her skin prickled. She felt blocked in, trapped, and claustrophobic.

As *The Harpy Queen* descended toward the huge glass dome

peeking through the water, it split to allow them entry. The ship settled onto the dock and the dome closed once more, leaving them covered in shadow. Gods, what a depressing place.

"We have to wait for them to raise the entrance pods and filter out the gases. It will be a few minutes, but you should probably get your things." Gwen smiled. "It will be great, sweetie. Just wait until you see my place. You'll love it."

Jenny forced a grin. "I don't doubt it." She wanted to be anywhere but here. Even the jungles of Sisilean were more welcoming than this place—and that was with the freaking man-eating lizards.

Speaking of... She poked her head into the triplets' room. "You guys ready?"

Caeden waved his new hand at her, the metal glinting. Ever since Mac hooked the thing up, it was as if a weight lifted off all their shoulders. Hells, even Shad spared her a grin, and gods knew that dude never smiled anymore. Hadriel signed, *We're packed and ready to go.*

"Good. As soon as we're set up in Gwennie's place, we'll do some dry runs and get a feel for this place." She ducked back into the hallways and headed for her room. As she suspected, there was a mess of mechanical crap covering every available surface except the bed. Strange how the sight had become familiar enough that it calmed her down. "I can't take you anywhere."

Mac spared her an absent smile, and then went back to playing with the link. She crossed the room to look over his shoulder. "What's cooking?"

Those elegant fingers flew over the controls, bringing up screens with more numbers than she'd know what to do with. "I'm attempting to hack into Sanctify's system. They've thrown up some new defenses since I was last inside their firewalls."

Good thinking. The more information they had before Oberon showed up, the better. "Can you figure out where Mr.

Big Bad is and how long we have before he shows up?"

"I can tell you what their reports *say*, but I doubt it's the truth. If I had time to decode—"

"Do what you can. I'm going to start packing. Let me know when you have something." Telling him they had less than an hour to disembark wouldn't do anything—when the man was focused on something, he was *focused*. It was one of the things she loved about him.

She froze, still bent over to pick up a handful of screws. Love. She didn't mean to think the "L" word. He was hot as hells and made her scream in the sack, but that was it. Okay, so he actually saw through her bullshit act, and didn't seem to care if she was a little bit fucked in the head, which was cool since he was pretty messed up, too.

He had changed so much of her worldview since he came into her life. Before the all-encompassing fear she'd felt when he'd suggested himself as bait, she hadn't understood why Boone made so many of the choices he did. It didn't make her like said choices any more than she had before, but she understood.

Mac had helped her do that.

And he'd listened while she ripped open the old wound her father's death had caused. He alone out of everyone she cared about made her feel like it was okay that she missed Dad even though she knew his death was the best for everyone.

Shit.

Jenny never fell in love. Ever. She played around, and then she flew off into the nearest warp point, never to be seen from again. Except, she'd already kind of decided not to leave Mac in the dust at the first available opportunity. She loved having him around, loved poking at him to see the way his mind worked at a problem, loved the way his perspective could cut through all the bullshit she threw up and get to the heart of the issue.

Hells, she just plain loved him.

Forcing herself into motion, she started tossing things into a bag, her mind still whirling. It couldn't work out between them. She was too out there and he was too steady, and they'd be at each other's throats within three months.

But what if they weren't?

She'd never thought to see the day when Boone would settle down with a woman, let alone a nut job like Ophelia, but what they had worked. And she'd never seen her brother happier than when he was bickering with his woman.

Longing hit her like a blow to her chest. She wanted that. A whole hells of a lot. She wanted someone who knew her and accepted all her crazy quirks, who was ready to take on the universe at her side. Her gaze skipped to Mac. Could it really work?

Time would bring forth all truths. That's what Dad would say. Except Dad was kind of a nut job all on his own. Gods, she was surrounded by insane people—she might be the most insane of all. Either way, she didn't particularly like the idea of sitting around waiting for time to tell if this thing with Mac was destined to work or just break her heart. What she needed was a fortune-teller to give her a definitive answer.

What she needed was a Diviner.

Ophelia would help, one way or another, which meant she wouldn't have to wait long for her answer. The Diviner never lied about a reading—Ophelia had told her that they couldn't or they ran the risk of bad fortune and death. As much as she'd like to chalk it up to superstition, Boone trusted the readings implicitly now, and that meant something. So maybe she could go out on a limb and try to trust them, too.

She had almost everything packed up when Mac finally grunted. "The check-in says he's just inside Keiluna's warp point—the secret one only Sanctify knows about—which would give us four days until he reaches us." He glanced up. "In reality,

I'd rather assume he's right on our heels."

"It won't matter. We'll have a brilliant plan that takes all factors into account."

He raised his eyebrows. "Oh we will, will we?"

"Of course." She kissed him. "We have a certified genius on our side. What could go wrong?"

He took her hand and gave it a squeeze as he stood. "I'm afraid you're giving me too much credit."

"Bullshit. You're one of the coolest people I know." She laughed when he swiped at her. "None of that, Sir Genius. We have to get moving—I'm sure Sadie is more than ready to get our asses off her ship."

He hoisted two of the bags, letting her take the smallest one. "Without a doubt."

They met the rest of her people in the hall and made their way down to the hatch. Sure enough, Sadie was waiting with her pretty little brother—the one with the broken tusk that Jenny had accidentally shown her goodies to—and she had a sour expression on her face. "Took you long enough."

Her brother casually smacked her arm. The impact would have sent anyone else sprawling. Sadie didn't even move. Scary. "They be guests."

Jenny pasted a brilliant grin on her face. "Don't you kids be fighting on my account. We'll just get moving and out of your hair."

Sadie turned chilly black eyes on her. "Remember what I said. We meet again and your blood is going to coat the walls."

"Sadie, what 'un I just say? You—"

Jenny laughed, cutting off the male Abura-Sumashi. "I love it when you talk dirty to me."

For once, Sadie didn't rise to the bait. The hatch opened and the triplets and Gwen filed out. Not wanting to press their luck any more than strictly necessary, Jenny towed Luc and Mac out after them. "I'll be seeing you, dollface."

Sadie growled, but whatever she would have said was lost as they reached the ground and the hatch retreated back into the ship. It was just as well. She didn't have the time or energy for another fight, and she wouldn't be able to back down if Sadie instigated one, despite not being fully recovered from the last one yet. Showing no weakness was seriously a pain in the ass.

She followed Gwen, her hand finding Mac's, the touch anchoring her even though she hadn't been aware she needed it. She glanced at him and earned a tight smile. This was the beginning of the end, whichever way it turned out. At least she was with him.

Now she just had to make sure he survived this fight.

Turning her attention to their surroundings, she took in the huge dome. Whoever had created it didn't care much about the mental health of the people who had to be inside it, because they'd left the walls and floor transparent, so it was all too easy to imagine that inky water rushing in to drown them.

Lights were set up around the perimeter, giving just enough illumination to see strange shapes moving in the darkness on the other side of the enclosure. They were huge and shadowed, easily the same size as *The Harpy Queen*. With a shiver, she turned back to the tunnel leading from the room. It was distinctly brighter, the walls a faded off-white that still showed too much of the ocean around them, but at least the floor was covered with a faded blue tile.

She wanted to ask Gwen exactly how thick the walls were, but she was afraid of the answer. Drowning was not on her list of ways to die. No, much better to go out in a great ball of flames, shot down out of space in a firefight, or in the middle of an actual fight, her gauntlets covering her hands…and she was turning into almost as much of a downer as Cole. She kind of missed the fur ball.

The tunnel opened up into a decent-sized round room—three cheers for more transparent walls—that contained several matching couches and a desk, behind which huddled a man. Judging from his pale, wrinkled skin and shock of gray hair, he had to be at least seventy, maybe older. What kind of place had an old dude as its gatekeeper?

Then she noticed the glass enclosures circling the room. Behind each was a bot nearly twice her size and outfitted in all the latest weaponry. Huh. She bet one push of a button and those nasties would shoot into the room and kill anyone who wasn't supposed to be here.

Guess this guy wasn't so helpless after all.

"David, darling, have you missed me?" Gwennie sashayed over to him. She bent down, offering him a good look at her cleavage, and air-kissed both of his cheeks.

"Miss Gwendolyn, it's a pleasure—as always." Even his voice was creaky. Those rheumy eyes turned in her direction. "You've brought guests? And so many."

"I decided it's been much too long since I visited. But this place can be a bit much for me all on my lonesome." There went her lower lip. If Jenny hadn't been watching, she would have missed the way Gwen's back arched and her fingers drifted over the back of David's hand.

The man sighed, obviously no match for her over-the-top charm. "Of course, Miss Gwendolyn. Shall I have the shuttle brought up?"

"Oh David, you're so sweet. Thank you."

"It's nothing. I'm simply doing my job." He pressed a button and Jenny tensed, half expecting an attack. Instead, the door behind the desk slid open to reveal yet another tunnel.

Gwen patted his hand. "And what an excellent job you do. I'll be sure to stop by with some goodies later on…if that's okay?"

He smiled, revealing startlingly white teeth. "You know what

I like, Miss Gwendolyn."

"That I do." After another kiss, she turned and led the way through the tunnel. They followed her, making Jenny feel like she was a kid chasing after her frivolous mother.

This hallway ended abruptly in a vertical shaft. Peering over the edge revealed nothing but a whole lot of air—kilometers of it—disappearing into darkness below. How deep did this city go? The sides of the shaft were perfectly smooth, preventing any aspiring soul from climbing either up or down. "Paranoid much?"

Gwen shrugged. "They take their privacy very seriously in Xaigh. I'm sure you understand."

Jenny couldn't suppress a shiver as a lift shot into view, stopping when it came even with them. The doors slid open and Gwen stepped in, obviously having no fears it would falter and they would plummet to an excruciating death.

Taking deep, even breaths, she walked onto the shuttle, fighting back panic when the doors snapped shut. It was fine. Everything was fine.

They shot down so fast the bottom of her stomach dropped out and she grabbed Mac's arm. Deeper and deeper they went, until she could feel the pressure pushing against her skull. When it was almost too much to bear, the shuttle stopped. This level was as different from the entrance as night from day. The floors were covered in a variety of beige and brown tiles, giving the impression of sand shifting over dunes. Rose and dusky purple bled across the walls, the warmth of the colors blocking out the darkness beyond and allowing Jenny to draw a full breath. If she concentrated, she could almost pretend that they weren't kilometers below the surface. "It's just like home."

"Yes, well…" Gwen waved airily. "There are times I do miss it—though they are few and far between. This way."

CHAPTER TWENTY-EIGHT

Gwen led them through a series of rooms, each with a rounded ceiling and walls—living room, kitchen, another hallway. It was practically a warren in here, which Jenny could appreciate. Even though she hadn't grown up sleeping in puppy piles in family tents like most Hansardians, she still had issues alone in large rooms.

After getting the triplets settled in adjoining rooms, she and Mac were shown to theirs. The same color scheme from the rest of the house carried over here, the bed covered in a patchwork quilt of burnt reds, browns, and beige. It looked so comfortable and inviting, it was everything she could do not to wrap herself up in it and take a nap right then and there.

She turned to the twins. "We need to try a few dry runs so we can a get a feel for the tunnels on your map."

"Jenny…" Gwen sighed when she caught Luc's glare. "Yes, of course. How about you get changed and we'll start dinner? We can do it after then."

"Deal." When they were alone, she turned to find Mac running his hands over the quilt. He looked at home here, surrounded by things that made her think of Hansarda. It was enough to make her wonder if he'd be as comfortable on the brutal sandy planet itself. She had to make sure they lived long enough to find out. "I'm not going to let him take you."

"And I refuse to be taken." He turned to face her. "We don't know how much time we have, but if there's an alchemist of some sort here, I'd like to stock up."

"More nerve gas?"

He smiled. "Among other things. As much as I hate to admit it, Gwendolyn's idea of coming here was a good one. It's even more fortified than Sisilean was."

She tried not to think too hard on how well *that* had turned out. "I'll take any advantage we can." It was on the tip of her tongue to spit out the realization she'd had back on *The Harpy Queen*, but she fought it back. To profess love right now reeked of desperation and a certain belief that she wouldn't have a chance to say it again after this confrontation.

Fuck that. They'd whup Oberon's ass, slip onto Keiluna under Sanctify's nose, and be back in Hansarda inside of a week.

She'd tell Mac then.

"You ready to see the rest of this hellhole?"

He opened the door and waited for her to walk through. "You don't like the underwater city?"

"I don't like anything that could kill me without giving me a fighting chance. One chink in this place, and we all go under. That's not exactly comforting."

"It would take more than one chink."

"And why does everything have to be see-through? As if I'm going to forget that I'm surrounded by water." She stopped walking so fast, he ran into her back. "Shit. I just forgot—I have to make a call."

"Do you want me there?"

The fact he asked instead of just demanding only reinforced

her feelings for him. Gods, she was so lost when it came to Mac. "I'm just checking in with Ophelia. Go ahead and figure out what the twins are cooking that smells so yumtastic."

He brushed a kiss against her lips. "If you need me, call."

"Will do." She could feel a stupid grin pulling at the edges of her lips as she wound her way back through the warren to their room. After palm-locking the door, she flipped on the link. It took a long time to connect…long enough that she was tapping her foot and fighting the urge to pace.

But finally the static cleared to show Ophelia's face. For the first time since she left—gods, how long ago was it now? She couldn't remember—the Diviner looked like her old self. Oh, sure, there were still nasty circles under her eyes from lack of sleep, but she'd had a sans shower recently and didn't look nearly as gaunt as she had before. Jenny whistled. "Looking good, big sis."

Ophelia sighed. "I'm not going to argue with you because we don't have a whole lot of time. You need a reading."

"How did you—"

"Diviner." She pointed at herself. "We kind of know stuff."

Oh. Duh. She forced a laugh. "I'd like a future with a lot of sun, water, and countless men whose whole purpose of existence is to make me happy." Even as she said it, she had to admit that future didn't hold as much appeal to her as it once had. There was only one man she wanted. Mac.

Ophelia had pulled out her cards. "Ready?"

Not even a little bit. "Sure."

The Diviner flipped over card after card, her brows drawing together with each one. She sighed. "Oh, Jenny."

She took a step back, hitting the edge of the bed. That wasn't a good tone. Hells, it was a scary-ass tone when coming from Ophelia. She wasn't going to be a coward—she was going to face this head-on. Jenny straightened, pulled her shoulders back, and lifted her chin. She ground out, "Hit me with it."

"It's a warning." Ophelia met her gaze squarely, those eerie purple eyes almost glowing. "Victory is in your future, the love of a good man, more happiness than you can imagine…but it's not without price." She held up a card. It showed a blond man carrying four swords on his back and a fifth sword—this one bloody—in his hand. What the hells? "And we aren't talking injuries, Jenny. We're talking death."

The room spun lazily. "I'm not liking this reading."

"I know." Ophelia took a deep breath. "However, if you abandon whatever plan you're forming right now—if you come home—you'll avoid all of it."

"Wait—so you're saying I can run home now, but I won't succeed, I won't get my love and other gooey stuff, and I'll be miserable for the rest of my life? But if I stay and go through with this, someone will die? What kind of fucking choice is that?"

"I don't control the readings. Do you think I want to be the harbinger of death and destruction? Ladydamnit, Jenny, but I'm sorry." She glared at the cards. "I wish I could say there was another way."

"Who? Who's going to die?" She'd seen Ophelia do things— know things—she shouldn't be able to. Even if she wasn't a die-hard believer in all things Diviner, she had to admit Ophelia had power.

"I don't know. Hells, I don't know if I'd tell you even if I did." Ophelia held up a hand. "Enough. I'm not going to ask where you are or what you're doing. But you have a decision to make."

It was always a decision, always her fault. Gods, sometimes she wished she'd been born the daughter of a trader or something. That role carried a whole lot less responsibility, and also had a much lower chance of people getting killed because of her. She swallowed hard. "I can't let someone die just so I can be happy."

Ophelia frowned, her gaze going distant. Jenny waited, not really sure what to do with a zoning-out Diviner. When the woman's attention snapped back to her, the expression on her face was terrible to see. "Hold on." She grabbed the deck and flipped it over, looking at the card underneath. "*Lady save us.*"

"What? What's going on?" Calling home was a mistake—a really crappy mistake. How was she supposed to sacrifice one of her people just so she could get her happily ever after? That was selfish on a psychopathic level. She couldn't make that choice.

"I…" Ophelia shook her head. "It's not just you."

"What the fuck are you talking about?"

"It's all of us. If you don't do this, it will mean Hansarda will lose to Sanctify."

The bottom of her stomach dropped out. "Are you seriously trying to tell me that the fate of the universe rests in my hands?"

The Diviner gave a wan smile. "Not the universe. Just our family."

"Oh great, *now* you admit you're really my big sister. Figures." Jenny gave in to the urge to pace, shoving her hair back. "This isn't fair. You can't put this all on me. All I wanted was a hot man to bang my brains out and enough alcohol to party hearty. I never wanted this."

"I know." Ophelia jumped as a door slammed somewhere in the distance. "Boone's coming. You have to go. I'm sorry I couldn't help more. I love you." The call cut off.

She swore and kicked the bed, then swore some more when her foot screamed in protest. She kept swearing when the palm lock flashed red, then green, and the door opened to reveal Mac. Of course a palm lock wouldn't keep him out.

He walked across the room and held out his arms. She didn't stop to think—she threw herself into them. He held her, whispering meaningless words as he rubbed her back. Her own words came without her meaning for them to, spilling out in a mess she was pretty sure sounded hysterical. But she kept going, needing him to understand what Ophelia's reading said. Needing someone else to know the decision that was suddenly weighing so heavily on her. She stumbled to a stop. "But she's wrong. She has to be wrong. I can't have the fate of Hansarda hanging on my decisions. It isn't fair." The plea of a child—Dad would have smacked her silly for even giving it voice.

He pressed a kiss to her temple. "I don't have answers for you. I wish I did."

"I thought you had all the answers." Her laugh was watery, and the first tear slid down her cheek. No. She wasn't going to cry. Absolutely not. She took a deep breath, and then another. "Why do all the decisions I make feel like they aren't really choices to begin with?"

"Because you're you, and you have the same vein of honor running through you that makes your brother such a formidable leader."

"Oh, just that." She straightened, and he let her. "I guess we better figure out our exit strategy, then, so we can save the day."

"I guess we'd better." He hesitated. "Jenny—"

And suddenly, she knew exactly what he was going to say. She shook her head. "Not yet."

Mac's eyebrows rose. "Not yet."

"No declarations until we're safe and sound. There's a rule that says that somewhere." She took another step back, because the urge to crawl into his lap and wait for this whole thing to blow over was so tempting, she could actually taste it. But it wasn't about her anymore—it never had been. It was about her crew, and Hansarda, and her brother, and making sure Ophelia and her questionably named niece didn't end up purified. She could be strong for them. She had to be. "But…I feel the same way."

His eyes flared green, and for a second, she thought he might ignore her warning and just tell her that he loved her. But then he nodded. "We'll talk about it when we're safe."

When. Not if.

"Okay." She braced herself. "Now, let's go round up the boys and do some dry runs."

CHAPTER TWENTY-NINE

Two hours later, Mac was grateful when Jenny called it quits. She spoke into her comm unit. "Luc, I think we're as ready as we can be. Let's get some rest and wait for him to show up."

"We'll rendezvous at Gwen's apartment."

She rolled her eyes. "Yeah, I know." She flicked it off and nodded at Mac. "Any news?"

He glanced at the handheld he'd been monitoring since they broke into two teams and took their respective routes down to the ship Gwendolyn had in the shipyard. "There haven't been any ships coming or going." Even if Oberon were able to mask his ship's signature, he couldn't mask the ship itself.

"Good." Jenny rolled her shoulders and poked Shad. "What did I tell you? This plan might actually work." He signed something and she huffed. "All my plans do *not* end in our probable death!"

The team climbed the maintenance ladder that would take them up to a hatch in the back of Gwendolyn's apartment. Mac didn't like the existence of a back door that anyone could find, but he had to admit that it was useful to their plans. Luc's team of Hadriel and Caeden would take a decoy out the front door, while Jenny's team would take the real High Priest this way. It wasn't foolproof by any means, but it wasn't terrible, either.

Mac pulled himself into the room and carefully closed the door behind him. It would be a hells of a fall if someone made a wrong step. He froze at the look of concentration on Jenny's face. "What's wrong?"

"I don't know…but something is." She drew her laser. "It's too quiet."

He'd spent too much time with her to ignore her instincts. "What do you need from me?"

"Stay behind us. I know you're not helpless, but just let me take the lead, okay?"

He hated the thought of her putting herself in danger, but she was also the most capable for it. "Okay."

"Shad, on my left." With that, she hit the palm lock and slid out the door, her footsteps silent on the tiled floor. Shad followed, his own laser up and ready, leaving Mac to once again take up the rear.

He'd barely made it out the door when cold metal pressed against the nape of his neck. "Put down your weapons. All of you."

He *knew* that voice.

Jenny spun around, and paled. "How—"

"Weapons on the ground, or I'll have to hurt the inventor." Oberon didn't sound the least bit hesitant about it.

Mac could almost see the gears turning in her head as she weighed the possibility of getting to the laser before Oberon shot him. He could have told her it was a lost cause—no one was that quick. Not even Jenny. She dropped the laser on the ground and nodded to Shad. When he followed suit, she crossed her arms over her chest and gave Oberon a saucy grin. "You know, you aren't supposed to be here yet. We had a fantastic welcoming party ready and now you've ruined it."

"I'm sure." Oberon moved sideways, finally coming into view. He was dressed in utilitarian dark colors and Mac counted half a dozen weapons he could readily see. Oberon motioned for them to precede him. "Shall we?"

"Wouldn't dream of holding up the party." She narrowed her eyes. "I have a traitor to deal with, methinks."

She'd hit on the same conclusion Mac was rapidly coming to. With all the alarms he set up, it should have been impossible for Oberon to sneak onto Lukrada—let alone into Gwendolyn's apartment. No, not should have been—it *was* impossible. The only logical deduction was Oberon was let in. And Mac had his suspicions about exactly who had done so.

In the living room they found a squad of Sanctify's men, as well as the rest of their party. Lucien, Hadriel, and Caeden were bound with mag-cuffs and sporting various bruises and injuries. They'd put up a fight. Gwendolyn, however, seemed to have spent considerable time on her appearance, wearing makeup, her hair curled and pulled into an updo. As if he needed further confirmation she was to blame for this, the blonde threw herself into Oberon's arms. "Hello, lover!"

Mac was still trying to process the fact that she was kissing the enemy when Jenny moved. She grabbed the blonde by the hair and whipped her around, dealing a devastating right hook. Gwendolyn went down and Jenny would have followed, but Oberon stepped between them. "Enough."

"Not nearly." She ducked around him and stomped on Gwendolyn's stomach, earning a breathless scream. Then one of the soldiers was there, grabbing her around the waist and towing her back.

"I said enough, damn it." Oberon went to a knee next to the

blonde, still keeping the laser trained on them.

But Jenny apparently wasn't listening. "You should have never crossed me, you stupid bitch. What do you think he's going to do to you now? He's going to fucking kill you. And if he doesn't, I sure as fuck will."

Oberon surged to his feet. "Keep speaking and, I swear to Ba'al, I will kill you myself."

No. Mac moved in front of her, slapping a hand over her mouth. "Listen to him."

"At least someone in this room isn't a damn fool." He nodded at the soldier. "Cuff them."

"Whmph thrf fmph." She struggled against his hold.

Gods, she was going to get herself killed. "Hush. Please." Mac tried to convey the need to remain calm and come up with a plan, but she was too far-gone. She only had eyes for Gwendolyn. He glanced at the triplets, but they were no help without their hands to speak—not that she would listen.

It was Lucien who spoke. "*Jennifer Lynn O'Keirna.*" When she jerked around to look at him, he said, "Stop acting like a spoiled child and do as this man says. Unless you want every single one of us dead?"

The fight didn't exactly go out of her body, but she went still. Cautiously, Mac took his hand off her mouth. "Luc, I love you, but you use my full name again and I'm going to kick your ass."

Oberon lifted Gwendolyn. "If she keeps talking, gag her." He waited while one of his men slapped mag-cuffs on Jenny and Mac, and then passed the unconscious woman to another of the men.

He led the way out of the apartment, taking a route different from the way they'd come in. They wound through a series of tunnels until even Mac's superior sense of direction was turned around. A lift took them deeper beneath the surface, so deep that his ears popped from the increase in pressure. The door opened to reveal yet another tunnel, this one ending in a shipyard—not the same one that housed Gwendolyn's ship—its huge dome reaching all the way to the surface.

Their destination was plain—the white warship crouched in the middle of the nearly empty yard. Jenny gave a harsh laugh. "You know, you might consider a paint job—white is so last season's color."

Gods, Mac wanted to kiss her and yell at her, all at the same time.

Oberon raised an eyebrow. "This is your last warning."

Her mouth closed so fast, Mac actually heard her teeth snap together.

They boarded the ship and were led to the third deck. Oberon nodded to the man carrying the blonde. "Put Gwendolyn in my cabin." He turned to Mac. "We'll be speaking once we reach Sanctus." And then he was gone, disappearing into the lift.

Their leader gone, the enforcers gave up all effort to be gentle. One shoved Mac so hard, he nearly tumbled over Jenny. Before he could recover, the door was shut and they were alone. A quick glance around the room found it completely devoid of furniture and painted—unsurprisingly—a gleaming white. She rolled her shoulders and started pacing while the rest of them sank to the floor against the wall across from the door. "We need a plan."

"I'm not sure if you noticed, but we have a distinct disadvantage at the moment. We have no weapons, and we're locked in and bound." Lucien raised his still-cuffed wrists. "Although if you have a way out of this, please enlighten me."

For half a second, Mac was sure she would go for his throat, but then she took a visible breath and shook her head. "I don't have shit, but I'll be damned before I bend over and spread my cheeks for Sanctify. I'd rather go down fighting, thank you very much."

Lucien sighed. "I'm listening."

"They'll come for us eventually—they have to when we warp." She started pacing again, shoving her hair from her face. "We jump them. Between the six of us, we should be able to overpower at least a few of them. Grab their lasers and do as much damage as we can before they take us out." She flipped her hair over her shoulder. "Hells, maybe the gods will smile on us and we'll kill everyone, take the ship, and show up on Hansarda as heroes just like we planned."

The probability of that happening was astronomically terrible, but Mac wouldn't be the one to voice the truth. Right now the only thing keeping them from ripping into one another was hope—take that away and they had nothing.

• • •

Jenny kept pacing for hours, until her aching body groaned in protest, until everyone else fell asleep, but she couldn't stop. Even as exhaustion added weights to her body, slowing her down, she kept moving, her thoughts tumbling over each other much the same way her feet were. Each step dragged as if she were fighting her way through waist-deep water.

This was her fault. Well, not completely—godsdamn Gwen to the lowest level of the seven hells—but she should have known something was wrong the second Oberon showed up at the party back on Sisilean. Because really, what were the chances of that happening? Coincidences might happen to normal people, but they sure as hells didn't happen to her. But it was *Gwennie* she was talking about. The woman didn't have a political thought in her head. How was Jenny supposed to know she was working for the freaking Master of Evil?

That was it, though. She suspected Gwen wasn't seeing the big picture right now. She probably fancied herself in lust or something, and even Jenny could see the appeal Oberon would have in general—let alone for a shallow creature like Gwen.

It didn't matter why she'd betrayed them, though—only that she had. For that she'd have to pay. But Jenny could plot revenge later. Right now she needed to get her people to safety, which was a serious problem since she couldn't begin to guess how they'd get out of this mess. None of the others believed they could. She'd seen it in their eyes. It didn't matter. She'd make it work even if she had to cozy up to Oberon. Her knees buckled and she slumped against the wall near the door. Damn. This was bad. Really bad.

The hours passed while she racked her brain for something that would give them a leg up. There was precious little. Oberon obviously didn't want Mac dead, but that didn't mean a damn thing for the rest of them—especially if he was taking them to Sanctus. Her crew was as good as dead, and she might as well be, too.

No, she wouldn't be that lucky. The High Priest was too smart to throw away an asset, and the only sister to the king of Hansada was a valuable hostage. That wouldn't save her from being hurt, but it would save her from death. Though she might wish for it before they were done with her.

She wasn't giving up hope. There *had* to be a way out of this.

The door opened, startling her awake. When had she fallen asleep? Before she had the answer to that question, white-robed men piled into the room, subduing them before they even had a chance to fight.

Way to go, Jenny. Just take a nap and lose the element of surprise. She glared at the man who hauled her to her feet, but she had no intention of being gagged, so she managed to keep her mouth shut.

The lift took them up to a cockpit set up similar to *The Harpy Queen's*. She got a good look at it when the guard shoved her into a seat and strapped her in. His hands were dispassionate on her body, and she spared a thought to thank whatever god was listening that she hadn't ended up with a lecher like the freak on T-II.

She glanced at Mac, but he only had eyes for the monitors over the controls. Good thinking. She turned her attention to it, taking in as much information as she could. It wasn't the same as *Psyche*, but she thought she could fly it in a pinch.

They just had to get free so she could find out one way or another.

Oberon barely looked up as he guided them into the jump with the ease of long practice. Apparently training to be High Priest came with the ability to fly his own damn ship. Good to know.

They hit straight space all too soon, and then they were jumping again. This time, when they left the warp point, she recognized where they were. Way too close to Sanctus. A few hours and any chance of them escaping would go up like so much smoke.

She held perfectly still as the guard came back to unhook her. With her arms cuffed behind her, she wasn't exactly in the greatest of positions to kick some ass, but desperate times called for desperate measures. She looked over and met each of her man's eyes in turn, silently telegraphing one word—*now*.

They moved as one, but she didn't stop to watch, instead focusing on taking her guard out. Jenny kicked him in the junk, and when he bent in half with a wheeze, kneed him in the face. She jumped out of her seat, ready to do some more damage, and stopped short when she came face to face with a laser.

A laser attached to Oberon.

"Enough." The command in his voice stopped everyone. Damn it, they hadn't been doing too shabby, either. Three members of Sanctify were on the ground, and another two were bleeding. If they'd had a few more seconds, they might have been able to actually get somewhere.

Apparently Oberon was thinking the same thing. He sighed. "You're growing tedious."

"Sorry?" She was going to try again the first chance she had.

He knew it, too. "Ba'al help you if I find out you're not worth all the trouble you're causing." He laser-whipped her across the face almost casually, sending her spinning to the ground. Her last thought before darkness closed in was that the bastard packed a serious punch.

CHAPTER THIRTY

*J*enny woke to the soft scuff of footsteps. She struggled to sit up—and ignore the way the room spun like it'd had one too many drinks. But her body wasn't working quite right, and she couldn't manage to move, let alone push to her feet.

She barely had time to notice that the room was empty when the door slid open and a figure walked through.

"Jenny?"

She blinked. Of all the scenarios she'd played out, Gwen's sneaking into her cell hadn't even made the list. Maybe she should just give up her life of crime and settle down someplace safe where her bad decisions couldn't hurt her and everyone else under her protection. "What are you doing here?"

Gwen turned, clearly not expecting her to be up against the same wall as the door, and Jenny saw that the entire right side of her face was a swollen mass of black and purple. Good. The bitch deserved it. "I'm here to help."

Unexpected—and suspicious. "Are you joking?" Jenny struggled to her feet. "What's Oberon's game?"

"I didn't know he was going to do this!" Gwen's lower lip quivered and two fat tears rolled down her cheek.

"Shut your trap and knock off with the waterworks—the dramatics doesn't work on me."

The tears kept coming, but she lowered her voice. "I didn't have a choice. You don't know what it's like being with a man like him. He's overwhelming and thoughtful and says the most wonderful things. He's my *patron*. I owe him so much." She looked away. "I didn't know he was going to do this, though. He said he wanted a chance to talk to you before things spiraled out of control. How was I supposed to know he'd take all of you captive?"

It took everything Jenny had to keep from hitting her again. "I don't know, Gwennie, maybe because he's the fucking High Priest of Sanctify? He's evil, which means—*shocker*—he does evil things. Like kidnap and kill people."

"He's not evil."

"Right. Of course. I bet the Big Bad Monster is really just misunderstood, too." She shook her head. "Wake up. He's using you to get to me, which will get him a first-class seat to Hansarda and my family. Gods, Gwen, why don't you ever just stop and *think*?"

"I'm thinking now. Why else would I be here?"

To draw them into a trap. But that wouldn't make sense. Oberon had them exactly where he wanted them. He might be a sadistic fuck, but he wasn't stupid. And letting them wander around his ship—and possibly find a way to actually cause problems—didn't make any sense.

All signs seemed to point to Gwen finally growing a few brain cells and realizing she'd screwed up. It didn't make Jenny any less inclined to punch her in her perfect face, but she could work with this.

Gwen wrapped her arms around herself, still not looking

over. "I know you think I'm stupid, and maybe I am. But I love him." Her breath shuddered out. "I'm sorry, Jenny. So sorry."

Now it made sense. She'd come here looking for forgiveness. She probably expected Jenny to welcome her with open arms and tell her how it was totally okay and she was justified in thinking her evil-ass patron wouldn't act evil and put them all in danger. Not happening. "You fucked up. You know that or you wouldn't be here."

"If—if I help you…will you promise you won't kill him?"

She snapped back her instinctive sarcastic response. As much as she wanted to smack some sense into the blonde, now wasn't the time or place for it. "We were never planning on killing him." At least not before they got him to Hansarda.

"Maybe not before. Promise me you won't now."

Like it or not, Gwen was giving her a chance to turn the tables on Oberon and possibly save them all. "How are you going to help?"

"I can get you out of the mag-cuffs—but only if you promise."

If she played this right, they could take the ship before anyone knew they were escaping. Maybe Ophelia's reading was wrong. Maybe they could do this without anyone she loved dying. She took a deep breath. First things first. "We won't kill your one true love."

"Thank you!"

She sidestepped the hug. "It doesn't mean I forgive you. You screwed up, Gwennie—big time."

"I'm sorry. Really, I am." She reached into the back pocket of her tiny shorts and pulled out a chip. When she pressed it against Jenny's cuffs, they gave a click and unlocked. Then she led Jenny to the next room over and unlocked it, revealing the men. It took all of two minutes to free them all. One thing down, only a half dozen to go.

She took the time to hug Mac. "Are you okay?"

"Yeah. We all are."

Thank the gods for small favors. She rolled her shoulder and twisted her bracelets, encasing her hands and forearms in metal. They had to do this quick and quiet or it'd be a slaughter. "Gwen, if you scream I'll kill you myself."

"I won't scream. Promise." She turned to Luc, but he wouldn't even look at his twin. "Luci, please don't be like this."

For all that she'd been raised on Hansarda the same as Luc and Jenny, she really didn't understand how things worked. Your planet came first. Your people came first. Your *family* came first. You didn't put someone who was good in the sack before those. Except Gwen had done just that. She'd thrown them all down the shitter for a man who was using her to further his speciesist brand of poison.

And that was just plain unforgivable. Jenny grabbed her wrist and yanked her through the door. They had to get moving or they'd miss this opportunity. "Where are the men?"

"How am I supposed to know? I just stay in the cabin." Gwen fluffed her hair.

She gritted her teeth, ready to shake answers out of the woman—the woman who *still* didn't seem to understand how much trouble they were all in—but Mac got there first. He smiled. "Maybe you didn't see them, but you know the layout of the ship. Where do you think they'd be?"

The idiot practically blossomed under his attention. "Oh. They'd probably be on the second deck in the cafeteria or their cabins."

"Very good. And Oberon?"

"The first deck. He likes to keep an eye on everything." She rolled her eyes. "He's kind of a control freak."

"Wonderful, Gwendolyn. Do you know where they keep the weapons?"

"Sure! This way." She turned and trotted down the hall. Jenny wanted to strangle her. They'd almost lost everything—might *still* lose everything—because the woman lost her mind when a gorgeous man came around. If they survived this… She didn't know what she'd do. Gwen couldn't just walk away after what she'd done, but the thought of accusing her of treason didn't sit well with Jenny. She knew what happened to traitors. As pissed as she was at this idiot, she didn't know if she could sentence her to that fate.

Life had been so much easier when it was just in black and white.

She nodded to the triplets, indicating that they should fall back to bring up the rear, and leave her to take point. They hurried to the stairs into the engine room. As Gwen opened the door, she almost ran over a white-robed man. "What are you—"

Jenny bashed him over the head and jumped back before he fell on her. "Hadriel."

Gwen shrieked when Hadriel snapped his neck. "*Oh gods. What are you doing?*"

Her lack of understanding over what had to be done should have made Jenny mad. Instead, she just felt tired. "Cleaning up your mess." She turned a quick circle until she found the crates marked with the proper label. Acquire weapons: check. So far things were going smoothly, which only made her worry that they were going *too* smoothly.

It took both her and Caeden, but they popped the lid, revealing state-of-the-art lasers. They were fancier than the one Mac made her, but they didn't have a stun feature. Good—she didn't need it. All these bastards were going to die.

Jenny took two lasers and waited while the rest of them loaded up. Between being armed and having surprise on their side, they might actually have a shot. Except… "I want you to stay here, Gwen."

"What? No."

Gwen still didn't understand what was about to happen. Even if they didn't kill Oberon, it was going to be a wholesale slaughter. She couldn't afford to risk the woman having third or fourth thoughts and letting a small army of Sanctify enforcers out of their cell. Which meant they had to die. "I don't have time for this. You—"

"Let her come." Luc shoved one laser into his waistband and grabbed another. "Let my darling twin see what her foolishness has brought."

"Fine." The longer they stood down here, the worse their chances got. She looked at Mac, standing there with a laser in his hand, ready to finish this. Damn it, she really, really loved his genius ass. *Later*, she promised herself. She'd tell him later.

She cracked her neck and started for the door. "Let's do this."

They bypassed the third deck and headed straight for the second. There were three men sitting around a table, playing cards. She didn't give them a chance to respond to the sudden appearance of seven people in the hallway. She shot two and Shad took out the other. Motioning for Caeden and Hadriel to cover them, she and Luc quickly searched the remaining rooms, coming up empty. Good.

As much as she didn't like splitting up their party, she couldn't risk someone flanking them. "You three stay here in case we missed someone." When the triplets nodded, she pointed a laser at Gwen. "No screaming, remember?"

"I remember," she whispered, wringing her hands.

As they moved up the stairs to the first deck, Jenny's heartbeat pounded in her ears until it drowned out everything else. This was it. It all ended here. She wanted to tell Mac to go back with the triplets, but he wouldn't listen any more than Gwen had. Inhaling, she blanked her mind and slid through the door. The bridge was set up similar to Sadie's—a whole lot of open space with the pilot's seat and screens opposite the door. And there was Oberon, his back to them, long dark hair gleaming in the low light.

She raised the laser, aiming down it at the man in the white robes next to him, but shout distracted her. A man flew out from the far corner and started shooting. "*Get down.*" Jenny dived, hearing the others do the same. The laser fire went over their heads and a feminine scream echoed through the room.

She knew that voice.

No. "No, no, no, no." She couldn't look, no matter how desperately she wanted to. With Mac beside her and Luc on her other side, she focused on her breathing, waiting for that piece of shit enforcer to poke his little brown head from behind the control panel... There. She squeezed off a shot, the sound of his body hitting the floor music to her ears.

Oberon stood, his hands raised, next to one enforcer still holding a gun. He wasn't even looking at Jenny. No, his focus was on something over her shoulder. She turned, feeling as if her entire body was immersed in taffy, and nearly cried out at the roaring that filled her ears. "*No.*"

Jenny crawled over Mac, ignoring the inventor's muffed warning, her entire being focused on Gwennie. She was sprawled lengthwise, her long golden hair a beacon in the shadows. It was fine. Everything was fine. She'd gotten down in time. She was okay. She had to be.

She reached Gwen and rolled her over, unable to grasp what she was seeing. It was wrong. So wrong. There shouldn't be blood. And what was wrong with Gwennie's neck? She pressed both her hands against the gaping wound, but there was no gushing blood. It was cauterized, she realized.

"Gwennie, sweetie, wake up. You have to wake up." She shook the woman, but it didn't change the blank expression on Gwen's face. "No. You can't be dead. *I won't let you be dead!*" But those empty brown eyes proved her otherwise. There would be no more shenanigans, no more petty fights, no more parties. *Nothing*. And for what? Another meaningless death in a war she wanted no part of.

I didn't even get a chance to forgive her.

She surged to her feet and shot the remaining member of Sanctify, leaving only Oberon. He still had his hands up, an unreadable look in his eyes. She turned, taking in the room. So much death, and for what? So he could purify another planet of any alien presence? It was such a godsdamned waste. She pointed her laser at Gwen. "Was it worth it?"

"That remains to be seen."

Red filtered over her vision. "She loved you!"

"Her death is regrettable."

Regrettable? "I'll show you fucking regrettable." She stalked toward him, changing direction when she caught sight of the laser on the ground next to a dead man. She knew that laser with its blue cartridge. Jenny picked it up and turned to Mac. He was still crouched on the floor, warily watching Luc train his own laser at Oberon. He, at least, seemed uninjured. "Are you okay?"

"Yeah."

"Good." She lifted the laser. "You're sure this won't kill him?"

"Not if it's set to stun."

A quick flick of her thumb and it was. She leveled it at Oberon. "I'm going to enjoy watching you die." Then she shot him in the face.

CHAPTER THIRTY-ONE

*I*t had all happened so fast. One second they were charging into the room, lasers blazing, the next Mac was surrounded by dead bodies. The blood staining white robes pushed memories he wanted nothing to do with to the surface, but there were bigger things to deal with than his issues from the past.

He pushed to his feet and picked his way through the bodies to where Oberon lay prone. A quick check confirmed that he was still alive. "Did you have to shoot him in the face?"

Jenny barely spared him a glance as she flicked through monitor after monitor. "I trusted you that it would stun him."

"I've never tested it on humans before." There hadn't been time.

"If I'd have killed him, it was nothing more than that shithole deserved." She took a shuddering breath. "I'm going to have a pretty little breakdown when all this is over, but we aren't out of danger yet."

Hadriel and Caeden got to work, hauling the bodies to one corner of the room. It was an ugly process, but better they end up in one place than scattered around like dropped toys.

The sole exception was Gwendolyn. Mac forced himself to look at her. She had been a frivolous, foolish creature, but she hadn't deserved to die. Luc knelt next to her, his expression terrifyingly blank.

Shad walked over and signed something. Jenny nodded. "There are two in the weapons room, but they don't know anything's wrong yet. No one else. Take care of it." Then he was gone, heading for the stairs leading down.

"There's some sort of lock on this." Jenny spoke so low, he had to move closer to hear her clearly. "It's set on autopilot for Sanctus. I need control of this ship, Mac."

Otherwise, it would all be for nothing. What was the point of all this if the ship was determined to deliver them to the very place they were fighting so hard to stay away from? He stepped up to her side and brought up the controls. "I'm on it."

"Thanks." She watched the monitors as he went to work, pulling up the system schematics. Normally, it would be a simple command to turn off the autopilot, but obviously Oberon had altered something on a basic level.

Command after command came up with nothing, while each minute brought them closer to Sanctify space. Finally, he found the trigger. Unsurprisingly, it needed a password. "Shit."

"How long will that stun keep him out?"

"It could be anywhere from five minutes to two hours. I haven't done enough tests." He rubbed a hand over his face. "You'll want to use the mag-cuffs on him sooner rather than later."

"I'm on it."

While she hunted a pair down and cuffed his hands behind his back, Mac started a program that would run every possible password combination. It took time, but there wasn't a better way to do it with Oberon passed out.

Shad reappeared, and he nodded when Jenny signed at him. Obviously he had taken care of the men in the weapons room. She motioned the triplets closer. "Look, this is going to get ugly. We're undermanned and outgunned if we get into Sanctus airspace. I need you to learn this ship, and I need you to learn it yesterday."

Hadriel nodded. "Shad says those cannons aren't too different from what's on *The Dutchman*. We can make it work."

"Then do it. I'll do my damnedest to get us out of here, but we're not lucky enough to do it without a fight."

She watched them go. "I'm getting us out of this alive, Mac. No matter what it takes."

He didn't ask her how she was going to do it or point out that the odds were even more against them now than they had been when she picked him up back on T-II. He also didn't touch her or ask if she was okay. She'd just watched a friend of hers get gunned down—traitor or not. She wasn't okay.

So he said the only thing he could. "I know you will."

A chiming sounded, so light and completely at odds with the grotesque picture the cockpit had become, as a call pinged through. Mac recognized the code—he'd been spying on them long enough. "It's a warship. They're hailing us."

"I don't suppose we have control of the ship yet?"

He double-checked his program. It was a little over halfway through the possible combinations. "No."

"Then I guess I'll have to stall." She closed her eyes, and when she opened them, she was wearing the Mad Jenny mask. Only her eyes gave her away, carrying a grief too large to encompass. "Put them through."

He obeyed, keeping an eye on his program so he could signal her as soon as the autopilot had been overridden. The center screen flickered, clearing to show an unassuming man in his middling years. His face showed the wear of a hard life and most of his dark hair had gone to gray, but there was still plenty of steel in his blue eyes. Those eyes went wide as they took Jenny in.

Mac could only imagine what he thought. He'd expected to hail Oberon, returning victorious, and had instead gotten a woman with madness in her eyes surrounded by bodies of his comrades.

He recovered fast, though. "Where is the High Priest?"

"Oh, around." She waved a negligent hand to where he still hadn't stirred. "He's just being a sleepyhead right now. He's not dead."

His mouth thinned. "Surrender."

"I don't think I will." She flipped her laser and caught it. "I have something you want, so I'm pretty sure you're going to do whatever I damn well say."

"That's where you're wrong."

Jenny raised her eyebrows. "Am I?"

Mac checked the program. Not yet. Godsdammit.

"You are." The man didn't look happy about it, but he leaned back in his chair. "The High Priest is one man, and he'd choose death over capture by the likes of you."

They weren't even going to pretend to bargain with her. Mac mentally cursed when a second—and then a third—warship showed up on the radar. And still the ship kept up its original course.

"You know, I don't think he'd agree." She nudged Oberon with her boot. "Why don't we wait until he wakes up and ask him?"

"Ba'al will forgive me."

The monitor beneath his hand pinged, releasing them to control the ship. "Got it," he murmured.

A short nod from her told him she'd heard. "Not to be a teller of tales, but I'm so going to let him know you said that." She smacked the button to end the call and threw herself into the captain's chair. "Hang on, people. This is going to be beyond ugly."

She veered so sharply, Mac fell against the wall. He caught sight of Luc hanging on to his twin's body, but he couldn't do anything about that. The only thing he could do was strap himself into the chair next to Jenny and hope for the best. They were hours beyond the nearest warp point, too far to flee. Maybe if they were in *Psyche*, they could have made it, but the three ships trying to pen them in were sporting similar hardware to the one Jenny was flying with such grim determination.

The force of the cannons shook the ship, but he couldn't tell if they had done any damage. He thought fast—*that* was something he could help with. He flicked through the controls, scanning the other ships. All were at full power, equipped with the latest gear. If Jenny was flying *The Dutchman*, with its antimatter gun, they would stand a chance.

Now? Now he wasn't so sure.

The ship shuddered again, but this time there was no mistaking its source. A quick diagnostics check confirmed his fear. They'd come at the ship from both sides while the third ship drew their attention. "Shields down to fifty percent. Another hit like that—"

"I know!" She cursed and slapped the console. "Hadriel, we have to do this one at a time. It's our only chance."

"Got it. Bring us in close and we'll do what we can."

"Consider it done." She flipped off the intercom. "We're not making it out of this. We're not fast enough, and they're just toying with us while more reinforcements show up." Her expression was bleak. "For all his talk, they don't have to shoot us out of space. They just have to take out our engines and we'll be dead in the water, waiting to be boarded." She pulled a fast turn, evading a spray of cannon fire. "Mac—"

He recognized the terrible knowledge in her eyes, but he

couldn't let her give in to it. "Not yet."

She cursed, diving below a ship and spinning so the triplets could open fire into its underbelly. "What if there's not a later? How am I supposed to sit on the fact that I'm pretty much madly in love with you?"

Her words would have brought him a hells of a lot more joy if it wasn't a confession that she didn't think they'd make it out of this alive. "You've sat on it this long. You can hold on to it a little longer." He reached over and briefly covered her hand with his. "But I love you, too."

Sanctify landed another hit, and his heart leaped into his throat as he watched the numbers decrease. "Thirty percent."

"Redirect power from whatever can stand to lose it. We need those damn shields or they're going to be blowing holes in us."

He went to work, pulling from the med bay, crew cabins, and entertainment rooms on the second deck. It bumped the shields up to fifty percent—high enough to buy a little time, but not much. "We need to call for help."

"Who's going to help us? Even if there were someone near a warp point, by the time they showed up, we'd be dead."

All the same... He put out a message to Gerard. He didn't expect the man to somehow make it out here, but information might be enough to turn the tide. He was about to say as much to Jenny, when new movement on the radar caught his attention. "What the hells?"

"What is it?"

"Another ship."

She yanked them into a barrel roll. "Fuck. Just what we need. Haven't they heard of a little thing called overkill?"

But there was something different about this one. He sent a ping, and the information that came back made him frown. "I don't believe it."

"Tell me."

"It's—"

Jenny cursed again. "*The Harpy Queen.*"

The giant red ship approached and the three Sanctify warships broke off their attack. Before Mac could figure out if they were welcoming or preparing for another attack, Sadie's ship opened fire. Her guns ripped through the first ship's shields like they weren't even there, blowing a hole in the side of the hull and sending it spinning.

"I loosened them up for her," Jenny muttered. Then she sent the warship hurtling back into motion, harrying the remaining two ships, until it seemed they didn't know which threat to face.

To their detriment.

Jenny kept them distracted while Sadie took them out, one after another. She didn't fully destroy them, but they weren't capable of flying by the time she was done with them. The chime sounded again. He swallowed, still trying to make himself believe that it might actually be over. "She's trying to contact us."

"Well, put the bitch on." At his look, she raised her hands. "What? She might have saved our asses, but that doesn't make her any more likable."

The Abura-Sumashi appeared on the screen, her expression stony. Jenny, of course, didn't waste any time. "I thought you said the next time you saw me, you'd paint the walls in my blood."

Sadie sighed. "Are you really poking at me when your life is in my hands? I could shoot you out of space as easily I did those bastards."

"But then you would have made the trip for nothing."

"Not for nothing. Boone owes me a favor now, and I'll be calling it in before too long."

What kind of favor could she possibly want? Boone might still have most of his contacts from when he was a smuggler, but as king of Hansarda, his range of influence was mostly confined to his actual planet. The same didn't necessarily hold true for

Azure Enterprises, but Sadie hadn't said *Ophelia* would owe her a favor. What game was she playing at?

If Jenny shared his concern, she didn't show it. "I'll let him know."

Sadie jerked her chin at the still-unconscious High Priest. "Is he dead?"

"Stunned."

"Pity."

Jenny laughed. "He won't be alive for long. He'll stand trial on Hansarda for his crimes against our people."

"A trial. How novel." Sadie sat back. "I have half a mind to follow you back to make sure you stay out of trouble. You're more of a pain in my ass than the Diviner was."

"Now you're just trying to turn my head with pretty words."

Sadie started to respond, but the chime sounded again. Jenny groaned. "We're too damn popular by half. Sadie, if you have a bug up your ass to follow us, then do it. I couldn't care less. Either way, I'm going home." She cut the call and answered the incoming one.

Mac started when Gerard's face appeared before them. He took the cockpit in with a single glance. "You still need information?"

Jenny glanced at him, silently giving him the lead. "I think we've taken care of the problem."

"Good." His gaze returned to Oberon and stayed there. Mac turned to see the man in question sitting up and shaking his head as if he was dizzy. The mag-cuffs didn't seem to bother him as he looked around the room and then finally at the man on the screen behind Mac.

Something flared in his eyes, some recognition. "You."

"Yes, him." Jenny stroked her laser like she wouldn't mind stunning him again. "Oberon Whatever-the-Hell-Your-Last-Name-Is, meet Gerard Leoni. He's been a thorn in Sanctify's paw for years, to hear tell of it."

Oberon's mouth twisted into something that wasn't quite a smile. "Would you like to tell them, or should I?"

Mac's looked from one man to the other, his mind racing to connect the dots. "What?"

Gerard just looked resigned. "His last name is Leoni. Oberon's my son."

CHAPTER THIRTY-TWO

$\mathcal{M}$ac's mind finally broke through the shock, the pieces falling into place so fast, it made him sick. This was the thing he'd been missing from the beginning, the reason nothing had quite fit before now—the reason everything Sanctify had done contained a taste of a personal vendetta. He'd thought it was because the old High Priest was killed on Hansarda.

He couldn't have been further from the truth.

"*What?*" Jenny spun around so fast, she almost knocked herself out of the chair. "What did you just say?"

"How's your favored child doing, Gerard? I hear that she spawned another Diviner brat."

"She's got nothing to do with this and you know it." Something filtered through Gerard's dispassionate demeanor. "Leave her alone."

"I'm a prisoner. What am I going to do to your precious daughter?"

That didn't seem to reassure Gerard any more than it did Mac. Oberon wasn't acting like a man who was chained and in fear for his life. Gerard sighed. "I'll meet you in Hansarda, Mac. It should go unsaid that you'll keep this information to yourself until I can talk to my daughter."

Oberon laughed. "Yes, let's not offend the poor girl's delicate sensibilities."

Jenny pushed to her feet and pointed at him. "You—shut up. And *you*—when were you going to tell us that the motherfucking High Priest of Sanctify was your son?"

"When it became relevant." Gerard cut the call, leaving them staring at each other.

He shook his head. "I didn't see that coming."

"I think it's safe to say that no one saw that coming." She flicked the intercom on. "Hadriel, I need you and Shad to escort our lovely prisoner to his cell, and then we're going to space the bodies." She looked over her shoulder. "Most of the bodies."

"Got it."

"Mac...I need to get us through that warp point."

He immediately understood what she needed from him. "I'll get Lucian to a room."

"Thank you." She turned back to the controls, but he didn't miss how tightly strung she was. She wouldn't stop going unless he dragged her away to grieve in private, and no one could afford that until they were through the warp points and closer to Hansarda.

He knelt next to Lucien, who hadn't moved except to prop himself between the wall and a nearby seat. He held his sister in his arms, smoothing back her hair over and over again. "Lucien. Lucien, look at me."

The man slowly raised his face. "She's dead."

There were no words that could help the grief the man had to be drowning in. Mac didn't try. "I know."

"I have to sit vigil." He closed his eyes, the breath shuddering from his body. "I know she made bad choices, but she needs to be buried with full rites."

"She will." He had no place to promise it, but he'd fight for it all the same. It was for Jenny's sake as much as for Lucien's. She might have mixed feelings about her friend now, but she'd regret it later if this wasn't done right.

"Thank you." He got slowly to his feet, keeping her in his arms the entire time. When Mac moved to help, he shook his head. "I need to do this alone."

He watched the man carry his terrible burden to the lift, and finally turned back to Jenny. She wouldn't accept his shoulder to lean on until they were through the warp point, and he didn't expect her to. After... After, he'd get her alone if he had to sit on her to do it.

• • •

Jenny's fury carried her to the warp point and through the four jumps it took to bring them to twelve hours outside of Hansarda. And that's when everything that had happened caught up with her. Her body shook so bad, she could barely manage to turn the intercom on. "Hadriel, can you keep watch for a while? I don't think there was pursuit, but I can't be sure."

"Sure thing."

She pushed to her feet and Mac was there, slipping his arm around her waist. He didn't say anything as they walked to the lift and took it down to the crew cabins. But once they were there, she couldn't face the thought of being surrounded by the possessions of a man she might have killed. "I can't."

He knew. He always seemed to know. He guided her back to the lift and took it down to the engine room. It was louder here, the hum of the engine soothing her in a way she never would have expected. It wasn't enough, not by a long shot, but it was something.

"I need...gods, I don't know what I need. There's the hole inside me and it keeps getting wider and I'm terrified it's going to swallow me entirely. I hurt so much I can barely breathe past it."

"Come here." He opened his arms and she dived for him, holding him so tightly, it felt like he was the last solid thing in the world. He cuddled her close and hummed something that sounded like a lullaby. Minutes passed and, muscle by muscle, she relaxed into him.

Gwen was dead. Oberon was Ophelia's brother. The universe as she had known it was altered. Nothing would ever be the same again. She spoke without lifting her head from his chest. "I need you to tell me it's going to be okay. That all this shit—the loss of Caeden's arm, Gwen's death—was worth it. Please, Mac."

He hesitated, as if debating his answer. "I don't know."

"Well, isn't that shit? I don't know either." She dredged up a smile, but it felt unnatural. "But we got the Big Bad and removed the sword hanging over Hansarda's neck, right?"

"Yes." He smoothed back her hair and cupped her jaw. "Oberon is in custody. He's not going anywhere."

"Not going anywhere but back to Hansarda, where we're going to blow Ophelia's worldview to shit."

"That's not something you can do anything about." He sighed. "None of us can do anything about it."

Knowing that didn't make it easier to think about the fact that one woman she considered a friend was going to be hurt by the news, and the other one was dead. It was a battle to be fought another day. Right now, she was so damn tired, she couldn't see straight.

The war wasn't over, but they'd stayed the writ of execution. Boone and Ophelia and her niece were safe for the time being.

It had to be enough.

She met his eyes, watching them shift from brown to green. "It's later."

"Yes, it's later."

It wasn't nearly as hard as she expected to say the words. "I love you, Mac Flannery. I can't imagine another man who'd be there for me like you have, or who's always so damn willing to call me on my shit. You're one of a kind."

He smiled. "I love you, too. And I'll always be here, Jenny, for as long as you'll have me."

Always. Not too long ago, words like that would send her panicked and running for the nearest warp point. Now? Now it sounded like the best thing she'd heard in longer than she cared to remember. Mac had stayed by her side through the hell they'd just gone through. Compared to that, spending the rest of their lives together should be cake. She laid her head back on her chest. "Gods, I just want to curl into a ball and sleep for seven days straight."

He lifted her hand and pressed a kiss against her knuckles. "How about if, after we see this through to the end, I'll take you somewhere—anywhere you want to go?"

"Anywhere?"

"I'd follow you to the lowest of the seven hells and back." She heard the grin in his voice. "But I was thinking something along the lines of a true vacation on a beach."

"Make it a nude beach and you've got yourself a deal."

"I think I can make that happen." He laughed, the sound doing a whole hell of a lot to dim the memory of too much bloodshed.

She lifted her head and smiled at him. "Gods, I love you. I love you so much, I'm willing to let you try to persuade me to let you make an honest woman of me."

His eyes glinted. "I'm more than up to the challenge."

Bonus
MATERIAL

ENJOY THE SANCTIFY PREQUEL NOVELLA

THE HIGH

Priestess

Entangled Publishing, LLC
2614 South Timberline Road
Suite 109
Fort Collins, CO 80525
Visit our website at www.entangledpublishing.com.

Edited by Heather Howland
Cover design by Heather Howland

Manufactured in the United States of America

First Edition March 2012

CHAPTER ONE

An unnatural calm blanketed the streets of Keiluna, as if its residents sensed a predator in their midst, searching for the perfect kill.

They were right.

Gerard checked his laser, white robe swishing against his legs with every step. He lived for this moment of the hunt, when the world narrowed to him and the comforting wall of his men at his back. Here and now, he could forget how close he'd come to losing his position, his boy, everything—all because he couldn't keep his damn mouth shut. Keiluna was a filthy cesspool, infested with aliens from every corner of the universe. Taking out a single cell of them wouldn't do shit for the greater good.

Too bad when he voiced his opinion to the High Priest, he'd been punished.

Gerard rolled his shoulders, his skin still feeling the sting of a phantom lash. It wasn't that he hated pain—it was one of the few constants of his life—but he wasn't a fan of being humiliated in front of the entire regiment. Those men looked up to him as a leader. Or they used to. Since the demonstration when he'd been whipped for publically questioning the wisdom of Sanctify's rapid expansion, many of the men he considered friends had fallen away, their greetings replaced by sideways looks and downcast eyes. Not Fisk, though. That idiot would stand by Gerard no matter what they were up against. Even the High Priest himself.

But this wasn't the place for distractions. His rage at the High Priest was far more useful at the moment. Despite his anger—or maybe because of it—Gerard found himself muttering Ba'al's Benediction under his breath.

> "Purity will protect you.
> Through the darkness of space
> Only Ba'al's light will shine;
> Cleansing the filth,
> Purifying the unclean,
> Spreading peace through his vengeance.
> In his light, forgiveness
> In his hands, life
> In the High Priest, truth
> In servitude, eternity."

As the words from his childhood rolled off his lips, calm settled over Gerard. Just like it always did. Even when things were at their darkest, his faith never failed to bring comfort. He might not have had a mother or a father while growing up, but he'd had Sanctify.

It was time. He nodded to Adam when they reached the coordinates he'd received, getting a toothy grin in response. The man loved killing more than anyone Gerard knew—except the High Priest—and there was bound to be blood spilled tonight.

Behind that sea-green door was a group of Bolkerian mercenaries driven enough to sign on with anyone working against Sanctify. If one of them hadn't had the support of a very generous backer, they never would have risen far enough to gain notice. A fatal mistake.

"Finish it quickly." At his signal, Adam and Fisk kicked in the door, pouring through to the room beyond. Gerard took in the room in a single blink—two Bolkerians against the far wall, two at a table near the other exit. All male. Thank Ba'al. The females were notoriously harder to kill.

Adam and Fisk moved to the right, taking out the first before it could respond. Attacking quickly was their only hope. Once these things got moving, there was no stopping them. Gerard sidestepped through the door, careful to keep his back to the wall, and followed Davis and Blaine left. Since both were only three months out of training, they needed more help than the other two. While the newbies shot wildly at the sitting Bolkerian, Gerard took aim at the standing one. The male spun toward him, meter-long back-spikes scraping along the wall in its attempt to move quickly. Its squinty black eyes peered over a furred muzzle a moment before Gerard pulled the trigger.

The body hit the ground, a crater where its head had been. He wiped his forehead with the back of his hand and sighed. After all this time, his emotions were bracketed by a wall of calm even killing couldn't touch. Just another pest put down to ensure the safety of Sanctify.

The newbies managed to finish off their Bolkerian, though the body was marked up with far too many laser burns. The only place laser fire could successfully penetrate a Bolkerian's thick, leathery shell was around its neck and head. To hit anywhere else was wasteful. He'd have to talk to them later about accuracy and weak points.

On the other side of the room, Adam and Fisk stood over the struggling body of the final creature. Adam pushed the shorter man. "Get out of my way."

Fisk shoved him back. "No. This isn't right."

Adam jumped forward, arm raised to deliver a blow, but he was forced to dance back at the last minute to avoid the back-spikes of the dying Bolkerian. With a growl, he turned to Gerard, blue eyes demanding. "Tell him."

Tension had been rising between Fisk and their blond squad mate for some time now. Gerard had hoped it would keep until they reached Sanctus again, but apparently that was too much to ask for. He pointed at the newbies. "Secure the perimeter and make sure there's no one else around." As they scrambled over each other to obey, he wondered if he'd ever been so young.

Turning back, he crossed his arms over his chest. "Explain. Now."

"What's there to explain?" Adam shrugged, his broad shoulders nearly taking up the entire width of the doorway. "Fisk's in my way. Hells, he's practically a sympathizer."

"Take that back." Fisk took a step in his direction, but stopped when Gerard held up a hand. "You can't honestly expect me to stand by and let him throw around those kinds of insults. I should cut out his Ba'al-damned tongue."

Obviously things were worse than he thought if Fisk was threatening personal injury on anyone—even Adam. Gerard wanted to tell them to stop acting like kids and stow their issues until they reached home, but a good leader didn't let something like this slide. "Enough. Both of you. Fisk, spit it out before I lose my patience."

The Bolkerian gave a low moan, its thrashing slowing. Fisk looked down, his too-long dark hair falling into his face. Damnit, Gerard had told him to cut it before it got him killed by obscuring his vision. "He was going to torture it."

Gerard blinked. "Elaborate."

"You're not stupid." Fisk motioned at the dying creature. "He wanted to play with it."

Adam gave a heavy sigh. "He's being dramatic. I merely wanted a chance to try out my new laser on its shell."

It seemed plausible enough—if they were talking about anyone else—but Adam had developed a taste for pain. Anyone's but his own. These days, even being in the same room as him made the small hairs on the back of Gerard's neck rise.

"We're on a mission, which means you don't have time for such luxuries. Fisk, put that thing out of its misery." Fisk obeyed instantly, shooting the Bolkerian point-blank in the face. It went limp, dark brown spikes hitting the floor with a heavy *thump*.

Another *thump* echoed through the ceiling above them.

Gerard had half a second to shout a warning before a ball of spikes came rolling down the stairs. Adam dove farther into the room, barely getting out of the way in time. The thing unfurled to a height of well over Gerard's two meters, its muzzle bared in a snarl, dull red eyes focused on him and him alone.

"A fucking female." Of course. How could his day get any worse?

Gerard regretted the thought as soon as the damn thing charged him. Claws, each nearly the size of his hand, swiped past his head. He ducked, trying to get an angle for a shot, but it closed the distance too fast. All he could see was chest fur and spikes and claws. Scrambling back, he hit the wall just as the thing kicked him, tearing into his side.

With a war cry, Davis came flying into the room, skidding to a halt in front of the creature. Then Adam and Fisk were there as well, taking turns firing, luring it away from where Gerard slid to the ground, his vision graying. He raised his laser, aiming carefully. When the Bolkerian turned toward Fisk, arm upraised in a move that would gut the man, Gerard pulled the trigger, taking it in the neck. The thing mewled and listed to the side.

"Out of the way." Fisk pulled Adam back just as the creature toppled.

Davis wasn't so lucky. One of the spikes pinned his leg. The female rolled, cutting off his screams as it covered him. Gerard stared at the thin river of blood curving its way from beneath the Bolkerian's body. It merged with the other pool next to the nearest male, the two reds exactly the same color.

What in Ba'al's name was wrong with him? It shouldn't matter if some aliens bled red. Why was he even thinking about this?

Shaking his head did nothing but make his dizziness worse. Each breath tore through him as if someone were sticking a poker into his wound. Bolkerians weren't poisonous, but the female had gotten him good. The bleeding wouldn't stop without formal treatment. He looked up at Fisk and Adam, their concerned expressions doing nothing to reassure him. Gerard opened his mouth to give the command to retreat to the ship when raised voices reached his ears. At first, he thought they were a hallucination, but both Adam and Fisk went still in front of him. Even straining, he couldn't make out the words, but the tone said enough.

They were in trouble.

Pushing to his feet nearly made him pass out, but his men wouldn't follow orders if they thought he was about to keel over. It was an effort to keep the pain from his voice, but he'd had years of practice. "Get to the ship and send a report to the High Priest."

Adam nodded and disappeared out the back door. Fisk was another story. He eyed Gerard, focusing on the hand he held against his side. The fabric was already soaked through, blood darkening the perfect white of the robe. "You're injured."

"Which is why you need to leave me behind. I can't keep up right now." As shit as that was.

For a moment, it looked as if Fisk would argue, but he finally nodded. "Let me at least help you out of the robe."

Smart. Gerard should have thought of it himself. That he didn't spoke volumes of his injury, but he just nodded and let Fisk help him out of the white cloth that marked him as a member of Sanctify. The shouts loomed closer, nearly to the front door. Gerard jerked his chin at the stairway. "Take the rooftops. I'll go out the back."

"There's a brother in arms who runs a bar about half a kilometer away. Follow the street and take your second left. It's called The Hammer. He'll patch you up while we wait for things to calm down."

The front door groaned as someone on the other side threw himself against it. "Go. Now."

Fisk nodded, but he waited until Gerard pushed off the wall and stumbled through the back door. The night, so calm before, was now filled with angry shouts. How disgustingly typical that these people would come out in arms to defend the monsters in their midst. Didn't they realize how dangerous aliens were? Any species other than humans wasn't to be trusted.

CHAPTER TWO

The back door led into a narrow alley used as a trash lane. Gerard held his side as he moved carefully around the disposal pipelines spiraling from the buildings into the ground. The giant tubes were easily large enough to fit a grown man. There were tales of children falling into the shoots and disappearing into the darkness, killed by either the fall or the incinerators beneath the surface, but Gerard didn't put much stock in stories.

It took longer than he wanted to reach the street and, as a result, his head was spinning as he rounded the corner leading to the bar. There were still sounds of a fight somewhere behind him, but Gerard didn't worry about his squad. They could take care of themselves—if they couldn't, they weren't fit to serve Ba'al in the spreading of purity and peace through the universe.

Too bad Gerard couldn't take care of himself in his current condition. The irony of that wasn't lost on him. Step by staggering step, he made his way to the flashing neon sign depicting a hammer and shouldered through the door.

Gerard blinked. The smoke saturating the place made it difficult to pick out the figures hunched over every table, huddling together in low conversation. He stumbled through the maze of chairs and half fell against the bar. The bartender put down the rag he'd been wiping the pitted counter with and leaned over. "Something I can help you with?"

Gerard put his hand over the other man's, praying to Ba'al that Fisk was right about a brother in arms. "I need assistance."

The man's eyes widened when he caught sight of the blood. "Of course." He jumped over the bar in a smooth movement and slipped an arm around his waist. The second the man put pressure on the wound, Gerard's entire world shifted sideways and went black.

• • •

When the stranger stumbled through the room, the impulse to do a reading rolled over Marianna. He was obviously injured, his hand never wavering from its place against his side, and every instinct screamed he was trouble of the worst kind—exactly the type of thing she avoided. She bit her lip, fighting the need to pull out her cards. This wasn't the time or the place for such things.

He swayed as Sven grabbed him, entire body going slack. Marianna was halfway out of her seat before she realized she'd moved. With a mental curse, she slid back into the chair and watched Sven haul the unconscious man into the back. It wasn't her responsibility to make sure he was okay.

The push got stronger, pulsing beneath her skin until it was everything she could do not to scratch at it.

She took a shaky sip of her drink. Why this man? Why now? With all the med gel and supplies they had on hand, he'd be fixed up in no time. She couldn't risk him emerging from the back room and seeing her cards.

But there was no change in the ants-under-her-skin feeling.

Marianna gritted her teeth. Fine. Unwilling—and unable—to deny the impulse any longer, her hand strayed to the worn cloth bag. The cards were her conduit to the Lady—to ignore their warning was to court death.

After a quick glance around to ensure no one watched, she slipped the cards free and shuffled them under the table. The deck had been her mother's before she died. Marianna still had her grandfather's spare deck stored away in a locked chest filled with some of her parents' things, but it had never felt as natural in her hands as this one did.

All the locals knew she was a Diviner, one of the Lady's people, but there were strangers mixed in with the crowd tonight. While Keiluna was a planet known for its tolerance of any and all alien life, Marianna wasn't willing to risk her health and well-being on that fact. There had been rumors of Sanctify ships spotted in the quadrant, and wherever those sadistic monsters went, alien blood flowed. And that was only for your typical, run-of-the-mill alien.

A Diviner's fate was so much worse.

Marianna sent up a quick prayer to the Lady for guidance, flipped over three cards, and sat back, tapping two fingers against her bottom lip. Usually a basic past, present, and future reading more than sufficed, but this reading wasn't particularly clear. The Star was simple enough—hope, helping an individual to prevail through hard times. Definitely her past. She'd gotten through her ill-spent adolescence on a steady diet of hope and, unlike so many of her childhood friends, went on to make a living in a way that didn't involve petty theft—even if she did retain quite a few of the skills she'd learned from Darla.

With a sigh, she moved on to the next card. The High Priestess indicated that she should trust her intuition. Fair enough. As a Diviner, she knew the truth in that better than most people.

The final card was The World. Sometime in the future, she would reach a new stage, and something would change fundamentally in her life.

Marianna sighed again. The reading was about as clear as mud. Definitely not worth the risk she'd taken by doing it in public.

With a final glare at the offending cards, she gathered them up and slipped the bag back into the pocket she'd sewn into the inside of her coat. Its two layers deterred all but the most determined pickpockets. Theft wasn't much of a concern with the way she was dressed—drab, too-loose clothing, her hair pinned up under a hat—but Marianna was always careful. There had been violence on the wind lately. It was best not to draw attention to herself with so many tempers riding hot.

Time passed and the bar's patrons came and went, several nodding to her though no one approached her booth. Finally, what felt like an eternity later, the back door swished open, and the stranger staggered back into the room. He must have been hurt worse than she thought for the healing to take so long. Even now, he was pale beneath his tanned skin, black hair sticking out haphazardly in a way that suggested he'd run his fingers through it recently. Lines bracketed his mouth, the only indication of the pain he must be experiencing. Those dark eyes certainly gave nothing away.

Drawn by an impulse she couldn't explain any more than the one that had pushed her to do a reading, Marianna slid out of her booth and skirted the wall, coming up between him and the back door. The desire to meet this man, to talk to him, pulsed beneath her skin in time with her heartbeat. The cards had told her to trust her intuition, and her intuition insisted he was important, vitally so.

She tapped his arm. "I've never seen you in here before."

The look he turned on her would have sent a different woman running.

Marianna just smiled. She'd seen far more terrifying things while growing up on the streets. "Allow me to buy you a drink."

Before he could say no, she signaled Sven to bring two glasses of the special liquor they brewed on-planet. Most tourists couldn't handle drinking it straight, but she had a feeling this man wouldn't have a problem with it.

"I don't want a drink."

She cocked her hip against the bar, picking up the closest glass. "While I'm inclined to respect your wishes, this isn't the type of bar you show up to and not drink." Marianna leaned closer, well aware that her billed cap shadowed her eyes, leaving him nowhere to focus but her lips. It was a trick she'd learned out of necessity. The deep violet color of her eyes marked her as a Diviner. It wasn't something she normally worried about, but a stranger—even an injured stranger—couldn't be trusted as a friend. Hells, for all she knew, he was a member of Sanctify.

Marianna shook off the thought as soon as it occurred to her. The Lady wouldn't push her into meeting this man if he meant to kill her. At least…she was reasonably sure She wouldn't.

He turned to face the rest of the room. It was difficult to tell, but she counted at least six people watching, all with varying degrees of hostility. The Hammer wasn't very welcoming of strangers, especially ones who mistreated Marianna. Even in this part of town, where aliens weren't completely accepted, people sought her out for readings. Getting a glimpse of the future was worth its weight in credits, even if most of them wouldn't admit to visiting her in the first place. Personally, that was fine with Marianna. Attention was all well and good—until things turned ugly and people wanted a scapegoat. Better to cruise below the radar and survive.

The man sighed. "Fine." He nodded at the booth she'd just vacated. "Shall we?"

Marianna allowed him to lead the way, giving her the opportunity to frown at a few of the old-timers huddled around the nearest table, playing with a deck of cards nearly as ancient as they were. Their expressions relaxed into grins that were all a few teeth short of a set, and they went back to their game.

After sliding in across from the man, she sat back and looked her fill. He had a harsh face that was strangely attractive, but there was nothing to indicate why she'd felt the impulse to approach him. The silence stretched between them as they sipped their drinks. When it was clear he wouldn't be the first one to speak, she asked, "So do you have a name?"

"I don't see why it matters."

What a prickly fellow. Marianna allowed herself a small laugh. "Well, generally when two people meet, they exchange names."

He made a face like he wanted to argue but, once more, she beat him to the punch. "The alternative is my calling you Stranger while we sit here and drink."

"You aren't going to quit, are you?" An unexpected grin deepened the brackets lining his mouth and sent an equally unexpected surge of warmth through her body. She hadn't felt something like this since...Lady, it'd been nearly a year. How extraordinarily depressing.

"Of course not. I bought you a drink—you're mine for the duration of it."

CHAPTER THREE

*G*erard had no time for women, especially ones with lips like hers. Hadn't he learned his lesson a thousand times over from Lizbeth? That female had been as mean as she was beautiful. She'd taken one look at Gerard and decided to have him for her own. While he wasn't originally opposed to the scenario—seeing as they both got something out of it—he'd never intended to have children. The universe was scary enough without bringing a helpless kid into it. And look how that ended up.

When Gerard shifted, it pulled at his newly patched wound, the discomfort bringing him back to the present. This woman, whoever she was, was no Lizbeth. It wouldn't kill him to share a drink with a pretty girl. It wasn't as if he usually had time for things like this.

"My name is Gerard." He leaned forward, ignoring the slivers of pain spiking through his ribs, and tried to see beneath the hat she had pulled so low. Everything about her was carefully chosen to blend in. All of her clothes were baggy, the jacket large enough that if he couldn't see the distinctly feminine line of her chin and curve of her lips, he'd wonder at her gender. The hair peeking out of the cap was an indeterminate length and silver-blond—not a color he saw often, which was probably why she kept it hidden. There was no telling what she'd look like if he could get her out of some of those clothes...

Gerard mentally cursed himself for even considering it.

Her smile was sweet and he felt it like a kick to the chest. "Gerard? That's quite the name."

How was he supposed to respond to that? "It's the one I was born with."

"The majority of them are." She held out a delicate hand, the skin so pale it was almost translucent. "I'm Marianna. It just so happens that it's not the same one I was born with."

Curiosity blossomed as he took her hand, careful to keep a gentle grip to avoid hurting her. She was so slight. Fragile, almost. Someone to be protected—

Training kicked in, demanding that he shut his mouth and leave. Nothing good could come from further conversation with this woman. But Gerard couldn't bring himself to move away from her. "What name were you born with?"

"It makes no difference." She shrugged. "That name died with my mother and father."

"You don't have any other family?"

Another shrug. "There's a grandfather out there, lost among the stars. He used to pop back in and make sure I was still alive, but he never stayed long."

"He left you." The thought of abandoning his own flesh and blood twisted something in Gerard's chest.

"Grandfather suffers from a severe case of wanderlust. There was no room for a child in his life."

"That's no excuse."

"Perhaps not. It's far too late to worry about it now."

So she was an orphan. Just like him. It didn't matter—hundreds of his brothers shared the same fate. Still, he found himself speaking. "My parents were killed by an Abura-Sumashi when

I was an infant." The High Priest was the one who had found him—he'd only been an enforcer back then—and taken him in. He owed the man—owed Sanctify—everything.

And now he had Oberon to take care of. Gerard owed it to the boy to keep his head down and obey orders, no matter if he agreed with the path Sanctify was taking or not.

"I'm sorry." She actually sounded like she meant it.

"Why? I never knew them."

"So what brings you to our humble establishment? Your injury?"

"Injury?" Gerard scanned the rest of the room, squinting against the smoke that stung his eyes, and wondered how many of them knew. *Fool. All of them.* It wasn't like he thought of that before stumbling through the front door. Just because the owner was a brother to Sanctify's cause didn't mean his patrons were. The rookie mistake burned in the back of his throat, heating his face until he was sure Marianna could see the blush spreading over his skin.

Her smile took on a sharp edge. "Yes, injury. You weren't exactly subtle about it when you passed out."

Which meant he needed to get out of here, and fast. If there were enemies among the crowded tables, they were probably waiting for the chance to knife him in the back. The spot between his shoulder blades itched at the thought. Gerard slid the link from his pocket, but there were no waiting messages, which meant his options were limited. He could stay here or wander the streets until Fisk or Adam gave the all clear. Judging from the way his head still swam, the latter wasn't the most intelligent plan he'd ever had.

He looked up to find her still smiling. An awful, idiot idea occurred to him, slipping out of his mouth before he could think better of it. "Do you know somewhere we can go?"

"To be alone?" Her smile widened, both teasing him and

inviting him to be in on the joke.

"Something like that." Gerard found himself smiling in return. "I was thinking of getting something to eat."

"You mean the beaten old InstaChef in the corner isn't tickling your fancy? The selection is quite nice—synth-beef, synth-brats, and synth-pork. Do you like meat, Gerard?"

He blinked. Surely she didn't realize how that could be construed? Then again, from the way she was smiling, Marianna knew exactly what she was saying. "I'm not overly fond of... meat."

She laughed, the sound reminding him of Sanctify's bells—totally and completely pure. "It would be a crying shame if you were. Come with me—I know the perfect place."

Gerard stood after she did, taking her outstretched hand without pause. A curious warmth spread through him, fueled by her touch. It wasn't until they slipped through the back door that he finally spoke again. "You aren't planning to lure me into a dark alley to murder me, are you?"

• • •

The flash of humor caught Marianna completely off guard. She'd simply been trying to get him out of The Hammer before one of the good old boys decided to brew up trouble. From the expression on Gerard's face as he'd examined their surroundings, he'd been about to kill someone. Marianna wanted to avoid that if at all possible.

Giving his hand another tug, she started walking down the street, watching the neon lights play on the cobblestones beneath her feet. Marianna loved Keiluna's bar district. The colors and old-world architecture gave even the slowest night a festive feel. Sounds of laughter and music drifted from the open windows, bringing with it a fascinating blend of sweet-smelling, blue-green smoke and perfume.

She glanced at Gerard as she towed him along, enjoying the simple feeling of touching him. When was the last time she'd casually touched another person? She couldn't remember. The realization made her feel lonely and giddy, all at once. Part of her wanted to withdraw, to run back to her shop and hide. This wouldn't last past tonight, after all. Whatever else Gerard was, he was still a stranger, and strangers rarely stayed on Keiluna longer than a few days. On the other hand, it had been so long since she'd done something for herself, sought any pleasure at all. The need to feel *something* was almost too much to bear.

The thought that he might be the wrong kind of stranger rose again, more persistent this time. Marianna pushed it away. Everyone knew members of Sanctify wore those hideous white robes, and Gerard was dressed in a simple pair of black pants and a loose gray shirt. Take in the fact that he was teasing her about luring him into a dark alley…

He wasn't Sanctify. He couldn't be.

She skipped forward a few steps, dragging him along behind her. "What a strange coincidence. A dark alley happens to be our destination."

He gave a wicked grin that sent a shock of lightning through her. Oh Lady, she couldn't turn down an opportunity like this. Gerard gave her hand a squeeze. "Then I lay myself in your hands. Do with me what you will."

The invitation, on top of everything else, was too much temptation to resist. Marianna pulled him into the nearest alley and pushed him against the wall. A little more forward than she would normally be, but the heat building under her skin demanded she do something. She paused long enough to make sure the shadows hid them from any observers and then leaned in.

Marianna captured his mouth, her tongue darting out to meet his. Whiskers rasped against her skin and sent delicious chills through her body. Gerard jerked back, inhaling sharply. Even in the darkness, she could see how wide his eyes were. She blinked—surely she hadn't misinterpreted his signals? More than a little stung, Marianna started to move away. If he didn't want her, then so be it. It wasn't as if she really needed another complication in her life right now, and this man was nothing if not—

He hooked the back of her neck and yanked her against him.

Cautious of his healing wound, Marianna tried to stop her forward momentum, but Gerard's mouth found hers and chased away all rational thought. His hands were everywhere, beneath her jacket, knocking off her hat, cupping her backside to draw her closer. Those Ladydamned whiskers would be her undoing. Or perhaps his tongue was the problem, twining with hers, tasting of the alcohol he'd been drinking. It left her light-headed, intoxicated with the chemistry screaming between them.

Marianna had a moment to wonder if she should grab her hat, but then Gerard gave a muffled moan, one hand tangling in the hair tumbling down around her shoulders, and her worry slipped away. She gave a moan of her own and slipped her arms around his neck, going up on her tiptoes.

Something vibrated against her hip, a chirping sound cutting through the night. Gerard pulled back, breathing hard, and leaned his forehead against hers. "Thirty seconds."

She would need a bit longer than that to regain her composure. Marianna rubbed her mouth with the back of her hand. "Of course."

Turning away, he fished a link from his pocket and spoke quietly into it. Too quietly for her to eavesdrop. To distract herself, she scanned the ground for her hat. It was too risky to walk the streets without it these days, not with word spreading of Sanctify's growing presence. They hated anything different from their purity-obsessed standards—so basically anyone who wasn't totally and completely human. And they had a special place in their torture dungeon for Diviners. She knew that all too well after what had happened to her uncles.

"Marianna."

She looked up to find him in the mouth of the alley, his hands clasped awkwardly in front of him. There was only one explanation for the apology in the way he said her name. "You're leaving."

It was what she expected. He was a stranger, and strangers came and went on Keiluna the same way the winter storms did — here one night to trash the place, and gone the next morning before the market opened — but she thought she'd have longer than this.

"I wish I wasn't." To his credit, he actually sounded as if he meant it.

"Perhaps in another life."

Gerard held out a hand and she took it, letting him pull her into the neon lights of the street, each announcing a different bar, a different special of the night. "I don't think I can wait that long. But next time my business brings me —"

Disbelief dawned on his face, quickly followed by horror. Marianna's instincts screamed at her to run, to fight, to do anything but stand still as his hold tightened to a painful level.

"*Diviner.*" The word came out like the vilest curse.

In that moment she knew, though her soul cried out at the unfairness of the Lady pushing her into this meeting. "You're one of those monsters, aren't you? Sanctify."

"I'm not the monster in this scenario." He pushed her back into the alley, peering down into her eyes as if they were the source of every problem that plagued his life. "Your kind is a blasphemy of the highest order."

Lady save her from murderous idiots like this one. Had she really thought he was attractive in a dangerous sort of way?

Gerard was just plain dangerous. "Let me go, and I'll take my blasphemous self from your sight."

"Let you go?" He was already shaking his head before he finished speaking. "No. Absolutely not. You're coming with me."

The first real thrill of fear coursed through her. "What are you talking about?" Surely, he couldn't mean what his words implied. And yet her Ladydamned instincts whispered that he wasn't joking.

"All blasphemers must be purified." His words came out hollow, as if it were nothing to threaten her with death by dismemberment and burning.

Panic sprang to life in her chest, its wings fierce as it tried to fly out her throat. "Please. No." Then she realized she was begging for sanity from a madman. Sanctify didn't see the humanity in aliens—they only saw the difference. There would be no mercy for her.

So be it.

She dropped to a crouch, pulling him off balance, and grabbed the shiv from the inside of her jacket. Switching her grip on it, Marianna struck out, aiming for his injured side. Even now, she didn't go for a mortal wound, instead hitting the outer edge of his hip. Gerard growled as he went to his knees, grip never faltering. She swiped at him again, but he knocked the shiv from her hand with no apparent effort. "Enough."

"Damn you." No matter how much she wriggled and fought, he refused to release her. "Let me go."

Footsteps echoed in the alley and Marianna twisted, opening her mouth to scream for help. The plea died in her throat when she saw the white robes.

There truly was no hope for her now.

CHAPTER FOUR

The Diviner looked so small and fragile once Adam took her coat and magcuffed her. She knelt, staring at Gerard with those unnatural violet eyes. He wanted to tell her to turn away, but it would show how uncomfortable he was and he couldn't risk that in front of the men.

"Here." Adam tossed over the jacket.

Thankful for something to distract himself, Gerard rifled through the pockets, coming up with another shiv, a lock-picking kit, and an old bag. There was no mistaking what the bag held—her cursed cards. He should burn them now, preferably with witchfire to make sure the job got done, but something held him back. "Get her to the ship."

Fisk sighed as he tossed her over his shoulder. Marianna didn't make a sound, though the impact must have jarred her something terrible. Gerard smothered a tiny thread of sympathy that threatened to bleed through him, his lips silently moving in Ba'al's Benediction.

Purity will protect you.
Through the darkness of space
Only Ba'al's light will shine;

Cleansing the filth…

Except Marianna didn't seem like filth. She seemed fragile and kind and innocent—well, maybe not innocent. Gerard shook his head and forced back the memory of her mouth going soft against his, continuing the chant.

Purifying the unclean,
Spreading peace through his vengeance.
In his light, forgiveness
In his hands, life
In the High Priest, truth
In servitude, eternity.

Odd how going through the prayer did little to smother the phantom feeling of guilt working its way through him. Guilt was a useless emotion. The Diviner would be his ticket back into the High Priest's good graces. Gerard needed her. End of story.

He pressed a hand to his side and winced. Those med patches hadn't held up when she cut him. Even now, Gerard could feel them peeling away from his skin, their seal broken.

"You okay?" Fisk wasn't even breathing hard as they walked down the street, but then, the woman couldn't weigh more than fifty-five kilograms soaking wet. With each step, it became harder to connect her with the monsters the High Priest preached of. While her use of the cards might be blasphemous, it wasn't as if she were capable of doing real harm.

"I'm fine." His wound pulled again, and he mentally amended the thought—she wasn't capable of *much* real harm. Marianna had the chance to do him serious injury when they'd struggled—he'd been wide open—and she'd chosen instead to wing him. It was more than a little odd, which doubled the doubt threading through his conviction. He smothered it—there was no room for doubts, not now. This was right, damn it.

"You don't look fine." Adam moved up on Fisk's other side, gaze roving over the Diviner. "Though she does. Think the High Priest will let me play with her?"

"*No.*" Under no circumstances would the man touch Marianna. Gerard rounded on Adam, barely fighting back the impulse to beat the teasing grin from his face. "Stay away from her."

Adam cackled, raising his hands in mock surrender. "Fine, fine. You can have the little bitch all to yourself. All you had to do was say you wanted her."

"I don't want her." Lie. He'd wanted her a whole hells of a lot until he'd realized what species she was. Ba'al be damned, Gerard could still taste her on his lips. "But the High Priest will."

"I can't hardly wait." Adam actually went so far as to clap his hands together. "I've never seen a purifying ritual for a Diviner before. Isaiah said there's nothing that compares to it."

Gerard had seen one. Once. And Ba'al forgive him, but he'd hoped to never see it again. The Diviner killed four of their men before they took him down, which should have made his death easier to watch. But, by the end, it had been everything Gerard could do not to turn away from the gory spectacle.

And Marianna was destined for the same fate.

Shoving the thought from his mind, he exchanged a look with Fisk. The other man had stood beside him while the last Diviner died, and Fisk hadn't liked it any more than he did.

Gerard checked behind them. "Shut the hells up, Adam. Let Blaine know we're coming."

He moved off, pulling a link from his pocket and speaking softly into it. Fisk shifted closer to Gerard. "Do you really mean to do this?"

"Do what?" Her blond hair had come loose of its bindings, falling around her face and hiding those eyes from sight. Like this, she could almost pass for a human they'd taken by mistake.

"Take her to Sanctus." Fisk lowered his voice further. "She's a woman—barely more than a child. Can you really stand by and watch her die like the last one?"

"I don't have a choice. She's a Diviner. You know what Ba'al teaches about their kind." The thought left a sharp pain in his stomach. It was the damned wound. Probably. It certainly wasn't blasted guilt again.

Damnit, no. He was on the path of righteousness—to question Ba'al's word was to question the very foundation of his upbringing. He pressed a hand against his wound, letting the pain roll over him, crystallizing his anger. *This* was what came of aliens mingling with humans. He might not agree with a full expansion into the universe, but Sanctify's mission was a holy one. Reflexively, he brought up the last part of Ba'al's Benediction—it usually did the trick with any worrisome emotions he didn't want to deal with.

In his light, forgiveness
In his hands, life
In the High Priest, truth
In servitude, eternity.

Fisk shook his head as if he could hear the phantom lines running through Gerard's head. "I won't try to stand in your way, but you better be sure before you do this, Gerard. Some things you can't come back from."

"I follow the law." Even if it sometimes stuck in his throat like a Ba'al-damned knife.

"The law isn't absolute and you know it." Fisk looked at Adam, who was still talking on the link. "Just say the word and we'll find a way to set her free."

A small voice urged him to take Fisk's offer. He didn't want to see her dismembered and burned to death. And yet…twenty years of training were nothing to set aside just because he made the mistake of kissing her. Even if it was quite possibly the best kiss of his life.

Adam shut off the link and rejoined them, grinning madly. "A Diviner. And here I thought this job was a complete bust. Bummer about Davis, though. At least we managed to get the body for burial."

It took Gerard a full thirty seconds to register what he meant. One of the newbies had been impaled beneath the female Bolkerian's spikes—something a good commander never would have forgotten. He swallowed, tasting bile at the back of his throat. "He shall receive the honor of the funeral rite. A proper burial with all the trappings of a warrior of Sanctify."

Adam snorted. "As if that ever helped anyone. Dead is dead."

• • •

Marianna fought off panic with every ounce of her control. They hauled her around as if she were a sack of laundry, and spoke of her death so matter-of-factly. A truly terrible death.

She lifted her arms until her hair hid her wrists. The magcuffs were standard issue, and easily unlocked—if she had her kit. But it was safely tucked inside the jacket now in Gerard's hands. No help from that quarter.

How fortunate that Darla taught her years ago to never keep all her tricks in one place. Marianna carefully pulled out the necklace hidden beneath her shirt. Inside the locket was an antitech device. It only had enough zing for one charge, but it would unlock her cuffs.

Which solved one problem, while still leaving three white-robed ones. Marianna wasn't much of a fighter—hells, she couldn't bring herself to take down one injured man, let alone another two healthy ones—but she had to try. Her death warrant was signed and sealed the moment they boarded the ship.

Inhaling deeply, she flipped open the locket and awkwardly pressed it against the cuffs, pushing on the button with her forefinger.

They snapped opened with a quiet *click*, and she scrambled to catch them before they hit the ground. Thank the Lady she hadn't bothered with a haircut in years.

Marianna moved before she could talk herself out of it, taking the cuffs in a two-handed grip, and twisting up and around, hitting her captor in the side of the head. He grunted and stumbled, his hold loosening enough for her to wiggle free. Hitting the ground hurt, jarring something in her shoulder, but she kept moving. There were cries of anger behind her, but she scrambled to her feet and started running.

Three steps later, a weight hit her from behind, taking her to the ground. Marianna screamed, partly in pain, partly in hope that someone would hear and come riding to her rescue. A vain hope, as it turned out.

The man who'd tackled her flipped Marianna over and backhanded her. As casual as the move looked, the sound of it cracked through the night and her head bounced on the cobblestone street. The last thing she heard before her world swam to gray was the sound of more shouting.

...

"What in Ba'al's name are you doing?" Gerard grabbed the back of Adam's robe and hauled him off Marianna, taking a precious second to shake the man before he tossed him to the side. Gerard went to his knees, scooping her up and trying to check for injuries at the same time. That thrice-damned voice inside him whispered that it shouldn't matter if she were injured—she was destined to die, after all. Gerard ignored it, smoothing her hair back to examine the wound oozing blood from her temple. A dangerous place for an injury, but since she still breathed, it was likely not fatal.

"Have you lost your damned mind?" Adam shoved to his feet, skin turning a mottled red. "She was trying to escape. I stopped her. Why the hells are your panties in a twist?"

"You had her down—there was no reason to hit her."

"Are you even listening to yourself?" Adam started toward him but then Fisk was between them, still clutching the side of his head.

"We don't have time for this." Gerard lifted his hand, which was wet with her blood. "People will be out soon and we're in no shape to take on anyone right now. Adam, take point."

"I'll take the girl."

"Like hells you will." Gerard clenched his fists and tried for a more moderate tone. "Fisk can take care of it." The way Adam had handled her attempted escape only solidified his previous stance. He wouldn't trust the man near Marianna in any way, shape, or form.

"What? But he's—"

"I'm fine. Take point, Adam." Fisk waited until the blond man started moving before he turned and glared at Gerard. "This is your fault. You never should have taken her, but it's too late now."

CHAPTER FIVE

*M*arianna woke cuffed to a bed. She started to turn her head and froze as pain rolled over her in waves. A few deep breaths fought down the nausea, but spots still danced across her vision. Ladydamnit.

All she wanted to do was curl into a ball and sleep until everything disappeared, but this situation wasn't going to go away simply because she willed it to. Which meant she had to do something proactive. She tilted her head, trying to see the bindings, and nearly cursed aloud when they revealed themselves to be magcuffs. Again. Given that her wrists were pinned on either side of the cot frame, it was unlikely she could get free, even under the best of circumstances. And these circumstances were hardly the best of anything.

The door *swoosh*ed open and the short, dark man from before came into the room. He did a double take when he met her gaze, mouth dropping open. "Those things really are eerie."

"Those things" apparently meant her eyes, since he couldn't seem to tear his attention away. Well, turnabout was fair play. She took him in, trying to figure out if this man was a potential ally. A foolish thought, to be sure—he was a member of Sanctify, after all—but the idea took root and demanded she put some consideration behind it.

He wasn't unattractive, exactly, but the pockmarks on his skin spoke of a difficult youth. His black eyes showed nothing, no emotion for her to capitalize on. And yet she couldn't shake the feeling the Lady was telling her this man was important—to what, though, was anyone's guess. "Hello."

"You shouldn't speak." He grabbed a cloth from the cabinet and crossed the room to crouch next to the cot. "I need to examine your head."

Marianna let him tilt her chin down, his fingers curiously gentle considering he was the enemy. "You mean I shouldn't speak so you don't see me as an actual person."

"You're a Diviner." As if that was everything he needed to know about her. It was a distancing trick, and a pathetic one.

Well, she was having none of that. "My name is Marianna. I'm twenty-four years old."

The stranger's grip tightened on her chin as he swabbed her temple. "I know what you're playing at, and it won't do any good. We've already spaced. Even if I was willing to help you—and that's not saying I am—there's nothing I can do."

"Then at least give me the decency of human conversation, since it seems my fate is already decided."

Gerard's voice cut through the room. "You aren't human."

They both flinched as he walked into the room, his expression so cold it was everything she could do to fight back a shiver.

"Get out of here, Fisk."

The smaller man stood, the bloody cloth still in his hand. "She needs food and rest. And to get out of those Ba'al-damned cuffs. It's not like she has anywhere to run."

Gerard glared down at her. "She's a problem-starter."

Fisk snorted. "She's a woman—they're all problem-starters."

Of course, the larger man found no humor in that. "We'll

speak of this later."

"I wait in suspense for that conversation." He paused in the doorway. "You know my feelings on this."

Again, a small flame of hope kindled in Marianna's chest. She tried to label it for the false beacon it was, and yet it persisted. "Fisk?" Marianna pitched her voice high and girlish, knowing full well how fragile it made her sound. As Darla had explained, when you weren't a fighter, you had to use what tools you had. Which meant Marianna had perfected blending in and, when she couldn't do that, developing a knack for making people want to protect her. If she could make it work with Fisk, it might be an opening.

"Yes?"

"Get out." Gerard's face was getting red again, but Marianna couldn't pass up this opportunity.

"Would it be possible to give back my belongings? Not the shivs, of course, but the rest of it?"

Fisk's dark eyes missed nothing. "You want your cards."

"*Out,*" Gerard said. "Now."

Fisk left the room without another word, but Gerard had enough to spare. "You will not speak to my men. You will not attempt to attack, coerce, or touch them in any way. For the remainder of this flight, you will sit your ass on that cot and keep out of trouble or, Ba'al help me, I will bind you again myself. Or—"

He pressed his lips together and turned away. A distant part of Marianna wondered if he would strike her, but instead he paced the room, seeming to take up more than his fair share of space, the threat of violence screaming from every line of his body.

A smarter woman would have remained silent, but it wasn't as if she had anything left to lose. Die here at his hands or later at someone else's; it made no difference. If she were to be perfectly honest, the former held more appeal. Gerard didn't seem the type to make his victims suffer.

"Or what?"

Gerard stopped in the middle of taking a step. "Excuse me?" His gaze skated over her body, eyes darkening with something like lust. Clearing his throat, Gerard resumed his pacing.

"I believe you heard me just fine."

"Did you miss the part where I said I'd bind you?"

Marianna rattled her cuffs. "Seeing as I'm already bound, your threat lacks a certain something. And, as you plan on ultimately killing me, what is my motivation for good behavior?"

The silence stretched out for a brief moment before he roared, "Do you *want* to stay cuffed to that cot for the next two days?"

She fought back a shiver, not completely sure if came from fear or desire. Marianna had never been ignited by anger, but there was something about Gerard that made her want to soothe away his pain. Because the man had pain—she could almost see it, pulsing beneath his skin. "Not particularly."

"Then be a good girl and shut the hells up."

"You won't hurt me." Where the absurd words came from, she hadn't the slightest clue, but they slid out of her mouth with the ease of a universal truth.

"Are you mad?" He scrubbed his hands over his face and up through his hair, the black locks standing on end. "What would possess you to say such a thing?"

"It's the truth." She watched him closely, taking in the way he made such a valiant effort to keep from looking at her body. Gerard still desired her, despite everything. He might hate himself for it, but he did. It was something she could—she *would*—use. "Unless you intend to assault me just to prove a point to yourself?"

"Assault you? I'll show you a Ba'al-damned assault."

Two steps and he was at the cot's side, fingers flying over

the magcuffs' controls. They gave way with a muted *click*, falling from her wrists. Marianna barely had time to relish the air on her chafed skin before he grabbed her shoulders and hauled her off the mattress. "Get up."

He let go of her so quickly, she stumbled, catching herself on the wall. Now, standing across from him with nothing but a small sink and a cabinet to use as distraction, a thread of doubt wound its way through her. What if she was wrong and he truly intended to hurt her? Marianna smothered the feeling before it could take root, lifting her chin. Nothing had changed.

He towered over her, easily a head and shoulders taller and twice as wide. "You are an idiot."

"Am I?" She lifted her chin higher, hands fisting at her sides. "I am not the one who murders innocents."

"And yet here you stand, so very alive." Gerard moved closer, bringing them nearly chest to chest. "You're playing in dangerous waters. Do not test me."

"Again I ask—why not? There is nothing you can do that's worse than what awaits me."

His short beard should have hidden those tempting lips. Instead, it only framed them to perfection. Dangerous, tempting thoughts circled her head—thoughts mirrored in his eyes. Gerard's mouth quirked, the sudden change of expression doing odd things to her stomach. "And again I say that you're a damned idiot."

Marianna licked her lips, achingly aware of the way his gaze sharpened on her. "You will not harm me." Perhaps she truly was a fool for believing in that so strongly—even if he didn't harm her, he would still stand by and watch her burn.

Unless she could convince him otherwise.

A perfectly mad thought blossomed in her mind. But this was the time for mad thoughts—they were all she had left. Marianna inhaled, her breasts rubbing against Gerard's chest. She didn't miss the way his breath caught at the touch. Perhaps it wasn't such a mad idea after all.

Instead of moving back, she ran her hands up his torso, careful to avoid his side, and slid her arms around his neck. When he didn't immediately resist, Marianna went up on her tiptoes and kissed him.

CHAPTER SIX

The woman cast a spell on him more convincingly than if she really were a witch. Even though he knew he should pull away, Gerard hugged her close, moving one hand up to cradle the back of Marianna's head as he devoured her mouth. No one should taste as good as she did, her tongue darting against his, the touch draining away his remaining willpower. Or maybe it wasn't her touch at all. Maybe it was those helpless little sounds she made as his free hand slipped beneath the back of her shirt, finding her skin so devastatingly soft. She arched against him, offering everything he could have ever wanted and more.

And he wanted. Oh, how he wanted.

Gerard tore away from her, shoving Marianna back onto the cot. He backpedaled until he hit the far wall, breathing hard. When she sat up, hair tousled and lips swollen from his kisses, it was everything he could do not to cross the room and keep going until they were both naked and coming.

He swiped the back of his hand across his mouth, but it did nothing to take away the taste of her. "Don't mistake me for a friend, Marianna."

Against the paleness of her skin and hair, her wide violet eyes stood out in stark contrast. "I wouldn't dream of it."

Her admission shouldn't have felt like a kick to the chest, but it did. Maybe it was him who was the idiot after all. Gerard pointed at her. "Don't make any trouble."

"I promise I won't try to escape again."

It wasn't quite the same thing as promising not to make trouble, but he chose to let it go. There were some battles he couldn't win, and if his instincts were correct, this was one of them. Gerard slid sideways to the door. "I'll have one of the men bring you something to eat soon." Any of the men but Adam.

"Thank you." She still hadn't moved from her spot on the bed.

"Don't thank me. You're still going to be purified. Nothing you say or do can change that."

Something sparked in her eyes—whether it was defiance or acceptance, he couldn't be sure. "I would expect nothing else from you."

"Good." Before he could make a bigger ass of himself—or kiss her again—he turned and walked through the door. After locking it, Gerard leaned against the wall and desperately tried to reclaim his calm. "Purity will protect you. T-Through the darkness of space. Only Ba'al's light will…" He searched for the next words but they eluded him, replaced by the memory of how good Marianna felt in his arms. Damn her.

He ground his teeth, wishing he could grind away his thoughts as easily. But they were still there, as persistent and nagging as the wound in his side. He sighed and went in search of Fisk.

The corridor stretched out before him, immaculate and shining. There was only one hallway on this deck, leading to a lift that ran from the engine room, all the way up to the hub. Gerard bypassed the lift, heading for the door to the stairs. After his encounter with Marianna, he needed to stretch his legs. The newly mended patches pulled slightly with each step. He ignored them. The gash in his side would be healed within three days or so, but in the meantime the damn patches were going to itch like crazy and drive him nuts.

Just as he expected, he found Fisk in the engine room, pacing. His arms were marked by grease all the way to the elbow, which meant he'd been working on something down here before he heard Gerard's approach. Fisk looked up, shoulders squared as if he expected a fight. "It's wrong."

There was no question as to what he meant. "She's a Diviner. It's the law." Gerard waved a hand when it looked like Fisk was going to argue. "It doesn't matter now—we've gone too far to turn back."

Fisk clenched his hands. "Fine. But I'm not going to watch it happen."

"Stop worrying about the future. Right now, what I am telling you to do is bring her food."

"Me?" He raised his eyebrows. "Since when am I on nurse-maid duty?"

Gerard leaned against the wall and crossed his arms over his chest. "Since Adam can't be trusted, and the new guy isn't prepared for something like this. He might give in to temptation." Just like Gerard almost had. The thought of Blaine pressing even so much as a single finger against her skin made him want to break something.

"And what's stopping *you* from doing it, oh fearless leader?"

"The fact that I'm the leader of this squad and you'll do what I say." Gerard allowed himself a tight smile. "But you're my friend, so I'm asking instead of commanding."

"Well that's something I don't get to hear often." Fisk grabbed a nearby rag and wiped down his arms. "Don't suppose I can get this in writing?"

"Don't push your luck."

"Fair enough. I'll take care of the girl."

"Good." Gerard pushed off the wall, wincing when his side twinged. "Don't take too long, though. I want a meeting within the hour."

"Then I'll get going." Fisk tossed the rag aside and strode from the room, moving toward the lifts. Gerard watched him go, wondering if this was all a grave mistake. Maybe he really should have let Marianna go before they ever made it to the ship.

• • •

Marianna wasn't sure what to expect when Fisk came into her room a second time, but the delicious smells wafting over from the covered tray he held chased away most of her misgivings. Still, she chose to be prudent and keep the cot between them as the dark man set down the tray.

They stared at each other a long, awkward moment before she cleared her throat. "Ah, thank you."

One corner of his mouth tweaked up. "There's really nothing to thank me for."

"All the same. Thank you." She stared at him, trying to place her finger on what it was that lulled her into a sense of false security. Certainly not his bulky fighter's body. Nor the haphazard haircut that was worn longer than the other members of their squad. No…it was something else.

He glanced over his shoulder as if he expected someone to have come through the door in the last ten seconds. "I brought you something, but it's best we keep this our little secret."

"Of course."

When Fisk pulled her cards from his side pocket, it was everything she could do not to burst into tears and profess her undying devotion. Instead, Marianna smiled and did the next best thing. "Would you like a reading?"

He jumped as if she'd electrocuted him. "What?"

She would have to tread carefully here, but instinct whispered for her to keep pressing. "I'm incredibly grateful to you for bringing my cards. I would like to give you a reading…if you'll allow it." While she waited for his answer, she found herself holding her breath. So much rested on this moment, Marianna was sure of it.

After one last look at the door, he turned back to her. For the first time, his expression thawed, a sliver of warmth showing through. "I've heard that your kind is never wrong with these readings."

"Our goddess speaks through the cards. There is some interpretation involved, but no, the cards never lie."

He gave a nod as if it was the answer he expected. "Then I would greatly appreciate a reading."

Taking a seat, Marianna patted the cot next to her. "It might be easiest if you sit. Would you like to know the past, present, or future?"

Fisk gave a low laugh. "Does anyone really pick the past or present?"

"It does occur from time to time, but generally people come to me looking for their futures." She shuffled the cards, each breath taking her deeper into herself—and closer to the Lady. Peace settled around Marianna, soothing away her fear and anxiety. "Please cut the cards, wherever you like."

Fisk cut them gingerly, as if he expected them to bite. "Gerard isn't a bad man, you know."

She went still. Where was he going with this?

"I've known him since we were kids in the academy. He's a true friend, a man of honor."

Setting the cards in front of her, Marianna met his gaze. "How did the two of you meet?"

"I've always been on the small side—especially when I was a boy—and my knack for not knowing when to shut up hasn't changed either. It got me in over my head, and he showed up in the nick of time." He sighed. "That idiot took on five boys who were all twice his size."

She found herself leaning forward, drawn into the story. "Did he save you?"

"Ba'al, no. He got his ass kicked right alongside me." Fisk shifted, lowering his voice until she had to lean forward to catch his words. "But he's saved my life half a dozen times since then. You have to understand that, while I don't agree with this, I owe him my life."

"I understand." And she did. Fisk owed Gerard in the same way she owed Darla. If the redhead needed her, Marianna would move every one of the heavens and hells to help her. How was his supporting Gerard any different? It was something to remember.

Marianna motioned to the cards. "Shall we?"

"Yes, of course. I apologize for rambling."

She flipped over three cards, face up. Marianna took them in with a glance, then did a double take. No, no, no. This couldn't be right. But there was no mistaking their meaning. In a desperate attempt to give lie to the reading, she turned the deck upside down to check the influencing card. *Death*. Dread spiraled up her spine, radiating outward. "Lady save you."

"What?"

She grabbed his wrist, realizing her mistake too late when he jerked away. Marianna made an effort to compose herself as Fisk stood, brushing nonexistent dust from his pants. "Please. Don't go before I give you the reading." She hurried on before he could change his mind. "There's a jealous woman in your life, someone ruled by her emotions and extremely high-strung. You will have a terrible fight, perhaps over an infidelity, perhaps because of a perceived infidelity."

Lady, she was losing him. Marianna could see it in the way Fisk shook his head, his expression icing over. "Listen. *Please.* She's going to try to hurt you—maybe even kill you—through nefarious means."

"Isn't all murder nefarious?" His joke fell flat, hanging between them.

Marianna sat back, pulling her knees to her chest and wrapping her arms around them. "I know you don't believe me, but please be careful. She's going to try to kill you."

"Leandra would never—No. I'm not discussing this with you. Thank you for the entertainment, but I will be going now."

"It is always a pleasure doing the Lady's work." Marianna waited until he left before she touched each of the cards in turn. Queen of Cups, Ill-Dignified. The Tower, Ill-Dignified. Five of Swords, Ill-Dignified.

All under the influence of Death.

The reading made her want to step into a sans shower to wash away the dread clinging to her soul. She placed her hand on the deck and closed her eyes, sending up a prayer to her goddess. "He might be a member of Sanctify, but he's not an evil man. Please, please, help him to heed the reading."

For once, her Lady's peace was nowhere to be found.

CHAPTER SEVEN

Every minute spent locked in the room dragged by even slower than the one before. When Marianna attempted to meditate, she couldn't sit still long enough to focus. She forced herself to remain on the cot, shuffling her cards, but thoughts and worries kept intruding. So she stopped trying to achieve calm and started pacing.

It was exactly ten paces from wall to wall, seventeen if she made a circuit around the bed. The sans shower held only the bare necessities—obviously a ship stocked by men—and the only food she had access to was what they brought her. To someone's credit—she suspected Gerard was the one making the decisions—meals appeared like clockwork, each a basic fare that could be found in most InstaChefs. If only her stomach would settle enough to eat.

Late in the second day, Gerard came for her. He gave her a cursory look before standing to the side of the open door. "We're warping now."

Questions bubbled up behind her lips, but only one wriggled free. "Why has it taken so long to reach the warp point?" She'd never had the resources or desire to fly before, but from what she'd overheard while picking pockets in the market, it was barely two days to the warp point everyone used out of Keiluna. While her timing might be somewhat off, she'd definitely been in this room more than two days.

"It's taken as long as it needed to."

That was no answer at all, but she was unlikely to get a better one. "As you say." Marianna jumped when he wrapped a hand around her upper arm, half guiding, half towing her down the corridor to the lift. They passed several doors that probably housed crew rooms, but there was no way to tell for sure.

She was fine until the lift doors shut, closing them in. A band of fear wrapped around her chest, constricting until spots danced behind her eyes. Marianna swayed, trying to temper her building panic. But the events of the last few days had worn down her hard-won control. A sob built in her throat, her skin feeling as if it were two sizes too small. Too close. It was too close in here. Impossible to believe there was enough air. She couldn't breathe, couldn't think, couldn't move. Time slowed, each heartbeat so loud in her ears that it drowned out everything else. Marianna tried to take a step away from Gerard, to achieve some space, but her knees gave out.

She never hit the floor.

He caught her around the waist, arms tightening to an almost painful level. Being closed in further should have increased her panic, but instead it beat back the waves of fear crashing over her. She closed her eyes, a single tear breaking free and sliding down her cheek.

"Don't cry."

The brusque command gave her the strength to open her eyes and face the tiny lift. It must have stopped moving while she was in the midst of her meltdown because the doors were standing open. "I'm not."

He released her, taking his warmth with him. Marianna chose

not to examine that the very man who signed her death warrant was the same one who comforted her when she was at her weakest. Without looking back, she stumbled into the hallway, arms wrapped around herself. The feeling of spinning out of control continued even though she was no longer in the lift, panic and fear and anger twisting around inside her, more terrifying than the worst of Keiluna's winter storms. Her shoulder hit the wall before Marianna was aware she was weaving. She clutched herself tighter, trying to hold in the sound demanding to be voiced, but it was no use.

Instead of the shriek she envisioned, it came out as a low keen. She slid to the floor, her hands against her face as if that would stop the tears. The sound kept coming, on and on, until she was convinced it would be the last sound she was capable of making.

This time, when Gerard touched her, she was having none of it. She would not find comfort, not from him. She scooted away, shaking her head.

"Marianna…please."

He reached for her again, but she shoved his hands away. The only warning she got was a hard look before he grabbed her around the waist and hauled her through the nearest door. It turned out to be a med bay, as she discovered when he dropped her on the nearest cot. The force of impact shocked her enough to stop that terrible noise coming out of her throat.

Gerard ran his hands through his hair, his jaw clenching. "The tears—you need to stop. I can't handle it." He opened a cabinet to grab a washcloth. After wetting it in a small sans sink, he walked back to her and, almost timidly, reached out to wipe her cheeks.

The absurdity of his comment gave her the pause she needed to fight for control. Marianna held her breath and closed her eyes, the strength leeching from her body as his thumbs traced over her cheeks. The man was so full of contradictions—one moment harsh and unforgiving, the next he was touching her as if she were the most precious thing in the universe. She finally opened her eyes and leaned back, unable to bear it any longer. "Please stop."

He dropped his hand but didn't move back. "I truly am sorry."

"It doesn't really change anything, does it? You can be sorry as much as you like, but I am still going to die horrifically." Unless she could convince him to set her free. Marianna tilted her head up, watching him watch her mouth.

She licked her lips as he leaned forward, intent clear in his expression. This time Gerard made the first move, his mouth crashing into hers. The barely restrained violence of his lips and tongue—and, yes, teeth—made her writhe against him, forgetting that *she* was supposed to be seducing *him*. Marianna gripped the front of his shirt, giving in when he pushed her onto her back and climbed on top of her.

Gerard settled into the cradle of her hips, moaning against her mouth when she wrapped her legs around him. His hands felt so big when he ran them over her body, stripping off her shirt in a smooth motion. Desire hardened her nipples as Gerard pushed up to look at her bare breasts, the move rubbing his length against her core. All worries and fears disappeared beneath the need to have him inside her. Marianna fumbled with his pants, finally giving up and ripping at his shirt instead. He gave a breathless curse and pulled it off, collapsing back on top of her and reclaiming her mouth.

Having his bare skin against her own was almost too good to bear. She needed more. So much more.

They both froze when the door slid open. Gerard gave a growl worthy of any Beshmaiite and snatched his shirt, using it to cover her nakedness. She couldn't move, pinned beneath his body, but Marianna got a good view of Fisk's shocked face before Gerard shouted, *"Out!"*

One look at Gerard's closed-off expression was all she needed. There would be no more chances for seduction in the future. Ladydamnit.

CHAPTER EIGHT

"*Y*ou know, I thought you had it under control. Obviously, you don't."

Gerard didn't need to follow the direction of Fisk's chin jerk to know what he'd seen. Marianna. Strapped in and ready for the ship to jump. Terrified. Oh, she didn't show it—hadn't shown anything since he tossed over her shirt and walked away—but he could see fear in the stiff line of her shoulders and the way she clutched her stomach as if holding something physical in.

"Leoni."

"I have it under control."

"No, you don't." Fisk grabbed his shoulder, preventing him from moving away. "Gerard, you have to stop. It's going to be bad enough, even without the extra complications, but you're making it worse."

"I don't want to talk about it."

"You're being a Ba'al-damned idiot." Fisk dropped his hand when Adam and Blaine walked into the hub. The redhead glanced at Marianna and blushed, moving to the chair farthest from her. Adam looked at her, too, but his gaze lingered in a predatory way.

"My, my, my, what a pretty little thing you are." Adam leaned down and brushed a strand of hair from her face, speaking in a low voice. "The boss has been keeping you from me, but soon enough we'll have an opportunity to be alone. Promise."

Gerard didn't realize he'd moved until Fisk stopped him with a hand to the chest. "Get strapped in, Adam," the other man said. "We're almost to the warp point."

Adam looked from Fisk to Gerard, his cool blue eyes seeing too much. "I'm aware of that."

"Then stop yapping and sit down." Gerard didn't move, forcing Adam to skirt around him to get into the cockpit. Fisk shook his head and followed Adam, leaving Gerard to take care of himself. The knot in his shoulders didn't loosen until the door slid shut between them.

When he dropped into the seat next to Marianna, he could feel the tension pulsing off her in waves. Every instinct Gerard possessed demanded he reach out—comfort her, hold her, protect her. It was only through sheer willpower—and Blaine's presence beside him—that he strapped himself in and leaned his head back without looking over.

They hit the warp point with no warning from Adam—typical—and the ship shuddered, all the bits and pieces rattling. If he hadn't heard it a thousand times before, he'd be concerned the damned thing was going to fly apart under the pressure.

Marianna made a small sound, a combination of a choked scream and a gasp, her hands grasping for the harness. It was too much. Gerard grabbed the one hand he could reach and pressed it against her lap. "All will be well."

"Please. Stop. Touching. Me."

"I will when we're through." He massaged her fingers, ignoring the tension there, and trying not to be bothered by it. The ship gave one final squeal and then they were back into straight space.

She freed her hands and rubbed at her arms. "So cold."

"What?" Gerard unhooked himself and turned to face her. All color was leeched from Marianna's skin, her breath coming in little pants as she attempted to curl in upon herself. It didn't work—the harness kept her from succeeding. He got her out of it as quickly as possible, which wasn't easy to do with the shivers racking her body.

"Come here." He lifted her, ignoring Blaine's wide-eyed look, and strode from the hub. Remembering Marianna's reaction to the lift, he took the stairs. By the time he hit the second deck, her shivers had lost their violence. Gerard stopped in front of her door, torn between the desire to let go and walk away, and the desire to go into her cabin and ensure she was okay.

Except she wasn't okay.

Marianna pressed a hand against his chest. "You can put me down now, Gerard."

He didn't want to, but he obeyed, then watched as she walked into her cabin without looking back.

. . .

Marianna sat cross-legged on her cot, shuffling her cards. She had managed to hold off doing a reading up until now for fear of what it might say, but it was time. The Lady had pushed her into this situation for a reason. She had to believe the end result wouldn't be another pointless Diviner death at the altar of Sanctify's bloodthirsty god.

Trying to ignore the way her hands shook, she dealt out a full reading in a *V* formation. It wasn't a spread she normally did, but it felt right for the situation.

She ignored the temptation to flip them all at once, instead starting with the card representing the past. "The Star." Well, that was no surprise—if Darla hadn't found her, saved her from those men, her life would have turned out a lot differently. The older girl had taken her in, taught her how to survive, offered her hope. Marianna returned the favor as often as she could, helping others whenever she had the capabilities to do so, but she was only one person, and some of them fell through the cracks. It wasn't something she liked to think about.

Moving on to the present, she was similarly unsurprised. The Hanged Man. Since she was in a situation where she couldn't move forward and was forced to simply react to others' actions, it made sense. The future seemed almost to contradict it, though. Seven of Wands. Continue soldiering on and fighting.

Frustrated, she flipped the remaining cards, taking in the reading as a whole. The presence of The Lovers seemed to indicate that she was on the correct track with her attempts to seduce Gerard. Good. And not solely because she longed for another opportunity to kiss him again. The man might be gruff and nearly unbearable, but he made her head spin and her blood heat.

The Emperor was an outside influence. She stroked the bearded face on the card. *Gerard.* It all kept coming back to him. He was her way out. The Nine of Wands made her think that perhaps her efforts weren't in vain. And then the final outcome—Justice.

Panic fluttered inside her throat, but she beat it back. There was hope of justice being served, but it was not without a price. She would not go to her death quietly—was grateful the Lady didn't ask such an impossible task of her. As she gathered up the cards, one fell out, landing face up.

The High Priestess.

She picked it up and tapped it against her knee, staring at the picture on the card. Trust her intuition. So be it. Marianna slipped her cards back into their bag, mind still preoccupied with searching out the different meanings of the Lady's message. There was a way out. There had to be.

CHAPTER NINE

"*I*t's time."

Marianna tried to compose her face, refusing to let any disappointment or fear show. With Gerard, she might have allowed a sliver of emotion through her shield, but Fisk was another story altogether. Ever since she'd read his cards, he acted as if she didn't exist. The redheaded boy—Blaine—did the same thing, but it hurt more coming from a man who had shown Marianna kindness.

She stood and smoothed her hand over her wrinkled clothes, wishing for the opportunity to change them. It would make no difference, though—her path was already laid before her and different clothes would only be an imaginary shield between her and her captors. Better to do away with such indulgences now. She was not safe—had never been less safe in her life, even when homeless and surviving as a pickpocket.

"I'm ready." A lie, but one he allowed her. Fisk stepped back and motioned Marianna through the door. Then he led the way to the stairs. They descended in silence but for the echoing of their footsteps. The engine room was the same as last time she'd been through, the huge machine taking up most of the area, leaving only a narrow space to walk.

She wrapped her arms around herself as they approached the ramp leading out of the ship. Beyond the doorway, it was daytime, the light so bright it hurt her eyes even from this distance. Marianna wouldn't allow herself to balk, though, and kept walking, head held high. Taking that last step into the outside world was one of the hardest of her life, but she pushed forward, refusing to let them see her fear.

They had set down in a shipyard, surrounded by other white warships. The entire area was paved, but on the outskirts of the lot, nature had already begun to fight back, weeds springing up between the cracks in the ground, the trees creating a wall of sorts, their roots opening the cracks even farther. A sweet wind kicked up to tease her hair from her face. Marianna closed her eyes and pretended it smelled of Keiluna, instead of this planet that had once been her people's homeland. But Sanctify had poisoned that in much the same way they poisoned everything they touched. Those monsters killed every man, woman, and child they could get their hands on and drove the rest of the Diviners to the far corners of the universe.

A hand in the middle of her back shoved her forward, sending her tumbling. She landed on her knees, cuffed hands barely coming up in time to keep her from skinning her face. She turned her head sideways in time to see a boot raised to kick.

Something snapped deep in her soul. Marianna gave a hiss to do any reptile proud and lunged, hitting her attacker around the waist. He cursed as they went over the side of the ramp and fell a full meter before hitting the ground. She reared up, catching sight of Adam's murderous look, brought her cuffed hands over her head, and slammed them down on that snarling mouth.

No more. She would submit no longer. Marianna managed two more hits before he flipped them and lifted his fist.

Then Gerard was there, tackling the blond man before his

fist could make contact. Marianna scrambled to her feet, ready to assist, but Blaine and Fisk grabbed her upper arms, trapping her between them.

Helpless, she was forced to watch Gerard and Adam roll around on the ground as they exchanged blows. Blood flew with each impact. The sheer violence of it drained away her own desire to inflict as much pain as possible on her captors. What had she been thinking to attack? It made her no better than the monsters who wanted her dead. Marianna bit her lip and struggled against the ridiculous urge to cry. Tears would solve her problems no more than violence had.

Truth be told, there was only one way out of this mess and he was now striding toward her, blood oozing from a cut above his right eye and another on his lip. She wanted to wipe it away, but the scathing look he sent her killed that foolish notion. Gerard nodded at Fisk. "Get her situated in one of the cells—*unharmed*. I will make my report to the High Priest and meet you afterward."

"Yes, sir."

He and Blaine turned her around and marched toward the low white building on the other side of the shipyard. It was nondescript, its edges rounded as if it stood here so long, the wind and rain had beaten even that much originality from it. But that was merely a fanciful thought—a few hundred years wasn't long enough to see that kind of elemental change.

Two white-robed guards stood near the entrance. Both perked up when they saw Fisk, seconds before their attention zeroed in on her.

"Ba'al be damned, Fisk, tell me that's not a Diviner?" The speaker was tall and lanky, not yet old enough to move past the awkward stage of adolescence. Beneath his black skin, his Adam's apple bobbed madly.

"Mind your own business, Drew."

Instead of obeying, Drew moved toward them. On closer

inspection, she noticed his skin actually had blue highlights. He was really quite pretty—if she ignored the zealous gleam in his eyes. He ducked down, face centimeters from Marianna's. "Never seen one of them in real life before. Is it true they actually believe they can tell the future?"

"We can."

She realized her mistake when his lips thinned. "No, you can't, you little bitch. Only Ba'al's High Priest has that ability. It was given to him—and only him—as a demonstration of Ba'al's love for us."

Marianna blinked, temporarily sidetracked. "Is that really what you believe?" Why in the Lady's name would a god restrict the future to only one person in the entire universe? It was the ultimate act of selfishness.

"It's the *truth*."

"Step back, Drew. Now."

For a moment, she didn't think he'd obey, but then he moved away, his gaze never leaving her eyes. She would do well to remember that most of these men weren't like her reluctant captor—they truly wanted her dead.

Fisk and Blaine guided her past the desks and down a long hallway devoid of any decoration. The unrelenting white raised the small hairs on the back of her neck, and the feeling only got worse as they descended a narrow set of stairs. Twenty-seven steps later, they reached a landing and turned left, the hall finally ending in a row of cells. Or that's what she assumed they were, judging from the unblinking red lights on each of the palm locks.

The last one on the right was her destination. Fisk nodded at Blaine and the redhead left them alone. He looked her up and down and sighed. "I'll have some clothes brought down for you—you can't wear that when the High Priest sees you."

"I'm to meet the High Priest?"

"Maybe." He shrugged, the move carrying a world of tension.

"Maybe not. It could be that he'll wait to see you until the day of the purification."

The world started to sway, but she dug her nails into her palm until it righted itself. "I see."

"Everything else aside, I truly am sorry it has to be this way."

Unable to look upon his guilt, she turned away. "I know." But sorry wasn't going to help her. "Will I see Gerard again before the...purification?"

"He's free to come and go as he pleases."

"I see." She could only hope and pray that he would come to talk to her sometime before then. As it was, her chances weren't looking good.

Fisk's footsteps started for the door. "Good-bye, Marianna."

"Good-bye, Fisk." She waited until the door slid shut behind him to whisper, "Lady bless you and keep you."

CHAPTER TEN

*G*erard knelt before the High Priest, fists clenching rhythmically at his sides as he tried to recite Ba'al's Benediction in his head. The words and the calm they usually brought escaped him. He couldn't get past the first cursed line. *Purity will protect you…*

"A Diviner, you say? Are you completely sure, boy?"

Gerard kept his head bowed as the old man walked a slow circle around him. He hadn't been a boy for ages, but damned if the High Priest would acknowledge it. "Yes, sir. She's definitely a Diviner. All the indicators are there—including the fact she carries a deck of their cards everywhere."

"Fascinating. I haven't seen one of their ilk in… It's been five years?"

"Ten years, sir."

"Don't correct me, boy. I know more than you ever will."

Heat built beneath Gerard's skin, and he was sure his face had turned a mottled red. He gritted his teeth. "Yes, sir."

"I believe we shall make an event of her purification. The autumn festival is in seven days. That shall be enough time to create quite the spectacle. Don't you agree?"

Seven days wasn't nearly long enough. Gerard bit back his knee-jerk response. Protesting wouldn't do anything at this point. Hells, it never did anything when it came to the High Priest. Gerard need only to think of his blood coating the stones outside the barracks while the High Priest droned on about the importance of expansion to be reminded of the fact. He refused to take that road again. The High Priest wasn't one to give second chances and next time it was sure to be significantly bloodier.

If only there was another way...

He shut down the line of thinking before it could go any further. "As you say."

"That's right, boy, as *I* say. Do not think I overlooked your previous disobedience. You disappointed me greatly." He gave a heavy sigh. "Rise."

Gerard carefully schooled his face before rising. The High Priest was well past his prime, shoulders beginning to stoop, his graying hair receding another centimeter or two a year. The lines that had once seemed to indicate a life lived with strength now were deeper and screamed weakness. Still, it was unlikely he'd die anytime soon. "High Priest."

"Go. Rest. We shall speak again before the purification ceremony."

Gerard turned and left the room before the man could change his mind. Darkness had fallen while he was kept waiting, cooling his heels while the High Priest did whatever it was he did when not meeting with his lieutenants. Gerard didn't stop until he passed the twin buildings where the dorms were located, rage rising with each step he took. He'd hand-delivered a damned Diviner to the High Priest and all he got was another reminder of his past punishment. He should have realized his disobedience wouldn't be so easily forgotten—no sin was ever forgotten in this place. If this encounter were any indication, it would be years before he could earn the trust of the High Priest again.

Which meant he'd sentenced Marianna to death for *nothing*.

Gerard doused the thought and its accompanying guilt. There was only one person he wanted to see right now, and he'd find him in the only pub the High Priest allowed to conduct business near the barracks.

Sure enough, Fisk was sitting in his customary seat, alone at a corner table the lights didn't quite reach. Gerard dropped into the empty chair across from him and ran his hands through his hair. "I talked to him."

"And?" Fisk's voice was completely devoid of emotion, which meant he was trying like crazy to keep something hidden.

"The…purification…is set for the autumn equinox."

"Seven days." Fisk drained his glass and set it on the table with a *thump*. He motioned the bartender without even looking. "A week."

"Generally there are seven days in a week." Gerard eyed the glass set in front of him. Three fingers of the best alcohol brewed on Keiluna. Ba'al be damned, did everything come back to Marianna? She was like a curse he couldn't shake, burrowing under his skin and wrapping around his mind until it was difficult to think of anything else.

"It's not all that long." Fisk lifted his drink and considered it, the amber liquid sloshing this way and that. "Are you prepared to watch Marianna tortured and burned to death?"

Gerard cast a quick look around, but the nearest patron was three tables away, well out of hearing range. "Purified."

"Pretty it up all you want, but that doesn't change the reality of the situation. She will be cut apart, joint by joint, each wound cauterized so she won't bleed out." Fisk leaned forward, lowering his voice until Gerard had to strain to hear, even though hearing was the last thing he wanted. "She will try to be strong at first and, knowing Marianna, she will last longer than the others. But then something in her will break, and she will beg and plead and, eventually, all she will do is scream."

"I don't want to talk about this anymore."

"You can't even talk about it and you expect to be able to watch it?" Fisk shook his head, staring off toward the door.

No, he didn't expect to be able to watch it and be unaffected. Even thinking about Marianna being hurt made a pit open up in his stomach, a dark place that he wasn't sure he could come back from. Gerard downed his drink in one shot, the liquid burning its way to his stomach. Sitting with Fisk hadn't settled him the way he'd hoped it would. "I'm going to get some sleep."

"If you can stomach it. I don't know that I can."

Gerard stood and wove his way through the tables, nodding at the men who met his gaze. There weren't many who would after watching Gerard whipped until he couldn't so much as stand on his own. Some refused to be seen as aligning themselves with him for fear that he would fall completely out of favor and bring them down as well. Others had lost all respect for him after seeing the public humiliation.

The night pressed against Gerard as he strode down the walkway, trying to outrun the demons chasing at his heels. It didn't work, but then, he hadn't expected it to. He never should have brought Marianna here. Hells, Gerard couldn't even bear to *think* about what was to come, let alone what his life would be like afterward.

His life. Something he hadn't spent much time contemplating as he grew older. Now, though, it stretched before him, blacker than the deepest abyss.

A figure detached itself from the nearest building and sauntered toward him. Gerard looked at the sky, wondering why Ba'al had chosen today of all days to make the world fall apart around him.

Lizbeth was exotically beautiful, her hair long and thick and blending in with the shadows around her. Men followed her everywhere, practically begging for any attention she'd give them. Once upon a time, she'd given her smiles to Gerard. Now her slanted eyes held nothing but disdain. "You've been gone longer than expected."

"I've been gone exactly as long as expected." Gerard wanted nothing more than to turn away and leave her standing there, but honor held him fast. This woman was the mother of his son—he owed it to her to at least attempt respect. "How have you been? How is Oberon?"

She cocked her hip, giving him a good view of the curves that had once caught his eye. Her dark gray shift couldn't conceal the fact she had nothing on underneath. "Come home. I've missed you."

It was a lie. Lizbeth only wanted the perks that came along with his position. Before, Gerard had been content to take what she offered. No longer. Not since he learned what cruelty hid behind the beautiful mask. It was years ago now, but he still remembered the disgust on her face when he had the audacity to want to lean on her after a particularly tough mission. It wasn't a mistake he'd make again. "I'm tired, Lizbeth. I'll come by tomorrow and see Oberon."

"You're so Ba'al-damned transparent." She looked him up and down before flicking her hair over her shoulder. "You got what you wanted—a son. What is left for me?"

"You have everything. Do you think I like only seeing my son on the rare occasions I'm allowed home? I want to be here."

"With *him*." Lizbeth slashed a hand through the air. "You care nothing for me."

Gerard looked around, grateful there was no one else out tonight. "You knew what I offered when we first met. I can't be a husband to you—to anyone."

"Liar. How could I not feel something for you when you held me just so, treated me so well?"

The worst part was that she actually had a point. For months after Lizbeth told him she was pregnant, he tried. Ba'al, how he tried. Gerard had grown up without parents, with only his comrades and teachers as his companions. Maybe if he could give his child a life with two loving parents, his son could circumvent the fate that had sucked Gerard in.

But Lizbeth had only seen him as a one-way ticket to a higher class of people. She didn't care about making a partnership with him—or the child growing in her womb. And so their relationship didn't last past Oberon's birth.

Looking at her now, Gerard might have actually felt bad if there were tears glittering in those black eyes. Instead, there was only hate. "I'm sorry, Lizbeth. I never meant it to turn out this way."

"No, I'm sure you didn't. Men never do once the child has come."

"That's not fair."

"I'm done, Gerard. Come by and see your son if you wish. This is the last time I try to make you love me." She turned and sauntered into the night, hips swinging as if she wanted him to know just what he would be missing in the future.

Funny. With all her curves and exotic good looks, Lizbeth didn't hold a candle to Marianna.

CHAPTER ELEVEN

Oberon was growing like a weed. Gerard tossed him into the air, the boy's giggles bringing a smile to his face. He was the only good thing that had come from the mess with Lizbeth.

Gerard let himself fall back onto the grass and roll down the small hill, keeping the boy sheltered in the bracket of his arms. They tumbled to a laughing mess at the bottom, Oberon sitting on his chest and raising his tiny fists to the cloudy sky.

Stretching, Gerard toppled him sideways. "I love you, boy."

Oberon sat up, babbling in a string of syllables that meant absolutely nothing to him. He reached forward and grabbed a handful of Gerard's hair, tugging on it. Whatever he was saying, it was of the utmost seriousness. Gerard grinned, meeting those large black eyes—his mother's eyes, but without all the complicated emotions. Just joy at spending time with his father.

A drop of rain splattered against his forehead, quickly followed by another. Soon it was pouring, soaking their clothing. Gerard stood, scooping up Oberon on the way, and hurried across the open ground. The village was a quick hover ride away, but he didn't want to take his son back yet. Their time together was already limited enough without him shortening it.

So he headed to his dorm room. The building was like a honeycomb, riddled with rooms and hallways that interconnected in ways only someone who walked it regularly would understand. Tossing Oberon on the bed made the boy break out in giggles again.

He barely had a chance to change and sit when his door burst open. Fisk staggered in, his skin an unhealthy gray color. "She was right. Ba'al-damnit, she was right."

Gerard moved Oberon out of the way before the other man could crush him and sat back, the boy settled in his lap. "Take a deep breath." He waited while Fisk followed the command.

"She was right. The Diviner."

"Marianna?" The black pit inside him got a bit wider. "Tell me what's going on. Slowly."

"She did a reading." Fisk held up a hand before Gerard could speak. "I know. I should never have let her do it—but I'm glad I did. She tried to poison me."

Gerard's emotional spiral skidded to a sudden stop. "What? Marianna tried to poison you? How in the hells did she manage—?"

"No, no. That's not what I meant. *Leandra* tried to poison me. She just... I thought she loved me. Things were so good with us." Fisk pushed to his feet and stalked from one wall to the other. "They were great. But when we were getting ready for bed, she goes crazy, starts accusing me of screwing around on her. Hells, she even named names. Where the fuck do women get this shit?"

Gerard hugged Oberon to his chest, thinking of Lizbeth. "I have no idea."

"Then, this morning, she's as sweet as pie, smiling and telling me she loves me." Fisk laughed, the sound full of despair. "She even made breakfast—my favorite."

That didn't sound like Leandra at all. From what Gerard had seen, she was a milder version of Lizbeth—only after the security

and financial stability of Fisk's position within Sanctify. "But...
she *poisoned* you?"

"She tried. Would have succeeded if not for Marianna."

"I don't understand—what does Marianna have to do with
this?"

"The reading, man." Fisk spun on his heel, throwing up his
hands and startling Oberon.

The boy burst into tears, wailing at the top of his lungs.
Gerard stood, rocking him until he calmed, screams quieting to
pathetic little whimpers. Oberon wrapped tiny arms around his
neck and said, "Dada."

Gerard blinked. "Did he just say what I think he said?"

"Sounded like he called you Dada. Can we get back to me?"

Gerard didn't want to. All he wanted was to cuddle his boy
close and listen to Oberon call him Dada again and again. But
life intruded, just as it always did. "Sorry. Yes. You were saying?"

"Marianna gave me a reading. She told me that things would
go south with me and the woman I was with. That this woman
would try to kill me, through devious means."

Gerard shook his head, finally tearing his gaze from Oberon.
"Wait—Marianna told you this? When?"

"Back on the ship." Fisk spun again, catching himself when
he started to yell. He continued in a quieter tone. "There's no
way she could have known then. Hells, there's no way she could
know now. *So how did she?*"

"I don't know. Maybe you're wrong?" The alternative was
mind-blowing. Instinctively, he reached for Ba'al's Benediction,
trying to draw it around him as he'd been taught from childhood.
Purity will... The words went up in smoke, disappearing from his
memory as if they hadn't been drilled there ever since he could
remember. He gave up trying, turning instead to the logical
conclusion of what Fisk was saying.

If the Diviners actually could tell the future... Gerard shook his head, rubbing Oberon's back. He didn't want to finish the thought, but he had to. If the Diviners actually could tell the future, then one of the very foundations of his faith was false. If they could actually tell the future, they weren't blasphemers. If they weren't blasphemers, then they were being killed for nothing.

Marianna would be killed for nothing.

And if one of the foundations of Sanctify was false, who was to say the rest were true? Gerard had killed countless aliens over the years and never thought twice about it—they were vile creatures, blemishes removed in order to contribute to the greater honor of Ba'al.

But…what if they really were innocents?

The implication nearly sent him to his knees. "You have to be wrong."

"I'm not wrong. I tasted the blood leaf before I spat it out. There's nothing else that has that same bitter flavor. Leandra tried to kill me, and Marianna saved me." Fisk froze, eyes widening. "I need to see her. To thank her. I have to go now."

"Wait—Fisk!" But it was too late. Fisk was gone.

Gerard stared at the open door for a long moment, and then looked down at his son, wondering how his entire world could collapse in the course of a week—all at the hands of a single woman.

• • •

Marianna was ready for him. As soon as Fisk appeared, all apologies and terrified thanks, she'd known Gerard would come for her. He wouldn't be able to stay away, not with his best friend acting the way Fisk was.

Still, when the door slid open to reveal him, her breath caught in her throat, and it was everything she could do not to throw herself into his arms and beg him to save her. But that wouldn't do. Instead, she dredged up a smile. "Good afternoon, Gerard."

His glower was so fierce she could almost see the emotional darkness plaguing him. "I don't see a damn thing good about it. You've ruined everything."

Well, that wasn't the best way to begin this conversation. It certainly didn't bode well for things to come. Marianna laced her hands behind her back, hoping he wouldn't know it was to hide their shaking. "What have I ruined?"

"Everything." He took up more space than was fair, seeming to draw in the very air in the room until she felt lightheaded. "Your reading saved Fisk."

"I know." And she'd thanked the Lady every hour since he left because of it. Sanctify or not, he was a good man and didn't deserve to die. Not like that; not at the hands of a vengeful woman.

"You obviously don't know what that means." There he went, running his hands through his hair again. "It changes everything. I have never questioned the way things are. *Never*. It's how I was raised—it was the truth I lived by. And now I can't stop questioning. This all started with *you*—if you can tell the future, then the teachings of the High Priest aren't completely accurate. If they aren't completely accurate…" He turned to her, and the torment on his face was a terrible thing to behold. "Do you know how many aliens I've killed, Marianna? Because I don't. I never even bothered to count. What if they've died for *nothing*?"

She wanted to take Gerard in her arms and comfort him—it was a tragedy to have one's beliefs rocked so thoroughly, even if he had been one of the monsters. Instead, she kept her voice light and soothing, instinctively knowing that he wouldn't take any comfort she offered. "There is nothing I can say to make you feel better about this. We can't change the past. We shouldn't even try. But the one thing that we can change is the future—only you have the ability to do that."

"What is that—more Diviner mumbo jumbo?"

"No." She gave a soft laugh. Far from it. She'd learned that from Darla, though the girl had put it a lot differently. "It's the truth. One that's very hard to stomach."

"I see." He moved closer, still staying just out of reach. "And if I asked you to tell my future...would you?"

Something told her that to know his future was to know her own—they were tied together. But what if she was wrong? Her chest constricted at the thought. "I would have to, or else risk falling violently out of favor with the Lady. But, please, don't ask me. I can't bear to know."

"To tell you the truth, I don't have any desire to know, either. Today is enough trouble without borrowing from tomorrow." Gerard sighed. "I have to go now, but I'll be back and we'll talk more." He left before she could decide if he meant the words as a threat or a promise.

CHAPTER TWELVE

*G*erard thought of nothing but Marianna for three days. Of the truth she represented. There was no other way to look at things. He'd been lied to from childhood, had been conditioned into being the perfect killing machine. The High Priest had pointed at a target, spouted Ba'al's Benediction, and Gerard had never once questioned it.

He really was one of the monsters.

But no longer. Marianna was right—he couldn't change the past, but he could start on a new future. But first he had to get her out of that cell. After that…well, he'd worry about that when the time came. But he'd take her and he'd take his boy, and they'd fly until the whole universe separated them from Sanctify.

He tried to spend time with Oberon, but the boy seemed to sense his inattention and became a squalling, shrieking mess when out of sight of his mother. Any other time it wouldn't have mattered, but Gerard was in no frame of mind to deal with a fussy toddler.

Finally, it was too much. He couldn't stay away from her any longer.

Drew was on duty, the boy lounging against the front desk.

He snapped to attention when Gerard came through the door, trying to pretend he wasn't slacking off. "Sir."

"Relax. I'm not here for an inspection." The best way to avoid suspicion was to keep everyone else on the defensive, so he made a show of looking around. There were scuff marks on the floor and a fine layer of pollen covered everything, brought in from the trees surrounding the town. "If I was, you'd be in some serious trouble. This place is disgusting."

"I'm sorry, sir. I'll get right on it, sir."

"Do that." While the kid was still sputtering out excuses, Gerard walked past him and headed down the stairs. Drew might be the darling of his superior officers, but he wouldn't go far enough to be a lieutenant. He was too lazy and he lacked the drive that made men shoot up through the ranks of Sanctify. A drive Gerard had once possessed. No longer, though. Not for Sanctify. Everything was changing, the world blurring and melting around him.

There was another guard sitting at the end of the white hallway where the prisoners were kept. He, at least, was alert, standing at attention with his hand on his laser. "Is there something I can help you with, sir?"

Damn. He hadn't put much thought into what people would think of him coming to visit the fabled Diviner. Again. "I need to question the prisoner. High Priest's orders."

The guard gave him a slow once-over, as if he couldn't quite believe it was the truth. In the end, though, he had no choice but to allow Gerard entry. "Do you need assistance?"

"No. I can handle one w—female. Not as if she's a Bolkerian."

They shared a laugh as the palm lock flashed green. And then there was nothing keeping him from her. Marianna stood as he entered the room, kicking something under her cot. The cards, no doubt. But he wasn't interested in them—had no interest in her future-telling abilities, either. If he was going to be honest with himself, the only reason he was here was to see her. She was the one who had started this storm in his life, and when he was with her was the only time he didn't feel as if he were about to be swept away. Gerard waited until the door shut behind him to speak. "How are you doing?"

She started to cross her arms over her chest, abandoning the motion halfway through. "As well as can be expected, I suppose."

"No one's hurt you?" His vision bled red at the thought of anyone laying hands on her. But she was shaking her head. Gerard made an effort to release the tension that wound through every one of his muscles. "Good."

"Gerard…" She bit her lip. "I, ah…"

"Ask." As if he could deny her anything within his power right now. The next three days lay before them, a timeline Gerard couldn't do a damn thing to change. Regret was sour on his tongue, burning from his throat to his stomach.

"Would you mind…holding me…just for a few moments?"

He blinked. Whatever he'd expected, it wasn't for her to seek comfort with the very person responsible for her situation. If it weren't for him, Marianna would still be on Keiluna, doing… whatever it was she did there. Ba'al be damned, it felt like she'd been in his life forever and he still knew next to nothing about her. "Of course." Gerard sat on the cot and waited for her to approach him.

For a long moment, it seemed as if she'd reconsidered, but then Marianna slid carefully next to him, perching on the edge of the mattress as if she expected to flee at any moment. That wouldn't do.

"You asked me to hold you." Without waiting for permission, Gerard scooped her up and settled her in his lap. She was so thin. Too thin. "Have you been eating?"

Marianna laughed. "I haven't had much of an appetite."

Of course not. He was an idiot for not taking that into consideration. Well, if he couldn't change their current reality, he could definitely distract them both for a time. Gerard scooted until his back hit the wall and stretched out his legs. There wasn't much space on the cot—hells, there wasn't much space in the room itself—but the only other option was the floor. "Tell me about yourself."

"I hardly think that's appropriate."

Now it was his turn to laugh. "I've seen you half naked—there isn't much that's inappropriate after that. Did you grow up on Keiluna?"

"You're not going to allow this to drop, are you?"

The echo of their first conversation hit him like a punch from a Bolkerian. Had it really been just over a week ago? "No. So you might as well submit."

"As if I haven't heard that line before." She started to relax, tracing her finger along his forearm. The innocent touch was distracting as hells. There was no hiding his reaction to it, but she didn't mention it, and he'd be damned before he willingly let her go. "Yes, I grew up on Keiluna."

"What was it like?" All he'd ever known was Sanctify, first the elementary dorms and school, then secondary, then on to officer academy. The only thing that really changed was the level of physical training. Everything else stayed the same, from the monochrome walls that he wasn't allowed to decorate, to the hard cot, to the harsh lessons.

"It was difficult at times." When he moved to look at her, she gave a half smile. "My parents died when I was a child, barely ten years old. Since I had no close relatives, I ended up in an orphanage, which wasn't completely terrible. But I was willful and thought I knew what was best, so I ran away. Through luck and happenstance, I fell in with a group of street children, and we looked out for one another."

He waited, drinking in the small smile she wore. "You enjoyed it."

"Yes, some days. I'm quite the pickpocket, though I haven't had reason to practice in years. But, there were times when food ran scarce or we were hurt by others—"

"Who hurt you?" Again, anger rushed through him, more heady and dangerous than Keiluna's homegrown brew.

Marianna leaned her head against his chest, the fresh smell of her hair wrapping around him. At least someone—probably Fisk—had ensured she was allowed to use the sans shower. "There was always someone larger or angrier. These things happened. It's just life."

"You have a very odd explanation of 'just life.' Were you ever…you know?" As soon as the words were out of his mouth, he shook his head. "Never mind. You don't have to answer that." He didn't know if he could handle it if her answer was anything but negative.

"It's all right. No, I was never hurt in that way. Just mugged a time or two."

He had a feeling her count was off by more than a handful, but Gerard made an effort to let it go. As she said, there was no point in nitpicking right now. The past was the past and there was no changing it, no matter how much he wanted to go back and save that willful child. What a ridiculous thought, considering their circumstances. Instead of traveling further down that mental road, he pressed a kiss to her temple. "I'm glad."

"Yes, well, everything happens for a reason." Marianna shifted, looking up at him until he was drowning in her violet eyes. "Do you believe in fate, Gerard?"

Unable to help himself, he traced a thumb across her bottom lip. "I don't know. Some days, maybe. Others, not so much."

She shivered, opening her mouth for him. It was all the invitation he needed. Gerard leaned down and kissed her, tongue tracing slowly along hers, leisurely, enjoying every second of it.

Pulling her closer, he slipped a hand beneath her shift, cupping her hip. Like this, she felt so fragile, almost breakable. Then she arched into him, her nails digging into his arm. "More. Please, Gerard."

He couldn't ignore a plea like that, not when he wanted it as much as she did. Gerard slid down, moving her until she straddled his waist. Giving a whimper that made him want to protect her and get her out of her clothes all at once, Marianna sat up just enough to look at him. "I need you naked."

Gerard could do that.

CHAPTER THIRTEEN

They made short work of his clothes and then hers, pausing frequently to kiss and touch. And then there was nothing left between them. Gerard's hands on her hips were the only thing keeping her from doing exactly what she wanted. He held her pinned even though she was on top, the angle all wrong to finish this. Desire beat through her body, rising higher with each heartbeat until all she could think of was touching him, loving him.

His free hand seemed to be everywhere at once, driving her out of her mind. Drifting over her ribs, light as a feather, down her spine, pausing to cup first one breast and then the other. She returned the favor, stroking his stomach, chest, shoulders. Scars covered his torso. She recognized a few knife wounds and other, harsher ones. Instead of dampening her attraction, they only increased it. This was a true man—a warrior. And, in this moment, he was hers and hers alone.

Finally, it was too much. Marianna dug her nails into his arms. "Gerard, if you don't finish this—now—I may just die."

"Trust me."

Gerard slithered down the cot as he lifted her and settled

her on his chest, her knees on either side of his head. Marianna straightened, looking down her body at him. The position was slightly awkward, but she didn't get a chance to say so before his mouth found her core. She slapped a hand over her mouth to muffle her shriek, but she was already too far gone to worry about being overheard. The pain of his fingers digging into her skin perfectly counteracted the pleasure of his tongue, heightening it until she wasn't sure where he ended and she began. And then it was too much—she shuddered, still trying to smother her cries even as he pushed her over the edge.

Marianna collapsed, barely catching herself on the wall. Aftershocks sparked as Gerard shifted, rolling them until he hovered over her. He smoothed her hair from her face, lips quirked into a smug smile. "Are you okay?"

As soon as she could form a coherent thought, she'd give him an answer. Or perhaps she wouldn't. Marianna kissed him, tasting herself on his tongue. She drew back long enough to say, *"More."* Then her mouth was back on his, teeth raking over his bottom lip.

Gerard found her with his fingers, first one and then two. It was too much. Too much and not enough. Even as she thrashed, she needed him there with her. "I need you."

"Yes." His fingers disappeared long enough to be replaced by exactly what she wanted. Gerard pushed his way inside her using slow, shallow strokes. He propped himself up on his forearms, dark eyes seeming to look into her soul. Desperate, Marianna grabbed his hips, trying to force him to move faster, deeper.

He groaned again. "You're killing me." Then Gerard slammed into her, withdrawing almost completely before he did it again.

"Yes. Oh, yes, *yes*." She couldn't seem to draw a full breath, her voice coming out in a gasp. Pressure started low in her stomach, building with each stroke. So close, so terribly close to what she needed. Reaching further, she dug her nails into his backside, driving him on. He kissed her as she went under, borne away on a tide of passion beyond anything she'd ever known. He kept going, finishing with a shudder that tore through his entire body before he collapsed on top of her.

Marianna wrapped her legs around Gerard's waist, trying to get him as close as possible, and ran her fingers through his hair. He responded by slipping an arm under the small of her back and kissing her again. "Gods, woman, how did you manage to turn my entire life on its head just by walking into it?"

"Because she's a whore and, as the past has shown us, you have a taste for whores."

There was nowhere to hide. Gerard didn't move except to turn his head to the door. Marianna followed suit, instantly trying to shrink away from the older man standing there. Every instinct went on red alert, screaming at her to run as fast and as far as she could.

"High Priest. How surprising." Ice was warmer than Gerard's tone.

"I shouldn't think so. You are in one of my cells, after all, seducing my prisoner." The man turned his attention on her. "You're quite a fetching young thing, aren't you?"

"Stay away from her." Gerard leaned over and grabbed his shirt, using it to cover her when he stood. "I'm to blame for this."

"Of that I have no doubt." The High Priest looked at her as if he could see through the flimsy fabric covering her nakedness. "However, the truth remains that she is, in fact, a Diviner. So your self-sacrifice is for nothing."

Gerard glanced at her, his gaze containing so many things. Things she had no name for. "No. Not for nothing."

"Guards. Take him. Strip him of his robes—he's no longer a lieutenant of Sanctify, though whether he's to be burned as a traitor remains to be seen." The High Priest waited while they did as he commanded. They marched Gerard from the room without a backward glance. The High Priest, on the other hand, lingered. "You are quite lovely for a creature whose very existence defiles our god."

Marianna sat up, careful to keep the shirt pressed against her chest. "Somehow, that does not make me feel any better."

"I imagine not." His smile held all the emotion of a reptile's. "Still…it would be a shame to let such a nubile young thing go to waste. Perhaps I can be…persuaded…to extend your life a bit longer."

Her skin broke out in gooseflesh at the very suggestion and she tasted bile on the back of her tongue. "I think not."

"As you say." With a shrug, he turned and left the room, the door sliding shut behind him.

Marianna hugged her knees to her chest. She pressed the fabric of Gerard's shirt to her face and inhaled deeply, taking in his scent. It was the only thing keeping panic at bay.

No, that was false. There was nothing keeping panic at bay— it hovered just beyond the edge of thought, ready to sweep over her and suck her under. There would be no going back once that happened. Which meant she couldn't let it get to her. Not yet.

She scrambled for her cards, dropping the shirt in the process. It didn't matter—there was no one here to see her, after all. When she tried to shuffle them, the cards flew out of her hands, scattering across the floor. Marianna crawled after them, the first tears slipping through her lashes as she tried to hold in her sobs.

This hadn't gone anything like she'd hoped. She thought seducing Gerard was the answer, but it had only muddled things further. Now, instead of him feeling softer toward her and willing to help, he was locked up as well. And Marianna doubted they treated traitors any better than they did Diviners.

He was going to die along with her, and it was all her fault.

CHAPTER FOURTEEN

"What a disappointment you've turned out to be." The High Priest moved slowly around the table where Gerard was tied, his hands laced loosely behind his back. "I had such high hopes for you."

"So sorry you're dissatisfied with my performance." Gerard pulled against the bindings, unable to help himself. He knew better, though—once you were tied to this table, there was no escaping.

"And yet you don't sound apologetic at all."

"Honestly, I'm surprised you haven't brought out the cat-o'-nine-tails."

"I have yet to decide if you truly are a traitor." He motioned to where Adam stood by. "It's time to begin."

Gerard knew exactly what would happen once Adam started cutting. They might not be ready to kill him, but there was a lot of damage one of Sanctify's enforcers could do without crossing that final line.

Adam pulled his wheeled table closer, lifting a knife so Gerard could see. "She's a new one—I've been wanting to try her out for weeks. How special that it's your blood we'll be shedding to pop her cherry."

Before Gerard could speak, Adam struck, cutting deep across his chest and down his stomach. Shuddering, he bit back a growl of pain, not sure if it was better that he knew where Adam would cut next, or worse.

Right arm. Left arm. Chest, again and again. Things faded beneath a haze of red as rich as the blood flowing from his body. It was almost as if he could feel his strength leeching away with every cut, but they would never make him scream. Never.

And then…it stopped.

He blinked slowly, trying to force his eyes to focus on the High Priest, standing just outside the blood pool. "What—"

"Best not to speak, as you'll only ruin your chance. I'm giving you the opportunity of mercy, you see. Not something we do often, I'll grant you, but I think in this circumstance, it's only fitting. That creature is quite beautiful, and the flesh is weak. You are only a man, after all."

Gerard tried to swallow past the dryness in his throat. "I don't understand."

"Well, boy, it's not as if you're getting away without consequence. That would set a bad example for the men."

Fear started at the base of his spine, spiraling upward. "What did you do?"

"It's not what I did—it's you who is responsible for this."

"What did you do?" He tried to sit up, but the bindings bit into his chest and the pain nearly made him pass out. "Tell me. Please."

It was Adam who answered, his voice far too smug. "Oberon."

His mind went blank for one perfect moment before reality set in. His boy. His giggling little boy. "You did not hurt my son."

"Of course not. What do you take me for?" The High Priest gave a dry chuckle and the bottom of Gerard's stomach dropped out. "His death was quite painless, I can assure you."

No. No, no, no, no, no. Please Ba'al, let it not be true. His breath rasped through his throat, the feeling barely registering against the well of emotional torment. It couldn't be true. Oberon was just a *child*. But Gerard knew better than most that no one was safe from the wrath of Sanctify.

"Not my son, Adam. *Not my boy*."

Adam crossed his arms over his chest, blood dripping in slow plops from the knife still in his hand. "It was the only way to make you see, Leoni. There are always consequences—just like the High Priest said."

The High Priest moved back into his line of sight. "Through your physical and emotional pain you have been cleansed. Now we can move past this small indiscretion and toward the future of Sanctify."

Gerard couldn't feel anything past the cocoon of numbness, couldn't speak, couldn't move as Adam undid his restraints and sat him up. The room swam, but he kept from falling through sheer strength of will.

"I will, however, need your word. You understand, I'm sure."

He looked at the High Priest, wishing there was enough strength in his body to leap off the table and kill the man where he stood. No, that wasn't right. He couldn't do it yet—Marianna was still a prisoner. It was the thought of saving her that gave him the strength to find the appropriate words. "Of course, High Priest. I live to serve. I now see the error of my ways."

"I had hoped you'd come around. Join me in saying Ba'al's Benediction and then we shall get you cleaned up, son."

"Of course." He bowed his head, staring at the blood covering the floor. His blood. The words flowed effortlessly off his lips but, for the first time in Gerard's life, they meant nothing to him. Less than nothing.

When he finished, the High Priest nodded. "There's a good boy." He turned and strode out of the room without a backward glance.

There was no way Gerard could walk. Adam seemed to know it because he scooped Gerard up as if he were no more than a child, carrying him through the halls and outside.

"It'll be just like the good old days, before that bitch came along and started screwing with your head."

Marianna. He was talking about Marianna. A part of Gerard tried to rise up and cast the blame on her. Things started to change once she came into his life. But that wasn't entirely true. What changed was Gerard.

Oberon. Oh Ba'al, his boy was gone. And there was only one person to blame for the loss threatening to eat his very soul.

The High Priest.

He took every ounce of his pain and stored it away in a little box inside him. There was no place for it here. Instead, Gerard embraced his rage, pulling it to the surface until it blacked out all else. This he could deal with. This he could use.

"You'll be a good boy now, right?" Adam helped him onto his bed and took a large step back. "I would really hate to have to go through this again."

Gerard braced his hands on his knees. "No, you wouldn't."

"You're right." Adam laughed, high and long. "I'd just *love* to have you on the table again."

Bastard. But he hadn't expected anything else. Gerard was the one who trained Adam, after all. He'd seen the monster beneath the man from the beginning and he'd done nothing. The man was just another tool for Sanctify to use as the High Priest saw fit. Which meant Gerard was partly to blame for what Adam had become.

"So sorry to disappoint, Adam, but you won't get that opportunity a second time." He'd be long gone before this monster had a chance to try for him again.

"We'll see. The old man, he thinks you're tamed. Me?" Adam

tapped the flat of his knife against his chin. "I think he just pushed you off the deep end. Can't wait to see the fireworks." With a final grin, he strode out of the room.

Gerard was going to kill that little shit one of these days. But not today. He let his head hang, drawing anger around him like a suit of armor. Nothing would get through it; no lesser emotion could stand against the wrath taking root in his soul. He'd kill the High Priest, but before he did, Gerard was going to take everything the man held dear. After all, he was only returning the favor.

His boy...

No, he couldn't dwell on that. Not yet.

First he had to save Marianna.

Something soft tried to worm its way through his hate, but he squashed it. Yes, she mattered to him, meant more than he could begin to describe, especially after such a short time, but until they were free of this place, he couldn't afford to feel it.

And they *would* be free.

But first, he had to find Fisk. And some med patches.

CHAPTER FIFTEEN

Even after drinking half his weight in supplements, Gerard was still weak as hells, but he couldn't wait any longer. It was too risky with the date of Marianna's scheduled death quickly approaching.

Fisk answered his call after three rings. "What?"

Gerard stared at the link in his hand, trying to decide how to proceed. In the end, he took the direct route. "I need your help."

"I figured this was coming. I'll be there in five."

Those five minutes were some of the longest of Gerard's life. He paced the room seven times, circling round and round. The motion made his head spin, and he had to catch himself on the edge of the bed before he fell. When Fisk finally walked through his door, Gerard was ready to burst from his skin. "Took your time."

Fisk held up his watch. "Actually, I took four minutes. I'm early."

"You're hilarious."

"I know, a regular comedian." Fisk leaned against the door and crossed his arms over his chest. "So are we breaking Marianna out, or what?"

"You know?" What was he saying? Of course Fisk knew. "Any ideas how to proceed?"

"Yeah. Rescue the girl, steal a ship, and fly off into the nearest warp point, never to be seen again." He laughed. "I figured you'd be planning something like this. I have a ship that's just been repaired. Made sure no one's scheduled on it for over a week, so you're clear on that."

"How convenient." He had the codes to get past Control. If they could get the thing airborne, they had a shot at the warp point... From there they could find a safe place to hide and start over.

"I think so. I also think you're going to need me to get her out. I figure you can stage a distraction. I'll send the newbie ahead to get everything ready for us, and I'll retrieve Marianna."

"You seem to have this all figured out." Which was a relief, because between the damn med patches and the supplements, it was hard for him to think straight. He wanted to itch at his wounds and pass out for a good twelve hours, but neither of those was an option right now.

Fisk shrugged. "Not exactly. You'll have to figure out something for the distraction."

"You leave me with the messy part and take the pretty woman for yourself. Typical."

"I know." He grinned. "We need to do this tonight if it's going to work. Even then, it's a long shot at best."

"You and I excel at long shots." Gerard swayed on his feet and glanced at the clock. "When?"

"Try to sleep for a few hours. We'll meet after midnight."

"Okay." Sleep sounded good, if he could manage to get his mind to stop racing. That didn't seem likely, but at the very least he could try to rest for a bit.

Fisk patted his shoulder. "It will be okay, Leoni."

Gerard reeled back, pressing a hand to his shoulder. It

throbbed where the needle had entered his skin. "Did you just… drug me?"

"It's only a mild sedative. You'll be right as rain in time to do some damage." He guided Gerard back to the bed and leaned over to set the alarm on the clock. "Don't forget—make it good enough to get everybody running."

"I'm gonna…kick your ass."

"Sure you are. Right when you get your legs under you again."

"Asshole," he slurred, unable to even lift his head to follow Fisk as he moved around the room.

"Sleep tight. See you soon."

• • •

Marianna sat in the dark, clutching her cards to her chest and rocking back and forth. Two days and it would all end—that's what she'd heard the guards talking about when they delivered the food she never touched. The big festival, in which the main attraction would be her torture and death.

Panic surged but she fought it back, clinging to sanity by her fingernails. Giving in would do nothing to help her now—it would only make things infinitely worse. And her situation was terrible enough without her turning into a weepy, inconsolable mess.

But all her brave thoughts didn't stop her stomach from twisting painfully as the door slid open. Her terror dissipated when she recognized Fisk in the doorway and the slumped guard on the ground behind him. Marianna took a deep breath, forcing back the fear. The cards had promised hope, even if she didn't quite believe it. "What are you doing here?"

He struck a heroic pose, chest puffed out and fists propped against his sides. "Saving the damsel in distress—what does it look like?"

"Um…"

"Get up, get up. We don't have a lot of time. Gerard set fire to the bar, but it won't keep them occupied for long."

"Fire?" She allowed him to pull her to her feet and hustle them to the door, wondering all the while if this were an elaborate trick by the High Priest. Doubt and fear were almost enough to make her turn around, but Marianna couldn't quell the hope blossoming. She had to try. What was the worst that could happen?

That question seemed to get her into trouble more often than not these days, but it wasn't as if things could get any worse. She followed Fisk through the halls, winding their way along a different route than he'd brought her in a week ago. He must have caught her questioning look, because he said, "I told them that I was sent to relieve the guard. If I come charging out with you, they'll know something's up." A shadow passed over his face. "And, as wrong as my brothers are, I really don't want to have to hurt or kill them."

Though she didn't exactly agree with him—plenty of these men deserved horrific pain—she didn't argue. Marianna just wanted to be free. She sent up a prayer to the Lady, begging for this escape to be successful.

Fisk stopped so abruptly she almost ran into his back. Voices sounded from around the corner in front of them. She slid back a step, her heart trying to beat its way out of her chest, when a high-pitched man's laugh echoed from behind them. "Oh, Fisk, I'd hoped you'd be a little more original than this."

Fisk went unnaturally still, hand on his laser. "Adam."

Marianna spun around and pressed her hand to her mouth. The blond man from Gerard's ship. The one he'd gone to such great lengths to keep from touching her. As she took in the sick smile on his face, Marianna decided she fully supported that plan. Judging by the laser aimed at her chest, it didn't seem as if she'd have much of a choice.

"Put the laser down, Fisk. I'd really hate to have to hurt you." He cackled again, the sound setting her teeth on edge. "Okay, that's a dirty lie. I'd love to hurt you."

She felt, rather than heard, more men come up on the other side of Fisk. They'd hurt Fisk and take her back to that cell where she'd wait to die. This was the end. There really was no escape. She was going to die.

The dismal thought snapped her back into the present. Was she really considering giving up without a fight?

No. She would *not* be taken passively.

Marianna dove for Adam's legs, taking him down the same way Darla had taught her all those years ago. The laser went flying, spinning down the hallway. Sounds of fighting broke out behind her, but she was only focused on getting that damned laser and making an end of this.

They rolled, knocking against the wall as he tried to shake her loose. Instead of letting go under the barrage of pain, Marianna went for his eyes. He screamed, swinging wildly and hitting the side of her head against the wall. For one terrifying moment, her muscles stopped responding, and she hit the ground hard.

If she didn't move, he'd calm down long enough to get the laser. Marianna had no illusions about her chances then.

While Adam flailed around, clutching his ruined face, she forced her damaged body to move down the hall when all she wanted was to curl up and be done with this. The laser felt foreign in her hands as she rolled over and pointed it at where Adam struggled to his feet. He turned in her direction, the blood running like tears down his face. "I'm going to kill you, whore."

"No, you're not." She pulled the trigger, the laser kicking so hard it nearly flew from her grip. The beam went wide, creating a crater in the plaster beside him. The bastard actually laughed at her. Marianna gritted her teeth, fighting back panic as he started toward her. Taking careful aim, she pulled the trigger again. This time the beam scorched his chest and knocked him into the wall. Adam slumped to the ground, the life gone from his body.

Marianna's breath hitched, her stomach lurching. A man was dead because of her, his life snuffed out, all chances of redemption extinguished. She dropped the laser, kicking it farther down the hall, all without taking her gaze from Adam. He was a monster, but he'd been a man, too.

When someone grabbed her shoulder, she shrieked. Fisk slapped a hand over her mouth. His eyes were dilated and blood stained his hairline, but he dredged up a half smile for her. "If they haven't heard us yet, we don't want to catch their attention now. Come on—let's get out of here."

• • •

The fire worked better than Gerard could have expected. He waited around long enough to make sure the flames caught and the shouts started, then slipped between buildings, keeping to the shadows as he headed for the shipyard. A gut feeling made him change direction, swinging around the dorms instead of taking the quicker way. He should trust Fisk to get Marianna, but the only thing keeping him going right now was making sure she got out of this alive. It was his fault she was here in the first place, after all, and she was the only one left for him to save.

His boy…

Gerard shoved the thought away before it could take root, picking up his pace even though it made his body scream in agony. He circled around the back of the holding cells, aiming for the secondary exit just in time to meet Fisk dragging Marianna out. Her eyes widened when she saw him. "Gerard?"

He didn't get a chance to respond before she shook free of Fisk and threw herself into his arms. Pain made the world go hazy, but he held on tighter, pressing a kiss to the top of her head.

"I've got you. I've got you."

"I know you're all happy to see each other and everything, but we need to keep moving." Fisk shifted from foot to foot, gaze jumping around as if he expected an attack at any moment. He looked like he'd been on the shit end of a fight, but at least he was still standing. "Your happily ever after is waiting."

There was no such thing, but Gerard would take whatever he could get. He nodded, keeping an arm around Marianna. "Let's go."

They wove though the warships, the eerie silence only broken by distant shouts as their brothers worked frantically to put out the fire. It wouldn't work—witchfire was notorious for resisting flame retardants. Fisk led the way, stopping in front of a beat-up old skiff. It wasn't pretty, but Gerard trusted his friend knew what he was doing. He had to let go of Marianna in order to climb the ladder to the hatch, and Gerard did so reluctantly. It was only then that he noticed the blood coating her hair. "You're hurt."

She raised a hand to her head, giving a shaky smile. "I'll live. Please, just get us out of here."

His perfect wall of rage cracked in the face of her bravery, even after all she'd been through—all of it *his* fault. "Marianna, I—" The words died somewhere around his throat, unable to be voiced. There was too much else wrapped around his heart, squeezing so tightly he couldn't seem to draw a full breath.

"I know." She kissed him, hard and brief, before turning and climbing the ladder, more agile than any squirrel. Gerard followed at a slower pace, grunting under the strain of pulling himself up. Tearing the med patches was guaranteed, but he'd worry about it later.

Blaine waited for them in the hub. He started to salute, but the motion died when he caught sight of Marianna. "W-What's going on? What is *she* doing here?" His brown eyes went wide. "You're breaking her out."

"Yes." There was no point in denying it. Gerard maneuvered

Marianna behind him in case the newbie tried to do something stupid.

"I can't let you do that." The redhead drew himself up, reaching for his laser. "By the order of the High Priest, I—"

Gerard moved before the newbie could finish the sentence. He stepped into Blaine, grabbing his head and twisting it sharply. As the boy hit the floor, the last part of Gerard tied to Sanctify died. Whether for better or worse, he was done with it.

He glanced up as Fisk came through the door. "It had to be done."

Fisk shrugged and headed into the cockpit, leaving the door open.

Gerard startled when Marianna touched him. She very deliberately didn't look at the body on the floor. "Would it be possible to remove him before we take off?"

Idiot. He should have thought of that. With a nod, he scooped up the body and staggered from the room, heading for the hatch. It was quick work to dump it. Gerard took one last look at Sanctus as the door slid shut. Ba'al willing, he'd never set foot on this planet again.

Fisk had the ship ready to go by the time Gerard made it back into the hub, his hands flying over the controls. "Better strap in. I'm going for a quick, rather than smooth, ride."

"Heard that line before." Gerard helped Marianna with her harness before he dropped into the seat next to her and strapped himself in.

The ship lifted off with a lurch, throwing them sideways. Marianna's hand found his, and Gerard held on to her as though she were his lifeline. Hells, she was. Without her, he had nothing else to live for but revenge.

"It will be okay." When he looked at her, she sighed. "Perhaps *okay* isn't the correct word. But it will get better."

"Some things never get better, Marianna." The boy—he couldn't even bear to think his son's name. The gaping hole inside him widened, just waiting for an unwary step to swallow him completely. Gerard had no intention of taking that step. Ever.

"We can argue about it later, if you like." She gave his hand a squeeze as the ship shuddered while passing through the atmosphere. "What will you do now?"

The future loomed, nearly as terrifying as the pit inside him. "I had hoped…we could spend some time together when you're not my captive."

"Would you like to come to Keiluna with me? It might not be much, but it's home."

Keiluna was the first place Sanctify would look for them—or maybe it was the last place. No one would believe he'd be stupid enough to return to where this all started. "I'd like that."

He wanted time with her, but he also needed to recoup. To gather his credits and connections and put into motion the plan starting to form in his mind.

Gerard looked at Marianna, her head tilted back and eyes closed. Revenge would take him far, but there was a spark between them that he wanted to explore. It was more than her beauty; she carried an inner strength he had never seen before. And the way she looked at him… Yeah, he wanted to see where this went, to see if they really had a chance outside Sanctify's hold. He brought their interlaced hands up and kissed her knuckles. "I've heard Keiluna is beautiful in the winter."

Those violet eyes opened and she gave a soft smile. "What about Sanctify?"

"I have a few ideas." There were so many rebel groups trying to fight against the inevitable tide that was Sanctify, but they were lacking in weapons and direction. He could supply them with both.

She arched an eyebrow. "We'll take on the devil together?"

"The devil, the High Priest, and anyone else fool enough to come after us."

ACKNOWLEDGMENTS

To God, for giving me the insatiable curiosity that drove me to write the Sanctify series.

To Heather, for helping me polish this beast of a book into something truly awesome. I couldn't have done it without you!

To Kari, for loving Jenny and Mac as much as I do!

To my beta readers on this one, Seleste Delaney and Lisa Basso. Your comments were beyond helpful!

To Tom, for the countless hours under the needle, and the amazing Tarot cards!

To the Rabble, for your unfailing support that never ceases to humble and amaze me! Y'all are too awesome to put into words!

To my family, for your boundless patience and total willingness to feed yourselves while I was lost in another universe.

And last, but far from least, to all the readers who took a wild leap with me into this adventure! You never know what you'll find beyond the next horizon--or through the nearest warp point.

For more page-turning books from Entangled, try these...

HONOR RECLAIMED

by Tonya Burrows

An interview with a runaway Afghani child bride lands photojournalist Phoebe Leighton in the middle of an arms deal. Forming an unlikely alliance with a ragtag team of mercenaries, she meets Seth Harlan, a former Marine sniper with PTSD. He ignites passions within her she thought long dead, but she's hiding a secret that could destroy him. Racing against the clock, Seth, Phoebe, and the rest of HORNET struggle to stop a ruthless warlord bent on power, revenge...and death.

DEATH DEFYING

by Nina Croft

After five hundred years, Callum Meridian, founding member of the Collective, is bored out of his mind. Until he realizes he's physically changing—into what, he isn't sure. Callum is determined to discover the truth, but his own people will stop at nothing to prevent it from coming out. He turns to Captain Tannis of the starship El Cazador. Sparks fly as they work together to make it out alive, but can Callum really trust the one woman hell bent on using him? Defying death has never been more dangerous...or more sexy.

EAST OF ECSTASY

by Laura Kaye

Devlin Eston, black-souled son of the evil Anemoi Eurus, is the only one who can thwart his father's plan to overthrow the Supreme God of Wind and Storms. But first, Dev must master the unstable powers he's been given. Distrusted and shunned by his own divine family, the last thing he expects is to find kindness and passion in the arms of a mortal. But Devlin's love puts Annalise in the path of a catastrophic storm, and in the final Armageddon showdown between the Anemoi and Eurus, sacrifices will be made, hearts broken, and lives changed forever...or lost.

A SHOT OF RED

by Tracy March

When biotech company heiress Mia Moncure learns her ex-boyfriend, the company's PR Director, has died in a suspicious accident in Switzerland, Mia suspects murder. Determined to reveal a killer, she turns to sexy Gio Lorenzo, Communications Director for her mother, a high-ranking senator—and the recent one-night stand Mia has been desperate to escape. While negotiating their rocky relationship, they race to uncover a deadly scheme that could ruin her family's reputation. But millions of people are being vaccinated, and there's more than her family's legacy at stake.

TANGLED HEARTS

by Heather McCollum

Highland warrior Ewan Brody always wanted a sweet, uncomplicated woman by his side, but he can't fight his attraction to the beautiful enchantress who's stumbled into his life. He quickly learns, though, that Pandora Wyatt is not only a witch, but also a pirate and possibly a traitor's daughter—and though she's tricked him into playing her husband at King Henry's court, he's falling hard. As they discover dark secrets leading to the real traitor of the Tudor court, Ewan and Pandora must uncover the truth before they lose more than just their hearts.

FIGHTING LOVE

by Abby Niles

Former Middleweight champion and confirmed bachelor Tommy "Lightning" Sparks has lost it all: his belt, his career, and now his home. After the devastating fire, he moves in with his drama-free best friend, Julie. One encounter changes everything and Julie is no longer the girl he's spent his life protecting but a desirable woman he wants to take to his bed. Knowing his reputation, he's determined to protect Julie more than ever—from himself. Can two childhood friends make a relationship work, or will they lose everything because they stopped fighting love?

SUNROPER

by Natalie J. Damschroder

Marley Canton joins Gage Samargo in tracking down the goddess who went rogue decades ago. Insane with too much power from the sun, she's selling that energy to Gage's younger brother and his friends. But Marley's ability to nullify power in those who aren't supposed to have it means that every time she nullifies someone, she takes on some of the goddess's insanity. Gage falls for Marley's sharp wit and intense desire to right wrongs. Once he discovers she's turning into her enemy, is it too late to back away?

TOUCH OF THE ANGEL

by Rosalie Lario

Night after night, Amara and her fellow succubi are forced to extract special abilities from the strongest Otherworlders for their psychotic master's growing collection. When Ronin Meyers, the gorgeous angel-demon hybrid she believed to be dead captures her, Amara is both stunned and elated. But the happily-ever-after Amara's dreamed about will have to wait. Before she and Ronin can find salvation, they must bring down the madman hell-bent on destroying everything—and everyone—they love. And Ronin and Amara are at the top of his list.